PHYLLIS BOTTOME

Miss Bottome's unusually rich writing career has confirmed her early recognition as one of the world's favorite storytellers. Her first novel was published when she was seventeen, and the ensuing years have produced many best-sellers. One of the most famous, PRIVATE WORLDS, was written while she was studying Alfred Adler's "Individual Psychology," first under Leonard Seif and later with Adler himself. This was a turning point in her life, Miss Bottome says.

For a writer, her career has been singularly varied. She has lived outside of England, her home, for thirty-nine years. The seven countries she knows intimately, plus her abiding interest in literature and psychology, have contributed to her latest career, as a noted lecturer. Her resonant voice and early training for the stage assured her success, and during World War II she not only worked as a novelist but was a prominent speaker for the Ministry of Information.

Miss Bottome's novel JANE is about a subject and character that have haunted her for ten years. She has studied at first hand the problems confronting such girls as Jane, and her warm sympathy and humanity, her deep and burning interest, make the pages of this book glow with rare human understanding.

Phyllis Bottome further rounds out her full life with a keen interest in politics. She is married to Alban Ernan Forbes Dennis, who practices as a lay psychologist and is the uncle of Nigel Dennis, author of the widely acclaimed novel, CARDS OF IDENTITY.

JANE

by the same author

*

AGAINST WHOM
BELATED RECKONING
MAN AND BEAST
FORTUNE'S FINGER
UNDER THE SKIN
INNOCENCE AND EXPERIENCE
OLD WINE
WITHIN THE CUP
LONDON PRIDE
THE MORTAL STORM
MASKS AND FACES
HEART OF A CHILD
ALFRED ADLER
SEARCH FOR A SOUL
THE CHALLENGE
NOT IN OUR STARS

JANE

by Phyllis Bottome

author of "Private Worlds,"
"The Mortal Storm," etc.

New York

THE VANGUARD PRESS

Library of Congress Catalogue Card Number: 57-7681

Manufactured in the United States of America

To

my friend

LACI ZILAHI

in love and admiration

Author's Note

I have studied the care of delinquent children in several countries, but no particular Remand Home or Approved School is mentioned in this book, and all characters in it are taken from the imagination and not from life.

The period written about is just after the Second World War when such Institutions were crowded out by bombing and suffered from special disadvantages. Nevertheless, the main errors in the psychological handling of these young people remain; and there are still more 'Miss Potters' than 'Miss Bartletts' in many such Institutions.

Phyllis Bottome

Acknowledgements

The author's thanks are due for the very great kindness shown her by Philip James Chellew, County Coroner, Clerk to the St. Ives Justices and Clerk to the West Penwith Justices, for reading the manuscript of *Jane* and revising technical flaws in law terms and procedure.

JANE

I

None of the other passengers in the 52 'bus, coming from Willesden Green, noticed the girl who got in at Notting Hill Gate. Her age was indeterminate, her make-up inferior but adequate, her clothes neat without being smart. She was not even on the edge of good looks nor was she so plain as to attract attention; yet the amount of detailed observation that went on behind Jane's mediocre brown eyes would have startled the whole omnibus.

In a flash while taking her seat Jane had gathered how many passengers the 'bus held, divided their sexes, reckoned their class income marks, and summed up the women's entire wardrobes. If, she thought, they looked like that outside, you could make a good guess at what they had inside their houses. Questions of character did not interest Jane beyond knowing whether a person were tough or soft.

Twelve of the fifteen years of her life had been lived in the United States, and three years of having adjusted herself to the slower paced lives of Great Britain had done nothing to check the quick-firing quality of her active mind.

Upon one woman in the 'bus Jane's attention focused itself with intensity. This woman was twice too heavy for her size, restless and undecided. Besides her own weight, she carried a large striped black and white bag from which a top-heavy cauliflower protruded; in addition she held a small suitcase, an umbrella, and a handbag. Twice she asked the conductor to put her down at the stop nearest Harrods; but when he went upstairs to collect fares, and the 'bus was momentarily halted by the traffic lights, she made a sudden decision to find out for herself. She hit one gentleman, absorbed in his newspaper, with the edge of her suitcase, and rapped another one's elbow sharply with her umbrella. At this moment the 'bus spurted on, and she would have fallen face forwards had Jane not deftly steadied her, gripping her firmly by the wrist. The 'bus once more slowed up, halted by an enterprising taxi still nearer Harrods, but well before its natural stop; the fat woman, entranced by her own velocity and supported by Jane's assistance, plunged forward on to the platform; Jane, by a swift acrobatic feat, landed her safely, all her parcels intact about her, between two irate but controllable taxis. Then with eel-like facility Jane re-mounted the 'bus and placidly took her place.

"What a kind, good gel that is!" an aristocratic Edwardian lady, who had not yet accustomed herself to the anonymity of buses, remarked in a high-pitched voice to the friend next her, "so unusual now-a-days to see good manners in gels— gratifying, very!"

She gave a gracious smile towards Jane.

Everyone in the 'bus now noticed Jane for the first time and gave her their complete approval. The fat woman might have fallen on them, she might even have caused an accident and delayed their journey, and now she was safe on the pavement; and the 'bus had once more swaggered into the middle of a traffic lane.

Jane felt the sudden wave of applause that greeted her action, and was pleased by it. Approval seldom came her way, and it roused in her a still rarer sense of self-satisfaction. Perhaps she *was* a good, kind girl after all, always ready to help the infirm and the unwary! But still it might be better to get out at Hyde Park Corner where there were always plenty of people about. Probably the fat lady had not yet discovered the loss of her gold wrist watch bracelet, and she was certainly not the person to have noticed the number of the 'bus if she had; still, it was always safest to be as far from scenes of action as possible.

The conductor came down from the top of the 'bus, and remarked to the universe in general that suicide was what ladies who got off 'buses between stops were asking for—if it wasn't murder, he added, looking grimly at the officious Jane, who blinked at the unpleasant word, but knew that whatever the conductor said, she had the opinion of the entire 'bus load upon her side.

"She'd have got out anyway!" a firm and portly old gentleman remarked reprovingly, "and had not that young lady helped her, she'd have landed on her nose!"

"Nah then!" the conductor shouted reproachfully, for he was not going to be put right by any member of his public, however well dressed and portly. "Nah then, if anyone wants ter get aht—'ere we are! Igh-Par!" With a grateful smile at the elderly gentleman, Jane slid gracefully out of the 'bus.

The trees in the open space opposite her were thick with unclenched buds, crocus in rings of orange and purple circled round their dingy bases. It was a rough March day and everything, even St. George's Hospital and the back of the retreating omnibus, looked fresh and bright. It might have been California, Jane thought, in mid-winter. The hard, shining air pursued her into the tube, where its place was immediately taken by sudden wild draughts of unchastened chemicals. Only, of course, it wasn't California; it was the skyless, dim, controlled and meagre life of London momentarily shaken into dramatic significance by the March sun and wind. Jane had adjusted to London, but she remembered California in spasms—not always with desire—sometimes with relief. London was an open book to Jane; it was almost the only book she ever read. She knew a lot, but what Jane knew came to her in a different way. She could read and write if she had to; but she had learned about life by living it, and beyond her personal experience there were, of course, the slightly enlarged and exaggerated visions she had imbibed from the Pictures.

Jane had also learned a good deal from George. George was known as Gentleman George in the circle he frequented, but not very well known because of the adjective. He was a highly skilled cat burglar who liked private houses better than shops or banks.

Jane, however, knew him in a different way—George was her whole world.

It would have been impossible to tell, and Jane had never asked herself, if she *liked* George or not. He was simply predominantly there, when no-one else was.

The disaster had happened before George; but there had been no disaster after him, and Jane never wanted to think about the old confusing horror. It had chopped her life in half, and left her at twelve coshed on the head and lying flat out, on the main motor road through the desert, near the Painted Mountains where George had his hide-out. There George had found her; and when she came round from a week's severe concussion in George's comfortable shack, she had found George.

Every now and then, when Jane saw daffodils in a flower shop window, or a particularly pleasant looking baby lording it in a pram, a quite peculiar pang struck at her very vitals, and she would think of Marlene. Marlene was her step-mother's youngest baby whom Jane had deserted to go out with the boys. But she needn't think about Marlene now; she was going back to George with a gold wrist watch bracelet which he would certainly like. In the open market such a watch might have been worth fifty pounds, for the gold was good and the watch the best Swiss, but for watches you take off other people's wrists, there was no open market. If George got twenty for it, out of old Daddy Fisk, he would be lucky. Jane gave a suppressed chuckle as she thought of the fat lady and the surprise in store for her.

Jane was coming out of the tube now, and had started walking along the Goldhawk Road. The incident was worth a laugh, but its success had cost Jane three years' intensive training. Probably, Jane thought happily, she was the lightest-fingered girl for her age in London.

Still, it wasn't only lightness and rapidity of touch that George had taught Jane. He had developed in her a special brand of emergency wits.

"You've got ter have *guts*," George often told her. "If you hadn't shown guts when I picked yer up—I'd never

14

have kep' you. The moment you came round you showed *guts*—and you went on showing it. Don't yer ever weaken, for if you weaken you'll bloody well get it, where the chicken got the axe, from me—as well as from the cops."

This was about as far as George had ever got, in showing any appreciation of Jane. He was a man without affections, and therefore his appreciations too were rare, and only likely to be expressed when they fitted into his scheme of things. Jane did not earn her keep for more than a year after George had picked her up; but George saw that she was going to earn her keep and more, therefore he had kept her.

She was his mascot and he thought of her as a pet animal: he had always been partial to animals and believed in luck, but the idea of love, or even pity, had not occurred to him. When he had picked her up, he had thought that she might be a remunerative "snatch", but he had soon found out, before Jane had even recovered consciousness, that far from being the victim of a kidnapping set-up, Jane was more likely to have done the kidnapping herself.

For, at twelve, Jane too was on the run. Probably, George thought, she had not shot both her step-mother and father, as the headlines of the Los Angeles Press said she had; but Jane was certainly with the two boys, slightly older than herself, who *had* shot them; and no doubt the boys had coshed Jane on the head and tossed her out of the car that they had stolen from her dead parents, when they saw she had weakened. But she couldn't, George came to the conclusion, have been very weak to have got that far with them.

George never went into the subject with Jane, then or later. Unless the past promised anything for the future, he thought it best left alone. He too was wanted, and proposed to cut himself off, with eager finality, from the people who wanted him. He had to wait to get a British passport and fix up a good smuggling contract with a tramp skipper; and then he was off.

"Seems you're on the run and I'm on the run", he told Jane. "Whadda yer say to us making a thing of it? No-one's going to look for us together—and that's one up for us!"

Jane had accepted this proposition with a nod. She hadn't much liked the look of George when she first came round; but she hadn't had anything else to look at, and by now she had become used to him.

The whole thing had gone without a hitch, and American Jane had become Jane Marsdon, daughter of George Marsdon, a British watchmaker, upon a beautifully faked British passport, and sailing in an ill-constructed but stubbornly surviving British tramp to a country that she had barely heard of except as behaving badly to the Irish and rather well to the Germans at a time when Germans were somehow or other markedly unpopular. Later on the British became more unpopular still and less kind to the Germans; but by then Jane herself had become British, and the opinion of California had ceased to form her own.

George was just old enough to be Jane's father, and he had preferred the relationship of father, to which he consistently adhered, to that of lover, liking to have his girls at a distance; and not too persistently attached to him.

Jane too preferred a platonic relationship ·with George, though she realized that if George hadn't preferred it, she would have had to put up with it. Jane was not afraid of George, but her gift for observation had soon told her that you either did what George wanted, or paid for not doing it, with anything, up to your life.

Physical intimacy was a thing Jane knew all about and thought very little of; nor did she connect it with Love.

Love went with diamond necklaces and a Rolls-Royce, and you discovered it in company with the latest film hero, at the end of every decent film.

Jane believed in Love implicitly and longed to possess it, accompanied by white satin and orange blossom.

As she walked down the Goldhawk Road with the wind blowing her along, and a blue gleam of pock-marked country opening out ahead, she was thinking about Love.

The Goldhawk Road is an open thoroughfare strangely and variously lined with sharp architectural surprises. You may find a row of squat little houses from Queen Victoria's

16

unsplendid century: dingy, self-contained, shy and deplorably uncomfortable but stout houses, some clinging together like shells and some standing alone, on a greenless plot just large enough to swing a cat in. Tall blocks of flats shoot up between such groups towards a visible expanse of sky, not of course scraping it, as they would have done in Jane's more grandiose and spacious land, but still presenting their close-pressed inhabitants with a modicum of light and air. There were all kinds of possibilities in the Goldhawk Road besides its nearness to Shepherd's Bush, where rents were low and outlooks not at all high. Shops, however, were cheaper; and you could buy almost anything for remarkably less than in some fashionable quarters. The things you bought did not last as long; but then perhaps you yourself wouldn't.

There were churches, chapels and all kinds of small and ugly institutes along this open thoroughfare; it was quite surprising to connect these buildings, however remotely, with Heaven; but they were, and Jane knew they were, portents of respectability. Jane had never known anyone who went either to church or chapel. God she thought of as an expletive, and Heaven as a rather played-out joke. Religion she connected with being forced to stay in over-time and sing carols for Hollywood Studios without being paid extra for it. Of course some of the studios just left gramophones on; but even they had to be cheaply looked after. In Hollywood, Christmas trees, exquisitely lit and coloured, spread like mushrooms from avenue to avenue for a few weeks every year, without any presents on them. The Christmas trees did no particular harm unless you were drunk and mistook them for traffic lights; but Jane hoped that Love would not turn out to be like those Hollywood Christmas trees.

So far, Jane had not experienced Love except in Pictures; but on this shining day, with her feet dancing under her, a sort of timeless song running through her heart and a gold wrist watch bracelet in her pocket, she wondered if Love might not be one of those things, promised her by George, which she could pick up on the Riviera when she was old enough to begin her real professional life?

II

Jane generally approached Ma's indirectly. There were
people she didn't like who might be coming in or going
out of the front door; and there was Ma herself who was
Jane's most intimate and persistent enemy.

Although, in her stuffy bed-sitting-room, Ma was always
found crouched over the fire, like an old witch brewing deadly
potions for unconscious victims, she yet managed to see everything that went on in the street outside, and inspect everyone
who went past her dirty window panes.

To Jane, who came from a sharply hygienic land full of
light and air, dirt and darkness seemed to have made their
permanent home in Ma's bed-sitter. Ma's huge inert person
drew them in and out as if dirt and darkness were a lively form
of oxygen vital to her existence. They were the only things
Ma was willing to share with anyone bold enough to enter her
den. She *could* go out-doors; and once a week she did, to
collect and bank her rents, for she very wisely didn't trust her
lodgers; but these excursions she took winter or summer
garbed as if exploring a polar landscape, wrapped in furs that
had managed to co-exist with moths, over an immeasurable
space of time.

Not that Ma was poor. She owned the nine-roomed house
she occupied with her lodgers, and a row of less affluent-
looking houses two streets away; and these, though small and
unobtrusive buildings, paid her a handsome rent, for they
were all illicitly over-populated.

Ma could therefore have afforded a modern luxury flat
instead of one crowded ill-lit room, but Ma used to say that
as she was half blind anyway, the little she could see with one

low-powered electric light bulb didn't matter—and no-one cared less for what she owned than she did; but anyone who believed this statement and acted on it was liable to very unpleasant surprises.

Ma's room was full of pieces of furniture she knew she wouldn't be able to sell at a small antique shop run by her inefficient son, but carefully supervised by Ma. It *was* an antique shop, but it was also a pawn shop, just at the edge of a district where pawning was a good deal in vogue, and yet where the tenants of quite respectable flats evinced a tendency to pick up what they fondly thought to be aesthetically cultural bargains.

All the surface of Ma's life appeared harmless and legally correct; it was only when you got into the depth, or dabbled in the illicit yourself, that the octopus unfolded its tentacles and dragged you down into its relentless maw.

Jane knew all about the depths in Ma, and she knew that only George—if George—was strong enough, once enfolded, to get out of them. George was not afraid of Ma, nor was Ma afraid of George: they just glared at each other in a challenging manner across a gulf of competitive corruption—knowing that neither of them would stick at anything, and that as long as it paid them to work together—and not an instant longer— they would consider each other's interests. Ma knew enough about George to hang him, and George knew enough about Ma to hang her, so that the temptation to give each other away was slight.

The Police, though they never liked the look of Number 27 Rostrevor Road, knew practically nothing of what went on inside it. They simply remarked to themselves that now a new man lodger had turned up with a very young girl; and they didn't like the look of that either. Still, what could they do about it? George was "in the money", though he kept this commodity in so many secret and anonymous places that the Police were quite unable to trace the amount or the sources of his income; nor—under the name of George Marsdon— had he any record. Tax collectors were warned, but even tax collectors could not get at the roots of George's supplies.

Perhaps he was not only a watchmaker. But he had a little shop on one of Ma's premises, and he sometimes sold watches.

George lived in the best room in Ma's house, to which he had added a bathroom, a kitchenette and a small hall-bedroom for Jane.

Ma's house stood at the end of a small and inconclusive street on the edge of a railway line. From George's point of view it was an ideal situation for a house. There were three doors to it; George had put in an extra side door leading to his own bed-sitter; and there was a skylight. It was semi-detached, so there were roofs to fall back on; while the main thoroughfare—an added attraction—was but a stone's throw away. George considered it even safer than his former hide-out in the desert under the Painted Mountains. Electric light and water supply had been a difficulty there, for once you had them in running order, officials might turn up. Here at Ma's George had both light and water, and yet the Public Authorities knew no more about his private life than they did about Adam's; indeed, it might have been easier to check up on Eden than on Ma's residential property.

There was, of course, Ma herself. In her girlhood—and Ma sometimes boasted of this when drunk—she had been taught knife tricks. It was a long time ago, but she had probably not forgotten the tricks; and Jane had discovered in the scullery two incredibly sharp-looking knives. Ma's bed-sitter had a mortise lock; and she never opened her safely latched windows.

Nor was George without his own lethal resources. He had not been called "Gentleman George" by one of Los Angeles' most famous gangs purely for gentlemanly attributes. It was a pet name founded on intimidation. Ma knew that she must keep her place if she wanted to keep George; and it paid her to keep George. He gave her ten times what she received from her other lodgers, and often put little jobs her way as well; so anything she could do for George, Ma made a point of doing; she even put up with Jane, but not very well.

Jane exasperated Ma almost beyond endurance. She aggra-vated Ma partly because she was observant and yet held her tongue, and also because she was unfledged—not promiscuous—and therefore not vulnerable to the inducements Ma could have offered her. But most of all Jane exasperated Ma because Rundle, Ma's cat, had taken a fancy to Jane.

As far as Ma liked any living thing, she liked Rundle. Rundle was a large, glossy black cat, male, redoubtable, and a perfect mouser. He had been left with her as a kitten by her favourite lodger, after whom she had named him. It was not likely that either of them would ever see Tom Rundle again, for he was unavoidably detained during Her Majesty's pleasure, and lucky—Ma thought—all things considered, to have got a lifer.

Rundle did not return Ma's affection, into which he had clawed his way—humping his infant back and jumping at her, spitting and swearing, as she fondly said, "like any Christian!" He had been deeply attached to his owner Tom, but, once weaned from his first love, he could not be got to care for a large clumsy old woman who drank quantities of gin and trod on a cat's tail.

The only qualities that appealed to Rundle in human beings were a certain gaiety and lightness of heart that matched his own; a willingness to leave an animal perfectly free to carry out its intentions, and sufficient insight into what these intentions were; to provide meals —and open windows or doors at required moments. Jane possessed all these qualities and practised them with lavish generosity. She was full of suppressed gaiety. She met Rundle's wishes—she left him free as air. So whenever possible Rundle deserted Ma and took to climbing up a pipe that led to Jane's window, which was always kept open for him. If she was there, she fed and played with him; and if she wasn't, he took the centre of her bed, curled himself into its soft warmth, and pleasurably awaited her. Rundle always gave George a wide berth because his instinct told him that George had no use for cats; and what George had no use for would not profit by his company.

When fine, and if he felt like being out-doors, Rundle would sit on the high wall at the end of Ma's strip of garden and watch for Jane. It was not an easy wall to sit on, since it was covered with broken glass, but there was just room for a clever cat to manœuvre a place for himself between these obstacles. From the top of the wall Rundle could see all over a strip of waste land, across the railway line, and up a parallel street down which Jane often came home, since by doing so she could avoid passing Ma's windows.

It was not a nice day for a cat to sit on an uneasily small piece of brick wall, ruffled by a high wind that flattened his ears against his head and violently tooth-combed his whiskers; yet there Rundle sat stoically, staring over the entire district emptied by himself of all other animals, until he saw Jane blown swiftly along in the right direction. He was secretly delighted, but he stared on, impassive and aloof, his opaque yellow eyes cold as the topaz which they resembled.

Jane was openly ecstatic and waved to him. She had hoped to see Rundle before she sought George's approval, partly because it was always lucky to see a black cat first, and partly because Jane knew that it would be more fun to tell Rundle about the gold watch, though gold watches were not in his line and he couldn't understand, than to tell George.

It would be more fun because Jane loved Rundle; and this was not a faculty that had hitherto been roused by anyone else whom she had met in England.

Jane came bowling on, swifter and swifter after she had caught sight of Rundle. The wind had whipped the colour into her sallow cheeks; her brown eyes looked larger and sparkled.

Jane was almost pretty as she stood under the wall looking up at Rundle. He was too high above her for her to have touched him if she had tried, and she wouldn't have tried, because she knew that he liked to pretend he wasn't pleased to see her. She simply said "'Lo Rundle!" with her heart behind it.

Rundle rose very slowly from his pyramid position and blinked disdainfully down upon her; then, without seeming to move one of his well clenched muscles, he launched his solid but elastic body into the air and landed on Jane's shoulder. He dug his claws in a little hard, because there was not quite enough shoulder to give him full security—and naturally a cat has to think of his own security first—then he began to purr; at first he merely made a low guttural mutter at the back of his throat, but this sound gradually grew more and more powerful as his joy churned up within him, until the volume of his purr sounded in Jane's ear like the triumphant note of an organ. "Call it a day! Call it a day!" Jane chanted back. "I gotta gold watch, Rundle! See! I gotta gold watch!"

Something, Rundle gathered, had gone right for both of them. Earlier on, about five o'clock that morning, Rundle had caught a mouse. There had seemed no way of communicating this pleasant fact to Jane, but perhaps the sense of it found expression in the protracted volume of his purr.

Their communication was complete enough. Here they were, two young creatures, who had by the exertion of great skill obtained desirable objects; that they were together—enjoying each other's company—doubled the value of their triumphs.

III

Jane was accustomed to approach George in much the same
way that keepers of affectionate, but unpredictable, wild
animals approach their pets.

She showed no sign of fear but she was wary; and she never
hurried him. Let him look her well over first, and see that
she came to him in a friendly spirit; and then if possible let
her produce something that she knew he would appreciate.

There was no reason to suspect trouble. Everything had
been left in order for George. The bread was sliced; cream,
butter and cold ham were in the fridge, and a row of eggs
stood on the shelf above it, in cardboard egg cups. The long
toasting fork stood prominently at right angles to George's
chair, leaning against the gas stove and flanked by a box of
matches.

George was under the impression that he did not ask much;
but he knew just what to do about it, if what he asked was not
provided. He would raise Hell.

As Jane entered, he lifted his heavy-lidded eyes and looked
at her as if she were not only an expected, but a welcome
visitor. Smiling was not his habit, but when he was not
frowning, Jane accepted it as a smile.

"Where you been?" he enquired almost genially.

"Oh jes' round!" Jane told him airily, "an' whadda yer
think mother's brought home for a good boy? Look—see!"

Jane held out the wrist watch triumphantly.

George's eyes and fingers acted together instantaneously.
For the fragment of a moment the watch lay on his outstretched palm, while he summed up its weight and make,
and then it melted into thin air.

24

"How come?" he demanded succinctly.

Drama seized Jane. She became the fat woman, the 'bus conductor, the portly protective gentleman, and each of the narrowly observed passengers in turn. Finally she was herself, retrieving parcels, whisking on and off platforms; and lastly a ministering angel, accepting the applause of the 'bus; then she leaned forward, took a piece of George's toast, buttered it profusely, and poured herself out a cup of tea, strong and bright as blood.

"You're good, Jane," George remarked, with the satisfaction of the creator for the thing he has created. "How come you slipped the catch without the Dame feeling it?"

"Well, I've practised on Wilfred's watches, he has quite a few," Jane explained. "I made him put them on, and then I took them off him, till I could do it without his knowing his wrist was touched. Boy, I never thought I'd get the chance on a 'bus! Lousy—the way those buses seat you. You gotta pair of eyes on you all the time. In the double seats you haven't an earthly, and not much of a break with those three opposite each other by the door. The clippies too—sort you out back to front, don't they? You can't hide the gum in your teeth from them. Seems as if they couldn't keep their minds off their passengers. A man conductor—he minds his own business, not noticing when you get in and out unless he has to! But the moment I see that fat dame, I knew she was just a sitting bird—the kind you can't miss! Public danger too—took everyone's eyes off. Once you get people thinking, what's going ter hit them next, you're in easy street. Why!—I could have walked off with the Crown jewels under their noses!"

"Yep—you're good!" George repeated slowly. Then with a sudden intensity of an M.V.5 hitting an invisible bull's eye, he leaned forward and asked, "How old are you, Jane?"

Jane stared at him. What was he up to with that sudden irrelevant question? She gave herself time before she answered, daintily licking the melted butter off her fingers one by one. She must find out without crowding George, so that if possible

25

he should not guess that she even wanted to know what he was up to!

"If you was right, George," she said at last, "an' those newspapers said I was twelve when you picked me up—why then I must be fifteen now, I reckon. Seems more like a lifetime than three years since I bin in this country."

Nobody had kept Jane's birthdays since her mother died, when she was seven years old; but she could quite well remember a strawberry-coloured cake with seven pink candles on it. It seemed to sum up the whole of her life with her real mother before her step-mother came. George's small, pale eyes were fixed on her with a peculiar look, as if he were not quite sure who she was, or whether she was fifty or fifteen.

"There was quite a lot of things I might have done to you when I picked you up", he said at last. "I might have left you where you was—ter be run dahn by the next car. I might have called the cops. I might have done you dirt. Well, I didn't do none of those things. I looked you over—you wasn't much shakes as a wardrobe, an' you had a work girl's hands—I saw there was no money in it from the start; but I picked you up and carried you—half a mile it was—thro' the scrub ter my shack, wot I got off a bootlegger as part of a deal. I hadn't made up my mind what ter do wiv you even then. You were as near dead as makes no matter—someone had coshed you good an' proper on the side of yer 'ead. If you'd waked up an' carried on like some girls do, who haven't no guts, I'd 'ave done you in myself; but when you came rahnd you look me straight between the eyes an' says, 'Who are you?' fierce as a cornered cat. I says, 'I'm George', an' you says, 'Well! I'm Jane!' and went off again. Long and short of it was by the time you'd come rahnd for keeps, I'd taken to you; an' I'd decided to carry on. I'd fahnd out by then that you was on the run— same as me. You was young enough ter be my chile and the cops knew I hadn't no chile—so that was one up ter me. An' you was being looked for wiv'aht a farver 'cos you or your boy fren' had shot your farver, so no one would expec' ter see you going abaht wiv one—see what I mean? My skipper he wasn't one ter arsk awkward questions, so it all went off like a piece

26

of cake. I never had no trouble landing nor nothing. There was you—my daughter Jane, right as a trivet on my passport; 'corse I'd paid extra for your name ter be put on the passport —but the passport was an extra too, if it comes ter that. You took ter lifting things as if you'd been born to it. I don't say you earned your keep, but you brought in somepin' from the start."

George came to an abrupt stop, as if startled by his own eloquence. It was laudatory too, and George's eloquence was seldom laudatory. Jane stared at him defensively—she too was startled. What was it he wanted to get out of her? He already had the watch.

George was not fond of referring to the Past. Jane hadn't even known that George knew her father was dead—far less that she herself, or the boys with her, had killed him. Her own memory was confused as to what exactly had happened, when she had decided to let the children shift for themselves— even the baby Marlene—and go off for the day with the two worst boys in the street. All George had told her, when she came round, was that the papers said she was missing, and that as far as he could see, she had better stay missing. Jane too had wanted to stay missing. She had not wanted to plunge into that queer black hole in her mind and find out what was at the bottom of it. The Police would make her do that, and she saw that she would have to choose between the Police and George; so Jane had chosen George.

"Well—what of it?" Jane demanded briskly, when the silence between them became excessive.

George's uncommunicative and lonely eyes left her, and fixed themselves on the toasting fork again.

"Hasn't no one ever made a pass at you?" he asked indirectly.

"Whadda know!" Jane retorted, "ain't I human? 'Course they have! But I'm no glamour girl—see? I don't get pestered by men! An' I don't go for rides on lorries or say 'Kiss me stranger' either!"

George's eyes rose from the fork, and once more slid over Jane cautiously; in a dim way he looked gratified.

"O.K.," he told her. "I only wanted ter make sure you got no boy fren's—'cos I don't like the idea of boy fren's—see what I mean? It 'ud be a pity if you was to start a boy fren'."

There was a long uneasy pause. "Who has been putting that idea into his thick head?" Jane was asking herself indignantly. "Ma?"

"Listen", she said finally, and with her usual snappiness, "do you want me to act all my life like that Virgin Queen you took me ter see at the Pictures? So old she'd have dropped dancing if it hadn't been for them corsets they wore in those days—that kinda kep' them in cages—so they couldn't drop even when they wos dyin'—and nothin' to it *but* dancing as far as I could see?"

"Nah!" George said earnestly, "I don't ask noffin' like that, Jane! Wot I want ter know is, if you're the right age for it, why not take me on? I ain't your farver, you know that well enough; I'm only thirty-six, and I haven't seen the roof yet I couldn't get up on—high or low—light or dark!"

Jane's face closed. This was the last thing she had expected; or wanted. Her lips tightened, her dark eyes hooded themselves so that George could not guess what lay behind them. It was her first serious proposition; and it came from George. She must not let George see that she was disagreeably surprised.

"Whadda know?" she said with a sudden grin. "An' what abaht Gladys?"

"Aw! Gladys!" George replied testily, "that bloody two-timer Gladys! She don't even add up!"

There was another pause. Jane broke it with cautious mildness.

"Well—it's O.K. by me, George", she told him. "Still, there's Adelaide—the one you do your Gentleman George act with the B.B.C. voice for! Gosh! I do like ter hear you! She thinks you're the cat's whiskers! An' you taking her out every Sunday! You must spend a lot of money on her, George—you don't do that for nuffin', do you?"

"This Adelaide," George said with less certainty than he

28

had dismissed Gladys, "we certainly gotta keep her well lined! If you and me is ter get ter the Riviera the way I've always promised you. She's got clo'es and she's got manners—she's a sales' lady—seems ter think she's the Duchess of Kent or somepin'—an' she can bloody well pass them on ter you—when the time comes. She don't know no more than what I tell her. I'm a widower and you're my chile—that's good enough for her. Chris'!—that Baby is so wild abaht me that she wouldn't see a herd of buffaloes walking dahn Piccadilly if I tole her ter look the other way!"

Jane let this picture sink in. It pleased George, and it gave her time to develop a sudden inspiration.

"What's the age of consent, George?" she asked him when she thought his vanity was sufficiently sated. "Seventeen, ain't it? Well —of course the Law don't mean a thing ter me! —nor ter you—may-be—but don't Ma know it? An' she knows my age too! I'm not saying she'd want to give you away, but I wouldn't put it past her to tip the wink ter somebody else ter do it! Why not us wait till I *am* seventeen?—then we'd be in the clear?"

This seemed a new but not unfavourable outlook to George. He was in no hurry. One girl to him was not wholly unlike another girl—except Jane. For Jane he had an almost super-stitious inclination. He had been in a corner when he first met Jane—and had got out of it, as he instinctively felt, through adopting her. Ever since, things had gone well with George. Jane did not take money out of George as other girls did—she brought it in. Snatching handbags in a crowd was child's play to her; and she seemed to know the right bags to snatch by a kind of instinct. Jane's attraction for him was very definitely not that of sex, but something between that of a comrade and a pet mouse. He could crush her as easily as he could have crushed a mouse; but he had no wish to crush her. He had never had a comrade, and if you have never had a comrade, a pet mouse goes quite a long way towards one; but it must be your own pet mouse. Ma had told him that he would lose Jane if he didn't make her his moll, so that George was pre-pared, but not anxious, for this new relationship.

Ma had also reminded him that he would save the price of an extra room.

George was not a person who noticed the reactions of other people to his suggestions, and never until he had first considered what his own might be, but being puzzled at the moment as to his own, he turned his slow attention towards Jane.

"Wot you feel abaht it?" he suggested. "Ma says you're lonely."

Jane laughed. "I'm not lonely!" she said. "I've got Rundle —an' I don't want Wilfred! The way it is with Ma—she *wants* me ter want Wilfred—'cos he has no guts, and don't get the marrow out of his shop like I'd sure do if I was wiv him— and pass money on ter her! That's what she wants!—and if that don't come off, she puts some kind of a lodger, most likely a spy, into my room like as not—an' the cat don't come up the pipe to my room no more neither! I'll tell you the truf, George. I like you O.K., but what I seen of sex in my home town Eldorado—an' I seen a-plenty—when I was a kid—it ain't never had no relish for me since! An' as far as that goes, I guess you aren't so keen either! That Gladys—well, she may have two-timed you once or twice, but she certainly is a glamour girl—an' if you'd got all *your* Dames wrote down with their dates—why, I know they'd fill a library! You're quite a Casanova, George, aren't you? An' Gladys not knowin' a thing about them—unless Ma told her!"

"Ma!" said George as if the word was an expletive. "Ma!"

A new idea occurred to him. He had forgotten about the age of consent; and Ma had not reminded him. Why had Ma not reminded him? Why indeed had Ma brought up the subject at all? Why had she pointed out to him that he would lose Jane, if he hadn't already lost her, the moment her adolescent eyes opened wide enough to take in the beauty of walking out with a young man? George's taking her to the Pictures once a week wasn't enough, Ma had told him. It merely wet her whistle. Probably there was a young man already, Ma had added, since Jane had turned up her nose at Wilfred. George discounted Wilfred. No girl in her senses would want Wilfred.

30

He was next to a moron; nor did he want an extra lodger put there by Ma; and he wondered that this had not occurred to him before.

Jane's eyes rested upon George with the crystalline innocence of a kitten. The horizon, he thought, was clear and George himself the only figure on it. But was it safe to wait two years? Yet was it any safer to force that tough little mascot of his to take a path that she did not wish to follow? Nor was George tired of Gladys. She had flaws, but she was on the whole the most attractive woman George had ever won. The very fact that he had not entirely won her added to her attraction; and then there were the police. Who wanted them butting in? For once Ma had over-reached herself; she should have reminded George that seventeen was the age of consent—or else she should have remembered that Jane might remind him. George got up.

"I'm orf ter play billiards", he told Jane.

She saw that her battle was won. Jane waited till the side door clicked behind him, and then, pouring out a saucer of milk and opening a tin of sardines, Jane went into her room and fed Rundle, whom she found well curled up, like a fried whiting, tail to mouth, in the exact centre of her bed.

IV

The chief difference between George and Ma was that George took to crime for professional reasons only. His aim was to ensure that he had what he wanted without earning it—that it deprived or harmed other people was a side issue for George, not an incentive.

Ma, however, loved crime for its own sake; no object that rose over the edge of her horizon shone by any other light. Her imagination was saturated with evil. Ma was even willing to lose money in order to do a friend a bad turn. Sitting hour after hour in her dimly lit bed-sitter, where all sorts of odds and ends of old furniture—too dilapidated even for the pawn shop of her only son Wilfred—had been collected, Ma chewed the cud of her life-long misdeeds, and planned fresh ones. As she sat there slowly sipping gin and bitters, the flavour of these long swallowed memories rose enriched by her imagination. Here she would take away a trifle, and there add a new enlivening touch. She loved to remember how almost invariably, through twenty years of married life, she had got the better of Henry, her first and only husband, the actual father—in spite of long and successfully practised infidelities—of her one child, that unfortunate Poop—Wilfred. Ma had to admit to herself that Wilfred himself was a misdeal. He had no objection to doing wrong—if only he had known how to do it! But he never learned. Ma had had to tell him, "Now you gotta go straight, Wilfred, 'cos you can't go any other way without being found out; and havin' the cops dahn on us is a thing I can't put up with! I shall have to put you into the shop ter mind it—you can sell and you can buy, but don't you dare touch anything 'ot! That you leave to me! Telephone—that's

32

what telephones is for—and I'll come rahnd. Nor you don't juggle wiv what comes in either—into the till every penny goes—an' aht it all comes every evening wiv me looking over yer shoulder—and all accounts kep'!" Ma had even let him pay his income tax.

There was another thing against Wilfred—he had a low cunning obstinacy. Anyone Ma wanted Wilfred to marry, he wouldn't touch; so she couldn't get even with him that way; and Ma wanted to get even with Wilfred. He was the only living being with the power to move her. She had always been, if not exactly fond of him, willing to trample on him with an eye for his own good; but what she couldn't forgive were the few words he had dared to say on the doorstep after his father's funeral. "Ma," Wilfred had told her, "I ain't ever goin' ter say noffin' ter nobody, but I won't ever sleep under your roof agin!"—and he actually hadn't. He had gone straight to his grandmother's—on his father's side—who kept a fish shop in Tooting. Now what did he mean by that? So uncalled for, since his father had died from a sharp attack of gastric 'flu during an epidemic; and old Dr. Bell had not made the slightest difficulty in signing his death certificate. No one in the street had ever had a handsomer funeral. Of course Albert had been talked about, but Wilfred must by then have got used to Albert. Henry was used to him, and after the first had made rather less fuss than Ma had expected. From a marital point of view Henry himself had not had a flawless past; but Ma would have agreed with Lord Chester-field—of whom she had never heard—that the escapades of a husband are not altogether a disadvantage to a wife who knows how to use them. Besides, Henry probably realized that Albert was only a flash in the pan. But what a glorious flash! Ma often thought hour after hour about Albert—the glory that was Greece and the grandeur that was Rome had been poured over him. He had shingled golden hair and eyes like clear blue icicles. Like David, he was ruddy and of a cheerful countenance. If Ma had known where to lay her hands on an ark, Albert would have danced before it. She had never seen a jitter-bugger to match Albert.

Ma had first met Albert in a Fun Fair, and lost her heart to him and nearly her head, to the sound of a juke box. Albert was a wide boy. He took in everything and everybody—even Ma for a time. How he spent, and what fun it was spending it with him! All Henry's savings vanished. Her own carefully owned public house, The Pig and Lilies, shook under Albert's lavish depredations; and then he began to touch Ma's private hoard which she had always kept separate. After Henry's death, Ma only just had the sense not to marry Albert. But how they had rampaged, drunk and danced! These were the peak years of Ma's life. She was in her late forties, but she was still good-looking in a slightly sinister over-painted way. Her blue-black hair was lustrous, her slanting dark eyes expressed her vigorous personality with dramatic fervour; her large, well-built figure kept in bounds, promised everything that Ma was more than ready to supply. Albert was Wilfred's age—not Henry's. The passion of love, played upon by Ma, was like an instrument outside herself—an instrument that gave her considerable pleasure but could be put aside at will. The passion of temper, however, when once thoroughly roused, was considerably stronger. Her temper was inside Ma, and it was what she acted on.

Albert should have known better than to have flaunted young Fanny in Ma's face.

It would be interesting, Ma sometimes thought, to know what had become of Fanny. She knew what had become of Albert—so did George. For George was no new affair in Ma's life—he was, although Jane did not know it, an institution.

George had been a unique event in Ma's long career, not ornamental but useful; incredibly, compassion had been its opening chapter. One snowy night, when an arctic wind seared the Goldhawk Road into complete emptiness, when there was no longer a footstep nor the belated whine of a skidding car, Ma, who was listening for Albert's late return, heard a faint knock at the door. Opening it gingerly, with ready vituperation on her lips, she was confronted by a frozen scarecrow of a young boy, starved through and through from cold and hunger. The child was blue and trembling, beyond speech. He was without threat or promise. His eyes vaguely claimed some human response to his needs before they closed forever. To her own surprise, Ma met this claim. She dragged George in, warmed him by the fire, and poured hot rum and milk between his shaking lips. She let him spend the rest of the short night on a mattress close to the kitchen stove. When she woke, she found that all the houses in the row were snowed up. The pipes had burst, and she was single-handed with no promise of Albert. The street reeled with its own problems and nobody in it was at all fond of Ma, or inclined to share male assistance.

The child on her doorstep, when well fed and warmed, proved a most useful contribution to her household.

George shovelled away snow hour by hour, mended pipes, and at length established a lethargic contact with the Gold-hawk Road. Albert failed to return until the weather became normal, and when he did, he was delighted by the advent of George. Here was just what Albert wanted, at this stage of his affections—a whipping boy—a scapegoat—a screen between him and his increasing and unpopular sallies. George ran errands, took notes, fetched beer for Albert at any hour of the day or night. He even arranged bets at street corners in an intelligent manner under the very noses of the Law.

George filled a gap in Albert's existence, and he did more than fill a gap for Ma. She found she could rely on him, for George supported her in all her roles; and Ma had many. There was the pawn shop. Wilfred, though he was officially its owner, could not have been said to move unsupported, far less run a shop. Ma owned The Pig and Lilies two streets away, but never wholly beyond the reach of Ma's eye and tongue; she also kept roomers with occult and unadvertised professions. She owned decrepit house property that paid her far beyond its intrinsic value; and she lent money under conditions which left her only just safe from the Law.

George became Ma's white-headed boy. He was practically speechless; but his mind as well as his body—worked. George knew that he had plenty to learn and he was learning it. He did not want to give away anything—not even his own intel-ligence; this kept him silent.

35

Ma never spoiled George as she had spoiled Albert. Life had taught her that she could tire of pampering young men sooner than the young men got tired of being pampered. She did not want to begin all over again with George. Yet Ma treated George with something that resembled respect. She liked a worker. She let him have hours off, gave him good food and good clothes, and bit by bit let him in to the outer courts of all her affairs. George always understood rather more than Ma told him, but he made no comments. His wits were keen, his ambitions silent but infinite; and there was this great difference in Ma's eyes between Albert and George: Albert expected to be kept, and George expected to keep himself.

When Ma became shocked and desperate at the irresponsible and pleasure-loving habits of Albert, and the increasing leakage from her savings, George put it into her head that she could get rid of Albert.

One night, when she and George were alone in the house together, eating fish and chips and drinking porter, George leaned across the table and said in his lowest, hoarsest voice, "Do you want that I should do him in?"

Ma stopped eating. She looked over the fluffy top of her glass of Guinness a long time, into George's small, deep-set eyes, before she replied. The one word she at last brought forth was "'Ow?"

Albert was not only young and beautiful: he was strong as an ox. If he had been capable of taking trouble or able to bear any pain, he would have made an excellent young heavyweight. Even as it was, he could have disposed of George and Ma with one hand tied behind him. Nor was Albert cowardly, as Henry had been; he was only unutterably silly. George knew this as well as Ma did; and he had a plan to make use of Albert's silliness.

Albert wanted a car. He was always alternately coaxing and brow-beating Ma to buy him one.

"Buy 'im a car!" George now suggested.

"Gawd, George", Ma exclaimed. "Are yer off yer bleedin' coker-nut?"

"Listen", George said succinctly; and Ma listened.

36

There was nothing Albert liked more than Dogs. He bet copiously and dangerously on every race he could get to, however distant, and almost always lost.

George had designed an accident for Albert on his way back from a special race, lit up, and supposedly alone. George and Ma would have cast iron alibis. Ma might actually never leave the table they were sitting at; she could have witnesses playing whist with her while Albert's accident took place; and George would see that Albert's watch was stopped at an hour when it could be safely proved that George was somewhere else. George would arrange with Albert a secret appointment on his way home; there were plenty of things Albert had to be secret about; no one would know that George was near the accident, till he was somewhere else.

The car, no doubt, would be unavoidably damaged; but it could be well insured. Albert would ostensibly drive it, while under the influence of drink, over a quarry and into a pond some fifty feet below. Actually George would drive it—and its contents—to the edge, and, after having coshed Albert, tip it over. There would be no fingerprints.

" 'Ow did you learn to drive a car?" Ma asked George suspiciously. "*I* never learned yer!"

George grinned. It was not a disarming grin, but it was, strangely enough, one that reassured Ma.

George had lived for four years under Ma's roof, and she knew that slow, economical grin.

George did not believe in luck. He took precautions, and one of the precautions he took was not to tell Ma how he knew what he knew; or even—unless obliged to—that he knew it. He was, however, obliged to admit to Ma now that he knew how to drive a car. He knew every last thing about cars. Ma was satisfied.

The death of Albert was the death of romance for Ma; but Ma had by now tired of romance, and she did not regret the death of Albert any more than she had regretted the death of Henry.

There had to be an inquest, but it all passed off without a hitch. The car was a total loss, and there had been a little trouble about the insurance; but that was all. The leakage to Ma's fortunes stopped. She was able to keep The Pig and Lilies, and even, from its profits, to start a dance hall. Yet somehow she and George, though their partnership was materially successful, were never again so happy together as they had been while conspiring against the living Albert. There were incidents between them, usually attributed to softer feelings, but not even in Ma's long reverberations of touched up memory could she call these incidents romantic. They had led nowhere—opened no vistas. The glorious flashing Past shared with Albert had never returned. The trouble with George as a male companion was that, though he occasionally took what Ma offered him, he remained secretive, self-contained and unpredictable, exactly as he appeared in any other relationship of life. You couldn't, Ma found, get the better of George, since there was nothing you could give him that—if he wanted it—he wasn't perfectly capable of taking for himself.

After a profitable year or two together, George told Ma that he had met two wide boys from Chicago who had offered him a worth while opening in their underworld. George thought that he would like to go to America—for a time at any rate. Ma discovered that she was not averse to George's departure. George asked her for a thousand pounds, but did not seem disappointed when Ma gave him five hundred.

They parted on excellent terms. Ma begged him to return whenever he liked and make her house his home.

George said, "Be good, Ma! and if you can't be good—be careful!"

He even turned to wave his hand as he crossed the gang plank.

On Ma's return home she found that George had taken the balance of the sum he had asked for from Wilfred's safe. Ma was very angry with Wilfred, but not really angry with George; she thought it had been very smart of him, and indeed just like him—no expostulations—no back-talk—just appropriate action.

But what she didn't like—after ten years of unquestioned

and prosperous freedom—was George's accompanied return. She might have stood George by himself—but why had he brought back Jane? Ma decided to take George in because he had obviously made a considerable amount of money, but she disliked the conditions he made. He insisted, while keeping Ma's best first floor double room, on building a garage adjoining it, and installing Jane in a room above the garage. In this way, George explained, he had three good exits as well as an up-to-date kitchenette and bathroom. In the United States he had learned to appreciate cleanliness and gadgets; now he could afford gadgets. And what was Jane, Ma had sarcastically enquired—was she also a gadget? She was too old to be George's child, too young to be his wife—what, then, was she? George replied that he was training Jane for professional purposes; there was probably no lighter-fingered child in London; and that she was besides a kind of mascot. He had had luck since he knew Jane.

If only, Ma thought, Jane had been a few years younger, she could have been controllable by a combination, curiously effective with children, of terror and pampering. Or had Jane been a few years older, she would have been still more vulnerable. A man's moll is always open to jealousy—either by feeling it—or by rousing it. But there was a cast iron quality about Jane that put Ma off. From the first Jane had been glowering and secretive. She had refused bribes and was too tough to frighten; and then she had enticed Rundle away from Ma. Rundle had never liked anyone before—not even Ma; but he had accepted whatever Ma gave him, and in return lain quietly and unobtrusively in front of the kitchen fire, neither hearing what Ma sometimes liked to say out loud to herself—nor even wanting to hear it. His indifferent presence had had a soothing influence on Ma; and sometimes Ma found with increasing age she needed soothing. She was not exactly afraid of anything. No one inside her own walls would do her any harm. Ma knew everything that all her roomers would have liked to hide from her; there was nothing in their whole ill-regulated lives Ma couldn't have laid a finger on, and held up against them, if they tried any funny business. But they wouldn't try any funny business. Just to be on the safe side, Ma had shown them how she could throw knives.

Like the three wise monkeys, Ma's lodgers saw nothing, heard nothing, and repeated nothing. They paid their rents like angels, and respected the rules of the house. It suited all of them; and up till now they had all suited Ma.

But what went on behind George's bolted door, or where he kept what he had undoubtedly acquired, and kept on acquiring, Ma did not know—nor did she know how she was going to find out.

She sat and stared unblinkingly at the place where Rundle should have lain, sipping steadily away at hot gin and bitters— she herself avoided cocoa—and considered how, upon the foundation of the Past, she could build a still more inviting structure for the Future. This structure, Ma told herself, might still contain George; but it should certainly not include Jane.

V

There was just a moment, while George was getting out his car, in which Jane could say goodbye to Rundle. He was lying, where a patch of April sun had caught him, in burnished glory on Jane's bed, slowly digesting two guilefully acquired breakfasts.

"Oh Boy!" Jane whispered into his neck. "It's wunnerful—it sure is! It's my first house-break with George! You be here when I git back, Rundle?"

Rundle slowly but reassuringly drove a sheathed paw into the round cheek close to his topaz eyes: the April light and Jane's soft cheek withdrew together, without disturbing his intent to slumber.

It seemed to Jane she had everything. George had bought her a new suit and allowed her to use her first really good make-up.

"If she's going to wear clothes—she must *look* like clothes!" Adelaide, who had chosen Jane's suit, had kindly informed him, "and what's more, George—she must *smell* like clothes."

So George, very reluctantly, had added a Lily of the Valley scent to round off Jane's outfit. The trouble was she didn't look like a lily, Jane thought to herself, after a last relentless glance into her looking glass, on her way to join George. She still had a boot-button nose, a wide mouth, and a complexion which might improve in time but badly needed clearing. She could not know that her grey-green eyes could sparkle like sunshine between their thick black lashes, and that when she smiled, it was difficult not to smile with her. George gave her an indifferent glance and told her to get in and look slippy.

It was the first time Jane had ever been alone with George on business in his sports Jaguar. She had an uncaged feeling, as if somebody had opened a door into the sky and let her free. Everything she looked at shone back at her—even George. The leaves on the small experimental trees bordering the arterial road, swirling with traffic, might have been made of real gold, if gold could swing as carelessly as new born leaves.

The rows of modern factories they shot by—glass and hygiene outside and chemicals and boredom within—were fairy tale palaces. Jane even believed in the swimming pools on pocket handkerchiefs of arsenical green grass that were never meant to be used at all, but which stood in front of the factories and were simply there to make you believe that everybody who worked there was having a wonderful time.

Jane watched with tender zeal—for she would have liked to take care of all of them—the babies in prams laid out for the air to harden, in front of the prim, neat new dwellings— each of exactly the same size and price, but made up to look a little different. Her heart was in her mouth for dogs nearly run over, or cats unduly hurried. She did not notice the petrol and dust-filled air—only the haunting scent of stubborn lilac bushes reached her eager senses.

The rows of houses and factories broke up. Fields spread round them, touched with delicate shades of colour, browns melting into pink, while living green struggled against grey winter grasses. Church spires shot up out of little villages built with rose-red brick or soft yellow stone. Small woods shot past them, like the palettes of painters trying in turn every conceivable shade.

The English countryside was like a picture on a screen, but not at all like Hollywood. There were no great empty mountains, no vast Pacific, sliding away from endless unlinked suburbs that were never quite a city. Nor was this delicate wind-ruffled light like the hard bright sunshine under which all Jane's early days had been publicly spent, for her home was a mere shell—the streets had been her life.

How much did she want to remember? How much out of that brawling, violent, yet stimulating time had ever been hers? Well—there was Marlene, a baby of a few months old, who would long ago have forgotten her. In fifteen years all Jane had ever had to love was a baby and a cat. They took what you gave them when they liked it, and let you know somehow or other if they didn't; but they were not what you could call resounding relationships. The future, not the past, was the thing Jane urged upon her bright imagination. She smiled confidently at George across its radiant possibilities; and George, his mind bent in a different way upon it, smiled reluctantly back. "It's a piece of cake!" George decided to tell her.

"This house we're going to open—it's convenient. The mink coat is in the main bedroom—same as the safe with the jewels. I got in and had a look-see last week, while they was all in church; but I couldn't stay, 'cos there was a cook that might have started prowling. You're sure you know mink by the touch?"

"I certainly do," Jane told him with pride. "Well—what I say is—every girl ought to know the feel of mink!"

George agreed. He agreed more readily with Jane now than when he had thought of her, a few days earlier, as a child. He looked at her as if she had become someone else—someone he was obliged—rather pleasantly obliged—to notice.

Jane herself, in a vague cloudy way, felt there was a change in George. Hitherto George had simply been Jane's climate; fair or foul, she had learned to put up with it. But it had never occurred to Jane to think of George as a person, or to hold him accountable in any way for his behaviour. Now she had taken a step nearer him as an individual. He had become her partner rather than her teacher. Jane had no longer only to carry out his lessons, but also to share his risks. A wall—the wall of her childhood—had been taken down; a protective wall, had Jane but known it; and though nothing as yet had been put in its place, there was open country between them.

"That mink coat", Jane demanded. "What is it worth, George?"

"A cool thousand", George replied. "The jewels are good too—what she has is O.K. though it isn't much. Pearl necklace, emerald pendant and two diamond clasps. Haven't seen them, but they sound good. The safe'll take me half an hour ter open; I've only opened one of them kind before—and it's

43

tricky—but you don't need jelly. People in the 'ouse won't be no bother. Old general plays cards every evening regular as clockwork—between 8 and 10.30. There they all sit glued to a table the opposite side of the 'ouse—no dog—not much staff. A fat girl, Emma, goes off home after washing up. Cook sits by her radio till bedtime. I danced with the fat girl lars' Saturday night—she tole me all I wanted. I wore a loverly scar—cost me a lot, that scar did—eyeglass and ginger 'air; and I took a bit of a tummy on! It don't do to be too crude in town—but in the country . . . Well—it won't be *me* they're looking for—after termorrer."

"Gee, George! You think of everything!" Jane said approvingly.

She was thrilled with fear—and rapture. Would she be good enough to match George? It was not the mink coat or the jewels which swam before Jane's eager eyes. She felt the promise and agony of a new opera star standing in the wings. Music ran in her blood; she was trained to her highest pitch, but would her voice come out all right? Would something stick in her throat and stop it?

Was George sure that Jane could get through that lavatory window? What if she opened a wrong door, or someone had an unusual errand that took him upstairs when George counted on his being down? It was a silent drive. George too had to think of his new risks. He was a matchless cat-burglar, but cat-burglars are used to working alone. George hated gangs. It was not only that he disliked dividing up, but he loathed the faulty mechanism of other men's minds. Jane's company was less offensive, but it was a new risk. If you were by yourself or had trained your girl as he had trained Jane, you did not have to argue, you just said. The rapidity of Jane's wits, her grasp of detail and her readiness to ignore risks gratified George. She had not even noticed that she was to get in first and get away last; and as for his plan and the careful drawings he had made—she knew them backwards. She wouldn't, he decided, be too bad a risk. She must begin some time.

The lovely golden day ran into a heavy shower of rain. George cursed and stopped the car to put the hood up. Rain

44

meant footsteps, and George didn't like the idea of footsteps at all, he told Jane. She mustn't forget, her shoes had got to come off before she climbed. She could wear them round her neck, same as he did, on a band. He'd brought two of them. He had his rope ladder with him, for getting away, because it didn't do to risk stairs too often. There was a magnolia trained against the bedroom wall, but not strong enough to hold either of them by itself. He didn't mind Jane getting out from downstairs, if they got through in time. Otherwise she must take to the ladder, and make no bones about it—torch in her teeth—same as he always did. She was used to rope ladders, wasn't she? Jane nodded. She *was* used to them; but in the dark they did sway something awful; and suppose the torch fell out of her teeth?

By tea-time they reached the outskirts of a large market town, a very handsome town, Jane thought, glittering under the slanting silver rain, with black-beamed houses, raspberry coloured bricks, a quick blue river under a grey stone bridge; and rising with effortless lightness, high above all the houses, the spire of a great cathedral, needling its thin way into the clear sky. The rain had stopped and every puddle glistened with gold or azure.

"We're going to have a slap up tea here", George told Jane, patiently pursuing a polite way through the huddled traffic. "In the biggest hotel—'cos where there are the most people you don't get noticed so much. But I don't want no garidge boy studying my car. I'll slip her in, on a side road—this'll do—between a Wolsey and a Standard and she'll park natural. Nah Jane, up wiv your chin and look grade A. That's what I bought you them party clothes for! I'll say you look swell in them!"

Jane bit her lips, threw up her head, and sailed into the lounge trying to resemble her favourite film star; while George, developing his gentlemanly side, sauntered nonchalantly after her.

George ordered the best of everything the hotel had to offer: tea-cakes and éclairs, cream and jam, slices of plum cake from Australia (rather gritty from its travels), savoury

45

sandwiches with limp pieces of watercress oozing between thin slices of bread and margarine; and one honest sardine sandwich on the top of the pile.

"Money speaks," George told Jane, "and what it says is that we aren't after anythink that we haven't got!"

They ate everything. George had been strung up while he drove, but now he relaxed—if to relax on purpose is to carry out its purpose. Gentlemen, George had noticed, generally appeared calm—polite to inferiors if well attended to—insolent at the slightest provocation—you-be-damned to all men; and smiling to all women.

George could do these things very well for a time; and if Jane had asked him for the moon, his smile told her that she would have got it. But Jane knew better than to ask George for the moon. She took whatever he gave her, and curled her little finger above the handle of her tea-cup. It was an uncomfortable position, but George looked at her approvingly. He would rather have had whisky, but he let Jane pour him out tea. After tea, George kindly suggested that Jane might like to have a look at the shops while he picked up a game of billiards. They need not start before six.

Jane found an opening between the shops that led through a great stone archway on to an empty grass space. On every side of this smooth green velvet carpet stood elegant and spacious houses; and in front of it was the Cathedral.

In the early evening light, the great building had a magic air. The stones out of which it was built were a pale fawn colour touched with pink, and there were swallows flying under it, very fast and high. Yet when Jane looked up between their arrowy flights, it was to see that the tower pierced far higher into the golden light than the flying birds. "Funny," she thought to herself, "it's only a church after all! It ain't a Studio!" Yet Jane had never seen anything more certain of its place in the sky than that thin spire.

There were glimpses of gardens through the iron gates of the mellow, generous houses. Jane could see daffodils and narcissi, hyacinths and beds of polyanthus washed with recent rain. They had not the rank and stateliness of the taller

46

flowers, but they shone like jewels, pushed up from the earth between their rough grey leaves. Herbaceous borders stretched away between grass paths, towards the narrow blue river in the distance. Jane longed to go inside the close-shut gates and look at them properly, but each garden seemed to have a suspicious little dog to bark gruffly at her.

She turned to face the spire again, to which the flowers, the houses, and the river itself, seemed to be drawn by invisible threads.

Jane could hardly tear herself away to get back in time to meet George. She had to run; and it was as if the spire ran with her.

George was already in the car, and he wasn't a gentleman any more. He told her, with a string of well chosen oaths, exactly what he thought of girls that kept men waiting; but Jane knew he wasn't really angry, and that she wasn't really late; George was only blowing off his nerves as if they were the froth on beer. When George was really angry he looked quite different, and seldom spoke. He did things; and it was then you had to be careful.

A few minutes later he said, "Getting on nah!" with fluctuating amiability.

"There's the Wiltshire Downs," he informed her, "off to yer left."

"Those green lumps?" Jane asked, but as they swung towards them, the low hills smoothed and opened out, like the high green backs of waves before they broke.

"That's—what they call their Park," George said in confidential tone. "We'll go down this side road—and pass the gate—'cos the lane beyond joins up wiv the main road—and I want ter leave her where nothing driving up can spot her. They don't have many visitors, but you never can tell. Here's the place to stop—far enough not to be seen from the house and near enough for a good get-away. You keep it well fixed in your 'ead, Jane, case we git separated!—'cos I shan't want ter mess abaht when I got the swag on me. It'll be dead dark in an hour. I ain't too fond of moons me-self. We won't talk out loud no more now. This is IT! Jane—you O.K.?"

"O.K. George!" Jane whispered trembling.

The curtain was rising. There was no sound in the misty Park, not a whine nor a whisper, no leaf stirred. Suddenly within a few yards—just above their heads—a great white thing swept by on silent wings, cleaving the darkness, and a voice like a bad child's shrieked in their very ears. Even George jerked back as if someone had struck him. Jane was fortunately too frightened to make a sound; she simply flung herself on George, who whispered not unkindly, while disengaging himself from her clinging arms, "Damn you, Jane—it's only a h'owl!"

Wet bracken and unseen bluebells curled themselves against their slowly moving figures. George, soundless as a shadow, led the way. A pin point of light from his torch shone downwards to save Jane from trees or hidden stumps. The dark bulk of the house rose suddenly above them. Jane held her breath. She knew George had left her side, but she could not see what he was doing, and she heard nothing. She knew that he was going to unfasten the catch of the lavatory window, through which Jane must climb in. That part would happen—but what would follow after? A chill, moist wind blew her hair into her eyes and tasted like tears against her lips. George's hand touched her shoulder; gently but inexorably he pushed her forward till Jane touched stone. A tiny light from George's shielded torch showed her a ledge high above her—to which she must climb. There was nothing to help her climb after the first steadying of George's powerful hands.

Her toes clamped themselves desperately into the interstices between the stones. Had she enough purchase to dare to draw herself up now on to this narrow ledge? What a weight her body was—her wrists seemed to break under the strain she drove down into them. But she was up at last; the struggle became more desperate still. She was small and her body was trained like an acrobat's. But was she small enough to get through that narrow gap—writhing and straining through the window, her torch between her teeth, her hands clawing at the cold walls? Suddenly she touched a pipe. Now she was safe; the lavatory seat was just beneath, and she dropped soundlessly on to it.

The door now. She pressed the knob with a firm, slow pressure, her body moving towards it; and then still more slowly, relaxed her pressure. The door opened without a sound. She was in a passage that led to the kitchen. There was a light under the door—and that protective universal voice of the radio—nobody in the kitchen would hear much through that voice.

In the opposite direction was complete darkness and no sound. But Jane could use her torch now. She could guess which were coal cellars, and brush cupboards; and she found at last the green baize door George had told her about, leading from the back premises into the front hall.

The hall, when Jane observed it through a crack, was full of light, but empty.

Haunting eyes from old portraits glared suspiciously down at Jane, and worse still, she stubbed her toes against the large bumpy head of a lion, and looking down appalled, met its glassy eyes threatening her. Who could have expected to have to walk about on lions? She got off the lion skin as quickly as she could, and there were the five doors George had shown her on the plan. She was to open the third one on the right. Could George have made a mistake? Behind one of the doors were people. She heard someone laugh. Jane was accustomed to loud laughter, silly laughter from drunkards, brutal laughter before or after a fight—but the sound of this laughter was new to her. It was as if someone had liked what had made them laugh; but Jane couldn't waste time listening to it, so she simply pressed herself against the third door.

This was the drawing room. Miles and miles of shining parquet floor stretched in front of her. She must cross this desert on her stocking feet and fumble her way through heavy damask curtains before she could find the latch of the right window for George. This was the hardest part of the whole business, because when she found the latch she couldn't make it move. She tried first one way, then the other; she put one hand under the latch, pressing her whole body behind it against the woodwork, and at last the latch moved, but not quite noiselessly. George's whispered curse might have been the voice of an angel, it so relieved the loneliness of Jane's hard-beating heart.

The cool air touched her cheeks with kindness. George was in, his whole taut body listening, beside her. How lightly he moved on the balls of his feet; he seemed to drift like thistle-down across the parquet floor. She had only to follow him; the stair carpet was thick and soft as heather under their feet. They were in the main bedroom. Now they had to move less carefully: the door was shut behind them. They could even bare their torches. The mink coat came next.

George needed half an hour for the safe, and without a glance at Jane set to work upon it. The walled cupboard was deep; it smelled like the Cathedral gardens Jane couldn't get into. The General's wife had a lot of clothes, and they were all good; but only one mink. Jane's hands ran over the smooth, soft king of furs with rapture. Gently she drew it from its padded hanger. She couldn't resist the silken sheath of the lining. She slipped into its rich, deep softness, and crept out into the room again.

If only she could see what she looked like! There was a tall hanging mirror, but from her small flashlight she could only get a garbled glimpse. She didn't dare ask George to stop and look at it with her.

What she ought to do next was to get straight out of the room, and guard the passage and the stairs; and it was what she did do; but she didn't take off the mink coat and lay it on the bed as George had told her. She just stood there, behind a bookcase on the stairs, a sort of queen, in the half darkness—mink endowed—waiting for George's releasing signal.

It came at last; and Jane crept back into the room again for further instructions. George preferred to make his entrances by a window on the ground floor and his exits from above by rope ladder. He said you didn't want to go marching about inside houses with the swag on you. But George didn't mind rope ladders swinging in the dark and taking your skin off against stone walls. Still, he hadn't made an awful fuss when Jane asked if she mightn't take the drawing room window herself instead.

"Mink!" George whispered hoarsely.

He hadn't looked at Jane. He was over the window sill—and she could of course have still slipped the coat to him. But she didn't; she just whispered back, "O.K. George. I got the mink. I'll go out the other way."

George said no more. The safe had taken longer than he meant it to take, and the ladder needed all his attention. Leaning over the sill, Jane could just make out George, a black lump, swinging to and fro till he joined an intenser darkness. She couldn't, she told herself, swing down like that with the weight of the mink. Her mind was made up for her: she must face the stairs again.

Jane turned at the sound of a faint click. Suddenly the whole room flooded with light, and she found herself staring into the steadiest pair of eyes she had ever seen. They belonged to Brigadier-General Despard, D.S.O. with a double bar. He was an old man between sixty and seventy, but time had done him very little harm.

"What the devil——!" he exclaimed.

He was considerably more astonished than Jane, for he had only come up for some change to pay his bridge debts, and had not expected to be confronted in his own bedroom by a strange little girl, half lost in his wife's mink coat.

The apparition leapt, not away from him but straight at him, like a boxing leopard, striking him first on one side of his head and then on the other. Jane further confused him by spitting in his face. Then she leapt backwards, the soft fur slipping through the hands he had stretched out to catch her, over the window sill, and presumably into forty feet of black air. Jane had remembered the magnolia. The ladder had gone with George; it would have been too slow a descent anyway; but the tree was there. Through it she scrambled, and fell—branches broke under her, caught at her, scratched, tore and bruised her—and at the end she had a sheer twelve foot drop.

"Gee—what a get-away!" Jane murmured to herself as she ran barefoot over the wet grass for the gate.

VI

The air, sharp with rain and pungent with wet bracken, closed over Jane like water. It was completely dark.

She stood for a second training all her senses to act for her, and then plunged towards the gates.

She guided herself by the sound of George's engine heating up for a start. The sound rose to its climax, dwindled, rose again, and died out against the silence.

Jane drew a long gasping breath and stood still. George had promised to wait for her; the Police Station was more than a mile away: he had found out on Saturday night just what time they could count on for escape. They might be separated —but whoever reached the car first would wait for the other. But George had not waited. In that blank moment of recognition Jane's childhood receded from her. She knew now that she had no one but herself to count on. There might be dogs let loose after her—there would be Police. She ran on, straight into the arms of a young man coming up the drive.

"What's your hurry?" he demanded, flashing a naked torch on her.

Jane knew that the mink coat was torn, and that her hair was wild. Something thicker than rain ran down her cheeks.

"Gotta catch a 'bus!" Jane cried. "Jes' heard my mother's dying in hospital!"

She tried to dodge past him, but he was a ubiquitous young man who could dodge as fast as Jane could.

"Isn't that just too bad!" he answered in a pleasant unconcerned voice, "but please don't worry. I can give you a lift in my car to the nearest 'bus stop—faster than you can sprint. But would you just mind telling me first, why you're wearing a mink coat two sizes too large for you, that looks uncommonly like my future mother-in-law's?"

Jane was silent. George had taught her to know when she was beaten, and what to do about it. You shut up and watched for the next chance to escape.

The young man seemed to know what was in her mind. He caught hold of both her wrists and drew them gently but tightly behind her back. She couldn't even kick him now—she was too close.

"I expect your poor mother will have to go on dying," he said with grim geniality, "just till we get the point about the mink cleared up."

The hands that held her were not rough, but they were cruelly strong.

The wild scented airs that blew about Jane's face no longer reached her senses. They were blocked by the knowledge that no escape was possible.

Shouts and telephone bells resounded; lights bobbed to and fro along the terrace beneath the magnolia tree, where no doubt they expected to find Jane's mangled remains.

The young man, pulling her reluctantly along, shouted out, "Hullo! I've got one of them!"

The long French window Jane had found so difficult to open was swinging wide, and the young man pushed her through it into the lit splendour of the drawing room. It must, Jane thought, have taken a lot of work to make a room of such a size shine so like a goldsmith's window. Besides the delicate-limbed, highly polished furniture, there were the People themselves—the ones she had heard laughing behind a shut door.

No one was laughing now. Suppose a cat—suppose Rundle suddenly found himself in a room full of strange dogs, would he not feel as Jane felt? Layers and layers of living, deepened by tradition, stretched by education, padded by money, lay between Jane's hard small consciousness and theirs.

The old gentleman she had banged about the head sat perfectly composed and at his ease, though both his cheeks were still bright crimson from her blows. His eyes met Jane's as if he were amused rather than angry. Sitting on a yellow satin sofa was a beautiful woman—presumably the General's wife, though she must have been twenty years younger—who looked as though the mink must belong to her. There was a young girl as well, a few years older than Jane, whose hair, shoes, and skin shone with a mysterious bloom. She glanced over Jane's head and gave the young man holding her a swift half derisive, half admiring smile.

Jane couldn't see how the young man returned this enigmatic greeting because he held Jane a little in front of him, facing the shining room.

Very gently, still holding her wrists with one hand, the young man disembarrassed Jane of the mink.

"This is yours, I suppose?" he asked the Lady on the sofa.

"Oh yes!" she sighed. "I'm afraid it *is*!"

There was a curious sound like compassion in her voice. Why the Hell, Jane asked herself, was the Lady afraid it was her coat? Didn't she want her mink back? Perhaps she would rather have had her jewels—yet the mink was something!

"She looks so terribly young!" the Lady said, and now there was no doubt that she minded less about the mink than she minded about Jane.

"Young enough to know better!" General Despard remarked drily. "I assure you she knows all the ropes!" but then he did a very funny thing. He deliberately pushed one of the delicate chairs towards Jane. "She even knows what to do when the ropes aren't there! Hadn't you better sit down", he asked Jane. "You must be tired after all that scrambling?"

The young man released her, and Jane sat down, but she knew that the young man still stood between her and the open window.

"I'm afraid," he said, "that I heard her mate making off down the lane just as I drove up; but of course I had no idea there was anything wrong, or I'd have taken his number. This young woman barged into me as if she'd been shot out of a catapult—just a minute or so too late for her romantic getaway."

There was a pause as if they were weighing up Jane's

chances, and perhaps regretting that she hadn't had that extra minute.

A motor cycle screeched up the drive, and a voice outside the door said, "The Police!"

There was no confusing magic about the Police. Jane knew all about them. They wouldn't be polite or look on the verge of tears because a thousand-pound mink had just been restored to them.

"Were you hurt at all?" the Lady asked Jane in a quick rueful tone, before the Police came in. "You must have had such a dreadful fall through that magnolia!"

"The mink tore," Jane told her abruptly.

In its way her statement was an apology. She knew now that she was bruised and sore all over, but she hadn't felt anything at the time. Even now it wasn't the bruises that she felt most—it was the loneliness.

The Lady said quickly, "Oh, the tear doesn't matter at all—it can easily be mended!"

"Don't be silly, Mother!" the other girl said sharply. "You forget what she did to Father. She's as hard as nails."

The girl hadn't looked directly at Jane before, but Jane knew from the first that she was the most hostile of the four strange people—and the least strange. But it was no use wasting her time thinking about her unnatural enemies—her natural enemies were now upon her. The Police were in the room.

The Inspector came in first, a middle-aged, hard-headed man as certain of himself as he was of the Law; following him was a simple, tow-haired young fellow, the size of a giant and agonizingly conscious of his boots and his hands.

Jane stared at them with a poker face. She knew what her rights were, and that they would try to get the better of her. Well—she would try to get the better of them too. Let's see which would get tired first.

"Now then", the Inspector barked, after polite exchanges with the General and his family.

"Who did you break into the house with? That's the first question for you to answer. And while you're answering it you

55

can stand up—and keep standing! It's no use trying to bluff me: I've seen two sets of footprints—and one set wasn't yours!"

"Perhaps she could just sit down for a *little* while", Lady Despard pleaded. "You know she must have fallen half-way through that magnolia tree; she must be very shaken even if she escaped an injury, and there's blood on her forehead."

"She don't look hurt to me, your Ladyship, and that's only a scratch to her forehead, I'm sure; but still, if you wish it, she can stay sitting down."

Jane, whose legs still shook under her, clung thankfully to her chair.

"You got me!" she said sharply to the Inspector. "I can't help that, can I? But that don't mean you can make me talk! Don't you run away with the idea that you're Go-bells—this is England!"

"Now, my girl," the Inspector told her, "you won't do yourself no good by backchat. You were caught with the goods on you. Your mate's got away for the moment, but we shall pick him up sooner or later—with you, or without you. All I want from you now about him is his name, his hide-out and the number of his car. When you've told me this, we'll see about you. If you tell us what we want at once, it'll be a lot better for you. I'm making no promises, but fair is fair, and if you help us, we may be able to help you. An' make no mistake, you'll need it! Stealing a mink coat at your age isn't a thing that's going to be easy explained to the magistrate!"

Jane gave him a long malevolent glance, but she said nothing.

"Speak up!" he said irately. "Where did you both come from?"

"I'm a messenger from Mars," Jane told him, after a pause, "and that was the Angel Gabriel that came along with me—and has gone back where he come from! You gotta cheek, haven't you—thinking I'd split on a pal?"

"I don't somehow think this girl is British", the young man behind Jane interjected. "She has a marked American

56

accent and she thinks quickly. I believe she comes from the United States."

The Inspector looked pained. He did not like untrained helpers who started up fresh problems.

Jane, however, herself released him from this dilemma.

"I'm not claiming to be American," she told him. "But if you want to know—my Ma—she was a Yank; and my Dad he deserted my Ma and me. She's dead, but he was Liverpool Irish—and Liverpool was where I was born—and my name's Jane McCarthy, and that's all I've got for you!"

"Nonsense," said the Inspector. "Less of your lip, young lady—and more of the facts—is what we want from you! We can take up your family history at the Police Station later on. What we want to know now is, who is that young man you're living with, and where's he off to?"

Jane smiled. "Oh yeah!" she murmured with infinite derision.

"I'll thank you for your address!" repeated the Inspector savagely. "You don't suppose, do you, that we shan't be able to pick it up somewhere for ourselves in time if you don't give it to us?"

"Well, you might," Jane admitted, "if I had one. But I haven't, not what you might call a *home* address. I live near an American airfield, and I camp visit." The names of the American boys whom she visited, except their first names, Jane conveniently forgot.

The People remained, and with them their atmosphere of cold fair play and irrelevant soft-heartedness.

Finally the Inspector turned to General Despard. "I think, Sir William, that we may take it this girl has an accomplice who has got off with the jewels. Still we shall have to take her to the Station in order to search her. My wife will look after her for the night and I think I can get hold of Sir Henry Melville and another magistrate to see her in the morning. Morely House must take her—though they're crammed full of bombed-out Londoners at present—a much wilder lot than any of ours—but I couldn't get her fitted in there so late at night. Do you think Captain Ransome could give us a lift

57

with her in his car to the Police Station? We've only got our motor bikes with us."

For people who knew so well how to behave, it occurred to Jane as odd that they should sit like so many stuffed owls and not get a move on. The General looked flushed and unhappy; Lady Despard had an expression as guilty as if she herself were in Jane's shoes; the Police Officers looked awkward; only Charles and Diana wore a detached and independent air, since they were in love and did not really care what happened to anyone but each other. Still, however detached they were, Jane thought, they would manage to stop her quicker even than the Police Officers if she tried to make a bolt for the window. It was best just to sit and stare at them defiantly in order to hide how sick, and sore, and shaken, she felt.

Lady Despard was the first to break the silence. "Diana," she said desperately, "this poor child must have something to eat and drink before they take her off to the Police Station! Will you take her into the dining-room—where there is probably still coffee—and see that she gets something to eat—while we discuss the whole matter with the Inspector?"

General Despard looked from his daughter to Jane and said briskly, with a curious glint in his eyes, "Well—why not? My daughter, Inspector, has been taught to box and she has done her full time during the war in the Service, so I feel that she is quite competent to deal with this young lady."

Diana led Jane into the dining-room. The shutters were shut. Jane observed that there were three possible exits and knew that, besides Diana, there were four men to guard them. There were a lot of silver cups on the sideboard. The great polished table shone like a mirror and in the middle of it was a silver tray with cups of pastel shades, each different in colour.

"I couldn't eat anything if you were to pay me to eat it," Jane said quickly, "but I could do with a drink."

Diana poured out a cup of black coffee and fetching a bottle of brandy from the sideboard she laced it with generosity.

"Now we are alone," she said, the asperity of her voice contradicting the generosity of her gesture, "I don't mind

58

telling you that I think you are a disgusting little brute—
knocking an old man about like that! You might have killed
my father. There isn't much to be said for stealing, but there's
even less for murdering somebody who has never done you
any harm!"

"What would you know about taking things—when you got
'em all already?" Jane replied tartly. "And what abaht my
get-away? Sweet Jesus—we wasn't playing no game of Tag,
your father and I—whichever caught the other was bound to
get hurt! You should worry about your Dad—he can look
after himself! But what do you suppose is coming ter me for
hitting him?"

"Nothing at all," Diana said contemptuously. "My father
isn't going to charge you with violence. I wanted him to—but
he won't! What you'll get—and it is a great deal less than
you deserve—is just for plain, clean burglary—and I don't
happen to think so much of that either."

"Holy Moses!" Jane gasped. "Why ever wouldn't he charge
me? He has the marks on his face—he could prove it! Sure, I
might say he'd assaulted me—but I wouldn't—there wasn't
time!"

Diana poured Jane out a second cup of coffee, without
brandy, and pushed it towards her in unsympathetic silence,
then she said, "Why, you little idiot, a man like my father
wouldn't touch you with a barge pole!"

Jane put down her cup and burst into tears. "You hadn't
ortta say that", she said, "you hurt my feelings!"

Everything had suddenly become quite awful, just as Jane
had begun to hope for the best—talking to another girl and
getting a good drink! Jane had felt so proud of her new coat
and skirt this morning, but she suddenly felt that the quality
of it had dimmed down and that the scent George had bought
was cheap. Diana, too, looked shocked—not this time with Jane,
but with herself.

"Like a smoke?" she asked hurriedly, opening a silver
cigarette case as thin as a wafer, and handing it to Jane.

Jane stopped sobbing. "Jee's!—I was kinda dying for one",
she admitted, and took a handful out of it.

VII

Jane postponed her tears until the door clanged behind the Inspector's wife, who had taken her in charge.

The hollow sound echoed on and on in Jane's heart, as if within its harsh emptiness was enclosed the defeated bitterness of all the prisoners it had ever shut upon; and yet Mrs. Bassett, the Inspector's wife, had not been unkind. She had told Jane she was not a prisoner in the ordinary sense of the word; but as there was nowhere else to put her safely for the night, she would have to sleep in the Station cell; but it wouldn't be locked and the Inspector's wife herself would sit in an armchair outside the door until morning.

It was too late to ring up the Remand Home where Jane would, no doubt, be taken tomorrow morning after the magistrates had seen her. She was only a child delinquent, well under sixteen, and the Police, beyond arresting her, would have nothing further to do with her. Miss Emsley, the Probation Officer, would come and see Jane in the morning, before the magistrates, and she was the person who would take her to Court later on and would, indeed, be put in charge of all her interests. Jane was not quite sure what her interests were but, no doubt, that was another thing she would find out in the morning. She saw by the face of the Inspector's wife that she had better not ask any more questions. Mrs. Bassett was naturally put out, having just gone to bed in a comfortable room at the back of the Station, to be hauled out, to sit wrapped in a blanket outside a bad girl's cell for the remainder of the night. Mrs. Bassett liked to help her husband, but she wasn't sure that she liked to help him quite as much as all that! "Of course", she finished, looking grimly at Jane, "breaking into a house at night is a very serious crime, whether you are under age or over it!"

Jane said nothing, because it occurred to her that the quieter she kept her tongue the more likely she was to get a better breakfast out of the Inspector's wife in the morning. When she was left alone Jane started to cry in a desultory way, and without much vigour, since there was no one watching her. She went on for some time, because the physical expression of her self-pity soothed the intensity of her discouragement. She was worn out, very severely bruised, and her feelings had been outraged in so many different ways, she hardly knew which hurt her most.

The bed she lay on was without a pillow or sheets, and her taut nerves pulled her towards the ceiling rather than let her relax into what little comfort there was. She had taken in every detail of the cell before the light went off. It was not dirty, but there was a smell in it of cheap chemicals and human misery. Dirty people had been afraid in it; and both their fear and their dirt had an indelible quality that would not yield even to chemicals. Besides, perhaps nobody had wanted it to look cleaner than was necessary. There was a wooden table in it fastened to the floor, a chair, a washstand with running water, a closet seat and a bed. Her window was very high up and barred, but a little of it was open; and through it the keen sweet wind blew in and helped to lessen the dingy, doleful smell.

Jane had seen a book on the table, but she hadn't opened it. She suspected it of being the Bible, a book that she knew nothing about except that you didn't open it.

Her uppermost problem was the singular behaviour of the Despards. Why had they treated her with such unexpected kindness—as if they liked her—and yet given her up to her enemies? What was the sense, she asked herself, of doing all that for her—and then not letting her go?

She could have found her way home—money or no money. Home to Rundle and her neat box bed above the garage, home to Ma—who hated her—to George, who had deserted her—home to all she had, anyhow, or knew anything about. The awful part of the Law was that Jane didn't know anything about it. "Never get caught!" was all that George had told Jane about the Law. It was not a subject that George liked to talk about and George never talked about what he didn't like. And now, on her very first house-break, Jane *had* got caught!

She thought it all over, step by innocent step; for they all appeared to her innocent, since they had been George's orders faithfully carried out. What had she done to deserve such a cruel punishment? She had watched the stairs, she had obeyed his signal from the room, she had found the mink in the dark by touch and smell. George hadn't told her to put it on, but he had seen she *had* it on—and he hadn't told her to take it off. He had given her the choice of the ladder or the stairs; and she had chosen the stairs, counting on the bridge party to stay where they sat. She couldn't have foretold the General's ascent to get his change. But how instantly and sensibly Jane had acted when the light went on! She had waltzed right in and wasted no time whatever—just biffed the old geyser silly. George had often told her, "Never you touch anybody if you can get away wiv'aht—but when you can't, rush 'em, and slap 'em! You'd be surprised wot two good slaps, right and left, do to anyone not expectin' 'em! What they're thinking of—is getting hold of you—so what you do is to git hold of them first—see! An' while they're thinking what to do next—you git aht!" Wasn't that *exactly* what she had done? It had needed some nerve to jump into the dark; and it hadn't been too easy, that tossed, jangled, broken flight through the magnolia, scratched and torn all the way down. Yet she'd picked herself up like a cat and gone straight for the gates—till she heard George's engine racing up—and then, cruelly, incredibly, dwindling into silence.

Could it be possible that George—with a good ten minutes in hand, for it took the Police all of that to get to the big house from the village—was a coward? He had practically nothing to risk, and all Jane's future and the mink to gain! Was that why he always burgled alone—not because he was more brave but because he was more cowardly? Because he was treacherous and only cared for his own safety? Was that why he never had men friends—only women whom he fooled or paid—and Ma, whom he both fooled *and* paid, whichever came handiest—and was it perhaps true that he was even afraid of Ma? Fear——? Jane sat up in the dark and hugged her knees thinking about fear. She'd had quite a lot of fear getting into the house—after that awful owl in the Park—and then in the passages, and when the latch of the French window wouldn't work, and when she was in the big cupboard, touching the soft furs. She'd got through those fears because there was always something to do about them; but now what could she do about tomorrow? A delinquent child! What was a delinquent child? What did the Law think it was? And what would the Law do about it—after it had thought?

She wasn't confused with self-pity now. She had stopped crying and was really thinking. She had been treated badly—badly by George—badly by the baffling Despards in spite of their kindness—and badly by the police, which was no more than she had expected. But was this all that was the matter—being treated badly? Wasn't there something—a hard, dark, frightening something behind her tears? Something worse than being badly treated?

The night was very dark. In the passage there was a dim light, but nothing in the cell was visible. Implacably memory reeled its pictures through her mind. She knew what they meant to show her: she was packed into that gold bright day when everything had stopped except her rage with her stepmother. She had been going to a school picnic. For once she was pleased with her pink rayon dress and nylon stockings. Usually she didn't wear stockings. It was her Dad who had given her the money for the dress and the stockings.

And then her stepmother said she couldn't go. She and Dad were going instead for a spree up by the lake, where they had a shack—and Jane must just give up the picnic and look after the children, and little Marlene who was only eight months old. She mustn't leave Marlene, whatever she did—not for a minute. They weren't sure how long they'd be. They left her five dollars to feed the kids on—and took a bottle of whiskey in the car.

An hour later the boys came round. They were terribly excited when they found Jane had five dollars, and no parents. It was wonderful. The whole blue and gold world lay open before them—except, Jane remembered at the last moment, except for Marlene. But after a while they made a plan, and all the children, including Marlene, went to the nearest drug store and had ice cream. Then the boys went off, promising to be back in an hour with a car, while Jane took all the children round to Grandma, who didn't like them—not her step-daughter's children—and not even Jane very much. The children all howled at the tops of their voices and Grandma swore and shouted after her; but Jane, fleet as a swallow, soon outpaced their noisy summoning. Maybe she couldn't go to the picnic, but she was going somewhere with the boys; and then she would come back for Marlene in the evening, and put them all to bed.

She hid up in the ravine behind the house till she saw the boys in a car—and whose business was it, whose car? Anyhow, they were off—five dollars intact—and one of boys had brought along his Dad's revolver. Well! a revolver was a wonderful thing to have in a car—going towards the desert and up into the mountains—and it was loaded, too! The boys had got another plan now. Why not go up to the lake—to her parents' shack—and frighten them into giving her more money? You can't go far on five dollars—you had to think of the petrol. Jane was still fighting-mad with her stepmother. She was always having to look after the children, clean the house, run the errands, tidy up for Drunks. She hadn't had the life of a louse since her mother died. She couldn't think of anything she'd like better than to frighten her stepmother with a revolver.

There was something gorgeous in everything the boys had suggested so far. Probably by now both her parents would be drunk; but the boys were cautious and crept stealthily—the way Jane showed them—round the shack; and there, just as Jane had expected, through the window, she saw them sitting on a bed, their arms round each other, and the whiskey bottle half empty on the table beside them.

Billy had suddenly pushed the revolver into her hands. She remembered how heavy it felt—and that she had smelt the oil—and then suddenly there was a tremendous bang, and her stepmother toppled straight off the bed on to the floor. Dad looked up and said, "Janie!—why, Janie——?" but that was all he said.

Everything happened so quickly after that. She wasn't holding the revolver any more. Billy had seized it, and shot twice. Dad got up and was walking towards the window, but suddenly his legs crumpled up under him, and there was a lot of blood everywhere. He scrabbled in it, as if he were trying to dig something up. The boys went into the room and turned out her father's pockets; but Jane sat down right where she was and stared at a chicken—she didn't know they kept chickens up at the shack, perhaps they were a neighbour's chickens—and then suddenly she saw the blood again, and heard her father's voice as if it would never stop—not a bit angry—just surprised: "Janie!—why, Janie——?" She saw his hands scrabbling on the floor, and she had a funny feeling as if they were her own hands. She hadn't loved her father very much, but she had loved him a little—you have to love something. She cried out suddenly and started making a lot of noise; and then the two boys came out and hit her and told her to stop. They pulled her into the car and drove away as fast as they could drive, but Jane couldn't stop screaming. It was as if the sounds came tearing through her throat—like a factory whistle that one day had got started and couldn't be stopped. She didn't know how long the noise, and Dick hitting her, had gone on. But she knew when they flung her out of the car and drove on into the desert.

There was a great blow, and then darkness. After that—perhaps a long while after—there was George's face—his narrow, pale eyes looking into hers, not kindly, not unkindly, just curious, as if he were reckoning up what, if anything, she would be worth to him if he took the trouble to help her stay alive. Well —he had taken the trouble, quite a lot of trouble, as he had explained to her afterwards—and expense! It was no use going back on George, whatever a Children's Court was like. But the thing that really frightened Jane wasn't the Children's Court—or magistrates—or Tomorrow: it was— what had made that gun go off that hit her stepmother?

VIII

Jane sprang out of bed as if a wasp had stung her. The sorrows of the night had slipped away from her waking mind, but a pang sharper still assailed her—she had no lipstick! What could she do during the long day before her without this hallmark of feminine respectability, and how could she face her accusers—two male magistrates—shorn of her red badge of courage? Even George at his cruellest would not have denied Jane her lipstick. Where was she to get it? The Inspector's wife had presented her the night before with a small piece of soap—completely scentless—and half a comb, remarking as she did so that to no ordinary criminal would she have offered such luxuries. What was the use of going to that bloody ashtray of a woman for cosmetics, Jane asked herself bitterly, as the rough unpainted face of Mrs. Bassett rose before her mind's eye! She gazed wildly round her cell till her eyes lit upon the book on the table. The Bible was bound in bright vermilion cloth. With the help of a few drops of water and the underside of her slip, Jane transformed herself, putting the book back almost reverently, on the side she had watered.

Nothing remained for her to do but to sit on the edge of her carefully made bed and blow the smoke of her cigarette out of the window, if possible. Jane had just had time to secrete a silver matchbox and cigarettes that she had picked up at the Despards', the night before, under her mattress while the Inspector's wife turned her back for a moment to draw Jane's attention to the printed Rules nailed to the door; then Jane, having nothing further to conceal, had submitted with great docility to a thorough search. "A nice, quiet child," the

Inspector's wife told the Probation Officer next morning, "more sinned against than sinning—if you ask me."

Miss Emsley arrived, after Jane had been given a bad breakfast on a tray, and then been ushered into Mrs. Bassett's parlour.

Miss Emsley, however, was not the kind of Probation Officer who would dream of asking an Inspector's wife anything. She was a retired Head Mistress who had offered her services as a Probation Officer during the war, and been so successful as to be asked to retain her post professionally, even when the war was over.

Miss Emsley knew the families of most of the girls in the neighbourhood. Some of the mothers as well as the girls themselves had passed through her capable hands as pupils. She therefore knew the homes from which girls were most likely to go wrong—and why.

Miss Emsley had great commonsense, some humour and a kind heart under an exterior which might not lead the observer to suppose she had any of these qualities. Her nose was large, both her chin and her eyes were formidable. She wore no lipstick and her perm—if it was a perm—was despicable; but she wore reasonably good clothes as if she were unused to wearing anything else.

Jane took in as much of this general impression as she could, sitting on the edge of a hard chair, and did not find it favourable. She had been waiting for some time before Miss Emsley was ushered in; and all Jane's observations had been unpleasant so far. It was a grim, yellow and grey morning, on the verge of rain. The spotted white curtains that covered the small tightly shut windows hid whatever view there was. The parlour was both full and cold. It was only used for formal occasions and totally crammed with useless objects: spikily carved inadequate brackets, shakily balanced insipid china ornaments, quantities of small brightly coloured mats were spread over rickety bamboo tables. There were a few prize books that had never been read; and vases, liable to leak, that had never held flowers. On the mantelpiece was a gilt clock that had stopped. Nothing, Jane thought, was worth

68

taking. Nor were there any gadgets that were usable. George had always supplied Jane with the best gadgets on the market. In their rooms, however sparsely furnished, taps turned, lights functioned, stoves heated; and what they wanted cold *was* cold, while should they want anything *hot*, it was hot. If they had needed a knife it would have been sharp; nor would they have filled a fireplace meant for coal with frilled pink paper in the shape of a fan.

"I wouldn't take nuffin' from this room," Jane finally acknowledged, "not if you was to spread a red carpet for me getaway!"

Jane had just made this summing-up when Miss Emsley came in.

"Have you had any breakfast?" she sensibly demanded.

Jane looked expressively at the door, closing on the substantial form of Mrs. Bassett. "I ate a slice of bread with train oil on it", she volunteered. "What I drank was boilin' water—though I wouldn't be surprised if she told you it was tea."

"Well —that is very much what I breakfasted on myself", Miss Emsley replied briskly. "You can hardly expect Mrs. Bassett to use her bacon and butter ration on a stray child. Like a good wife she probably gives them all to her husband. You're not even a prisoner, remember —in fact, you've no right to be here at all. However, we'll soon put that straight once the magistrates get here and empower me to ring up the Remand Home. Miss Bartlett, the Matron, will make you as comfortable as she can, but you mustn't forget that it's still wartime conditions and I'm bound to say the Home is very full and not with the kind of girl our county is accustomed to! We have a pack of bombed-out Londoners at present."

"I'm a Londoner myself", Jane admitted, and then was rather surprised that she *had* admitted it. She corrected her statement after a moment's pause by saying, "Anyhow, I drove out from London same as anyone does who wants ter git anywheres."

"That is one of the things the magistrates will want to know", Miss Emsley said with a satisfied air. "We'll just run through a few of them before they come, so as to save time. Where do you come from, child, and who do you live with— your parents, I suppose? We must get your background clear before I can help you, because that is what I'm here for. I am the children's friend. Now, did you really take anything yourself at the Despards'? Or did the man you were with just slip you inside to open a window for him?"

"No one put me anywhere!" Jane said with cold pride. "I git where I want ter be. An' it's no use me claimin' I didn't pick up that there mink coat 'cos they saw me in it—an' I'm covered wiv bruises from head to foot fallin' thro' a tree from a top winder. An' if you were to want to show a livin' rainbow at a circus I could qualify, 'cos that is what I look like with me clo'es orf."

"I shall take you straight to the doctor", Miss Emsley said, "as soon as we have finished with the magistrates. I'm not at all sure you oughtn't to have seen a doctor last night. Are you sure you have no bones broken?"

Jane shook her head. It was no use claiming what might be proved untrue. "These magistrates", she asked, for she began to feel as if Miss Emsley was, after all, on her side, "what kind of a sentence will they give me, anyway? I didn't git nuffin' aht of what happened last night! I tore the mink, it's true—but I didn't never mean ter tear it—it was them branches I fell thro'! Those Despards, they looked kinda sorry for me—but they couldn't reely 'ave been sorry, could they—or else I wouldn't be here?"

A queer gleam that might have been fellow feeling shone for a moment in Miss Emsley's non-committal eyes. "You won't get any sentence at all this morning", she said reassuringly. "They will just take a statement from the Inspector and send you to the Remand Home for twenty-eight days, while they think things over and find out all about you. Now, Jane, I must tell you that they really *will* find out, so I do strongly advise you to stick to the truth if they ask you a few questions. They may be satisfied with what I tell them but, in any case, they're quite kind, sensible men, both of them. And if Miss Poole comes, too —she's one in a thousand, though she is even less likely to be taken in by lies, being—besides unusually intelligent—a woman. Now, what we have to get straight is—have you got a home at all—parents—grandparents—uncles, aunts—anyone you could be with—not just a burglar with no proper background for a young girl at all? Because if I *can* keep you at home, I will—and if I can't, then you'll have to go to an Approved School. There is nothing to be said against them; indeed, some of them are very good indeed and give an excellent education, but I am not going to pretend that I wouldn't rather send you back to your own home and I'd do my best to keep you in it, if you will stop breaking the law. There is nothing in law-breaking at all!—take my word for it—compared to earning your own living in some sensible way with no one running after you or getting you into trouble."

Miss Emsley paused. She was considered a good talker but she was an equally good listener, and she had found that by talking a good deal herself she could often elicit considerably more than people who talked less. Jane appreciated her conversation very much, but she had no intention of changing her own story. It was George's story, and it had got to hold water or else she wouldn't be able to get back to George; and, after all, George was all she had, while beyond George shone the Riviera.

"I haven't no parents," Jane said firmly, "nor no relations, nor no one. My Ma died when I was twelve—at Liverpool, that was. She was from the U-nited States, she come over to visit relations and met my Dad. My Dad was Liverpool Irish, named McCarthy. I guess they got married or somepin'. My Ma's name was O'Shane—so was her relations an' they was all killed in the bombing. Since then I lived with American boys, like I said, in camps—an' you can't think how good an American boy is till you've tried."

Miss Emsley hadn't tried, but she endeavoured to look as sympathetic as if she had.

"Mostly they hid me in huts", Jane went on, after a short pause. "Often I got aht by day and went back evenings. That was how I got money fer me eats and me clo'es. More'n that I

71

never asked fer—not from any boy—and wouldn't 'ave taken—not in wartime with them boys maybe dyin' fer you on the next draught—not wild horses wouldn't have made me take their money more nor what I needed. That night at the Despards was me first 'ousebreak. Maybe there was a man wiv me—but no names, no pack drill. They don't torture you in this country, do they?" Jane eyed Miss Emsley searchingly. "I 'ave 'eard say abaht hair-singin' and beatings-up", she ventured cautiously. "Wouldn't say there was much in it me-self—would you? I jes' would like to know."

"You say 'this country'", Miss Emsley replied cautiously. "Jane, I don't think this is really your country, is it? For I've never heard anyone say 'this country' unless they have another. No, you won't be tortured, but you'll certainly be penalised for having committed a crime."

Jane felt a slow colour creep towards her hair. She couldn't remember ever having blushed before, but she felt sure this strange, hot feeling was blushing. Why, this old armadillo woman had actually caught her out!

"I *never!*" Jane said passionately. "This country was where I was borned. Me Pa was Irish-British an' I'm British! You can't turn me into nuffin' else try as you may."

"I'm not going to try if you really are British," Miss Emsley said reassuringly, "but before the magistrates come we must get hold of what they call 'evidence'. Can you tell me the name of the school that you were sent to in Liverpool, for instance —or some friend's name who has an address, where I can enquire further about your parents?"

Jane shook her head. "I never went much to school an' that's a fac'", she said with easy candour. "I kin do sums an' I know 'ow to read and write. I don't know as I need much else. Don't you worry abaht me, lady. I kin get by. Jes' you git me aht from under these magistrates' hoofs—sendin' me ter schools they maybe approve of—but Gawd, he knows, I shouldn't!"

Miss Emsley said, with sudden severity, "This won't do at all, Jane! You were not sent straight into a cabbage when you were born, nor found on a doorstep! Now, you tell me

72

straight—who were you staying with before you were arrested? Your birth must have been registered; your school would know something about you; your mother or your father presumably worked. Well then, where did they work, and for whom?"

Jane considered this list of awkward questions in silence. "My Pa was torpedoed," she then advanced, "nor we weren't told the name of his ship. We was notified ever so nicely that he was dead—well dead, seemingly, he was—fer he never come back no more. My Ma—if you want ter know the truth— I think she took up wiv black markets. She used to go abaht a lot at night—but I don't fink it was men so much as markets from the look of the fings she brought back. I must say we lived well till she got the new-monia an' died. I don't mind tellin' you that I didn't like the look of things at all then— Inspectors on the top of doctors—so I lit aht afore they could git hold of me. I 'ad me friends in the camp, like what I told you —but I'm not interested in names—no use your askin' me—nor the camps neither—me mem'ry has been so bad since that bombing. You sho'ld er lived on the Merseyside as we did—me Ma and me—mostly under a table every night."

Miss Emsley knew all about the Merseyside. She had often visited it during the bombing so she decided to drop the subject. She began to ask for information about the camps instead. Here, however, George had been before her. Jane had a complete list of the American camps that she declared she had visited, their routine, and any possible break in the extremely good order in which they were usually run. Jane had been well coached and she took a gruelling examination from Miss Emsley, who was an adept at asking awkward questions. Miss Emsley saw at last, at the end of an hour and a half exhaustive questioning, that there was nothing she could do but accept the appearance of the magistrates who depended upon her for all their information— without having obtained any.

It was a most unusual situation for all of them and only Jane got any satisfaction from it.

The interview between Miss Emsley and the two magistrates took place in Jane's presence but rather above her head; and she decided, perhaps wisely, not to take any active part in it.

"Very well, then, Sir Melville," Miss Emsley finally said. "I see there is nothing else for it but a visit to the psychiatrist."

Jane did not know what a psychiatrist was, but she felt that probably Miss Emsley had good reason for her evident dislike of the species.

IX

D r. Martin Jessop was a young doctor who took both his
profession and himself—in that order—very seriously.
Having just finished adding a psychiatric degree to his
medical one, he had been appointed to the Farminster
Remand Home. He now had to make up his mind whether
Jane had told the magistrates the truth or not.

If she had told them the truth she was almost certainly a
V.D. case and must be treated as such; if she had lied, then
hers might be merely a hygienic burglary, and would require
quite another form of treatment.

Owing to shortage of staff and housing difficulties due to
the bombing, all female delinquents under eighteen were lodged
in Morely House until they could be sorted out and sent to
their appropriate destinations.

Two forms of examination were open to Martin, physical or
mental; and the Probation Officer, a middle-aged woman with
a nineteenth century approach to morals, must be shudder-
ingly present at either or both. Miss Emsley, Martin already
knew, would be mortally affronted by his modern methods,
and probably report him to authorities with the same medieval
outlook as her own.

Still, after living a quarter of a century, he told himself, a
man should be able to solve any human problem for himself,
while ignoring all merely ignorant criticisms.

Jane, shepherded into his office by Miss Emsley, wore the
mask of hate common to all trapped animals. Most trapped
animals are healthy; few have any knowledge of pain. They
just can't get out; and their own instincts, as well as their
experienced mothers, have taught them that when trapped,

something even worse than not being able to get out is going to happen to them.

There was nothing in Jane's mind but ignorance and rage. She hadn't even undue vanity, so that she felt no desire to please the young man in front of her who was to help decide her fate; and was therefore unable, as well as unwilling, to help him find out anything to her advantage.

"It would be better to be an animal," Martin thought, "then you wouldn't have to be asked questions. You would be just let out—or done in—and not have to be bullied into adding to your own punishment!"

He instantly decided against making a simple physical examination of Jane, which would have settled his question and eased his responsibility. Instead, he would make a general examination, when she would have had time to get used to him; and try to make his decision out of the use of his own wits. Inwardly Martin flinched at this increase of responsibility; but Jane, her eyes hard on him, did not know that he was flinching.

Jane did not dislike the look of the young man. He was clean but not tidy; he had a big, generous mouth, thick eyebrows, hair the colour of wet seaweed, and clear grey eyes which looked straight at her, as if he thought she was just as much a person as he was.

"You had quite a fall last night, I hear," he observed to Jane. "Feel a bit stiff this morning, don't you?"

"Sure," Jane agreed, "so would anyone else feel stiff that had taken a toss through that blasted ole tree. An' I don't see what business it is of yours whether I'm bruised or not!"

"Well, that's all right", Martin reassured her. "I don't want to take your bruises away from you! I might have a look at them later on just to see if they're free of dirt. You see, I'm a doctor, and it's supposed to be my business to find out what—if anything—is the matter with you."

"I'm not looney, if that's what you're after," Jane told him briskly, "but whether I'm sick or not I wouldn't know—after what I've just been eating in what they call a caffy fer my elevenses. What I ate wasn't what I'd call food; an' what I

76

had to drink I *know* wasn't coffee! I don't blame Miss Emsley
—she had the same!"

"I think you're being rude, Jane, and you mustn't be",
Miss Emsley intervened. "Dr. Jessop is a Psychiatrist, and
he is talking to you in his official capacity. He doesn't want
to hear what you have to say—except when he asks you a
question."

"I will stop her talking if I want to", Dr. Jessop said without looking at Miss Emsley.

Miss Emsley disliked the direct way in which modern young
men spoke to young girls, and she was trying to keep awake
to see if anything worse would happen. Dr. Jessop had given
her the only comfortable chair in the room; she was worn out
from overwork and, after a meal composed mainly of starch,
she felt ungovernably sleepy. Both Martin and Jane were
silent for so long that Miss Emsley actually fell asleep before
the conversation began again.

"What's biting the girl most?" Martin was asking himself,
and finally, as nothing else occurred to him of greater importance, he repeated the question to Jane.

" What's biting you most?" he demanded. "I know you've
had a shock, and a fall, lost your mate, and been caught out
in a spectacular, unescapable burglary. But what is it that you
mind most about in coming all these croppers?"

"Being shut up!" Jane said, with a baleful glare at her
sleeping Protectress. "Shut up for a month or more—wiv
dull ole bitches herding you round—and a bunch of nitwits
for company. Wouldn't that make anyone feel sore?"

"I gather you haven't had an awful lot of schooling previously?" Martin ventured.

"I've had enough", Jane replied viciously. "Wot do I want
ter be educated *for* anyway? I know my onions."

" Well, that's more than many of us do," Martin admitted,
"but what I want to find out is if you *really* know them. Even
the cleverest of us can fool ourselves sometimes. What do you
know about sex, for instance?"

Miss Emsley started wide awake and turned rigid. She had
to listen—she was paid for it—though not paid very much;

77

besides, she always did listen when anybody spoke about sex.

Jane replied with a grin—for this was the way in which the subject was, in her world, universally greeted. Sex was what Jane had learned all about, even before she knew George, in her Californian childhood. What was there but sex and drink in that lonely, broken, sunny city founded on gold and exile?

"I know every damned thing about sex," Jane replied, "and then some!"

"Then—what is a hormone?" Martin asked her in a calm objective tone that made Jane suddenly feel a little less certain of her acquired knowledge. The word "hormone" was both unprovocative and unfamiliar to her. When she shook her head, Martin defined it for her, and went on with the same considerate indifference to tell her quite a lot about sex that neither she nor Miss Emsley had ever known existed. Miss Emsley kept awake quite easily now; but although she recognised that the explanation was purely biological, she still felt shocked.

Jane, too, felt embarrassed, but for a different reason. It was not Martin's knowledge that embarrassed her, but her own ignorance.

"Gosh!" she said at last. "You know a mouthful, don't you? But it can't all be like pickin' oakum in stir! There must be a little merry hell to it—to make sense—mustn't there?"

"You can add that for yourself by-and-bye", Martin told her. "What I want you to remember are the functions, symptoms and consequences of the various sex relationships: then you can't be caught out by not knowing what you are up to. There's just as much human nature in one place as there is in another, and it's up to you how you tackle it! Sex is natural to all of us; and a good life should have a good sex life in it in order to *be* natural! A woman who doesn't want a man and children isn't normal; but too much fooling round beforehand won't help her to get either of them. Sex isn't the whole of education by a long chalk; you've got plenty of other instincts to learn to develop properly. The time won't seem so long once you get the hang of it. I've had fifteen years education myself and not found it enough—and I don't

78

suppose my schools were much freer than yours will be either. Approved Schools can be quite good nowadays, and I expect you'll have as much freedom in them as you can manage without getting into fresh trouble. Then, when you're fully trained, you'll come out again, knowing some job you can earn your living at, on the level. If you want to go below the level by taking what doesn't belong to you, you will still know a lot more than you did before you went to school, and can do it better. Only, it'll be at a bigger risk. You won't be a child delinquent when you get caught again—you'll be a common criminal; and believe me, though there's a lot I don't like out of jail—there's still less I like inside it!"

"Gawd!—Have *you* done a stretch?" Jane asked him with awed sympathy.

Martin shook his head. "Near enough," he told her. "I've looked after a prison hospital for three months. The hospital and the library are the plums of prison life. As a prisoner you're lucky if you can get into either—but if you weren't a prisoner—you wouldn't think yourself so lucky!"

Jane nodded. The hooded look had fallen from her eyes, so that Martin could at last see plainly her eagerness for life —her fear—and her innocence. He was silent for a long time thinking her over, before he suggested taking a look at her bruises.

Jane made no objection now; it had even occurred to her that this young man really did know something about life— perhaps more about it than she did; and that, in spite of what he knew—perhaps because of it—he was not hostile to her.

When Martin had finished his general examination and shown a superficial interest in her bruises, he went back to his seat behind the desk to make up his own mind, on what facts he had. He saw that he must make—as all scientists sooner or later have to make—a plunge into faith. His was a mind that was only at rest dealing with concrete facts—now he must make up his mind without them. He had indications, inferences and reassurances—but no facts.

He looked at Jane with an amused, kindly, almost conspiratorial look.

"See here," he said, laying down his pen, "those boys—American airmen—airfields—camp life and so on: they don't add up! They're all my eye and Betty Martin—aren't they? I mean, you've never been near any of them in your young life—have you?"

An answering gleam met him from Jane's eyes.

"When Jonah was away from home three nights and three days an' his wife asked him where he'd been—he had to tell her somepin', hadn't he?" Jane demanded.

"I'm sorry, Dr. Jessop," Miss Emsley said firmly, "I don't want to interfere, but I must say I can't allow this child to make fun of Holy Writ—whether you're talking psychologically or not!"

Dr. Jessop shook his head as if he were brushing off a fly.

"Nonsense," he said equally firmly, "it's quite à propos, that story, and helps me to make up my report. Now, Jane," once more he leaned forward, his whole attention fixed upon the child in front of him, "it's not my job to find out *who* those people are that you were with! But I suspect that you have lived with someone—related or not—who took pretty good care of you physically. Apart from those bruises—you're all right. Your organs are in good order—you're clean as a whistle; and there's nothing for you to be frightened about —going or coming! Miss Emsley will now take you to Morely House with my report. Perhaps I'll be along one day to see you, before they pack you off to a School. But, believe me, the School can be the best part of the business! I'll give you some ointment to put on your bruises; and there's just one thing more I think you ought to remember—for the rest of your life. Don't you ever hit an old person over the head again! The Police Sergeant didn't put it in the evidence, because General Despard wouldn't charge you with it, but over the 'phone the Sergeant told me what you had done; and what you did to that old man wasn't cricket. If you'd killed him—and you might quite well have killed him—you'd have had what you deserved—a pretty poor time of it! Murder isn't the kind of thing—whether you're hanged for it or not— that leaves a nice sweet memory in a young girl's mind!"

Martin was surprised as well as frightened by what followed. Jane gave a kind of yelp like a dog that has been run over and fell off her chair in a dead faint, on the floor.

It took Martin five minutes to bring her round; and when her eyes met his, the dreadful mask of hate and fear had closed over them. She didn't speak to him again, and she wouldn't shake hands with him when he tried to say goodbye to her.

Miss Emsley, feeling highly sympathetic towards Jane and fully justified in her disapproval of psychology, led her triumphantly from the room.

"Extra sensory perception seems to be the operative phrase", Martin said to himself with some discomfort. "Queer how psychologists bump into secrets they're not looking for! Either that kid's killed someone—intentionally or not intentionally—in her short time, or else she's got a pretty vivid memory of watching a murder done! The worst of it is, I'll be no good to her from now on. However, I'm prepared to go to the stake she hasn't got V.D. and now I've told her how to avoid it—so that's something. Perhaps it's worth losing my lunch for!" It was now close on four o'clock and Dr. Martin Jessop had eaten nothing since breakfast. But he was right about the value he set on his interview, for it lasted Jane for the rest of her life.

X

She could, Jane thought, as they stood waiting in a 'bus queue, escape from Miss Emsley far more easily than from a police woman. Police Officers wore whistles and had disciplined muscular reactions; but Miss Emsley, though morally a tower of strength and no fool, shared none of their physical advantages. Besides, since Jane had fainted, she had had a headache and felt dizzy.

It would be better, she thought, to try the Remand Home first, and start escaping when she felt more like it. At present, she would simply pay sharp attention to landmarks so as to remember the way back. The intensity of her visual observation relieved her from listening to Miss Emsley, who was doing her duty by trying to tell Jane, above the noises of the motor 'bus, as tactfully as possible, what a Remand Home was like—without all the other passengers discovering that it *was* to a Remand Home that Jane was being taken.

A huge red lump of a building, indecisively Gothic, stood on rising ground half a mile from the main road, encircled by high walls.

Jane guessed before the 'bus lurched to a halt that this was Morely House. It might equally have served as a jail or as a lunatic asylum, since the remedial impact of beauty upon moral or mental sickness has not yet reached the governmental mind.

Jane thought it worth while to listen now to Miss Emsley.

"There it is, dear!" Miss Emsley was saying. "Beautiful air and quite large playgrounds, far better in some ways than more ordinary schools. I've known schools for normal children that had no playgrounds at all! Nothing but a yard, with

82

lavatories and cloakrooms as part of them. Now we shan't be long!"

Even an approach to Paradise might have seemed long to Jane, walking uphill and still feeling queer. Nor had Jane any delusions about Remand Homes being Paradise, when you got there, in spite of Miss Emsley's reassurances, which grew more and more emphatic as they neared the high iron gates.

"I believe they have wonderful high teas," Miss Emsley rambled on, ringing the bell with deceptive cheerfulness and relief, "flowers sometimes on the table—and cold ham. But we don't go straight up to the house; we stop at the Lodge to sign papers."

A woman with a very hard mouth and chin, carrying a large key, came out of the lodge and nodded to Miss Emsley. She did not seem to see Jane at all. She unlocked the gate and let them both in, as if this part of her duty was considerably easier than letting anybody out.

"Fetch her along!" she told Miss Emsley shortly. "The wash woman is still here—though it's late. We have to sign her in first, you know, before we can begin!"

Miss Emsley and Mrs. Parker, the lodge keeper, signed several papers in triplicate while Jane wondered what *would* begin afterwards. Then Miss Emsley held out her hand to Jane.

"Now dear," she said, with the false heartiness of one about to escape an ordeal, to the one who must endure it, "you be good—and I'm sure you will be happy here! I've known plenty of girls who have come out of this Home re-made!"

"Hell!" Jane told her savagely, seized by mingled panic and derision, "how come you think I want to *be* re-made?"

Miss Emsley gave her a reproving, but by no means unkindly, look and backed decisively away. She did not guess that Jane was making conversation because she wanted her to stay. For whatever Miss Emsley wasn't, Jane realized at this last moment, she was a kind woman and would have liked to help Jane if she had known how; while Mrs. Parker—even if she knew how—wouldn't enjoy helping anyone.

83

There was a short, hostile pause after the office door had closed behind Miss Emsley.

"Now you come in here!" Mrs. Parker said sharply.

Jane found herself in a room with a big stove, a large boiler and several cubicles containing baths. There were no chairs.

"Mrs. Watson!" Mrs. Parker shouted. "Here's the last one!"

A slightly less forbidding and much stouter middle-aged woman came out from one of the cubicles and said: "Well!— there isn't much more hot water—but I dessay it'll do!"

"It'll have to!" Mrs. Parker replied. "There's been enough coal used already and I'll not waste another shovel-full more on this girl. Besides, it's past teatime."

Jane's eyes glanced incredulously from cubicle to cubicle.

"Baths!" she said. "What for? I'm quite clean, thank you! Where I come from, people *wash!* I have a shower every morning, and when I want a barf I take it at night!"

"Well—here—you all have baths whenever you come!" Mrs. Watson told her tolerantly.

Mrs. Parker laughed a loud unpleasant laugh, and went back into her office.

"You take your clo'es orf," Mrs. Watson explained, "stack 'em here on the table, and I'll look thro' them. Posh, that coat and skirt, I will say! You wash your 'air in the barf and then I'll run through it with a fine toothcomb, jest ter see if it's necessary! You can go on up to the big house after that for your tea. It won't take long."

"It'll take longer than you think!" Jane said, breathing rapidly. "If you lay as much as a hand on me, you'll be sorry for it! There's nothing to my hair *but* hair—see! An' as for a barf in the middle of the afternoon—you go barf yer gran'-mother an' see how *she* likes it!"

"If you don't come quiet, I'll have to call Mrs. Parker," Mrs. Watson warned her, "an' you won't like that—no one does—she's 'arsh, 'aving 'ad a tragedy in 'er life with a man that ort by rights ter 'ave been 'er 'usban'—and turns out ter be one of these 'ere bigamists you read about in the papers— comin' to 'er full of 'istory an' none of it showing in 'is face!

84

Wot I say is, it 'ad ort ter be compulsory men wearing wedding rings same as us. No sense *we* showing orf—while they're 'iding up—is there? C'mon Ducks, and git this over, and then we can 'ave our tea in peace!"

But Jane's heart was far from peace. She had been through too much indignity in one day to stand any more. She gave a swift look round the room. Beyond the cubicles against the wall, if not part of it, was a solid looking dresser hung with cups, and holding plates. Shelf rose above shelf, and all were full of china. Jane made a running leap. The cupboard shuddered, but withstood her light weight. She climbed deftly upwards like a cat from shelf to shelf till she reached the top; then she faced round with a cup in one hand and a teapot in the other.

"Nah!" she said triumphantly to the agonized and yet fascinated Mrs. Watson, who hovered beneath her. "If you move one step nearer this dresser, I'll break everything on it —plates and all! Jes' ter show you I mean business—here goes this cup!"

A cup crashed to the floor. Mrs. Parker entered as if by automatic suction.

"What's going on here?" she demanded.

Then she saw Jane, aloft and threatening, her favourite teapot brandished in her hand.

"Down you come, you little wild cat!" she shouted furiously, "or I'll spank you till you've nothing left to sit upon!"

"C'mon an' try!" Jane answered, waving the teapot still higher.

They glowered at each other, equally conscious of an animosity so fierce that nothing but physical combat could appease it.

"We don't want no trouble!" Mrs. Watson urged, "do we, Mrs. Parker dear?"

"Trouble!" snorted Mrs. Parker, "this isn't trouble, my girl—this is just a slum cat that's never been house trained, that's all! No! don't ring for *Her*—you never know how she'll take it! Now, you see here—what-ever-your-name-is! Children in this place really *get* what's coming to them! It's what

85

they've needed all their lives, or they wouldn't *be* here. Corporal punishment is still used—praise the Lord!—and when I say punishment, I *mean* punishment! Not to mention a cell—which many like even less—and where you can be shut for twenty-four hours on bread and water—and reported to the Police, if necessary, to keep you there longer! Now come down—or you're for it!"

A plate skimmed, rather unfairly, past Mrs. Parker's nose, and cut Mrs. Watson's wrist. Mrs. Watson started screaming. Mrs. Parker, blind with rage, advanced a step. The teapot caught her shoulder and smashed at her feet. Now nothing could stop her. She moved relentlessly forward upon the dresser, while a hail of cups, saucers and plates fell all about her, some of them hitting her.

She was a tall woman, and she finally succeeded in catching Jane by the ankle. This brought Jane, with the remaining china, on the top of her. Jane was in a good position to claw at Mrs. Parker's hair and face, and she took every advantage of it. They were by now both on the ground together, rolling on a sea of broken china. Jane clawed and clung ferociously, knowing that she must eventually succumb to Mrs. Parker's greater weight.

Suddenly Mrs. Watson stopped shrieking. The antagonists fell apart as if by magic. No sound had reached them, but a penetrating silence, more potent than sound, slackened their hold upon each other. Jane eeled away from the solid form of Mrs. Parker and leapt to her feet.

Mrs. Parker, much more slowly and bleeding profusely from cuts and scratches, rose from the floor, clinging to the table for support. Mrs. Watson sat down on a stool in the nearest cubicle.

"If it isn't an artiary—wot is it?" she sobbed, wrapping her apron round her streaming wrist.

A very small erect lady with white hair stood in the doorway. She might have been nothing but a little old woman, and yet she was considerably more than a little old woman. It was the acute quality of her silence that had driven the fighters apart. She now moved forward purposefully towards

Mrs. Watson, held her wrist under the cold tap, and then bound it expertly with a strip of apron that she had ruthlessly torn into a bandage.

"Mrs. Watson," she said, with a clear enunciation that made the low voice she spoke in more effective, "this cut is not serious. It will soon stop bleeding, and you shall have a new apron. Now I think you had better go home. You can come again as usual, but do not use your wrist until I have examined it again to-morrow. Mrs. Parker, those scratches on your face need attention. I should advise you to see about them at once. After you have done this, please telephone the House and say that I shall not be free for some time. Miss Potter can take tea with the girls. You need not return here."

Both women longed to unpack their outraged feelings with words. Mrs. Parker went so far as to open her mouth, but meeting Miss Bartlett's cold steady eyes, she shut it again. It was as if the door of a refrigerator had closed upon their senses. Mrs. Watson went out of one door, and Mrs. Parker retired into her office by another. After they had gone, nothing took place for a long time.

A tap dripped audibly; and the clock ticked steadily on. There didn't seem anything else that Jane hadn't broken. The glow of battle slowly died down in her. Miss Bartlett neither looked at Jane, nor spoke to her.

After a time, Miss Bartlett stooped and began to pick up the larger fragments of the broken crockery and put them on the table; and Jane found herself helping her.

"It is better not to touch the smaller pieces with our hands", Miss Bartlett said at last. "In that cupboard by the door you will find a dustpan and brush."

Jane found it. Miss Bartlett took it from her, and swept the floor clean.

When she had finished sweeping, she washed her hands and returned to Jane. Her eyes meeting Jane's had a speculative, but not unfriendly look.

"What didn't you like about taking a bath?" she then asked her; "you look quite clean."

"That's just it!" Jane replied promptly.

87

She found herself burning to make some convincing explanation of her conduct. "I *am* clean! I don't never take a barf in the afternoon. I take a shower night an' morning, and a barf when I feel like it at night. As for things in me head, it's much more likely those Dames had them themselves!—ole-fashioned sluts! Why, even girl guides brush their hair twenty-five strokes a day—an' they're religious! I've read about them in a magazine. It ain't nuffin' ter the way I brush mine! More like fifty strokes a day, if you ask me!"

Miss Bartlett smiled.

"Well—it does look very nice and glossy, I must say!" she remarked, "but I don't suppose for a moment that you have insects in your hair. It's a mere precaution, and if you'd seen some of the girls who come here, you wouldn't be surprised that we take it. It is always a pity to spread dirt or to catch things. Indeed, it wouldn't be fair *not* to take every precaution, seeing that we are responsible for all the girls here. But I am sure you would agree with me that it would be very unkind to force a dirty girl to take a bath and let the clean ones off, just because perhaps she came from a bad home, or had had no soap to use for washing. She'd feel very sensitive, wouldn't she?—and afraid of being laughed at for being dirty?"

Jane saw that Miss Bartlett was not only saying a correct thing, but that she meant what she said. This was a woman who would not rob even a delinquent child of its dignity.

"I don't know as I would", Jane agreed uncertainly. "No one said anything about the other girls ter me—I only—well, I suppose I only thought of myself. I knew I *was* clean!"

Miss Bartlett made no direct answer.

"While you are taking your bath", she said after a pause, "I will write a list of the broken china so that we can replace it for Mrs. Parker. I will pay for her china myself. Then we can go and have tea."

Jane went into the nearest cubicle and turned on the water. The day had been hot as well as exhausting, and the cell she had slept in the night before had certainly been far from clean. It was refreshing to take a lukewarm bath behind a curtain. There wasn't a looking-glass anywhere, but Jane had remembered to take her handbag into the cubicle with her, so that she could make up her face by the little glass inside it. When she was re-dressed, no one would have dreamed that she had just had a sanguinary fight.

When Jane rejoined her, Miss Bartlett was looking out of the window towards the distant downs.

"It's a beautiful evening", she murmured, without turning round.

Jane hesitated, and then she said with a rush, "I got four shillings and sixpence the Police lady didn't find lars' night. Whad'ja say—I hand 'em over to you to help pay for that china?"

It was a great sacrifice: it might hamper her get-away. Jane hoped, the moment she'd spoken, that Miss Bartlett would let her off it.

However, Miss Bartlett simply said, "I think that would be quite a good plan"; and took the money from her.

On their way up to the House, Jane could see right through the open door, into a big dining-room where twenty or more girls were sitting round long tables eating their supper.

She was thankful she did not have to face all those strange girls at once. Instead she went down a long corridor to the back of the house, where there was a room with long French windows. It seemed cut off from everything else, and had a piano in it, and pictures. It wasn't a grand room, and the furniture in it was made of very simple unpolished wood, but it was comfortable and clean and had an open-air look. There was a kitchenette next door to it, rather like her own, kept as she and George kept theirs, all polished steel and electric gadgets: it might have been a Californian kitchen in an ideal home. They made themselves a plate full of hot buttered toast, and there was a good cake to eat after it.

Miss Bartlett asked Jane no questions. It was Jane who did all the talking. She told Miss Bartlett about the magistrates, and even the house-break; and how sorry she had felt about tearing the mink on the magnolia.

She even said, while she was helping to wash up the tea

things afterwards, that where she had lived there was a cat called Rundle.

Miss Bartlett told Jane that she had a dog called Tito, and they looked out of the window together and saw the dog. Tito was a fox terrier, glossy white with golden brown ears and face. He was playing with a tennis ball and several girls. They fitted together and flew apart like the pieces of a kaleidoscope. They tore round so fast—flying ball, leaping dog and racing girls—that Jane could hardly keep still as she looked at them.

"Gee—he is cute—he'll never let them have it!" she murmured, as Tito, tennis ball in mouth, shot between the legs of the swiftest girl.

"You can join them later," Miss Bartlett told her, "but before you are introduced to the others, you had better see your room and get your things unpacked. There are eleven other girls in your room, and each girl has a locker beside her bed where she can keep her own things safely locked up. I will give you a key; and here's a ribbon to fasten it round your neck."

It was a new idea to Jane that her things might be stolen from her instead of her stealing other people's things. Miss Bartlett had not said that the other girls stole, but she looked at Jane as she spoke about the key as if she knew all about stealing.

She wasn't a soft woman like Lady Despard—nor yet a hard woman; she was something, Jane decided, different; so that you couldn't be sure how she'd turn out if you tried to fool her.

At the foot of the main staircase Miss Bartlett called to a girl who was half way up.

"Elsie—this is a new girl—Jane McCarthy! Will you take her to the green dormitory and show her everything?"

Elsie turned and looked down at Jane. A miracle took place between the two girls. Neither could have said what happened, but each of them suddenly felt at home with the other.

Miss Bartlett disappeared.

There was only the late April sunshine filling the hall, and another girl standing on the stairs and looking down at Jane; yet it was enough. It was more, indeed, than Jane had ever had.

90

XI

As they climbed the stairs together, suddenly freed from restraint, and yet half embarrassed by their freedom, Elsie gave an awkward little giggle, which Jane found full of music.

"'Coo", she murmured. "Fancy '*Er* letting me show you over everythink! Why! I'm one of the lepers—I am! She must 'ave forgot—or else gone crackers!"

"Whadda mean—lepers?" Jane asked.

She had a vague feeling that there was something inimical in the sound of this strange word.

"They was people who had to walk rahnd wiv bells on their necks ter get people out of the way—'cos wot they 'ad was catching—see?" Elsie explained. "Bits fell orf 'em! Must'er been orful when you come to think of it! V.D. isn't that bad— still it's bad enough—you get abscesses, an' sore froats, an' yer eyes run; but Nurse Grace, she says she don't fink it's all that easy catching it. We're allowed ter go ter prayers, an' lessons an' P.T. wiv the other girls, but we eats and sleeps at the top of the house by ourselves. There's eighteen of us an' jes' now I'm the youngest. We'll be sent to a different School soon to ourselves, but our School is full nah—on account of the bombing—so maybe I'll stay 'ere as long as you! It's better 'ere than at them Schools. We get good grub, work's not ser 'ard and you get a square deal if you arsk Miss Bartlett for it! Nurse Grace 'as pets—but that don't matter ter me—'cos I'm one of 'em. Miss Potter's the narsty one—nosy and noisy, I calls 'er."

Elsie, who was a wit, and enjoyed her own examples of it, giggled again. Her teeth were a beautiful chalk white, and shone like sugar. Jane thought she had never seen so sweet and gay a smile.

"That Miss Bartlett," she asked cautiously, "she's O.K., isn't she?—the one wiv the white hair that sent you wiv me? She let me make toast wiv her and gave me cake."

Elsie considered this question carefully.

"She's *good*", she admitted at last. "When I first come I was sick as a cat, an' she was awful good ter me—better than Nurse Grace. I can't never forget 'Er comin' up nights wiv cool drinks, an' doin' lots of extra work so she could keep me in bed. She dressed all me abscesses 'erself—I screamed when anyone else touched me; nor she's never made me feel I was dirt like Miss Potter does. But Miss Bartlett, she's Boss orl right. You 'ave ter do what she wants when you don't want ter; you can't get by like you can wiv the others sometimes! 'Ere's where you 'its the 'ay!"

The room was large and clean. Three windows looked out over the spring world, but there were bars to the windows. There were twelve narrow beds in a row, and by each bedside was a painted green locker. Six fixture washstands with running water lined one wall, and beyond them was a lavatory door that you could shut but not lock. The lavatory too had a window, without bars, but so small and narrow that Jane thought it a doubtful method of escape.

The girls sat on the nearest bed, inspecting each other's clothes. Each was a new world to the other, a kingdom in which excitement, curiosity and kindness played equal parts. Elsie felt no envy of her friend's new clothes. She liked everything for what it was in itself, and did not connect herself with it beyond the curiosity it excited. She had long ago given up all thoughts of ownership; even her own body had not belonged to her.

Elsie was only fourteen, but she had had a good deal of experience in human relationships. She was in need of protection, but she already knew that protectors do not always protect people from themselves. Sometimes her protectors had snared her by their strength, and then tortured her by their jealous adoration, till in despair she had sought some new protector more accommodating than the last, who would relieve her not only from all her burdens but from her former protector; still, she always hoped that this next adventure might be pleasanter and more lasting than the others.

"How come you got this V.D.?" Jane asked her. "You let some man git the better of you?"

A faint flush spread over Elsie's delicate face, her eyes looked bluer and more wistful, her lips trembled. She gave a long helpless sigh. She found it difficult to trace her path backwards. Looking into a vague series of pictures, mostly unpleasant, which she knew as her memory, 'she felt that these pictures themselves might perhaps have been pleasanter if she had been different; but who can tell what truth lies in circumstances and what in the self that is enmeshed by them? Is it the rabbit's fault that it does not fight when cornered? There was no doubt about it that Elsie had been cornered.

"It was orl right", she said at last, "jes' as long as I 'ad me Dad. 'E was a loverly Dad! 'E ain't ever 'it me—nor 'e didn't come 'ome wiv'aht 'e bought me somethink! A chimbley sweep 'e was, an' I used to watch every h'evening till I saw 'is little brushes sticking up over 'is 'ead, and then run like 'ell till I got ter 'im, fer fear Muver might stop me. I fair 'ated Muver's guts and she fair 'ated mine! My Ma was orful— drank the roof orf, Saturday nights, she did—an' when she was sober—dahn right crool. She kinda didn't fancy me Dad —'cos of the smuts. Said the pillars were orlways black where 'is 'ead laid. But 'e couldn't 'elp the way smuts clung to 'is 'air, could 'e? There wasn't never an ole man as clean as me Dad. Orl 'e ever wanted, when 'e come 'ome, was 'ot water an' soap. My Ma took with other men be'ind his back. Young Frank—'e was always rahnd when my Dad wasn't there— one of these 'ere spivs—a regular Teddy Boy—'e was out er work, an' livin' off 'is molls most of the time. I didn't stay ter 'ome ever, when my Dad wasn't there. When I wasn't at school, I was on the street, and people orften giv' me things ter eat till my Dad come 'ome evenings, an' then I was orl right—see? But then one day 'e didn't come 'ome! Maybe 'e'd got fed up. But 'e never come 'ome ner more! Nor 'e

93

didn't say where 'e went to, nor never sent me no message. 'Is friends was always good ter me, an' 'e 'ad lots of fren's! They give me things, nylons an' sweets an' ice cream, an' took me to the Pictures. I didn't mind the petting either—nor what come after the petting begins. You know how 'tis with men, don't you? Even if you've never 'ad V.D., I s'pose you've 'ad a Boy? I didn't mind pleasuring them arter they done ser much fer me. Why should I?"

Jane shook her head. "No, I never", she admitted. "I jes' wouldn't! Seen too much of it when I was young, I 'ad. I fought if I 'ad to—but mostly I got left alone. I 'ad boy fren's—fac' is I never 'ad girl fren's, jest boys till I got 'it in a accident; 'bout twelve I was then, and that's how I got took up, by George. George is a lot older than me: I was jes' his mascot. I brought him luck. Till larst night we was on the up and up, both of us! Everythink was fine and dandy, till an old man turned up that hadn't ought ter 'ave been there! So—I got cotched! George got orf wiv the swag—he had to! It wasn't no use waiting for me, it was a fair cop. Ser when I git out—an' I *shall* too—like a celluloid bat from Hell, the moment a chance comes along—I can go straight back to George!"

Though this prospect sounded bright, Jane's voice died down, and the light in her eyes went out.

"Is he good to you?" Elsie asked suspiciously. "D'you like him ser orful much?"

Jane hesitated. She had often asked herself the same question, and had never yet found a satisfactory answer.

"George?—why, he's taught me everythink I know", she said slowly at last. "I couldn't do no lifting if it hadn't been for George. I can keep myself nah, but he kept me till I learned. I look after his rooms and cooks for him—you might say I'm George's housekeeper. He has heaps of girls of course, much older than me, but he likes them on their own. He says women's place *isn't* the home—not if you're working your way to the top—the way George is! I'm going ter the Riviera wiv George one day—then we'll go in for the big money—pearls and such like. I fink George'll still take me—it wasn't my fault that the General popped up ser sudden like 'fore we

94

was clear—Yeah!—I *like* George all right—sure—I certainly do—but yer have ter be keerful wiv him—he's dangerous! I mean he might slap you up, soon as look at you, sooner if you crossed him."

It was like Hollywood, Elsie thought, listening to Jane. There she sat, steady and composed, with such bright eyes, and hard hands, and clear words; and look what she'd got in her handbag—compact, lipstick, two Arden bottles (foundation and night), as well as a round box of Coty's powder; and all this Jane had collected unpaid for, without undue effort. No wonder George appreciated her talents! Elsie did not mind George being rough; she loved to hear about fierce people so long as she herself escaped their attentions; but she was glad that Jane was not too soft on him.

In her day-dreams Elsie was always a Gunman's Moll; but the Gunman never treated her to his professional brutalities: she was his Princess, and to her he behaved like a Prince. She had a queer impression now that the real Gunman's Moll might have to get knocked about and share his risks; she might even look hard and rather plain—like the interesting girl who so appreciated her own gentleness.

"I don't want you to like George *too* much!" Elsie said after a pause. "'E's your bread ticket, of course, ser you got ter go back to 'im! But while you're 'ere you might take on wiv me—if yer cotton ter me the way I do ter you! All the girls 'ere 'as fren's—if they can make 'em!"

"I like you better than George nah!" Jane said fervently. "I shall always like you better! There won't be any more of those dirty ole men rahnd wiv me handy. I know the sort they are! They can keep their candy and their nylons to theirselves!"

Elsie smiled. She hadn't really liked the old men herself much, but she had liked what came because of them—in those precarious days when she had to choose between her mother and the police. In the end the police had got her; and they had been kinder to her than her mother. They had led her to the hospital; and afterwards to this security which had every comfort—except freedom.

"One thing," Elsie said with a reassuring little laugh, "I never 'ad no baby—I 'ad that much luck! Now Nurse don't fink I ever will. My fren' Mabel—upstairs—she's 'ad two babies, an' she isn't sixteen yet. Careless—that's what she must 'ave bin; but she's 'ad churchyard luck wiv 'em, I will say that! She lorst 'em bof—one was born dead, an' the other, 'e died jes' as she began to git fond of 'im!"

"This Mabel," Jane demanded with severity, "what abaht her? Is she yer girl-fren' steady—like a feller?"

Elsie considered this question carefully. If she confessed that she had once cared for Mabel and now no longer did, would she not appear unreliable to her new friend? But if she said she still cared for Mabel, would this not provoke trouble—trouble of a kind she preferred to avoid? To cast off Mabel altogether might not yet be practicable—or if practicable, even desirable? A good deal, one way or another, still came to Elsie from her friendship with the devoted Mabel. Perhaps the safest plan was just to acknowledge Mabel—as the victim acknowledges the executioner. The keen eyes fixed on her looked, Elsie thought, as if they might soften towards victims in whatever situation these debatable sufferers found themselves.

"Mabel," she explained to Jane, "I wouldn't say she was a queer eggsactly, 'cos queers don't orfen 'ave babies; but she's got one of these yer pashes for me—and she's the sort that it don't do ter upset too easily—kinda like your George maybe! She'd 'it back, somethink *crool*, if I didn't go wiv 'er. Nor I wouldn't want ter upset 'er too much anyway, 'cos I'm kinda sorry fer the girl!"

Her guilty sympathy tailed off into silence under Jane's reproachful eyes.

"If she got over losing that baby," Jane said firmly, "she can git over losin' you—the way I see it—someone's got to be lost——! You and me don't want ter git losin' each uvver, do we?"

Elsie shook her head emphatically. She didn't want to lose Jane, that was certain, but she meant to leave the whole thorny subject of getting rid of Mabel in Jane's capable hands.

As she reached this conclusion and expressed it by a sweet, wavering smile, the door burst open and a horn-rimmed tornado burst in upon them.

Sin came into the room with Miss Potter—sin and retribution. Elsie could almost hear the beat of the Devil's hoofs as she slid off the bed and stood cringing before Miss Potter.

To Miss Potter two bad girls were always worse if taken alone together. She could not have got rid of this impression had she found them on their knees saying their prayers. When she shouted "What are you doing?" it was a purely rhetorical question, for she did not give them the benefit of the doubt. Miss Potter knew with every quivering nerve of her self-righteous being that they were doing wrong.

"Elsie, how *dare* you come into this dormitory?" she hissed. "In broad daylight too—when you *know* how strictly forbidden it is! Report yourself immediately to Nurse Grace!"

Jane too descended from the bed, but she did not cringe. It was to defend Elsie that she descended, not from fear. She stood in front of Elsie.

"She was *sent!*" Jane exclaimed belligerently. "The Boss sent her—to show me the works—see! So what call have you to start slam-banging round at her—or me either?"

"New girls wait till they are spoken to", Miss Potter told Jane sharply. But her severest indignation was reserved for Elsie.

"What *you* have done," she told her, "is *seriously* wrong! Miss Bartlett may have told you to indicate this new girl's dormitory to her—but never to *enter* it yourself; and as for sitting on one of the girl's beds—you know very well why not! Such a thing is downright wicked! No punishment is too bad for you!"

Elsie began to cry. It was the simplest thing, she felt, to do; while crying, she slid past both Jane and Miss Potter, and was out of the door before either of them could stop her.

"You're crool," Jane told Miss Potter dispassionately, "that's what you are! Jees', jes' becos things haven't happened to you, you think they shouldn't happen to girls like Elsie— girls that's got what it takes! Your face is your fortune, that's what saved *you*—if you ask me!"

For a moment Miss Potter was too astonished for speech. Her cheeks, naturally red, became purple; her eyeballs stood out like over-ripe gooseberries; consternation as well as rage stiffened her figure like a board.

"Jane McCarthy", she said at last, "your remarks are as unseemly as your conduct. A girl could be sent to the cells for such behaviour here! But you are new, and I will merely report you as insolent. Read the rules by the door, and never let me find you in such a situation again. Nurse Grace is coming to attend to you presently; you are to undress and go to bed immediately and remain there until tomorrow morning, when you can get up when the other girls do, and come down to breakfast with them."

Miss Potter left the room and Jane heard the key turn in the lock.

She was, however, much less disturbed than Miss Potter, for she had said what she enjoyed saying, and did not mind being left alone; although after a moment or two she dissolved into tears. They were not the tears of anger or grief, however, merely an agreeable outlet for her long exasperated nerves. It had been a day of too many sensations. Now at last Jane was alone and in silence, where no one could see her, and she took the luxury of crying in peace.

Jane's head swam, her bruises ached, her heart—a deep and vulnerable portion of her—was acutely stirred by this new affection. How could she save and help Elsie? Life would no longer be worth living to her if she could not save her!

Perhaps Jane already knew that Elsie would do nothing to help Jane solve this problem, but this did not deflect her from her purpose.

It was a queer time to go to bed, in the middle of a long golden evening. The peaceful silence after Miss Potter had gone was only broken by far off sounds: the last call of birds, a voice floating up from below, the chink of china; then no sound at all, only colour deepening round her.

The green of the painted lockers and the swinging curtains were lit by the sunset light, till Jane felt as if she were floating on a sea of green and gold. At home she always had the radio on when George wasn't there, but in this strange place you could not hide your thoughts under other people's voices. Jane had to re-live her day, and plan her future, alone. How could she reach Elsie? Would George forgive her for being caught? Something nagged her beneath all these fragments, something in the place itself which might have a secret of its own to reveal to her. Soon she and Elsie must escape together —but not just yet. They would find out everything they could first. But one thing they couldn't find out, Jane reminded herself, even if they'd learned everything that the Home could teach: they couldn't find out what kind of an escape it would be if they *did* manage to reach George.

XII

Through her sleep Jane heard the terrifying, insistent clamour of a bell. Pursued by its brazen clang, she ran through sheets of scarlet flame. "Fire! Fire!" she shrieked —only to awake to a room full of derisive laughter.

"Garn'—yer bloody looney, that's the getting-up bell— an' when you 'ear it—scram!" a tall red-head shouted across the room at her.

Maudie was a big hefty girl of seventeen with a round face covered with freckles, a low forehead and no eyelashes. She was evidently a person of authority. She arranged which girl was to wash first. On her rested the amount of noise tolerated; by her disputed rights were settled, and very occasional mutinies sharply quelled. So strong were her limbs and so tyrannical her impulses that no one in the dormitory had hitherto questioned Maudie's sway. She had grasped enough morality to know on which side her bread was buttered: and she knew that it was buttered by Miss Potter.

She therefore saw that Miss Potter's dormitory rules were carried out, except when she wished to violate them herself and could count on evading discovery.

As Maudie met Jane's eyes she felt for a moment an obscure challenge; but it passed, for Jane turned obediently towards the washstand Maudie had indicated; she was not going to expose herself by back-chat in a new situation. She was simply taking Maudie in. Behind Maudie were the docile shrieks of all the other girls. "You can't shape up to a gang", George had once told Jane. "You wait till you get your feller alone— then you waltz in!" Undeniably Maudie was stronger and heavier than Jane, but had she staying power or wits?

George had taught Jane both to box and to practise the knowledge he had gained in ju-jitsu from a Japanese wrestler; but it was not upon these skills alone that Jane counted. Maudie's eyes as well as her carroty hair were fiery; but had she the kind of self-stimulation that lasts under extreme pain? Jane had. She thought it possible that she might be able to make short work of Maudie.

The girl at the next wash basin told Jane that her name was Esther, and gave Jane various hints about the processes expected of her. Esther had the narrow, predatory face of a rat. Her hair and eyes were a bleak brown; her lips were thin, her nose and chin sharply pointed. Esther always began an acquaintance by being pleasant. It cost her nothing; and later on, when she found it necessary to become unpleasant, it often paid her to have paved the way by an agreeable approach. She gave a few hints to Jane from lips that had already learned the prison trick of appearing moveless while she spoke; her words passed almost without sound into Jane's listening ears.

"She's boss!" Esther murmured with a crafty eye on Maudie. "Don't fergit it! If you don't mind what she says you get told orf by Miss Potter—yer might lose yer breakfas' or get kept in! A prime bloody Pet—that's what our Maudie is! No use complainin' of 'er either! 'Er lies are better than our words! Look at them two loonies—ort ter be in a bin, they ort—Maudie she 'as a down on them that's somepin chronic!"

The two "loonies" were painfully obvious. All the natural processes of life were slowed down in them. They couldn't find their wash rags, soap slipped from their hands on to the floor; their clothes confronted them as inextricable mysteries. Shoutings and cuffings from Maudie merely dazed them into greater clumsinesses. Bewildered, half-washed, with hair insufficiently combed, they trailed in panic-stricken oblivion at the end of the collected line of girls towards the stairs. Jane felt a brief spasm of pity for them. They did not know what was up; and they were never going to find out. Jane also faced the unknown, but she knew that she was going to find out what there was to know; and then, when she had found out, she would be able to stand up to it. She would never sink to the level of these two girls, snuffling and tearful, gnawed at simultaneously by guilt, hunger and fear. This was not where they belonged—if they belonged anywhere.

At the foot of the stairs a long counter spread, between the kitchen and the dining-room, covered with trays. Each girl's exact portions were placed on her tray and taken by her to her assigned place at table. There were three long tables— two for ten girls and one for eight, and at the head of each table stood a teacher. Miss Potter, the deputy-head, had charge of the first table where the eldest girls sat: their ages ranged from fifteen to eighteen. These girls were the best behaved, although they were the most determined delinquents with the longest records; but they had usually attained a certain maturity of outlook.

Like Maudie, they had discovered that it paid them to meet authority half way. A few of them were insolent to the less capable supervisors; most of them were lazy; and all of them were out to snatch any advantage they could get, from their companions or their supervisors; but unless they were mentally defective—as two or three of them were—they fully realized that it would profit them in the future, and might even shorten their sentences, if they could reach the standard of behaviour required of them—or appear to reach it.

The middle table, to which Jane was directed, was looked after by Miss Anne Plunket, a stocky good-natured blonde who took the physical training and dancing classes. The girls at her table were from twelve to fifteen, and considered the most difficult and least co-operative in the House. They broke down more easily, and could be expected to supply more tears, dramas and tantrums than either the younger or older girls. They were less assured in the arena of crime than the older delinquents, and less amenable to affection than the younger ones. However, Miss Plunket was the most popular of all the supervisors; and they found in her a robust control and commonsense which often steadied their wilfulness, and sometimes supplied them with the confidence they lacked.

The eight youngest children from nine to twelve were supposed to be the easiest and most innocent in the Home, but this supposition frequently broke down. They were the most active and also the least predictable, and Miss Plunket had very often to be called upon to protect the badgered and distracted Miss Davis, their main victim, by physical coercion.

Miss Davis was elderly and bilious, and might not have been used for her present purpose except for the general war shortages, which still lingered on in the pockets of our reputable state. Miss Davis taught preliminary subjects to which little importance was attached, and did whatever nobody else had time to do. She was not popular, but she could be relied on, except where human contacts were concerned.

Punishments, by small deprivations of privileges, or slight extra duties, were allowed to all the supervisors alike; but any girl, of whatever age, requiring severer correction, was sent to interview Miss Bartlett. It was never known exactly what happened at these interviews, but it was soon discovered that only the most hardened culprits failed to avoid a too frequent repetition of them.

Miss Bartlett did not appear at breakfast. It was a silent meal, brief and meagre. Each girl had a cereal with a small · jug of milk which must suffice for her tea as well; two slices of bread, one white and one brown; two thin disks of butter or margarine; and besides a little powdered sugar for her cereal, two small lumps of beet sugar for her tea. There was besides some variety as to "extras", Esther, who sat beside Jane, explained from the corner of her moveless lips: Monday they had prunes instead of cereal, Thursday they had potted meat instead of marmalade or jam. Friday they had a kipper or a piece of smoked haddock, and no jam, marmalade or cereal. While on Sundays they reached the dazzling height of an egg and bacon. It was considered a great privilege that each girl was allowed her own pot of tea and could use her milk and sugar at will. Tuesdays and Wednesdays were slightly enlivened by a tomato or an apple as the season suggested.

They all had elevenses—cocoa or milk, and biscuits. After breakfast each girl returned her tray to the counter. Miss Carter, who managed the breakfasts, ran the kitchen. She was a general favourite—young, breezy, exact but genial. She came in by the day, and seemed part of a freer and alien atmosphere.

On the counter—with their names attached by a tape—were now piled three heaps of square blue veilings to cover their heads.

"Wot is those for?" Jane demanded, of the helpful Esther. "Ter keep the dust out of yer hair?"

"Nah!" Esther retorted with a derisive grin. "Chepel."

They lined up again, and waited.

"Wot are we waitin' for?" Jane whispered.

"Lepers!" Esther told her with a still more derisive grin.

Looking upwards with eager eyes, Jane beheld the eighteen isolated students of civilization, descending the staircase in pairs. They were dressed exactly as the others were, nor did they look any different, except that the proportion of half-wits among them was distinctly higher.

Elsie shone out from among them as their only beauty; her blue veil brought out the astounding blueness of her eyes; her bright hair, a crown of gold, rose above the pink and white of her oval face. No young madonna meeting the angel of annunciation could have had more innocent delight in her welcoming eyes as they met Jane's; yet Elsie must have known that to Mabel, who walked beside her, this signal of new joy was a bitter business. Perhaps Elsie could not help the dimple sliding out from the tender hollow of her cheeks, nor the parted lips which revealed the almond whiteness of her teeth; but perhaps Elsie smiled on purpose to punish her tyrant companion. Who can tell what mingled motives lie behind the sweetest smile? It must be admitted that Elsie was not loyal, and that Jane rejoiced in this collapse of her friend's integrity.

The whole day shone for them both in that swift smile.

Silently—for all their supervisors upheld and enforced this silence—two by two the girls paced into the chapel, where they were to meet the religion which had been provided for them.

XIII

When Miss Bartlett said: "Come in!" she said it sadly, for she knew that behind that eager knock stood her friend Emily Potter, anxious for a nice long talk.

Emily *was* a friend, since she shared with Susan Bartlett all the responsibilities of their hard task with conscientious zeal, and gave her chief unflinching support. Yet she was, as well, all the things that Miss Bartlett neither was nor wanted to be. Emily was devoted to Susan; she was self-assured; and dead-locked in a sense of her moral superiority. Miss Bartlett was not devoted to Emily; she was not sure of anything, least of all perhaps of herself; and she had no sense of moral superiority to anyone.

She did not want to have a nice long talk; she would have liked to read a book or listen to a gramophone record, preferably Elizabeth Schumann singing one of Heine's songs.

Emily came in with a rush, and sank onto a footstool at her feet.

"My dear," she said, "how tired you look. I will make you a good cup of tea! I expect it was that awful scene I heard about from Mrs. Parker with that appalling new girl! You will hardly believe me when I tell you what I found her up to yesterday evening: I've only just had time to report it to you! She was actually *sitting* on her bed *with* Elsie Cummings, in my dormitory!"

"Thank you—I've had my tea," Miss Bartlett said after a pause, "but do make yourself some if you haven't! I suppose they had to sit somewhere. I forgot Elsie wasn't supposed to go into your dormitory. I happened to see her going upstairs, just as my telephone bell rang, so I told her to show Jane McCarthy her room. I hope you didn't scold her for what was after all my fault?"

Miss Bartlett did not say "for carrying out my instructions", since that might sound as if she were reproving Emily. Still there were times when Miss Bartlett, who usually hated reproofs, would have enjoyed reproving Emily.

"She knew very well that wasn't what you meant!" Miss Potter replied reassuringly, for she felt her friend had been careless and needed absolution. "She simply took advantage of a chance remark to disobey one of our most important rules. Think of the moral risk—let alone the physical one—of those two girls in a bedroom alone! And I spend half my time keeping the V.D.s away from the others—even in the *public* rooms!"

Miss Bartlett said, stirring uneasily, "I do wish we didn't have to keep them apart! I mean, of course, we should *never* have had to have them mixed up in one community: it is bad for both types of girls, if you can call them types, when each is a separate individual with different problems. But I don't think you need worry about little Elsie; she is so plainly a victim of circumstance, she won't hand on any alluring spectacle of a life of sin—she didn't like it!"

"You don't know *what* they may have been up to," Miss Potter urged with resolute disgust. "Jane is older than Elsie and such a little savage, and with that atrocious accent too, picked up no doubt from living in camps with American airmen—a shocking case history!"

"Dr. Martin Jessop satisfied himself that she made up that whole camp story", Miss Bartlett roused herself to say. "There was nothing in it at all. He thought that she had been well taken care of by some burglar—perhaps her father."

"You know what some fathers are like. Our worst cases——" Miss Potter began, but Miss Bartlett checked her a little tartly.

"Most fathers—*aren't!*" she said. "I have had two talks with Jane, one after she had broken Mrs. Parker's crockery, and one after chapel this morning. I rather like her. It won't do Elsie any harm to have a little iron introduced into her system—and Jane is full of iron. But I am afraid it will cause trouble with Mabel. Still, Mabel shouldn't be such a tyrant. Nurse Grace says she won't let Elsie call her soul her own. Of course Elsie *likes* not calling her soul her own—that's part of the trouble. She makes herself into a sort of prey to be eaten up by the first monster she comes across; and then, finding it dull being swallowed, she starts looking out for a *fresh* monster. I am afraid Elsie is what is called a murderee. I have always believed that they are responsible for a good third of our murders."

"I don't quite know what you mean, dear", Miss Potter said with a shade of disapproval in her voice. "Lack of self-control is of course the main trouble with all our girls. We have never had any actual murderers here as far as I know, and I have worked here for fifteen years—unless you think that Mabel *was* responsible for the death of her baby—and you know the magistrates thought it was simply ignorance and neglect. She was quite broken-hearted about it, Nurse Grace told me."

"No—no, Emily, I didn't mean that", Miss Bartlett said hurriedly, "I am talking of murder in the abstract."

"Oh, the abstract!" Miss Potter said with polite resignation. "I'm afraid, dear, I always take the sins of these poor girls rather too deeply to heart to feel interested in the abstract! Not that I can say that I greatly pity Elsie: I have a horror of those girls upstairs. We should certainly *never* have been asked to house them under the same roof as our poor, merely delinquent girls!—whatever the war demanded. Far better to let them stay in a bombed district, and *be* bombed. We may be able to save these others from their sins—though I can't say I have much hope for a hardened type like Jane. Criminal is written all over her! But once sex has reared its ugly head, I don't believe the poor little horrors can ever quite recover from what they have learned; though we must do what we can, of course, to help them!"

"I think you'd be surprised", Miss Bartlett said in a voice that she restrained with difficulty from exasperation, "to realise how little they have learned or even—some of them—

have been harmed, except physically, by their experiences! A little happiness of another kind—some sort of skill to restore their self-respect and give them a new incentive—is all a great many of them need! You see, whatever they've experienced has been, not only a failure, but a *painful* failure; so that if you can give them something else instead, they really don't *want* any more of it! Whereas these physically free children— thieves in particular—have all had some successes before they got found out. They are most of them simply pining to try again. They've only been 'unlucky' on the way to a life full of opportunities for gain. They have not had to face a cruel illness nor perhaps seen into the jaws of death—lost their self-respect and the respect of others—and gained nothing at all but the miserable knowledge that men forsake what they have once desired—or, worse still, that a life that was part of their very own flesh and blood has been denied to them forever!"

Miss Bartlett spoke with such bitter sadness that Miss Potter stopped eating her piece of cake and gazed at her with horrified surprise.

"My dear," she gasped, "you might have been one of them yourself to talk like that!"

"Sometimes," Miss Bartlett told her drily, "I feel that I *ought* to have been, in order to deal fairly with them. It is as if I had shirked something."

"You *are* over-tired, dear", Miss Potter said, continuing her cake with relief, since physical explanations soothed away her sense of shock. "You really ought to take more time off: these sad cases get on your nerves! After all, our business is simply to carry out what we know to be right for the little community under our charge—and leave the rest to God."

Miss Bartlett, who did not have that kind of God, refrained from answering her friend.

"I daresay some suffer worse than others", Miss Potter conceded after rather a long pause, "but girls *are* responsible for having lovers, aren't they?—if you can call them lovers— in most cases anyhow; some girls are even *more* than half responsible, Nurse Grace thinks; so they must just take the consequences, mustn't they?—and the little thieves the same!

But what I'm quite sure is that they ought to be kept apart, and while under *our* charge not learn anything worse from each other than what they know already!"

Susan, who struggled in a perpetual conflict between uncertainty of faith and deep compassion, almost envied her friend her pat and easy securities. It seemed strange to her, however, that a friend who had so much unnecessary devotion to herself should have so little imaginative kindness in her heart for the children they both spent so much energy in serving.

"You know," Miss Bartlett said at last, groping towards something that they might agree on together, "I can't help believing, Emily, that within reason we should encourage friendships between our girls—not possessive ones perhaps, like Mabel's for Elsie, and not what is called 'inordinate affection' which might lead to vice. I know that you are right, and that we must safeguard what is left of their innocence—although we can't of course *know* what *is* innocent—to them! Yet if we believe that God is love—isn't it a kind of sacrilege to deny it to them, for each other? How otherwise are they to learn what love is? Even the little stagnant backwaters of affection—mixed up with jealousies and perhaps dangerous sentimentalities—must be better than no love! I know that I like to see the look in a child's eyes when she is smiling at another child!"

Miss Potter drank the rest of her tea in silence. "Dear Susan", she thought, "is a great deal too emotional to be the head of an institution such as ours! It was a great mistake—after I'd been here more than twelve years—to put someone in from outside over my head—even if her father *was* a bishop—which of course makes a great difference, I can quite see. And God knows how loyally I accepted her, and would have done even if he hadn't been. But I must say that Susan with all her beautiful qualities hasn't got commonsense. Fortunately I am always at hand to help her!"

"Dear," she said with tactful solemnity, "what you said to the girls in chapel this morning was *most* touching and impressive. I was quite moved by it, and so I am sure were the girls. It's a pity you have to limit these little talks of yours to three minutes—by-the-by you were just over four this morning—I timed you. I think they sang their final hymn even better than usual—and with such gusto! It did me good to hear them. We must, I think, trust that whatever is necessary in the way of love will reach them in their religious life. Fortunately divine love is quite safe for them!"

"If they know what it is—or where to find it," Miss Bartlett said, looking still graver, "or how to use it if they find it! But Emily, if we pigeon-hole it away from human love, how can they find it? While I was arranging Jane's classes with her this morning—to find out what she knew—she suddenly asked me what chapel was *for*. Of course she knew that churches and chapels existed, and she had often heard sacred words used as expletives, but she had never heard any other value attached to them. She had never been to either Sunday School or Church, and I gather her family never had either. She had heard a few perfunctory prayers in the schools which she had attended, but they were without meaning for her. She had seen a Bible, but had never opened it. I am telling you this, Emily, because you will now see what—in a Christian country, with a church nominally supposed to govern equally with the state—a child can find to help it live a Christian life—or even a legal one!

> 'Go, little creature
> Formed for joy and mirth—
> Go—live without the help of anything on earth!'

Blake was quite right when he wrote this sombre poem, more than a hundred years ago; and unfortunately he is *still* quite right about it!"

Miss Potter said, after a shocked pause, "I really feel quite concerned at the way you take these things, dear Susan. I feel you don't go quite deep enough! I have been here for longer, as you know, than you have, and I assure you many of our girls have a really satisfactory faith, and *like* going to church. I shouldn't be surprised that *if* Jane made up those stories about American soldiers, she hasn't lied also to you about what she believes—or has been *taught* to believe! She certainly must have realised how wicked it was to break all that china and to attack poor Mrs. Parker like a wild cat! I must say I am thankful that I have my good strong Maudie in my dormitory, to prevent Jane's bullying the other girls. Now do go and lie down, dear, for a bit, before touching the bills!"

Miss Bartlett shook her head. "No", she said firmly, "the accounts are just as much my duty as Jane's religious faith, and I'm bound to admit I find them a great deal easier to tackle!"

XIV

When Jane joined Elsie outside the chapel door in the free, mixed moment of their unveiling, she only just had time to whisper, "Where we goin' to meet?" and to hear Elsie's low-voiced reply, "'Levenses—'ere, by the counter", before she found herself swept forward into a class room.

It was the first time Jane had ever been inside a British school. George had thought that at twelve her education was sufficient, and that a place where you had to fill out forms was at all costs to be avoided. Her first reaction to the class room was contempt. Where were the huge windows, like doors into the sky, universal in California? Where were the modern chairs and desks suited to the human form, for sedentary purposes? Where was the extensive stage for the teacher, the bright colours, the innumerable external signs by which education should be supported if not entirely conducted?

There was only a blackboard on a small platform containing a chipped desk, a teacher's chair, and the supervisor herself. Miss Plunket wore an ill-made coat and skirt, no make-up, and her hair was badly permed. She seemed a part of the antiquated, ineffective look of the whole class room. It was swept out every day, and yet the look of dust had sunk into it: not new dust, but old dust never drastically cleaned out that seemed, through its constant, unmarked presence, to have become a spiritual entity and to stand between even the most eager scholar and her wish for knowledge. Very few of the girls were eager. They knew they had to sit there for an hour and listen to things being said that they didn't care to hear, and probably have to answer questions it had never occurred to any of them were worth asking—even if they had known the answers. Yet there was one surprise in this discouraging atmosphere. Miss Plunket was nothing like as ineffective as she looked; and if there was a mind open to receive knowledge, she could make a bridge to it, by the full use of her own.

Almost instantly she made the bridge between Jane and herself; and crossing it, Jane felt for the first time the thrill of a disinterested thought. She was actually using her brain to find out something that wasn't going to pay her, and that didn't involve either her appetite or her appearance. It was a very curious sensation—this mastery without desire; and it made her suddenly think of the young doctor she had seen the day before, who had said that fifteen years' schooling wasn't enough for him. But this new form of enjoyment soon palled when Jane found a way to meet Elsie's eyes, by dodging the head of a tall girl who sometimes had the grace to bend her head over her desk, so that Jane could catch even across the gulf of space the vision of Elsie's Mona Lisa smile.

They were far apart; but there must be ways, Jane's ingenious mind told her, of getting together, and she proceeded to let English grammar go and set herself to solve the more immediate problem.

Two determined young creatures, lit by love, can break through the strongest barriers as a knife cuts through butter. Miss Potter could not spend all her time trying to thwart them; the maddened Mabel might do what she could to destroy their blithe interchanges, but Elsie knew by heart the best moments for evasion. There is a certain forethought caused by fear in natures habituated to defeat which is very nearly impregnable. Elsie might be incapable of defending herself in moments of danger, but no one knew better how to dodge such occasions. As for Jane, it was to be her invariable role in the enterprise of friendship to play a part of perpetual activity; risk or no risk, she could count upon her own emergency wits.

Half way through the first hour's lesson, under Miss Plunket's not ungenial sway, Jane succeeded in getting herself moved to the next desk to Elsie, on the plea of being sick if she wasn't close to a window. She really looked sick, Miss Plunket thought, for Jane's sallow complexion had assumed a vague green tinge, her eyes rolled up, and she panted a little; though she became instantly relieved when allowed to sit by the quiet Elsie—a bad pupil but, so Miss Plunket thought, a decent, non-conducting girl. Perhaps, had Miss Plunket not considered Jane to be an intelligent girl, she would not so readily have allowed a change; but in the long run, Jane thought, even intelligence pays.

It was a pity that Jane's next class was taken by Miss Potter. Jane didn't like her, and was therefore unable to learn anything at all from her. Nor was there any ruse that Jane could think of that enabled her to bring herself near Elsie again, under the protuberant and active glances of Miss Potter.

Soon, however, Jane found sufficient pastime in playing ducks and drakes with the information placed alertly before the class; for Miss Potter was an excellent teacher, and prided herself upon interesting her pupils. With an air of misleading concern, Jane asked reasonable-sounding, but disruptive questions that set the whole class giggling. These were ecstatic interludes in which Miss Potter became desperate, and the whole class learned nothing, except that Jane could fool Miss Potter.

History and geography were Miss Potter's subjects, and upon them both Jane had preconceived notions which did not harmonise with Miss Potter's. Jane believed that history dated from the moment when George Washington licked the British. This one great and important historic victory had slid into Jane's mind and obliterated every other incident. Everything else either dated from it, or came back to it. As for geography, Jane had grasped that England was a small island, some way off from America, in which everything—except perhaps George—moved more slowly than she had been accustomed to at home. This Island, Jane felt, had only been saved from complete insignificance by having recently become an air base for American bombers; and she wished to share this view of her subject with the highly patriotic Miss Potter.

Elevenses broke up the gathering storm.

Mathematics and literature were Miss Bartlett's main subjects; and Jane readily became enthralled by figures, that she felt would in the end add up to something. Millionaires based their fortunes upon an understanding of how to use these elusive quantities. And as for literature, Jane loved the sound of words as well as the ideas behind them. The atmosphere of Miss Bartlett's schoolroom was strangely different. Miss Bartlett, a remoter figure than Jane expected, appeared to be more interested in her subject than in her pupils. She looked at them as if they were the mere background of an experiment. The experiment was in a sense *for* them, but it would be just as interesting and just as valid—should they not be there. They, indeed, might miss something by not attending to what was before them: what they would miss would be the challenge of the explorer. In Miss Bartlett's classes, even the stupidest or most discouraged child saw itself as a "stout Cortez", and was given—if it could take it—its brief moment, "silent, upon a peak in Darien".

Jane's first day was a series of such exciting moments. She had a very good brain, and it had never been released before. She was stunned by her success in the art class.

None of the girls painted more vivid pictures than Jane found herself painting. The active subjects of her imagination burst through her ignorance into lively forms, and magic colours. Even when she was told to paint a ";still", it never was still: a jug handle cleaved the air like a scimitar; a shut door appeared in the act of opening; a bunch of flowers fluttered to one side as if attacked by a gust of wind.

Elsie did not take kindly to any of Jane's favourite subjects except dancing. She liked music if it was the sort that could be utilized; and she did not object to being read out loud to, while she was sewing, in the evenings.

David Copperfield had been chosen by Miss Bartlett, and led to lively discussions.

Jane dispensed with David's child-wife, Dora, very rapidly. Indeed, she thought, Dickens' heroines—doubtful even in Victorian times—were completely bogus, when compared with "Chippies". But Jane, and even Elsie, shivered real shivers over the Murdstones, and followed Steerforth's sordid career with eagerness; though Jane had an uncomfortable feeling from time to time that Steerforth might be a refined edition of George in his less pleasant moments.

Jane felt the whole nineteenth century seethe and rock through her enraptured mind. Here in this book was London— a London where people were really hungry, dirty, angry, playing tricks on others, committing crimes, embarking on enterprises she could follow and understand. How plainly she could see Ma drinking gin in one of those sordid, foggy rooms—hatching plots out of people's hearts and lives with deadly gusto! The gusto of Dickens had lasted, and some of the pity—intense as the gusto—that went with it reached Jane's generous imagination. Then how wonderful the storm was on the way to Yarmouth; and that modern film hero, Steerforth, handsome, arrogant and false—born to ruin little Emily and disconcert Rose Dartle—and in the end washed up on the beach, drowned by a sea stronger, and more cruel, than himself! Jane generously agreed to share Steerforth with Elsie, who accepted her half with submissive gratitude. Elsie thought that it would be very nice indeed—though not likely— to meet someone just like Steerforth in a dance hall.

Every kind of man came to dance halls, she explained to Jane, who on this point was considerably more ignorant than she was. "But if they're Lords or real posh", Elsie admitted a little sadly, "they don't let on to be, 'cos they reckon you'd try to get more money out of them if you knew who they wos—an' nah they 'av'n't got it! They 'ad ort to—'cos they do know 'ow ter spend it—I will say that for them! Somefin' chronic being poor is—when you fink you 'ad ort ter be rich!"

"I *am* going to be rich", Jane informed Elsie loftily. "You only have to learn how, and when I know I'll teach you."

Elsie thanked her enthusiastically, but she privately thought that it would be better for Jane to acquire the riches by herself, and then for them just to spend the money together. There was quite a lot Elsie could teach Jane about spending money—but nothing at all about earning it.

The other girls, as the brisk days passed, melted round them in a misty landscape of separate insignificances. Some of them were paths Jane might have liked to follow, had her eyes been less glued upon the magnetic figure of Elsie—"a lovely apparition sent to be a moment's ornament"—but not, had Jane known it, of any more lasting substance.

There was one very small girl in her own dormitory, whom Jane noticed because she picked her up in an outdoor scrimmage just as she was in danger of being trampled on by a girl the size of an elephant. After this Jane often found the child following her at a respectful distance like a friendly dog. She had deeply enquiring eyes, and was called "Snoutie" though her real name was Esmeralda Jones. Esmeralda was not the kind of name by which you could think of her, while Snoutie was; besides, anyone could see how much it hurt her to be called Snoutie; and these were hard girls who liked to hurt each other.

One day Snoutie said to Jane, whom she met full tilt in an empty passage, "Please—do you fink a girl with a long back, short legs an' a turned up nose can ever get *anywheres?*"

Jane, who was on her way to a secret rendezvous with Elsie, stopped short to consider this question seriously. She fully realized the desperate urgency that lay behind it. It was as if Snoutie's very life hung on Jane's answer.

"Any guy can get anywheres if he sets out", Jane said at last with desperate optimism, "but you don't get no rockets sent up to help you!—you have ter be tough! That's wot a fren' of mine says—an' he hasn't half got on in the world! You be tough! 'Course you're small, I admit—but there's bantams as well as heavyweights, aren't there? Whadda yer say—I learn you somepin I picked up—so you can crack an' crumple up a big guy by jes' lettin' go and seemin' soft in the right place—and then you weigh in and punch his lights out?"

117

"'Jees—that would be gorgeous!" Snoutie answered, breathing fast and hard.

"On the strict Q.T. mind!" Jane advised her, "so no one sees yer on to it! That Maudie—I kinda noticed she got a down on you, hasn't she?"

Snoutie drew a still deeper breath. "She's orfle 'ard on me!" she admitted. "She fair 'ates me guts! It's 'cos I won't 'oller when she 'its me! Well—I won't never! If that's what she wants, I ain't given it 'er—see? I kin die, carn't I?"

Jane nodded appreciatively. That, she thought, was the spirit, and then Elsie appeared, smiling her sweet enigmatic smile, and Jane forgot all about Snoutie.

XV

While Jane had lived with George every day had had a curiously wide open quality. There were no consecutive hours for certain actions. There was no certainty at all. George might go out at midnight and return at dawn; he might go out at dawn and not return before dusk. He might not go out at all; or, even more likely, he might not stay in.

Freedom was a quality that woke with daylight and had had an indefinite expansion. There were tasks which George expected Jane to perform, but they were not pinned to hours unless he was on the spot to exact them. He expected Jane to be in not too long after dark, unless he himself took her out in the evening; so that it might be said that nightfall closed one end of the timeless expanse, but not with any sense of fixity about it. Extraordinary things might happen in the house even after nightfall. Once Jane, coming in late from a cinema, saw Ma running round her kitchen table after a belligerent black man, whom she had, no doubt, cheated, and who had too sharply resented being cheated. Ma had a knife, and the black man had a razor—but Ma cut off half his ear before he could slice her up. Ma had escaped, scot free, though shaken.

Jane, feeling far more sympathetic to the black man than to Ma, ministered to him to the best of her ability. Finding that not even Ma's tablecloth and half a sheet were sufficient to stop the dramatic flowing of his blood—exactly the same blood, Jane had observed, in colour and texture as her own—she ran with him hand in hand to the nearest surgery, and forced a terrified young surgeon to carry out his duties, without sending for the police. Jane had a good story made up as she ran, and the size of the black man, and a sense of physical urgency, did the rest.

At Morely House there was no open sense of time, and nothing unpredictable happened. The flight of hours fixed itself into objects of attention that couldn't be contracted or expanded. Activities were communal and planned beforehand; no task could be postponed or evaded; and each hour, with equal tread, succeeded to the last. Sometimes Jane thought that she could not live through the twenty-eight pigeon-holed days, weighed down by suspense for what still stretched before her after the days were over. Not even the fact that every waking hour was shot through by the sense of Elsie's rainbow presence could alleviate the sense of ordered time.

Whenever the girls were free to talk they discussed their sentences. Jane soon learned that there were three possible prospects before her. She might be put back where she was for another twenty-eight days. This was the best thing that could happen; and it might continue to happen every twenty-eight days, until, in the far mists of time, a place was found for her elsewhere. If the home she came from originally was considered suitable she might be allowed to return there, with Miss Emsley, or another nearer Probation Officer, visiting her from time to time. This, Jane privately realised, was not, in her own circumstances, a real possibility. If her home were found entirely unsuitable, she could be boarded out in a family where she could work out her sentence attached, like a dog on a lead, to the visiting presence of Miss Emsley. Or Jane might be removed from both Morely House and Miss Emsley and sent to an Approved School for an indefinite period. Considering that Jane was listed as a first offender's case and that she was admitted to be, at her age, rather a stooge than an accomplice, it was the general consensus of opinion among the girls at Morely House that Jane would get off with a minor sentence.

On exactly the twenty-eighth day Miss Emsley reappeared in her neat little baby Austin. Jane was sitting in the hall waiting for her; but not even the fact that Miss Bartlett had allowed her the full use of her handbag, filled with cosmetics, could take away from Jane the cruel sense of impending execution.

They reached the Town Hall at eleven; and it wasn't like a Court at all, just a small room used for Councils, with a table down the centre and nobody there but themselves. Then three Plush Horses, as Jane in her mind described them, came in; the two magistrates whom she had already seen for a few tongue-tied minutes in the Police Station had a lady with them. There wasn't much to be said about the lady at first glance, except that she looked as if she really was one, and didn't much like being there.

There was no sign of a policeman or woman, but they wouldn't be very far off, Jane fancied. The police never were, even when they had said they would be.

Before the magistrates began to talk, the Inspector himself came in, dressed in ordinary clothes and trying to pretend he was a clerk in a bank which, except for his boots, he might have been. He was asked to make a statement about the burglary; and when he had made it—it was just as unfavourable to Jane as if he had been in uniform—he was told by Sir Henry Melville that he could go; and went.

"An' I suppose he's got ter change his clo'es agin!" Jane thought, "first thing in the day like—arter his breakfus'—that's twice already! Pity I couldn't have known where he keeps his uniform an' got a boy friend ter fill 'em full of bed-bugs! That wud 'abeen a treat!"

This treat having been denied her, Jane fixed her piercing eyes on Sir Henry Melville, a benevolent local magnate, who sat at the head of the table in a big armchair. He was a family man, whose children had given him no trouble. They had been very well brought up by his wife and sent to first-rate schools. On his left sat Mr. Victor Jackson, a retired civil servant, who had held an important post in the tropics. He was unmarried, but it was supposed that his "dominion over palm and pine" would make him a particularly suitable person to deal with a delinquent child. Jane had already seen them in Mr. Bassett's parlour, but they did not look as if they wished to remember the meeting.

121

Upon these two magnates and an unknown lady, Jane's whole future depended. On Sir Henry's right sat Miss Edwina Pole. Although unmarried and in her late forties, Miss Pole, alone of the three, had had first-hand experience of children. She even knew the difference between a Problem Child and a child with problems too difficult for it to solve. Both men felt confidence in her judgment, coupled with anxiety, for it often seemed to them that she was too severe when they would have been lenient, and too lenient when their own impulse would have been to be severe.

There was no blandness in her, and when she spoke, her directness sometimes shattered them, much more than it seemed to shatter the child.

They all said "Good morning" to Jane, and Sir Henry asked her very kindly to sit down, which she had already done.

Sir Henry opened the proceedings. He had a deep resonant voice, between a bellow—when he was excited—and a mild booming when he was at ease or wished to put those beneath him at their ease. He boomed now at Jane.

"Well now, Jane," he began, "Jane is your name, isn't it? —Jane McCarthy, we have already met, haven't we?—and I see you're fifteen? You're not at school now, I understand, but perhaps you'll tell us where you went to school?"

Jane shook her head; she let her voice shake too, because she realised that Sir Henry would be nicer to her if she appeared frightened.

"Please, I didn't know their names—them schools——" she murmured. "We moved about terrible—an' I left before Mother died!"

A dead mother, Jane felt, would be a good note. Sir Henry made a sympathetic rustling sound.

"And how old were you then?" he questioned.

"Twelve", Jane whispered.

"And where were you then?" he asked, more kindly still, for it happened that his own youngest daughter was twelve and had just been sent to boarding school.

"We was at Liverpool", Jane told him. "My father left us when I was a kid—I don't know exactly when—but then the war started an' there was the bombing. We was evacuated, but went back to Liverpool arter a bit. I didn't go to no more schools. Men was what my Ma lived on."

"Surely, black markets, Jane, was what you told me?" urged Miss Emsley, in distress.

"Men—an' black markets", Jane amended.

There was a pause. It was rather a long pause. The men looked shocked. Miss Pole looked mildly interested. Jane saw that she did not believe a word of it, and respected her accordingly. Mr. Jackson polished his single eye-glass, fixed it firmly, where he really needed it, and remarked rather drily:

"The night of the burglary—as, no doubt, you realise—you committed a crime. To break into another person's house and steal his property is a punishable offence, and whatever your parentage was, or your schooling may have been, you have committed a serious offence in the eyes of the law. You will not be sent to prison for it—since you are beneath the age when the law orders imprisonment—but you will certainly be placed under some milder form of restraint. We are not here to scold you, but we are here to see that you understand what you have done. To be a thief is to break the laws of your own country— if we are to believe, as you have stated, that this *is* your native country. If not, you have a right to be returned wherever you belong, and to be tried by their law."

"Morally", Sir Henry interjected, "you are a thief whatever country you belong to, my poor child. The moral law is every-where the same."

Jane made up her mind before she spoke that it was no use listening to Sir Henry—he didn't make sense—but that she'd have to be careful of the other man.

Then she said, "I'm English all right".

Miss Pole leaned forward. Her eyes were very clear and rather cold, and her voice was like something held in very tight that couldn't get away.

"You look to me extremely intelligent", she observed to Jane, "so you had better try to take in that thieves get caught sooner or later—and that when they do the rest of their lives is likely to be unpleasant. Now you needn't have an unpleasant life—you can learn in the next few years how to earn your living, so that you needn't be afraid of anyone—nor of the police, because if you keep the law they will be on your side—nor of anyone else who may have made you break it. You can be free—no one will interfere with you—or hurt you or lock you up ever again! Wouldn't you like to try?"

Jane looked at her carefully. Miss Pole must have spent, misguidedly, quite a lot of money on her clothes; but being rather beige looking, she should have avoided wearing iron grey. Her hat was much too hard for her vigorous and pronounced features; and her perm—or the hair itself—was poor.

"Lots of people", Jane told her, "don't get caught; and if you're alone, you can earn more by breaking laws than keepin' 'em! Granted you gotta learn—and I did *git* caught! But things was against me—they certainly was! How'd I know that ole geyser'd come upstairs unbeknownst, when he'd orta bin playin' bridge?"

Sir Henry made an uncomfortable noise in his throat; Mr. Jackson remained impassive; but Jane paid no attention to either of them. She was at grips with this strange woman to whom she had suddenly—and unexpectedly to herself—told part of the truth.

"You couldn't have known", Miss Pole agreed, "but the point is—if you hadn't been there uninvited and stealing his wife's coat—it wouldn't have mattered. You wouldn't be here now—and you *would* be free. What we all want is for you to be kept free; and you can only be free by learning to earn your own living instead of stealing it."

Was this woman really talking sense? Was she herself so blessed—so happy—living her single unattractive life within the law? Anyhow, it wouldn't have been any use George taking *her* on the Riviera, to get under people's skins and find out where their jewels were kept! She was safe—all these three Plush Horses were safe, and didn't need to steal because they were already rich. They had roofs and meals anyway, and money in banks; and as for education, they knew things Jane didn't; but Jane was prepared to bet her bottom dollar that she also knew things they didn't!

Jane decided to discard the uncomfortable and slightly doubtful feeling produced in her by Miss Pole. She lifted her eyes to the ceiling and switched off her attention. She wondered if, when they got out, Miss Emsley would let her have an elevenses. Sir Henry's voice boomed on, graver than before, but not unpleasing, like the radio when you were reading an exciting book and not listening to it. Suddenly she heard him say the words "American airmen!" and sprang to attention again. He was repeating all that stuff she'd made up about camps and airfields, which he had probably got from Miss Emsley, and got all wrong, even as a story.

"We are all three most anxious to keep you away from such evil and immoral influences", he said.

The blood rushed to Jane's head. Her boys were being abused—she didn't know them, but they were her boys—and she wouldn't hear a word against them—unless she needed it for her own getaway.

"Listen!" she said sharply. "Those boys is good! They aren't here for what they can git! They take risks—maybe they'll get done in one day by Russians. Anyhow they're helpin' ter take care of all of us. What do you want ter grudge them a little fun and games for? You tomato-coloured old Doughnut! I wouldn't put it past you—ter run after a young skirt on the sly yourself and get what you could out of her! Fambly or no fambly!"

Sir Henry turned purple; a faint but quite unmistakable twinkle flickered in Victor Jackson's frosty eyes. Miss Pole took out her handkerchief and blew her nose; it was a large one and covered her mouth as well.

"Insolence will get you nowhere", Sir Henry said in a voice that had lost its booming quality. "You are too young for prison, so we have all three decided to send you to a school—an Approved School. You will there have a chance, as Miss Pole has so kindly pointed out, to learn how to live a decent and useful life, if you are capable of taking it!"

"How long?" Jane demanded breathlessly.

"For your own sake it must be long enough," Sir Henry told her, much more grimly than he had intended to tell her. "We have decided on three years."

Miss Pole thought that she would never forget the child's sigh—as if her heart were crushed by the weight of their judgment, "heavy as frost and deep almost as life". Even Victor Jackson felt uncomfortable. None of the three knew how to break the silence after the child's sigh.

"Why, you're crazy! You're all three plumb crazy", Jane shouted suddenly, raising herself from her sense of absolute defeat. "What have I done to git three years *for*? Why, I only wore that mink half an hour! You ask Lady Despard if she minded it being tore! I didn't touch her jools! You all know that! Wasn't I searched? You can't do this to me! You can't— you can't! You bloody ole stuffed dolls—you aren't human! Gawd blast an' damn you all to Hell!"

Jane's voice broke into sobs. The almost reassuringly familiar voice of Miss Emsley sounded in her ear.

"Come along with me at once, Jane", Miss Emsley said sternly. "We don't want to have to bring the police into this——" So Jane had been right—the police must have been near all the time.

Jane was led out of the Court into hard bright sunshine— without having had a chance to hit back at anybody. She knew now what being a delinquent child meant.

XVI

It was a quiet night. The May moon, an amber-coloured ball, rose high over the hushed fields. The air was full of the mingled scents of unseen blossoms stirring the blood. Swift winged bats replaced the darting swallows. The fifty young girls in the old Manor House were restless with the closed off spring.

None of them had been told beforehand that Miss Bartlett was to be away for the week-end. Yet there was a strange feeling in the air as if something highly charged, but safe when under control, had broken loose and was now dangerous. A ship whose captain has been suddenly called ashore has such an atmosphere. Another, perhaps as capable an officer, is in control, but he is not the captain.

None of these girls had any certainty in themselves. They borrowed what certainty they had from their surroundings. Even Jane, though George had taught her self-mastery in action, only practised it for short intervals, from acute self-interest and because she had known that worse would happen if she didn't. She did not know what might happen now. It might not be worse. There might even be more chances of meeting Elsie unobserved; and yet the feeling of looseness in the air was sinister rather than inviting.

Miss Potter took their short evening prayers; and after prayers were over, as the girls filed off to their dormitories, her eyes met Maudie's.

Miss Potter had just finished a private prayer that God would give her the necessary courage and good will to carry through her great responsibility for the week-end with justice and mercy; she did not by this glance send Maudie a direct

127

message to the contrary, nor would she have dreamed of actually saying to her: "Now we are free to punish this insolent chit who has dared to rebel against our authority!" Yet what Maudie took from Miss Potter's glance was just such a message.

Maudie had stood a fortnight of Jane's unsubmissive presence; but she had only just stood it. What she could do to make Jane uncomfortable and to provoke disorder she had done; but the truth was Jane would not break rules—not ones that would put her in the wrong in the dormitory; she reserved her lawlessness for the moments she could snatch with Elsie. She did not believe in being jumped on for taking the wrong risks. She simply met Maudie's small wicked eyes with glances that disposed of them with derision, ignored the tones of Maudie's shouted orders and meticulously performed the duties expected of her, as if she were acting from her own volition.

There had been near misses to rows—the splash without the hit; sometimes everyone in the room had shuddered with the sense of the storm that hadn't broken. It was like watching the long preliminaries to a dangerous dog fight—the bristling up, the looking over, the first studied snarls—and then suddenly one dog or the other postpones the ordeal—sighs— and walks away, saying to himself, "Not this time—anyhow— but the next!"

Esther whispered to Jane as they walked upstairs together, "'Oly Jesus—yer better mind yer footsteps ternight, Jane! Miss Potter, she got ter sleep downstairs in Miss Bartlett's room: there won't be no one near our dormitory ternight. Our Maudie can send up rockets ef she wants ter!—and by God, she *will* want ter!"

Jane nodded. She had secretly prepared another arrangement for tonight. She meant to wait till everybody was asleep, and then to take her way up to Elsie's floor, unlocking both dormitory doors with a cleverly contrived tool, half hairpin, half gimlet. Elsie was prepared to find her door opened after eleven, and to make her way into the bathroom, where they could sit and talk for hours, as easy, Jane had assured her, "as picking peaches off a peach tree!"

128

This prospect now looked a trifle dim, for if a row came on, everybody might *not* be fast asleep at eleven o'clock.

A good deal can be done to avoid a row, though it is a mistake to suppose that it invariably takes two to make a quarrel. Still, if one of the two has definitely decided on avoiding it, the approaches can often be blocked. Jane decided instantly to block them. When Maudie stood in the doorway and wouldn't let Jane pass her, Jane waited humbly till Maudie got ready to move. She made nothing, when Maudie deprived her of her turn at the one small looking-glass, of this injurious omission. Jane was prepared to be deprived of practically everything tonight, except her hidden will; but she had not reckoned on what Maudie would do to Snoutie.

Having to give up a direct challenge, Maudie decided on a sadistic byway.

"Girls," she said in her loud, bullying voice, "Snoutie cheeked me today—she's for it—come on over 'ere, yer bloody little bitch—Snoutie!"

Snoutie, pale green and trembling, obeyed the summons. She knew something awful hung over her, but not quite how awful.

Maudie produced a long cord, tied it round the child's thumbs, twisted it back over her wrists, and fixing the other end of the cord over the lavatory door, pulled the cord tighter and tighter till Snoutie's toes barely touched the ground. The strain upon her lifted arms and strapped thumbs was excruciating: Snoutie could not help a feeble yelp.

"Nah girls—'it 'er!" Maudie told them exultingly. "Take yer slippers, and slap her fanny—it won't show in the morning!"

Eight girls out of the twelve were prepared to hit Snoutie—two of them were the Loonies.

But nobody had time to begin. As soon as Jane saw what Maudie was going to do, she jumped for her locker, got out a knife, and cut Snoutie down. She heard the thud of the little body falling through her hands on to the floor, as she turned round, just in time, to face the outraged Maudie.

"Now it comes!" she thought, as a man might think who

hears the roar of an avalanche and looks up to find the great wave breaking over him.

Maudie was so large and strong that she had never been faced before, and for a moment she was taken aback by Jane's mere decisive stand. A stream of filthy language poured from her lips. The other girls stood back, in a safe ring, thrilled with expectation. The long boredom of the day was over—something was going to happen—and not to them. Most of them hated and all of them feared Maudie; but she was the Devil they knew—Jane was an unknown Devil—and a midget compared to the buffalo confronting her.

The storm of obscene speech passed over Jane unanswered. She licked her lips and concentrated on the huge figure above her, meeting the small eyes, hot with hate, by an observant, dispassionate scrutiny. Then the avalanche fell upon her: the flail-like arms beat at her, the ham-shaped hands seized her, and the overpowering weight closed over her. Jane had one chance and she took it; like a mouse jumping to the soft breast of a cat she gave herself up into the embrace of the huge swaying bulk. She sought a deeper embrace, a closer grip. She was tossed to and fro, but her hold never slackened. Once she crashed into the wall and her senses flickered; but still she clung. She moved deeper in—past all guards—to the vulnerable spot she sought for: her thumbs closed on Maudie's windpipe. The red-headed monster started a curious, whining growl unlike victory, the huge figure tottered, shuddered throughout its bulk, and fell crashing backwards on to the hard wood floor.

Jane, disentangling herself neatly from the inert form of her adversary, looked down on her with contempt.

"Gee!" she said when she got her breath. "Why!—that girl's lather! She ain't nuffin' but a pair o' glamour-pants on legs made outer wool!"

The admiring audience surged forward.

"Jees, she's dead!" one girl shrieked; another started violent hysterical screams; a third banged on the locked door with a chair leg. There was a rush of feet on the stairs, a click of the lock, and Miss Potter stood among them. Part of her prayer had been answered, for Miss Potter felt courageous and looked composed: but the other—the unspoken part—had missed fire: for it was Maudie, and not Jane, who lay outstretched upon the floor at her feet, a Goliath laid low by a pebble, and so completely and efficiently laid low that Maudie had no tongue with which to accuse her small impertinent David.

There was Snoutie, too, with badly twisted thumbs, trailing a long cord, and crawling to the feet of Jane as if they were the feet of a saviour. It looked as if Maudie had rather over-punished Snoutie; but Esther, a docile, reliable little girl, came forward to give just the explanation that Miss Potter wanted to hear.

"Snoutie cheeked Maudie—somepin orful! It don't bear speakin' of!" Esther informed the silent audience.

Jane was—from the first moment Esther had seen it—Jane was a "queer"! Her bed was next to Jane's—*she* ought to know! First there was that Elsie—now Snoutie! Maudie was simply doing her duty by separating the two—rather over-poweringly perhaps—but who could have told in advance that Jane was a trick fighter? Esther looked anxiously about her. Would the rest of the dormitory support her? They supported her; only Snoutie's feeble moan protested and was overborne, because after all nobody cared much about Snoutie, since all of them knew she couldn't do them any harm.

Miss Potter gave the order the whole room longed to hear. Jane was to be frog-marched to the punishment cell—there to remain for twenty-four hours on dry bread and water.

Miss Plunket had by now joined them. Under her expert eye, the two strongest girls dragged Jane's arms behind her, and frog-marched her away.

Jane still hoped that Miss Plunket would ask what had happened; but it wasn't any use if she did, for Miss Potter had by now arranged what had happened. This was Miss Potter's dormitory, and Maudie was Miss Potter's favourite.

Snoutie was taken away to be examined by Nurse Grace, persistently wailing a truth no one wanted to hear.

Maudie recovered slowly. She was lifted on to her bed and given, first smelling salts, and then brandy; but she attempted no explanation—nor was any asked of her. There was an uncomfortable feeling after authority had left the room.

The moon had climbed above the long, firm curve of the Downs, washing their sides with silver. The magic of the spring night spread a feeling of guilt over the girls' hearts. They were not fully responsible for what had happened, and yet each one felt that she had played a part she could have resisted playing. The hangover from deliberate cruelty made them feel as if they had lost something precious; and it was a long while before any of them, except Maudie, could fall asleep.

XVII

Jane lay flat on her back in a grim little attic with a sloping roof, her world in chaos. All the light and air that came to her was from a sky-light so far overhead that she could not have broken the glass, even if she'd had anything to throw at it. Her mind churned round and round in horrified confusion. For where was justice?

This was a house of punishment for doing wrong—and she had done right, risking her life to do it; and yet she had been punished for it. What kind of place was this?—What kind of people were they?—Jane passionately asked herself, when not one person in the place came up to any scratch, and all hated the sight of a courage they hadn't got?

She lived over and over again Miss Potter's blind entry, and heard her deepest feelings dragged meanly in the mud with Elsie's—and poor little Snoutie's too—and everyone in the dormitory lying in chorus to support a charge they knew to be false! No one had challenged the accusation, except the unheard Snoutie in her agony from the floor feebly moaning, "'Taint so! 'Taint so!" and no one had listened to her.

Not Miss Plunket, with her breezy acceptance of authority; not Miss Potter, hoodwinked by her sense of inviolability; not Nurse, who had ministered to Jane after dealing with her other patients, but had been sternly non-committal; and worst of all, not Miss Bartlett, who in this crisis had been absent altogether. In this atrocious storm the compass was missing. Nor could Jane know which way to turn in her tormented bitterness. Even the image of Elsie dimmed before her eyes.

She slept at last; but she was tortured in her sleep by dreams in which everything she loved was lost, and nothing that she fought for could be saved—yet Jane still fought. Above her rose Maudie's great body, abrupt as a cliff; and her red, cruel eyes bored into hers to find fear—the huge flail-like arms battered Jane down towards the floor. She woke before she reached it, woke and tried to remember that she had freed herself in freeing Snoutie. Jane had *not* lessened her grip; the lessons George had so patiently—for George—drilled into her had been well and truly learned. There had been that one short moment of victory over Maudie—before all that Jane had learned of civilization shut her up in this dark, airless cupboard.

Even when the light came, there was nothing. No sound; nothing to look at; and no hope.

The hours hung over Jane without a landmark. She couldn't get up and dress because Nurse had taken away her clothes; and she couldn't tear or break or throw anything because there was nothing to tear except the pyjamas she had on, and her blankets: there were no sheets; and there was nothing to break —because there was nothing to throw. She was alone with her own mind, and very little in it except dread. Bread, and water in a celluloid cup, were pushed through the door, but by a hand with no voice attached to it—for the door shut on Jane's cry before she could get it out. She drank the water, but she could not eat the bread—a sick anger prevented her. She felt that it would have been like giving in to her punishment.

Her love for Elsie raced in her like a bitter thing, for well she knew that no whisper from Elsie would reach her from under the heavy door. The sparkle and shimmer that had flooded the world when Elsie smiled did not rest upon the foundation of an equal love. Elsie was not a villain, but she could "smile and smile" and not risk anything. And yet it was not only Elsie who had let her down.

Jane felt as if in this queer place, full of restriction and control as it was, there had been fresh possibilities. New activities of the mind and body had given her unknown interests and pleasurable excitements. There was, too, a sort of kindness in the air: some people were trying to give Jane something she wanted to take. She had—for the first time in her life—trusted something outside herself to act for her; and now it had acted against her—and the trust was gone.

Jane had fought to save Snoutie, but she hadn't saved her. Snoutie was safe for the moment because Nurse had taken her upstairs to look after her; but Maudie would be worse to Snoutie next time she got hold of her. "A bloody sight worse!" Jane reminded herself, "'cos I shan't fight her next time— I've had enough of it! I certainly won't! The whole School can be hung up by its thumbs, but there won't be no atom bomb up me sleeve nex' time—no sir-ee! They can cut their flowers for their own funerals!"

The day did not seem to move. Time was like a weight on Jane's chest. She said over all the things she'd learned at school, and perhaps that took up an hour; then she re-stole all the things she'd lifted. She dared not think of the games she'd played with Rundle, because thinking of Rundle made her want to cry. But the best thing of all, and what took up most time, was planning all the things she'd do, to Esther, once she got out.

Jane saw at last that the light had changed. When she first woke it had been like a spear in a corner, with the rest of the cell in deep shadow; then the spear had moved and widened into a slow pool drinking up the shadows. There were none left at last—only—for hours and hours—a dull light, while above her head she could see a handkerchief of blue sky. No cloud touched its blueness—no aeroplane roared across it, no bird flew. More bread and water was put into her cell twice, but still Jane only drank the water; for not eating was a protest more satisfying than bread. Nor did Jane feel exactly hungry—only empty—like the sky.

The light began to grow softer than gold; it filled the room with its fugitive deep colour, before it retreated, and let the shadows in. When it was quite dark again, Jane knew that she had been forgotten; no one had risked anything; no voice had whispered outside the door, as her own would have whispered if a friend had been inside; and probably she *would* never get out. For if everyone was her enemy, why should Jane be let out? Nurse had not been in again, though

135

now her bruises had grown into lumps, huge purple and black bruises—quite resplendent and probably dangerous—where Maudie had hit her.

Jane had no fresh courage to meet the dark. Instead, she kept seeing Ma's face, or that sudden look George sometimes had, as if he might be going to do something awful, without any sense, just for the pure hell of it.

Sleep came at last, and there were more nightmares, worse than waking dreams. She was buried alive and couldn't breathe. She did not want to go to sleep again; but sleep came from somewhere else, and when it wanted you, it took you; and at last she slept till dawn.

This time, when Jane woke up—if it wasn't only another dream—Miss Bartlett stood in the doorway looking at her. Something clicked back into her world of chaos when Jane met that look. It was trust; and the queer part of it was that it was not only Jane's trust in Miss Bartlett—it was something deeper that made Jane feel at home in the world again—it was Miss Bartlett's trust in Jane.

The look Miss Bartlett gave her was not a particularly kind look, and it did not pretend that nothing had happened; it was as if Miss Bartlett knew—knew not only what had taken place, but what Jane had felt about it—and understood. She was *with* Jane.

She said at last, although by this time it was hardly necessary for her to say it: "It was a mistake, of course. But now get up, and come downstairs with me, and we'll have breakfast in my room."

Hardly knowing whether she was awake or still asleep, Jane got up and followed Miss Bartlett. The whole house was silent, and full of that mysterious first light of day which seems to be making everything anew. Miss Bartlett drew back the soft green curtains and opened the long windows which looked on the garden; and all the garden, the full chorus of the birds and the flowers with their scents, came into the room with the sunlight. It was wonderful to pick out the birds' different songs—blackbird, thrush and linnet—and even see their wings flickering between the leaves and the light. Blue tits and King

136

tits were hanging upside down in a bush of honeysuckle; and far off, invisibly, a cuckoo signalled his flight, cool and mocking, from the empty corners of the sky.

There were hedges beyond the garden full of golden gorse, and May blossoms so white, no snow, fresh-fallen upon far-off peaks, could have matched them. The world might have been made over-night, by someone quite different from whoever had made it the day before.

When Miss Bartlett said, looking into the garden without turning round, "It's all right really!" Jane suddenly knew that she was awake.

"Where *was* you?" she asked reproachfully.

"I suppose I was coming back", Miss Bartlett said, "driving in the rain. I had been visiting my mother. I have to do that sometimes, but I don't go very often. I *wanted* to get back. Now we'll get breakfast. Will you make the toast and tea, and set the table here by the window—while I fry eggs and bacon?"

The eggs and bacon did not sound any better than they tasted.

The breakfast felt less real than a dream because Jane knew what the rations were, and yet she found herself eating two eggs and two rashers of bacon, besides a round of toast and butter with jam. She could have had marmalade, but there was cherry jam. She went on eating and eating, with the scent of the air and the songs of the birds mixed up with it, while Miss Bartlett sat at her desk reading letters and making lists. She explained that this was what she always did, before anyone was up, so that afterwards she needn't hurry; and that was why, too, she didn't take breakfast with the girls. Jane had often wondered why she didn't: and now she knew.

It was not until Jane had quite finished, and put away the breakfast things, that Miss Bartlett turned round to talk to her. "You see," she said, "I thought you might wake up early because you'd had nothing to eat the day before. Strictly speaking, whatever anyone has done, they don't sleep a second night in the punishment cell; but I came back so late that it was thought best to leave you where you were. Besides, I rather wanted to find out everything first—before I saw you."

Jane did not ask Miss Bartlett what she had found out because it did not seem to be necessary; she merely nodded her head. The second night had been terrible—more terrible than the first night—but perhaps Miss Bartlett's night had not been a good one either.

"We must not think Miss Potter to blame, because she did not come in until everything had already happened," Miss Bartlett went on after a pause, "and then you see all those ten girls lied to her. They were all afraid of Maudie—so they did not tell the truth. I have often noticed that people who are afraid seem to need lies. But of course lies are very misleading; and Miss Potter *was* misled."

Miss Bartlett paused again; she was wondering if she could say more for Emily than that, but she came to the conclusion that there wasn't any more she *could* say. Jane's eyes, boring like gimlets into her face, knew that there wasn't.

"I have seen Esmeralda," Miss Bartlett went on. "She was awake still earlier than you, although Nurse had given her something to make her sleep because of the pain. It would have been worse if you had not cut her down in time; and I am glad that you had that knife which you had no business to keep in your locker."

"Well—I wouldn't go nowheres wiv-art a knife ef I could help it", Jane murmured modestly. "I jes' picked it up—arter they'd searched me—on me way aht when the Inspector's wife wasn't looking. Her potato knife I 'spect it was. I faught ter myself—it might come in handy."

Miss Bartlett accepted this explanation in silence.

"I shall see Esther", she continued, "after morning prayers, and then I will speak to the dormitory. I think it will be better to send Maudie away, and fortunately I found a letter this morning to say there is a vacancy in an Approved School, where I can send her. You and Esmeralda can go into Miss Plunket's dormitory—and two of her girls into yours. I want you both to have a new start, and you might not be able to over-look what you have both suffered in Miss Potter's dormitory."

"No sir-ee—nor I wouldn't overlook it!" Jane agreed warmly. "I'll take the tiles off that Esther's head—if it's the lars' thing that happens to me—I certainly will!"

"Well now—I was coming to that", Miss Bartlett went on, her strange, hooded eyes sending a piercing look into Jane's watchful ones. "It was, of course, a great mistake to punish you for fighting Maudie in order to protect Esmeralda. But Jane, you have been violent too often. If Miss Potter had not already known that you had hit an old man to save yourself, and attacked Mrs. Parker for no good reason, she might not have mistaken your fighting for Esmeralda—for just such another wanton attack. Does it not strike you—that twice you have deserved punishment and escaped—and only once have you *not* deserved it—and had it? I want to remind you of these times, because—while we must fight if there is no other way to save a wrong being done—you will find there is almost always a better thing to be done than fighting: it is a question of taking the trouble to find out what better way there is. Otherwise, if you don't take this trouble and always rely on violence, you will get into such great trouble that nothing—and nobody—can save you!"

There was a great deal that Jane thought of afterwards—to combat this way of looking at things, or at least to explain why she herself often took an opposite way—but she couldn't at the time think of anything conclusive. She simply knew that what Miss Bartlett had said hurt her.

The colour rushed into her face, her eyes filled with tears, and she felt herself tremble; yet she was hurt, not angry. Miss Bartlett looked at her with kindness, but she did not take back anything that she had said.

She only added after quite a long pause, "I want you to give Esmeralda her breakfast soon. You will have to feed her, because she won't be able to use her hands at all for several days; both her thumbs are in splints, and we are keeping her in bed for shock. She is in the isolation room next to Nurse's. Nurse will give you your clothes, and I have told her that later on you may visit Elsie with the other upstairs girls, and then come downstairs to prayers as usual with them. Perhaps Nurse will let you sit by Elsie—and as for Esther—do you not think you could safely leave Esther to me? She has had a very bad home—a much worse home than many of the rest of you— and since she has only seen people doing each other harm, she believes that it is quite natural to do harm without any sense in it, to other people. If you do her more harm, she will believe it still more. I shall try to make her see things in some other way—and it will help me if you promise to leave her quite alone."

Jane hesitated. She still felt the bashing of Esther's head in might be the most effective way, but she decided that Miss Bartlett might after all know better. There was, however, something even more on her mind than punishing Esther.

"What Esther said," she began uncertainly, "abaht me an' Elsie—that don't *have* to be true, does it—jes' 'cos we like each other? I sure do like Elsie! But I feel as if Esther had kinda spoiled it all—saying them things! I won't touch Esther if you say not—but I do feel she's kinda mucked the whole thing up fer me an' Elsie!"

"No, I don't think she has", Miss Bartlett said reflectively. "I don't think what anybody says need spoil anything real. Only what you do could spoil what you and Elsie feel for each other. What Esther says—or does—can only spoil Esther— nobody else!"

Miss Bartlett got up decisively, and Jane saw that she had forgotten to drink her tea. She had put it beside her on her desk while she was writing or thinking, and she had not touched it.

It occurred to Jane that perhaps Miss Bartlett hadn't only been reading her letters or writing her list; she might have been thinking what she should say to Jane when Jane had finished her breakfast.

Miss Bartlett having forgotten her tea seemed to make what she had said to Jane strangely important.

XVIII

Elsie quickly explained, to Jane's entire satisfaction, why she had been unable to whisper, even once, outside the door of Jane's cell. Mabel, she told her, had followed her about like a dog biting at her heels all day long, and ready to tell on her, if she as much as dared to ask to go to the lavatory. At night, when at last Mabel slept, the door between the upstairs floor and the comparative freedom of the rest of the house was always locked. They were not called lepers for nothing. But Elsie had cried—there were outside witnesses to her tears—by day as well as by night. She had refused to eat; she had successfully agonized Mabel by these tactics; and even Nurse Grace—favourite though Elsie was—had accused her of "creating".

When Jane, after she had fed the speechlessly enthralled Snoutie, dramatically entered the lepers' main room, Elsie gave a shriek like a startled peacock and flung herself into her friend's arms, under the outraged eyes of Mabel. They could not, of course, say much to each other while their every word was being taken down, by indelible shorthand, in Mabel's burning memory. Everything had to wait till the happy oblivion of prayers was over; but they sat side by side in the Chapel room, their little fingers touching; and the sense of harmony between them rose like a song of thanksgiving. If all the hosts of Heaven, winged with the spirit-shaft of Fra Angelico's exquisite signature, had broken upon them through the roof, they would still have had eyes only for each other.

As far as the lessons that followed were concerned, like Paulo and Francesca, "they closed the book and read no more that day".

When "elevenses" came, they wandered arm in arm into the Elysian fields, exchanging the pageant of their dramatic experiences, under the watchful eyes, but beyond the ears, of Miss Potter.

There was one faint shadow over Elsie's joy as she gazed in rapture into Jane's heroic eyes; she could not help thinking that it would have been better all round had Jane fought for *her*—rather than for Snoutie. She wouldn't have fancied having her thumbs torn out by the roots—for so the description of the battle scene had reached her—but as an adored victim, she would, she felt, have been a far more authentic heroine than Snoutie; while had Mabel played the part of Maudie, she would have been probably less severe on Elsie's thumbs.

"May be", she said with a gentle sigh, "you'll 'ave ter fight Mabel one of these days. She's so sore at you, she'd like ter tear yer eyes aht! I don't know what's got in ter Mabel—I don't reely! She 'asn't a good word ter throw at a dawg, an' when I wanted ter cry on 'er shoulder, she pushed me 'ead away!"

"Jees, she 'ad ort ter have somepin ter be sore abaht," Jane said rather tartly, "if you put me *firs'*, the way I should think you would!"

"O' course I puts yer firs'!" Elsie exclaimed tenderly. "I slapped Mabel's fice an' I never ate nuffin'—wot more could I do ter show I'm soft on you? Mabel says I shall go to 'ell when I die fer throwin' her over! Do yer believe in 'ell, Jane?"

"Hell", Jane repeated reflectively, for Hell was a word she used times without number, but without attaching any special significance to it. "A hot word", she ventured at last, "wot yer say if yer kind of riled, ain't it?"

"'Ot's correc'", Elsie agreed with her slow, sweet smile. "It's a plice yer go ter if yer lived a gay life, and yer burn ferever and ever—arter yer dead, of course! My Pa had a fren'—one of my fren's 'e was too when my Pa had gorn away —kep' a parrot that cussed loverly—'nuff ter make a cat larf, that parrot was——! 'Go ter 'ell, yer bloody bitch!' 'e'd scream! Tort 'is parrot that—'e 'ad—ter speak ter 'is wife, wot left 'im fer anuver chap, an' yer can't 'ardly wonder; but I did 'ear 'e cut 'er fice open wiv a knife an' spoiled her looks. Yer 'ave ter be keerful abaht men, Jane—they're that spiteful! I arsked Nurse Grace wot she fought abaht 'ell—you can arsk Nurse anyfing—an' she said she didn't rightly know if there was such a plice, but anyhow it was best ter be on the safe side an' keep clear of wot would get you there! Sounds sense ter me—but I ain't goin' ter give you up fer it, no-how!"

"When you're onct dead", Jane replied authoritatively, "there isn't anything goin' ter start up fer you—hot or cold. No Sir-ee——! Wot's dead stays dead—I've seen it. Tellin' yer that abaht Hell is just one of Mabel's tricks ter put you orf me—that's all Hell is!"

This was a comforting reflection for both of them. They went to their next class in blissful accord, and maddened Miss Potter, who had naturally separated them by the width of the class room, by their frequent attempts—some of them successful—to pass notes to each other.

On the next occasion that Miss Potter was alone with Miss Bartlett, she asked her despairingly, "Aren't you going to do *anything*, Susan, to separate those two girls—Jane and Elsie? It's the most flagrant case of—at least incipient—Lesbianism that we've ever had here. Surely—surely it ought to be put a stop to! Think of the example to the others—and now that you've re-instated Jane in such a public way, it's worse than ever!"

"I did nothing to re-instate Jane", Miss Bartlett objected. "We know a mistake was made about her punishment, and all I did was to let her take her place again, as she had the right to do. The change of dormitories was for everybody's sake. I wish we didn't have to use classical or medical terms for these girls' emotions for each other. We know that they are being shut up—some of them for years—away from all their natural objects of affection; and what do you suppose they can turn to, Emily, but each other? It's not particularly good for them to take passions for us, is it?"

Miss Potter shuddered. "That would be *too* terrible", she agreed, "you know how I guard against it!—and I often warn our younger helpers—Nurse Grace, for instance——"

"She eats sweets and reads detective stories—I don't think she does any worse", Miss Bartlett interrupted rather impatiently. "She's not fully trained, but she's a good nurse—and you know how hard they are to get!"

"I don't ask you to get *rid* of her", Miss Potter said with a delicate sniff. "It's the *class* of woman she is that I object to. Whatever may be said for her nursing, she's not refined—*and* lazy. Still—what I mean about those two flagrantly behaved girls, Susan, is that we are told to avoid the very appearance of evil; and you can't deny the appearance is there!"

"Yes, yes," Miss Bartlett murmured in an exasperated tone, "they are *very* fond of each other certainly. But unfortunately we're not told what *is* evil or even if what seems like it mayn't be an approach to good. I'm very sorry, Emily, I know some things are as clear as day to you, while I'm lost in a fog. I've seen what you've seen; but I can't help remembering that I have to deal with two girls—one who has been physically degraded almost below the reach of affection, and one who is in grave danger of knowing no affection at all, going from violence to violence which may end in murder, through *lack* of affection. Here—perhaps for a few weeks, or even days, for they may be separated any day—they have a chance to learn a little of this most perplexing but surely *creditable* instinct of human love. If this feeling, mixed or not with sex stimulation, can make Jane gentler and give Elsie some self-respect, why should I check it? I simply cannot bring myself to do it!"

"We have seen such sad cases of what this kind of thing leads to, dear, that I think you must admit that it should be checked when at least it is as flagrant as this case is", Miss Potter replied firmly and gravely. "Tragic, no doubt, these long sentences are—in the girls' removal from all home ties during adolescence; but then we must remember that most of these homes made a misuse of all such influences, whereas some at least of the Approved Schools are excellent places, and give the girls a real chance for reform. It is what we are attempting here—even though in a Remand Home our time is short and our influence has but a brief time to take effect; but this I feel—and I am sure you agree with me—but doubles our responsibility!"

"Yes—I think we are—responsible", Miss Bartlett said in a low voice, without looking at Emily, "very responsible indeed, Emily."

Miss Potter moved uncomfortably on the footstool she had drawn to her friend's feet. She liked the affectionate humility of this position, but she did not like the feeling that any advantage should be taken of it.

She said a little stiffly, after a pause that Miss Bartlett showed no intention of breaking, "I do realise, and I have confessed to you, that I was over-hasty in my judgment of Jane while you were away. In cutting down Snoutie, she only did what was her duty—though of course she should never have had access to a knife! But I am sure that she had maddened my poor Maudie first, before Maudie could have dreamed of taking such a fearful step as to hang little Snoutie up by her thumbs! It was all a most terrible affair! I acted too quickly—I see that now—though what was I to think, when the whole dormitory supported Maudie? When I heard Esther's fearful accusations about Jane's sex activities, I was overwhelmed with horror! I know you think them untrue, Susan, but we must admit that they are not yet disproved."

"I think we must expect these children to be a little lurid sometimes", Miss Bartlett said, not unsympathetically, "they so seldom have sufficient drama here, after what they have been accustomed to on the streets; and as for evidence, the support they gave Esther was withdrawn as soon as they all knew that Maudie was not coming back again. Still, you should not blame yourself for what happened before you came upstairs. Nothing you did afterwards could alter the attack that had taken place on Esmeralda, and I suppose nothing before could account for it; or had you any reason to suppose that there was something beforehand that *may* have influenced Maudie to act as she did?"

Miss Potter was unexpectedly silent. She believed that she was a good woman, and she had some evidence for this belief in herself; but this evidence shook under the probe of Susan's question. Had she not had *any* part in what took place *before* the attack on Snoutie?

Of course, Miss Potter told herself vigorously, this was an absurd idea. She hadn't had the slightest notion that Maudie would attack Snoutie. Miss Potter could safely tell herself, and Susan, that she was innocent of any such intention. What indication could she have had before she heard that awful screaming that had sent her flying upstairs to take her rightful part in any emergency—and at great personal risk to herself—that anything injurious to anybody was going to take place? Unfortunately it is the penalty of a strict conscience that it cannot always persuade itself that it has been strict enough.

Miss Potter did not meet her friend's eyes; she looked away from her before she said at last, "Perhaps, dear, Maudie's undue influence upon the ward, which you rightly complained of to me when we first discussed this matter, *is* something for which I must blame myself! It is possible—I see that now—that I may have put too *much* confidence in Maudie."

She would go as far as that, Miss Potter told herself; and then surely—surely she needn't go any further?

Miss Bartlett let her off. She said with a sigh, "My dear, I am sure we are all of us—always—to blame for something! Let's go to bed."

But it was not so easy for Miss Potter, when in bed, not to go on with that awkward question, to which (before she went to sleep) she did not want, even if it kept her awake all night, to find the answer.

XIX

In the weeks that followed Jane was happier than she had ever been in her life. Her old dormitory mates, relieved of Maudie's presence, were prepared to accept her as a heroine, and from her new dormitory, where she reigned supreme, she was free to enjoy without a check the increasing rapture of her love for Elsie.

To Jane, Elsie was mysteriously wonderful, she had a magic that touched with delight every act and expression that emanated from her.

To see Elsie at the ironing board was a breathless joy. Even Miss Carter said, when she beheld the feathery vision that was the ultimate result of Elsie's skilful hands, "Goodness me, Elsie—that blouse might belong to one of the little Princesses!"

Jane's pride in Elsie rose higher than any pride she felt in herself. She depreciated her own increasingly exciting school work. The more she put her answering mind to a lesson, the more vast and complicated the whole subject became. Learning was like watching a wave move towards the shore: behind it rose following wave on wave; if you tried to count them, one merged into another, and all Jane was finally left with was the spinning foam at her feet. But that did not lessen her excitement. She worked so hard that it was only every now and then, when they were running round the yard with Tito or the summer sun grew too hot in the class room, that the itch for freedom attacked Jane; and then she knew that she could not bear for much longer the high walls; and Mrs. Parker; and the locked gate.

There was one other cloud that lay on Jane's horizon. She

loved Elsie so deeply herself that she hadn't quite liked it when Elsie flipped her ironing board off its stand, to the other side of Jane, away from Mabel's. Jane had seen Mabel's face whiten as if Elsie had struck her.

Miss Carter excused Mabel shortly after this incident; and Elsie, fixing her blue eyes upon Jane's while her iron reheated, said—in a way that made Jane feel that Elsie could never have meant to be unkind—"I wouldn't want you to 'ave no trouble, of course, but it wouldn't do no harm like, Jane, if you was to say in passing as 'ow you'd 'ave 'er lights an' 'er liver art ef Mabel so much as looked at me. It would be a relief like to know she was warned—she do give me sech narsty looks!"

"Yeah, p'raps I had better warn her," Jane agreed doubtfully, tilting her iron to catch the last line of her cuff, "but if I was to be hoofed out away from you, I guess I might look kinda narsty—myself!"

Everyone had finished ironing before Jane, so that Miss Carter said she might stay by herself to do the last of her blouses. Jane was absorbed in her work, but try as she might the fine, deft handling of Elsie evaded her. Still, she didn't mind being left alone in Miss Carter's kitchen; on a sunny day with the windows open and all the cooking and washing tidied away, it was a beautiful place to be in, and a very quiet one. The kitchen only needed a cat, Jane thought, to be quiet with you.

Into the warm stillness a noise broke like a smothered sob. Or was it perhaps a cat shut up somewhere in a cupboard shouting for delivery? Jane made a careful search. None of the kitchen cupboards held anything but kitchen utensils, but she remembered that in the scullery there was a big cupboard where the girls kept their rubber boots for rainy days. When Jane opened the cupboard, she saw a girl lying face downwards among the rubber boots. She wasn't only sobbing: a great red streak ran away from her. She had cut both her wrists with a sharp kitchen knife, and kept saying over and over to herself, as if it were one word, "I-wish-I-wos-dead! I-wish-I-wos-dead!"

Mabel was too far gone in grief and weakness to know who had found her. She only knew that at last someone was touching her with gentle hands and saying, "Wot's it? Wot's it, Mabel?" as if she really cared.

Mabel didn't say what it was, but she let Jane bind up her wrists tightly and effectually: although they bled profusely she had not reached an artery before her courage failed her. Mabel felt vaguely glad when she felt someone's arms round her, and her head laid against a friendly shoulder, instead of on rather gritty boots.

She sobbed louder.

"You don't want to take on this way!" Jane told her, tearing a few more strips off the kitchen roller to wind over the still bleeding wrists. "You'll only get orful sick—an' you *can't* die—there's no sense in it, you're too young!"

"I ain't that much young!" Mabel sobbed back. "I've 'ad two babies—they were young orl right—but that didn't stop them dying!"

Suddenly she grasped that the arms that held her were Jane's.

"Oh you——!" she cried in horror, and struggled to get out of them.

"I ain't no enemy of yours", Jane told her impressively, "I'm a fren'! I sure am! I don't want yer ter be hurt and I don't aim to hurt you. Jes' you listen ter me! 'Corse I fink an orful lot of Elsie an' so do you! Listen! Why can't we *bofe* fink an orful lot of Elsie—an' keep our hair on? There!—the bleedin's stopped comin' froo' the bandages. That's good! Why don't you have her as your fren' *upstairs*—an' me for my fren' *downstairs*—no bones broken either way? I had to share a cat onct with an ole woman I fair hated. But it didn't do the cat, nor me, no harm! No Sir-ee, it didn't! Matter of fact the cat had its meals double—an' liked it!"

Mabel sobbed on helplessly, but she no longer struggled to free herself from Jane's protecting arms.

At last she muttered between her sobs, "It ain't only Elsie— I never could 'old on ter anyfink! There was my boy fren'— Harry. We was ever so 'appy tergever, 'im and me. 'E 'ad blue eyes jes' like Elsie's—an' larf—'ow 'e larfed! An' my best fren' pinched 'im—jes' one night Pub-crawlin' an' juke box dancing—under me very eyes—she pinched 'im! Nor I wasn't never like the other V.D.s—they ran rahnd! Believe it or not, I 'ad a good muvver and she brought me up ever so strict. Onct when I was thirteen I went to a cinema by myself: my girl fren' couldn't come wiv me, an' a man got hold of me. 'E put 'is 'and over me mouf—an' there wasn't nobody near, back of the cinema in the dark. I fort 'e was killin' me—but 'e wasn't, and then 'e let me go an' slipped aht. I ain't never seen 'im no more, nor I didn't know wot 'ad 'appened. I tole my Ma, an' she says, 'Say noffin abaht it—or your Pa'll 'alf kill you!' 'E was an orful good man, my farther—went to chepel regular—so we never told 'im noffin; an' when it did come to somepin, my Ma got me away to 'er sister wot lived in the country. She was orful good to me, my Auntie; an' I 'ad me firs' baby wiv 'er. Only I nearly died on it, 'cos I wasn't big enuff seemingly—'an 'e died—pore little cuss! We wos glad 'e went—Ma an' Auntie, an' me too! An' I got better some'ow an' I fort it was all okie dokie. So did Ma. My Dad, 'e never fahnd aht abaht it. I was fifteen before I met up wiv Harry. 'E was different. 'E was my steady. I'd 'ave done anyfink for 'im.''

Mabel stopped. Through the open doorway the last brilliant beams of the sun crept across the floor and touched the red pool of blood into a magic colour. Mabel didn't seem able to say anything more about Harry; she just stared idly at the blood.

"How come this boy lef' you the way 'e did?" Jane ventured at last. "Didn't you put up no fight fer 'im wiv yer girl fren'?"

Mabel shook her head. "There wasn't no fight in me", she explained. "I felt orful ill—wiv this new baby comin'—an' my looks' ad gorn; you can't altogether blame 'im. 'E wasn't earnin' big money neither, and I couldn't work. An' then this fren' of mine—she was new like—'e 'adn't done 'er no 'arm! This time me Dad fahnd aht. Things 'ad gone wrong wiv me from the firs' on account of the way they'd been before. He took on somepin orful an' turn me aht of doors—jes' the way they do in books. But I knew when he went ter work an' when he come back, an' my muvver, she stood by me, an' took me in, daytimes. My Auntie, she'd married, so she couldn't help me no more. It was evenings, an' the nights, that were 'ard. Sundays too, we couldn't meet up nor nuffin wiv me Dad 'angin' rahnd. But I fahnd a church I'd 'eard tell abaht near Charing X, where they took me in nights an' let me sleep in a crip', they called it, an' they give me a 'ot drink when I come in, an' when I lef' in the morning. They wasn't like they *was* religious, an' they got me into a 'orspital when my time come. This baby—'e lived, an' we calls 'im Noel on account 'e was born on Christmas Day. An' when I got abaht, the bombs 'ad begun to drop, an' I fahnd 'alf a 'ouse—I sleep in it better than under the arches—an' my muvver she keeps 'elpin' me orl the time—same as before. Noel—'e 'ad red 'air an' blue eyes—an' larfed—natural as a lark 'e larfed! 'E was ever so loverly! People used to say so in the streets, an' arsk why I didn't take 'im aht er Lunnon 'cos o' the bombs. Truth was, I was afraid 'e might be taken away from me—an' my muvver she bought all 'is clo'es fer me; and we washed 'im and kep' 'im tidy. Me Dad got good pay nor he never knew Ma went froo' 'is pockets reg'lar an' took wot we needed. 'E never fahnd aht 'cos she'd say, 'You lose yer money every Saturday night drinkin',' an' 'e wos a crool 'ard drinker—though religious the way I said—so 'e thort no more on it. Ma, she earned too: she cleaned business orfices in the early mornin's—ser we 'ad enuff."

Mabel stopped again, and this time Jane thought she'd better go and find nurse, for Mabel looked as if she might pass right out; but instead Jane got her some water to drink, and wiped up all the blood, so that Mabel needn't lie and look at it any more.

After a while Mabel started again. "'E wos a 'eavy baby," she said, "an' I always carried 'im in me arms, in the streets evenings—sat by the river too wiv 'im, on those seats near it. You'd think—I wouldn't 'ave minded so orful much lettin' 'im go—but I did. I couldn't work nor nuffin carin' 'im. 'E cort cold—croup it was—couldn't git 'is breaf no'ow! We nursed 'im good an' proper, me an' Ma, in the daytime, but come evenin'—an' me Dad gittin' back—wot could we do? The church let me in same as before—but they wanted me ter take 'im ter the 'orspital, an' I was afraid they'd make 'im stay there—or send 'im away outer Lunnon, on account the bombin' was somepin orful—made you wonder wot was goin' ter 'appen next!—it did reely! So I 'ad ter tell them at lars' I'd fahnd a home ter take 'im to, tho' I 'adn't fahnd noffin! People are good ter you orl right when you're up against it, but not the way it's any use their bein' good ter yer—see?"

Jane saw. She remembered the way that the Despards had been good to her—and even the Probation Officer—but got her shut up all the same—for three years—behind bars.

"You gotta git rich", Jane said after a pause. "The way I done is best! The stuff's rahnd all right—when yer knows how to lift it."

"When I was little I went ter Sunday School an' all", Mabel said rather apologetically, "sort of puts you orf stealin'! Ma, she managed ter git me a bottle wiv chloroform in it, ter keep 'im quiet like, an' it did seem ter 'elp 'im. 'E'd drop orf ter sleep an' stop 'is chokin'. I fort 'e was all right—till one night 'e got 'eavier all of a sudden, an' then cole! Gawd, 'ow I cried! I wanted ter frow meself, an' 'im, inter the river, but the light come up, an' there was Police abaht—so I went 'ome instead. Seems I didn't care no more if me Dad saw me! Matter of fac', I ran right into 'im on the doorstep. 'E didn't beat me neither—tho' 'e saw I was holdin' the baby. 'E looked at me kinda pitiful, an' 'e let me in. Bein' warm an' all wasn't no good ter me then—but my Ma was there."

Jane held her closer. "I had a baby onct", she said after a long pause, "she wasn't rightly mine—she belonged ter my step-muvver, but I had all the care of her. I won't never forget the way she looked at me when I lef' her. Seems as if they feels you could give them the earth, don't it?"

"That's jus' it!" Mabel agreed passionately, "an' I would 'ave given 'im the earth too—if I'd 'ad it ter giv'! I would reely!"

Miss Potter burst into the kitchen with an outraged air.

"Whatever has happened to you two girls?" she exclaimed angrily. "Don't you know it's long past teatime?—and here you are—actually together—in the boot cupboard. You *will* get into trouble!"

The two girls stared up at her from the bottom of the boot cupboard. They stared quite shamelessly and unafraid, for they had reached a place where authority could no longer frighten them.

XX

Jane never paid much attention to what took place in chapel. Prayers and hymns sailed over her head like passing clouds. It was her first sight of Elsie during the day, and there was always the excitement of finding out whether it was possible to change her seat for one with a better view of her, or of passing a note, already neatly folded inside Jane's blouse, through skilled and friendly hands.

Still, every now and then Jane listened to Miss Bartlett's three minutes' talk. She liked the sound of Miss Bartlett's voice, and Miss Bartlett would sometimes say something that stirred her and left her with a feeling of friendliness. Not that Jane accepted the idea of God; for what, she asked Elsie, was the sense of speaking to, or even about, a Person you never saw or heard?

"There's the radio", Jane argued, "an' television—why can't He be shown up on them—if He's anywheres?"

One day, when Jane hadn't been listening at all, because it was hot, and she was remembering a bathe she'd once taken in the Serpentine, and wishing she could have one today—even if she couldn't take back the loot she had acquired for George on the previous occasion, besides two hair combs and a scarf for herself—Miss Bartlett had finished her talk. She'd been saying something about a boy with a thorn in his foot running a race and getting a prize for it. Far better have taken the thorn out first, Jane decided, when suddenly Miss Bartlett's words became alive and struck down on her heart with the weight of stone. "I think I would like to tell you while you are here in chapel together that tomorrow there is going to be a great change here", Miss Bartlett was saying. "Our upstairs girls are going to leave us for a real Home of their own, a Home where they will have no difference from anyone else, but all be getting well together. They have been our house-mates ever since the bombing because, until now, no other place could be used for them. I want to tell them that I think we have all enjoyed having them; and I hope they have been as happy here with us as they could be anywhere. Now they are going to a place where they won't be cut off from anyone else, and where I hope they will be still happier."

Miss Bartlett paused. The silence was electric, it was almost terrifying. There was not one girl in the room who had not already learned that change might be no improvement. Yet none was so old that there was no room for hope.

Jane's heart, riveted upon Elsie, had only mastered the one fact that she was going to lose her. How could Miss Bartlett do this thing to her and Elsie? Miss Bartlett, who after Mabel had cut her wrists, had had all three of them together in her room, and talked with such strange under-standing and friendliness about a new way in which they could all get on together—a way, too, which had actually *worked*? Elsie had been a little suspicious at first, until she found that having two tyrants whom she could play off, one against the other, merely meant that each became more thoroughly enslaved to her—and all the time this infamy of parting was going on behind their backs! What did Miss Bartlett mean by it? Never had Jane felt so angry, and so impotent. She longed to tear the blue veil off her own head and off the heads of all those round her, to throw every prayer book within reach through the glass windowpanes, and to shriek curses loud enough to drown the rising notes of their wind-up hymn. But what if she did all these things—and worse? The inexorable Law that had got her where she was could quite as easily carry out its purpose whether it broke her heart in the process, or not.

Jane's fierce eyes glued themselves on Elsie's piteous blue ones, swimming in tears; but was there not behind those tears a faint gleam of pleasurable excitement? Was Elsie unhappy *enough*? Is it possible for those who go to suffer as acutely, or finally, as those who stay? Jane could not cry. As for her lessons—knowledge collapsed under her. Class after class found her staring at her supervisor with burning eyes that looked through her into the blankest of silences. Reproaches and penalties pattered against her consciousness like raindrops on the other side of a pane.

At last came the break for elevenses. During this pause any girl who wished could tap at Miss Bartlett's door and claim her attention. Very few ever did, because they might lose their elevenses, and get rather more attention than they had claimed. But today, a direct attack was all that Jane desired. She stood before the neat desk, her eyes blazing, her hands clenched.

"You das'nt do this to me!" she began, and then out streamed the obscenities, the prolonged and intricate curses that even George might have envied, and which she had been preparing all the morning.

There was no interruption. Miss Bartlett sat and listened without even lifting her eyebrows. Her colourless eyes met Jane's without flinching, but without indignation. She might have been listening to the multiplication table.

At last the stream of filthy vituperation dried up. Not one curse remained untrapped to escape into the clean little office. There was really nothing left there, except Miss Bartlett and Jane.

"Sit down, Jane", Miss Bartlett said; and Jane, her legs turning to jellies beneath her, sat down. What she trembled at now was not rage—nor was it fear: it was a curious sense of loss, as if she had met something stronger than herself, and could not go on meeting it.

"It can't be helped", Miss Bartlett said gently. "I have to obey orders just the same as you do. There are rules about these Homes that have to be kept. Try to remember that these girls—who call themselves lepers—have felt like lepers here simply because they had a different kind of trouble from yours. You are all here for some kind of trouble—trouble you have made for yourselves or that has been partly made for you—but theirs, they have felt, was a worse kind of trouble, perhaps

156

I should say—though I don't myself think it—a less respectable kind, and this has been extremely painful for them. We
have always known—and so have they—that a Home of their
own, where there were no comparisons, would be better. Well
—now it is found; and the friends you have made among them,
you will have to part from—I don't say 'lose', because no one
need lose a friend by having to part from them. Perhaps it will
make it easier for you to know that in a few days' time you will
be leaving here yourself, and Esmeralda with you. I have been
able to arrange that, and I have taken some trouble to do it.
That is the best I can do for you, Jane. You must do the rest
for yourself."

"Wot rest?" demanded Jane scornfully. "Have you never
had no Special, a guy you thought the world of, and wanted
to be wiv for ever? Tork abaht marriage, that's one thing—you
blow up when you marries—but carin', real honest to
Gawd carin'—why, there ain't a thing lef'!—if you take orf
Elsie!"

Jane's breath failed her. She laid her hand on the desk
in front of her, while sobs shook both her and the desk as if
they were an outside force that could get hold of anything and
rend it to pieces. Miss Bartlett put out her hand to steady
the desk, but she made no effort to comfort Jane; she just
waited.

At last a pause came between the wrenching sobs, and then
Miss Bartlett said, "These things pass", but she did not say it
as if she thought such things passed easily.

Jane sat up suddenly as if something had reached her that
made her want to sit up straight.

"She'll go wiv Mabel", Jane said slowly and bitterly.
"It's Mabel that's sitting pretty nah—not me! Mabel 'ull
git her away from me. She won't never wanta come back,
Elsie—she's the sort yer had orta hold on to—they'll take that,
—but they won't take being let go of! See?"

Miss Bartlett saw. She said after a pause, "If she doesn't
come back, is she worth so much heartbreak? If she is worth it
and sticks to you, then you have no need to break your heart at
all, have you? You have only to learn patience."

"Patience!—How come you think patience so much of a catch when what I've got is three years?" Jane passionately demanded.

"Patience *is* worth learning," Miss Bartlett told her, "and it is only one of the things you have to learn. You have been here three months, Jane, and you have learned a lot. I shall be very disappointed in you if you stop learning. You might remember, too, that Elsie isn't the only friend you will leave behind."

Jane stared at Miss Bartlett incredulously.

"You mean *you're* me friend?" she asked in an awestruck voice, "arter wot I tole yer orf abaht—an'—all?"

Miss Bartlett nodded. "And you're going to take another one with you", she reminded Jane. "Esmeralda is your friend too. I should think myself she is rather a good one."

"Wot—Snoutie?" Jane asked with astonished contempt. "Thet lil'——" she checked the name on her lips and hung her head.

"Well—'course Snoutie, she's O.K.!" Jane admitted after a pause, "but she ain't anyfink much, if you know what I mean—jes' a natural pick-up, like a dawg that's broke its leg. I ain't ever *felt* anyfink fer Snoutie!"

"But perhaps she has for you", Miss Bartlett observed mildly. "Now your next class is due. As Elsie leaves tomorrow, I think I could arrange for you to have half an hour's talk together in my sitting room after chapel this evening. Try to get through the rest of the day as well as you can."

Jane got up; her legs felt quite like legs again now. She looked doubtfully at Miss Bartlett, uncertain what to say to her, and yet vaguely feeling that something more ought to be said. Gratitude had not even occurred to Jane. Her sorrow was not lessened, and she still felt wronged and resentful, but confidence had been restored to her. She should not, Jane felt, have let loose so great a flood of aggressive language upon a person who was not directly responsible for the sharpness of her sorrow. She knew now that this quiet person in this quiet room had not meant to harm her.

"Wot I said," she remarked, once she had reached the refuge of the door, "it jes' came aht natural like, 'cos I'd got Elsie snatched orf of me! Nah!—I know you ain't done no snatching. I'm kinda sore I said it—I certainly am! Nor I won't fergit you gave us that half-hour tonight neither——"

XXI

The moment Miss Bartlett closed the door behind her and the two girls found themselves alone, Jane grasped Elsie's wrist. "Listen!" she said sharply. "You stop cryin' right away! We got somepin better to do than yell—we gotta plan! We ain't goin' ter stay here bein' pushed rahnd and druv apart—no, Sirree! If we got ter git aht, we gits aht tergever—a real break! I got it all thought aht!"

Jane pulled Elsie down on the sofa beside her. She could not see Elsie's face very clearly; every colour and shape in the room was shadowy and soft. Miss Bartlett had left only one small reading lamp turned on. It was eight o'clock in the evening, and the August moon had not yet risen over the dark mass of the downs.

Elsie's wrist felt limp in Jane's hand.

"You ain't got ter *do* noffin!" Jane explained urgently. "You lie still an' keep awake, till I touch you, an' then you creep arter me to the door. You know what the room feels like an' where the furniture is an' all better than what I do! See?"

Elsie saw, but she did not like what she saw.

"Miss Bartlett," she ventured cautiously, "she'll be awful mad at us, Jane, if we wos ter run away. I fort as 'ow you liked 'er?"

"She don't mean no harm, Miss Bartlett", Jane agreed impatiently, "she's pushed rahnd same as us——! She's a Lady an' noffink ain't ever happened to her. When a kick's comin' ter Ladies—they git kicked; but when I know a kick's comin' I light aht—and let somebody else take it! That's me!"

Jane paused, partly for breath, and partly for a reaction from Elsie.

The french window was open on to the garden, and the scent of the tobacco plants, sweet and penetrating, filled the room. It wasn't like a room in a Home: it was more like a room in the Pictures, only emptier. It seemed to expect something from the person who was in it.

Elsie's head was half turned away from Jane. There was no reaction; it was as if she were asking to get away, and expecting the room to help her.

"Oh, Jane!" she whispered at last, "I'm a-feared!"

"Wot you afeared of?" Jane demanded suspiciously. "You do wot I tell you—an' yer won't see noffin—nor meet no one ter be afeared on! Miss Bartlett, she'll be asleep—an'¹ so will all the uvers. You ain't afeared of *me*, are you?"

Elsie slowly turned her head to face Jane. Her big blue eyes swam with tears, her lips trembled. She did not tell Jane, but she wanted to let Jane see, that she *was* afraid of her. Her tears splashed down on their clasped hands.

"If you fink I carn't git yer aht of here wiv'aht trouble, you're all wet!" Jane assured her, for she still could not quite grasp that what frightened Elsie was not simply the method, and the risk, of their escape—but the escape itself.

"I got a rope on me—here it is under me cami-knickers— feel it! The barf-room pipe's dead easy ter slide dahn—I tried 'em—an' ter shinny up them walls is a piece of cake. All you got ter do is jes' wot I say. I'll go ahead—and hold on ter yer! Once aht—I know how to keep aht! If we wanted him—there's George, but I don't fink somehow as we're goin' ter need ter hang on to George. You an' me'll take our pickings for ourselves. Might have to sleep a night or two in barns or haystacks till I can git clo'es that won't mark us, and then we'll be okie dokie! I guess I'll be a boy—maybe we'd better *both* be boys 'cos wot the cops'll be arfter is girls. Lucky we don't bulge at the back—neither of us!"

Elsie gave a faint giggle. She drew a deep breath.

"Jane," she said, "I dares'nt! I couldn't! I'd fink it wrong!"

"Wrong?" Jane inquired indignantly. "Whaddha mean— wrong?"

"Well —stealin's wrong!" Elsie said, to Jane's amazement, for stealing had never seemed wrong to Elsie before, when it had not involved any activity on her part. She withdrew her wrist and spoke with a trembling air of superiority.

"Nurse Grace says so! She says wot *we* 'ad done ter us—upstairs—we giv'—somepin for nuffin' as you might say! It was wrong, but we wos too young ter understan'—it wos the men's fault mostly—not h'ours. We 'ad ter pay for wot they took. But she says girls who stole—like you dahnstairs girls—wos worse than us really 'cos you knew you wos takin' somepin what belonged to someone else."

"Holy Moses!" Jane said crossly. "Nurse Grace has a nerve, I will say! Fancy her figuring us all aht like that—an' not true neither! Anyone that risks—earns, that's my motter! I risked a lot, didn't I?—ter git that mink—an' I got free years! An' you only got two—fer all your carryin's on! Tell that to the Canaries!—you lepers bein' better 'an us! I shud larf! Arter all, men can mostly be got away from if you have the spunk!"

Elsie gave a long, soft sigh. There was regret in it, a certain wistfulness for unforgotten benefits; and no bitterness whatever. Elsie knew she hadn't had the spunk to resist men; but she would have liked to have had it, when she found out what the consequences were of not resisting. She thought she *had* the spunk to resist Jane, because Jane loved her. She leaned her head on Jane's shoulder and whispered, "I don't never want to steal, Jane. Nurse Grace says I'll learn dressmaking or somepin' at this school I'm going to, she says it's quite a free school reely—they let you use lipstick; an' arterwards when I'm aht, she says, I'm young and a good looker an' maybe I'll marry. She says, once I'm well, to let the dead Past bury its dead sort of—an' then I'll never 'ave the Police arter me no more!"

"Cops!—who cares wot cops is arfter?" Jane said contemptuously. "I weren't cort by no cops. A young man that had been a Commando—he cort me! He knew his onions, that young man! You think I'd let a cop ketch me? An' who wants ter git married? Carn't I look arter you same as any man?"

A sense of clashing moralities rose between them: both began to feel secretly outraged by the very qualities they had most admired in the other. Jane felt her innate capacity to face the world shaken by Elsie's belated belief in honesty. All her pride was in the skill with which she could earn her living by her wits. Elsie's pride lay in her incapacity. What had happened to her hadn't happened because she chose it—it had been thrust upon her by life: and now Jane was actually suggesting that Elsie *could* have avoided it, and might still change an easier and more supported destiny for one of greater risk and uncertainty. Elsie nearly hated Jane. She sat and trembled, but only half her trembling now was fear: the other half was moral indignation. Jane, feeling her tremble, threw her arms round her in an instant agony of compassion and tenderness. Wasn't this, after all, her friend—her Elsie—and hadn't she the strength for the two of them, whatever happened?

"Don't you cry, Baby!" she implored, "an' don't you worry abaht wot's ter happen. I'll see to it all! If you don't want ter take fings—you needn't! I'll take a plenty for bof of us! I'm some provider, Elsie! George 'ud never have held on ter me if I hadn't bin. He wasn't one for an also-ran! Believe you me, he wasn't! When he picked me, he knew he'd picked a winner!"

Elsie, while believing Jane and warmly returning her embrace, felt indisposed to act upon George's judgment. Once she had enjoyed the thought of meeting George, in a dance hall for instance, with plenty of money on him and a huge car to take her off to realms unknown, where she could sit on a red velvet sofa and drink champagne. There might be revolver shots in the distance. But now, when being a gunman's moll could really take place, she began to realise there might be another side to this glittering picture. There were the Police: and whether Elsie had to depend on Jane's illicit gains, or George's, the Police would be unsympathetic to their main sharer. Besides, sleeping in haystacks in the rain or where rats sometimes slept near you—or, worse still, *didn't* sleep—was not a tempting prospect.

Elsie's mind was an accommodating place, where facts turned up when, and as, she wanted them. She now remembered her illness. She wasn't quite well yet; an abscess might break out again—and who was going to look after her, when the pain came and the fever? The outside world did not draw her into it, as it drew Jane. Jane longed to be on the other side of the wall between her and the open downs; but Elsie was glad when she remembered the wall that stood between her and insecurity.

"Jane," she said at last, summoning all the courage she had in her and wishing that it was more, "Jane, I carn't come wiv you! I ain't ser ter speak properly well yet. I got ter 'ave me medicines, an' sleep an' eat where I git kind of looked after. I 'ave ter—reely!"

The truth in Elsie's voice reached Jane's heart. It even checked her plans for a moment, but not for more than a moment.

"That's O.K. by me," she said jealously, "I'll look arter you, Elsie! There isn't anyfink Nurse Grace does for you I won't do better. The way things are now, hospitals have gotta look arter you when you needs it. I'll see ter that! There's that church, too, that Mabel told us abaht near Charing X. I'd make a bee line for that church if you wos to be took ill. I'll do it anyways, ef you wants me to! We'll go straight ter Lunnon, 'cos I know Lunnon. It's big an' there's lots to it. An' I'll arsk that bloke that helped Mabel ter help us, ef we need it! I'll do it instead of askin' George. I can't say no fairer than that, can I?"

"You 'adn't ort ter go ter church ef yer don't believe in Gawd!" Elsie said reprovingly.

This, she thought, was one way out of it. Jane was always so excited about playing fair.

"Gawd's one fing!" Jane replied shortly, "and men that git their livin' by Him—they're somepin' else again! He's their meat ticket, ef you know wot I mean. They gotta be kind ter lost women; an' that's wot we are, ain't it?"

Elsie gave another sigh, but this time it was tinged with impatience.

"I carn't do it, Jane," she said miserably. "I carn't slide dahn no pipes—nor climb no walls—nor sleep in no 'aystacks; and I aren't lorst ef I stay right 'ere where I am! You don't know wot bein' lorst is like. You've 'ad George or a 'ome. But I 'ave *been* lorst—so's Mabel. You wos only cotched!"

Jane gave her companion half a shake and half a hug. The truth of Elsie's experience shook her with pity, but it could not take from her determined hopes their unreality.

"You don' need ter git lost again!" she said with greater tenderness than ever. "Not if I'm wiv yer! Jes' let one of them old men look at yer agin! One of the fings I'm goin' ter pick up is a gun! There's a boy called Wilfred that keeps a shop—soft as dough, that boy is—and I know where he keeps his guns. I'll take a gun orf him!"

"Men aren't always old", Elsie suggested. She nearly said, "George isn't old", but she reminded herself in time that Jane had no idea that Elsie had already taken George away from her, in her mind. If they were ever to come across George in reality, it would be better for Jane to have no knowledge of this intention.

"'Ow kin yer git into our flat upstairs in the night?" Elsie now suggested. "Nurse Grace locks the ahtside door an' sleeps wiv the key under her piller, an' she don't sleep 'eavy either!"

Jane gave a short laugh. "I don't let a little fing like a door stop me!" she boasted, not untruly. "I fort aht this get-away firs' night I come, an' nah I got orl I need ter make it. Then I sees you, an' I had that talk with the Boss an' I kinda fort I'd play erlong wiv this place, till I see wot's up. No harm in a little education either, jes' so long as yer don't let it freeze you!"

"I don't fink education's much meself", Elsie said, glad to find a subject that postponed immediate action. "Still, it's better ter learn somepin' yer can make a living by, isn't it? This new school I'm goin' to, Nurse Grace says, turns out every girl independent like when 'er time's up—an' she gits good clo'es, too! W.V.S. helps over the clo'es—an' the most of 'em are posh."

165

"You ain'ter goin' ter no sech school!" Jane told Elsie in an ominous voice. "Elsie, how come you speak as if this goin' away's ser good—when it means we gotta part fur ever an' ever! Ain't you my girl fren' ner more?"

"'*Cors* I'm yer girl fren'!" Elsie said with a pronounced sniff that partly contradicted the assertion. "But that don' mean I 'ave ter do every bleedin' thing you says—like I 'ad ter wiv Mabel—does it?"

There was an awful pause. Worse than conflicting moralities, they now had to face conflicting wills. Jane was the one who trembled now, for the bitter truth assailed her that, though her strength was enough for two, it could not be used unless the weaker of the two willed it.

"Elsie," she whispered, "Elsie, don't yer *wanta* come away wiv me?"

At last they had reached the point at issue; and as they reached it, the door opened and Miss Bartlett came in. Suddenly they knew that the decision was now taken away from them. They would not run away; nor would they ever forget that they had separated from each other before their parting took place.

XXII

Frenzied with thwarted longing, Jane's wild eyes met Miss Bartlett's. This was her enemy. Was there not freedom beyond this slight, unarmed figure between her and the door? She trembled violently, as an animal trembles before it springs.

"Sit down, Jane", Miss Bartlett said, brushing aside her fury. "What Elsie said was quite true: she isn't well enough to run away."

The tension in Jane's taut figure relaxed, the trembling ceased; she wavered and sat down.

Miss Bartlett moved to the open window and looked out over the moonlit garden. Every flower stood erect and still, haloed in silver. The harvest fields beyond were stripped and white beneath the dark curves of the Downs. It was the unconcern of the universe that Miss Bartlett clung to at that moment. Surely, she thought, if she were unperturbed enough, its cool serenity might reach Jane's troubled heart.

Jane put her hands up to her aching throat. She felt suffocated, as if she could neither speak nor swallow. Perhaps she was going to die; but before she died, she must somehow tell the truth to Miss Bartlett.

"Thet's not it", she heard a harsh, strangled voice cry out. "She didn' wanta——! Gawd, Miss—she jes' didn' wanta!"

Miss Bartlett turned and sat down. "I know," she said, "that's part of it, Jane. Elsie isn't that kind of person—but perhaps you wouldn't have liked her so much if she had been. It is no use trying to make people, who are different from us, act the way we want them to act. They can't! We aren't any of us the same."

"But she wanted to be wiv me, an' there weren't no way of bein' wiv me but runnin' away—was there?" Jane urged, longing for the support of her flagging intent.

The compulsion of running away seemed strangely less, not more, in the company of the person she had a moment or two before wanted to kill. Miss Bartlett seemed to have slipped away from the laws she was there to represent. It was as if she was part of the freedom to which Jane wanted to escape, rather than the force that prevented her from escaping.

"You have learned such a lot here in these three months", Miss Bartlett said, as if she were thinking out loud. "It seems a pity to stop learning."

These words beat in vain at the door of Jane's mind: all of it was still fixed on Elsie. Elsie was more present than when she had left the room, crying loudly to excuse the fact of her departure. She had seen more plainly than Jane had seen what it was best for her to do. If there was going to be anything to face, Elsie wasn't going to face it. But absent Elsie ceased to be a coward: she became instead a victim: her value was suddenly enhanced to that of a lady for whom knights fought, and whose gloves were to be retrieved at any price, from lions. Separation from her was acutest agony.

"Free years!" Jane shouted desperately, "Free years! You think I'm goin' ter stick it in a bleedin' school for free years, when I got legs an' the guts ter use 'em?"

"But apparently you haven't the nerve *to* stick it", Miss Bartlett said regretfully. "Well—I expected that you had! Of course you can run away if you want to. Probably the Police will bring you back; but you might even manage to escape them; and then you'll never learn anything any more, except how to steal—and you'll never be free again, for there will always be prison just round the corner waiting for you—and the record against you."

"Well—wot if it is?" Jane replied, her voice feeling less and less restricted as the tension in her lessened. "See wot happened to Mabel wiv'aht money—lorst her baby, didn't she? An' Elsie—she didn't need to get sick nor go with orl those dirty ole men wot gave her nylons, did she?—not if she knew how to pick them up herself—she didn't! O' corse, there's work——", Jane admitted defensively, as Miss Bartlett made no immediate reply, "but it's orful dull, work, nor you don' make much by it. Wot you git comes reg-lar—I grant that. Gladys—she wos a fren' of mine—said onct she'd *rather* work the way she did than take fings like we uset ter; but she couldn' have got herself that fox fur out of her earnin's—the way I picked it up for her come lars' Christmas. Jees—she wuz orl over herself in that fox fur! She sure was a good-looker, our Gladys! Not that I like that brassy hair meself— you carn't help but know it comes aht of a bottle, can yer?"

Miss Bartlett smiled. She agreed about gamboge hair, and it astonished Jane to find herself smiling back. It had not seemed conceivable that anyone could smile again, after what had taken place in that haunted room.

"I think perhaps it will be easier for you, that you are going away so soon yourself", Miss Bartlett said encouragingly. "Everything will be new and different from this in your new school; new faces, new lessons—a new world! I know three years is a terribly long time, but you've had three months off it already, and every girl of your age has to go to school somewhere and be learning something. By the time you're eighteen you'll be the usual age for going out into the world and living on your own. You will go to the job you have chosen. They will find one for you—one that you've learned how to do—and you may like it. I like my job."

"Do yer?" Jane asked uncertainly, "like herdin' of us up in here behind bars and keepin' of us dahn—them lepers an' all—so we carn't git aht!—not ever? Why—I'd think you'd hate it!"

"Well, that isn't all there is to it", Miss Bartlett explained. "Those girls upstairs weren't safe outside. They'd have died if they'd gone on living the way they were when they were brought to this home. The only way to help them was to lock them up till they got well, and to try to put a little courage into them, so that when they can go out again they'll make a better fight for their freedom—their real freedom, I mean! It's the same way with you, Jane. It's your freedom that I really want. If you break laws that were made to keep everybody safe—why!—then you lose your own safety. You wouldn't have liked it, when you came here with all those nice new things and that pretty handbag, if the other girls had stolen them and got away with it! That's why I gave you that key. Of course, you can steal again when you get out. No one can stop you. But after that—if you get caught again—you'll be sent to prison—and prison is a cruel place, much worse than these Schools are, a place without friendliness or laughter. I should hate to have you sent to prison, Jane!"

"I wouldn't have sent no girl to stir that pinched me bag", Jane said with virtuous conviction. "Gawd, no! I'd jes' have pinched it back—an' I might have slammed into her as well, jes' to learn her! I don' say I wouldn't!"

Miss Bartlett seemed to think no reply was necessary.

There were a great many things in Miss Bartlett's room that Jane might have considered stealing, if she hadn't been thinking of Elsie. She felt a curious pang as she looked watchfully about her, not because she would not have another opportunity of stealing them, but because she wouldn't see the room again. She wouldn't see the white, soft carpet, nor the curious clear pictures on the pale golden walls, nor the clean odd furniture that wasn't grand, but that she liked looking at because of its shape. She wouldn't be likely to see Miss Bartlett again either.

"Tomorrow," Miss Bartlett said, "you and all the other girls, after early chapel, can stay in the hall and say Goodbye to the upstairs girls and watch them go. A 'bus is coming for them; it'll be like a sort of treat, going out into the world again together, and it will look like anybody else's 'bus. I hope they'll like it."

Jane found it hard to swallow again, remembering that Elsie would most certainly like it.

Miss Bartlett got up and held out her hand to Jane, as if she had been a proper visitor. She evidently did not intend to punish or even to reprove Jane for wanting to run away. No one, Jane thought, could have been easier to run away from than Miss Bartlett. Jane could escape still, if she wanted to, that very night: she had the rope upon her, and later on there would be no one about. It would be easier to escape by herself than with Elsie.

The three years stretched ahead of her just the same, the loneliness and the bitter sense of lost opportunities; and yet Jane knew that she was not going to try to escape them.

XXIII

When all the downstairs girls came out of chapel, delivering up their blue veils carefully folded on to the tray held out to them by Miss Davis, it was to find the hall full of happy and expectant lepers, waiting to say goodbye. Each leper carried a suitcase containing all her worldly goods; none of them was a large suitcase, but in addition they also had brown paper parcels containing the farewell presents of their friends. Twenty packets of sandwiches hygienically packed in cellophane, flanked by ten Thermosfulls of tea, came up from the kitchen, to be carefully counted over and stored away in a hamper by Nurse Grace.

Their 'bus would stop at a halfway inn for the driver to descend for his lunch, but the girls would eat theirs in the 'bus. They would be escorted afterwards in couples, by Nurse Grace, to the Ladies' Cloak Room, a place where anyone else went who wanted. If it was not exactly freedom, it sounded extraordinarily like it to those cooped-up young creatures.

They were going outside, into an unlocked, open world, bathed in September sunshine. Their actual destination was immaterial to them, and indeed unknown, but they were going to a Home where they would no longer *be* lepers; and now, for a whole blissful, carefree day, there would be no walls, no locks, no Mrs. Parker, no warning bells; and to crown their joy, until they were off they were enjoying the unfamiliar interest and affection of the downstairs girls. It was really astonishing how many friends in this aloof aristocracy they now found they had. The whole staff was on the stairs, or standing in doorways of classrooms, to wish them luck; even Miss Potter, who for the last few months had shrunk from the mere sight of them, was in danger of falling into the whirl-pool of St. Peter's vision of charity—and ceasing to think evil of them.

Miss Bartlett had already said her goodbyes to the girls singly, and was no longer visible; but Tito dashed madly from one friendly group to the other, leaping up at each girl with rapture, his abrupt white tail twitching to and fro incessantly, while he gave vent to constant yelps of excitement. Not that he had the slightest intention of going with them, for well he knew from the corner of a vigilant eye where Miss Bartlett had gone, and where he meant eventually to join her; his heart remained with his treasure, but that was no reason why he should not share the possible rats and rabbits of his friends' adventures—his blood would go with them, even if his faithful body remained prosaically behind. In a final volley of darts and barks, he would follow their 'bus as far as the gate, threatening the legs of his enemy Mrs. Parker, while she was too busy to deal with him.

Jane's eyes rested for a moment on Tito; she was his greatest friend next to the mistress he worshipped, but if she saw him at all now it was as an obstacle to be pushed away. Stubbornly and without joy, she was searching for a figure she did not see in any of the waiting groups by the hall door.

Suddenly a scream rang out, like the high, empty note of a peacock, and down the stairs darted a slender figure in a pink and white cotton dress.

"I don' wanta go! I don' wanta go!" shrieked Elsie, flinging herself into Jane's arms. "I won't never! never! *never* forget you!" she sobbed, her thin arms wound around Jane's neck. "Oh Jane, never!"

Even as she spoke, Miss Potter's inexorable hands removed her from Jane's fierce clasp.

"Elsie—Elsie—come away at once, you forget yourself!" Miss Potter said sharply.

But had Elsie forgotten herself or had she remembered Jane, with sudden helpless intensity? Or was she seeking in a final moment of whipped-up drama to recapture the heart she had lost yesterday?

Jane had held Elsie in speechless silence, as if it were life itself to which she clung; and when Elsie was torn from her grasp, she stood immovable and unresponsive to the shouts and cheers of the Home girls speeding their parting guests.

She did not join them on the steps to watch the 'bus drive off. She did not hear the classroom bell's challenging ring. It was not until a friendly girl dragged her by the arm that Jane let herself slip into the leaden routine of the day. She would not let herself feel, until all the other girls were asleep, and it was dark enough to cry. She cried then; but it was hard for Jane to know what she was crying about. Elsie had gone, before she had had to let her go. Saying goodbye wasn't terrible at all, compared to not having the Elsie she had loved, to whom to say goodbye.

It wasn't just that Jane had lost Elsie: now she had started crying and came to think of it, it was having no Elsie to lose, and all the other loved objects of her life lost as well. Marlene, Rundle, and that unforgettable look in her father's face, before he fell in the crumpled heap upon the floor—that surprised look, when he saw that Jane had held the gun. He wasn't surprised at death: what he was surprised about was Jane's having had anything to do with it. What *had* she had to do with it, Jane now asked herself? She had never meant to shoot even her step-mother. Had she had any choice in the matter? She had never fired a gun before. Was it she, or was it one of the boys, who, that last time, pulled the trigger? They had both stood behind her, egging her on; she could feel their eagerness and their admiration. Was it because she had wanted to be a sport that she had let them kill her father? And why should she think about him now, when her heart was fixed on Elsie? Of course she *had* killed him: about this Jane had no real doubt whatever. There is very little difference between firing a gun and letting someone else fire it. Probably God was punishing her by taking away Elsie. She had heard quite a lot about God in the last three months, and although she did not actually believe in Him, she was aware that as a sort of spoil-sport some great Power existed. Then there were all those talks about Jesus, talks that Miss Bartlett herself obviously had swallowed. Jesus was crucified, Miss Bartlett had said, because He loved people. It happened two thousand years ago—but it was history, like Julius Caesar, Napoleon Bonaparte and George Washington. He died to save everybody, and to make them good; but it hadn't. Still Jane could just believe in the Crucifixion. It was cruel; but after all people did do cruel things: people got hanged and there was the hot seat in America. George said that if you were a burglar you must never forget the long drop and the hot seat—because killing anyone set the Police off more than anything.

Jesus hadn't killed anyone. On the contrary, He had died for them. But that was like the Police too—they were stupid. They were always wanting to pick on somebody—so they'd picked on Him. But when it came to the Resurrection, Jane simply didn't believe it, even though Miss Bartlett had said that there was just as much evidence for it as for many other facts in history, which people find it possible to believe. Once you were dead, you stayed dead, Jane told herself. Her father had looked surprised, and then hadn't looked anything. To believe anyone came alive after they were once dead, Jane told herself, was like believing she could ever feel the same about Elsie again. She couldn't—not now—not in spite of that last kiss. There was something unreal about it, when before everything had been real. Two days ago, nothing in the world was as real to Jane as Elsie. How could you believe in the sun again if one day when you woke it wasn't in the sky?

Jane heard a sniff quite near her. It was a conscious sniff: Snoutie must be awake. Jane looked round her cautiously. Snoutie, too, was crying.

"Wot you yellin' fer?" Jane whispered across to her with severity, "you ain't got nuffin' to lose, lightin' aht from here! It's a picnic ter you!"

"I lose me 'ome!" Snoutie whispered back. "This 'ere is me 'ome."

"What a scream!" Jane announced scornfully. "You ain't got ner home. No one ain't ever bin kind ter you here. You'd better get anuver fink comin' ef yer wants ter yell!"

"They been kinder 'ere than when I wos wiv me Aunties",
Snoutie told Jane. "Me Aunties said I wos a trick, an' none of
'em wanted me—said I took the bread out of their moufs; but
it weren't much bread they guv me, only left-overs like, an' I
slep' on the kitchen table. 'Ere I've 'ad good food an' me own
mattress an' piller an' all—an' a fren', a real fren', I've
'ad 'ere, better 'an your glamour-Puss any'ow!"

"Who's your fren'—me?" Jane demanded suspiciously. "Ef
it's me, I'm goin' away wiv yer, aren't I? Nuffin' ter make
no song and dance abaht as far as I can see!"

"I don't mean you", Snoutie said with sad sincerity. "You
don't kere for me, I know! I wos just an accident ter you.
You wos orful good ter me—I might er died else. I won't
never fergit that. But my fren' she loves me as well as I love
'er. She tole me so—an' she's comin' ter see me in the nex'
summer holidays—she's promised—but it'll be an orful long
time afore nex' summer!"

"Who's yer bleedin' fren'? I never knew you had one!"
Jane asked rather crossly. "You don't go rahnd wiv a fren'—
an' no girl here gits vacations anyways!"

"Miss Bartlett, she's my fren'," Snoutie said with pride;
"'corse she's too busy ter go rahnd wiv me, but she's my fren'
jest the same. Why, she'd come up an' sit hours, nights, wiv
me, when me thumb wos ser bad an' they didn' want ter give
me ner more dope. An' she don't never call me Snoutie—she
calls me Esmeralda, an' she told me abaht Jesus—an' I'm
goin' ter believe in Gawd—strike me pink if I ain't—no matter
wot you say—ser there!"

Jane was speechless with surprise. Of course she knew that
Snoutie had spunk, but not so much as to speak to her—a sort
of heroine—in the middle of the night, with such a fury of
defiance. It was an astonishing amount of courage for a little
girl of thirteen to show to a big girl of fifteen who had saved
her life; and besides, Miss Bartlett—what did Miss Bartlett
mean by making such friends with anyone but Jane? Promising
to go and see Snoutie, when she hadn't said anything about
seeing Jane again—it was worse than astonishing. It actually
took Jane's mind off Elsie.

176

"Blime, Snoutie—you have a nerve!" she said at last. "I'm doggone staggered wiv you—girl er your age too, ter speak ter me like that!"

"I 'avn't ner more nerve than wot I want!" said Snoutie reasonably. "Some of these schools, wot girls like us gits sent ter, are 'ells on earth—I've 'eard—an' I can easy believe it!"

Snoutie sniffed again, but without suppressing it this time; and the second sniff roused Jane's compassion. She said, after a pause for reflection, "Well, I'm wiv you, Snoutie, don't fergit that. No one's goin' ter git tough wiv you while I'm arahnd—let 'em bloody well try! You only gotta holler, an' I'll lay their 'earts an' livers on the floor an' trample on them! There won't be no girls in no Hell I can't lick if I gotta!"

"Thanks a lot, Jane", Snoutie said in a subdued voice, and stopped sniffing.

Jane lay in silence for a while, turning over in her mind what Snoutie had told her.

At last she said, though she wasn't quite sure if Snoutie heard her, for she made no answer, "Ef I remember," Jane whispered cautiously into the friendly darkness, "ef I remember ter, Snoutie, I'll call yer Esmeralda too!"

XXIV

This was Jane's last day. The sharp, tuneless urgency of the getting-up bell had nothing more to say to her. The cheerless, sleepy girls in the dormitory, pulling themselves reluctantly out of the freedom of their dreams, were no more than shadows. Jane did not really care if she beat them to the wash-basins or not. A glance through the open window showed her that it was raining in a dull, indeterminate way. The downs were a dark smudge against the sky, and Jane felt the same lack-lustre feeling as the desultory raindrops; she too did not care whether she was coming or going.

Jane was perhaps for the only time in her life without expectancy. Yet she knew that she had good clothes to wear; her compact had been reluctantly restored to her by Miss Potter overnight; she could paint her face and use her powder and lipstick, whereas Snoutie, who had been picked up poor and possessionless, must go out into the world in an old cotton frock acquired in the Home, and a drab green sweater.

Snoutie swore miserably to herself in a low undertone, but Jane felt beyond swearing. An unreal Elsie danced before her eyes, inaccessible and no longer desirable. A punctured reality may still contain life, but a dream that has been punctured shivers into nothingness like a toy broken. Jane could not even pretend that she wanted to see Elsie again.

After breakfast in the hall, as Miss Potter was shepherding the girls into chapel, Miss Bartlett appeared swinging a beautiful red handbag. It was for Snoutie as a parting present. No girl in the Home had ever had a parting present like that before—and Snoutie rose out of her grief like a phoenix from its ashes, resplendent in her new enchantment. She did not feel that she was leaving her home now; she was taking the living promise of an established affection with her. Miss Bartlett did not give Jane anything. Even when she shook hands with her she only said, "You will both be gone when I come out of chapel. I want to say a queer thing to you, Jane— see if you can understand it: I don't want ever to see you here again! Prepare to go out into the world in this new school of yours—and then go out into it armed—but never come back here."

Jane said nothing. Their departure was as dull as the day. Nobody assembled in the hall to see them off; the girls had cleared themselves out for the departure of the lepers, and were now regretting their impulsive generosity. Jane could hear their chapel voices in the distance. "Trust in God," they sang without much conviction, "And borrow, Peace for heart and mind." Borrowing had not been their strong point. "More likely—lifting", Jane thought to herself, as Miss Potter came up to shepherd them towards the waiting Miss Emsley and her car.

"Now, Esmeralda," Miss Potter said, "you sit behind and Jane sit in front with Miss Emsley. It is a great treat for you both to be going to this new school in Miss Emsley's private car. Few Probation Officers would do so much for you. And I am sure, Miss Emsley, that they will behave properly and give you no trouble."

Jane leaned out of the window and looked hard at Miss Potter.

"We ain't your Pekineses", she observed dispassionately. "We was house-trained before we struck this joint, an' I guess you know just as much abaht us as a monkey knows abaht its own behind! I don't know where you was borned to—nor who borned you—but what you look like is somepin one of these frogmen brought up from the sea floor by mistake and forgot to throw back!"

After two frantic efforts, Miss Emsley got the car started. Mrs. Parker was at the open gates; and Jane, her head still out of the window to watch the effect her parting words had had on

Miss Potter, spat in Mrs. Parker's face. Jane then leaned back in her seat, satisfied with her leave-taking.

Miss Emsley knew that there were no more partings to take place; and rightly guessing that some of Jane's execrable behaviour was due to suppressed excitement—even perhaps to grief—she devoted herself to driving and made no comments on it. Miss Emsley had had three talks with Jane, after her Court sentence, at weekly interviews. In none of these talks had Jane shown much interest, but she had not been rude. No liberties had been taken with her, and she had taken none back. A fellow self-respect had acted as a bond between them. Each was watchfully aware of the other's hidden strength.

Miss Emsley drove well, and Jane watched her with envy. Before they reached the main road, a big black car swished close past them.

"Gawd, I bet that was a Cadillac—U.S.A., sure enough", Jane murmured. She had not caught sight of the driver, but a strange home-sickness gripped her; for if you haven't any home, Jane told herself sternly, what have you got to be sick about? And yet these tame skies, these sodden brown fields and dried-up autumn leaves, made her long for the huge round hills, wide streets and blazing lights that had filled her childhood.

There was Snoutie sitting behind her, clasping her red bag first in one hand and then in the other, happy as a bird on its first flight. They were both "out" in the open world without locks or bars—they were even in a private car like real ladies. Jane could not explain to herself why she must feel so broken down and miserable.

"I'll take you a nice country way on a side road where there won't be so much traffic", Miss Emsley said encouragingly; "the autumn colours are lovely." Both girls preferred the traffic to autumn colouring, but were too polite to say so; nor did they care for scenery unless it had cowboys in it.

Jane was the first to see the small car that shot out of a side road straight at them. There was an unavailing shout from the young man, a tremendous lurch, and there they all were mixed up with broken glass at the bottom of a ditch. No one was badly hurt. Miss Emsley had turned off her engine before the car struck her; and only Jane had seen that the young man driving the car had meant to run into them.

Miss Emsley had been jerked forward on to her steering wheel and had the breath knocked out of her. Another car drove up rapidly from the same side road as their aggressor's. This car was the Cadillac Jane had observed earlier. The man driving it sprang out to help them, and gave the faulty driver a sharp piece of his mind.

He was well-dressed, but his B.B.C. voice and his gallant manner, backed by a moustache, dyed hair and a monocle, did nothing to prevent Jane's instant recognition that he was George.

"I'll go straight off", he told Miss Emsley solicitously, "to the nearest Police Station and tell them to get a tow for you and bring it right along. You stay here, young man, till the police come. I've got your number and am a witness to your reckless carelessness in dashing out of a blind road. Hullo! Hullo!" he added in a concerned voice, "looks to me, Madam, by the way that young lady's hand is hanging, that her wrist is broken. She'd better come with me. I saw the doctor's surgery next door to the Police Station, in the last village I came through. I'll see she's well looked after till you can pick her up."

A cold feeling crept up Jane's spine; a wild sense of exhilaration fought with dread in her divided heart. She just had sense to hold her now dangling wrist in her other hand and let an expression of stoically borne anguish cross her features, before George swept her up into the seat beside him.

Jane caught a last glimpse of Snoutie's forlorn white face. She was cut about the forehead and the blood was running down her cheeks; but she wasn't thinking of the blood, or even of the red handbag which it had been her first thought to save undamaged, but of Jane's fast disappearing form. George had kept his engine running, and they were off at ninety miles an hour. Snoutie knew there was something funny about the whole business, if Miss Emsley didn't, and that the fun involved the future of Jane. Snoutie had never heard of George, but the men in the world Snoutie had once lived in had not been unlike George.

It was impossible to tell whether George was pleased to see Jane or not. She could only see the line of his jaw and the gleam of his pale eyes under his cap. He was making time and keeping his eyes fixed on the flying ribbon of the road, no sooner before him than it was under him.

"How come", Jane ventured at last, "you knew where I was goin', George —so as to pick me up?"

George spoke out of the corner of his mouth; he seemed to have left his accent and his grand manner behind him, with the dishevelled group he had pulled out of the ditch.

"I took notice—see?" he explained. "I knew where you was from the firs', but no use trying a get-away while you was locked up. I knew when they was shipping you—milkman told me when that crew of V.D.s was off. Bought their clinic milk from him—drink a herd of cows dry a day—those V.D.s would. Must orl 'a been nursin' muvers, come to think of it! I followed their 'bus erlong the day they was orf, and when they stopped for an eat, I cort the eye of a Glamour-Puss. She and I watched out for a chanct. There wasn't only two dames with the load, and when their backs was turned, I arsked her did she know a girl called Jane that talked American-like, and she said 'yerse'—you was her best friend, and getting out today with a private car, name of Emsley driving. Then a Screwy come up, and I ducked from under. I spotted the right dame in the telephone book, an' hung rahnd. That fella wot ran into your car—'e's a smash-and-grabber I use sometimes—see? The way we fixed it—I was to pass you—and turn off up a likely blind, and 'e was ter follow me. We roosted up easy—the way we'd planned—and wot ever way the accident went I gotta good story.

"Bill, 'e'll be orf when he sees the lars' of us, an' your little caravan can sit tight waiting for the next pick-up. It won't hurt them any—waitin'."

"You took a chanct", Jane said reprovingly. "He might have killed one of us."

"Well—it wouldn't have been you", George said nonchalantly, "'e knew his business—same as I do mine. An' it wouldn't 'ave been the firs' time people's been killed in a road accident either."

Jane was silent. She knew that she must adjust to George. She always had adjusted to him, and it had worked. He was the same George. But there was a new element to the situation which she couldn't overlook—she wasn't herself the same Jane. Something had happened to her at the Home; she wasn't quite sure what, but it took her further away from George. In a sense, she told herself, George was her saviour. There wasn't going to be three years locked up with ladies teaching you to do things that wouldn't be any use to you afterwards. Now there was going to be what she had long been used to—and had learned to like—or had lumped, when she hadn't liked it.

The same path was still before her, only the chief figure on it meant differently to her. She looked again at George. It wasn't only the disguise, she thought, that had changed George: the lines of his face were harder, his eyes were bleaker, his nostrils more pinched in. He could still look like Gentleman George when he wanted to—smiling away and sparkling up his eyes, talking like velvet; but when he wasn't putting on an act, he didn't look very nice. The sweet, haunting face of Elsie, and her unvarying gentleness, pricked Jane's heart. She turned her eyes resolutely away from George, back to the flying road.

"We goin' back ter Ma's, George?" she asked.

George deftly scraped past a huge lorry and, with the smoothness of poured out cream, slipped into the traffic of the London road. He had plenty of time to get to London before the police began calling up cars; he could take a good straight run and then turn off it again; and, finding a turning that he had planned to take, he idled along looking for a good hide-out, where he could change his plates. He would go back to the London road later on, but with fresh numbers on the plate behind him.

"You ain't heard, o' corse," he replied at last to Jane's question with casual unconcern, "mewed up there like a hutched rabbit—but Ma's passed on."

"Ma—dead?" Jane cried incredulously. "Why, George—you don't say? How come?"

It was inconceivable to Jane to think of all that lively evil at an end.

"But you kep' Rundle for me, George?" she asked with breathless urgency, "you sure kep' Rundle?"

"I *would* er kept 'im," George admitted, "but she knifed 'im first. The night you was copped, when I got back, she had Rundle hangin' on the wall with knives stuck in 'im, like a pickshure. I broke 'is neck in a split second—so 'e didn't suffer ner more, poor brute! An' was I mad at Ma? She was crool, Ma was—when she hadn't no need to be. 'No sense in that,' I orften tole 'er."

"George," Jane said in a low scared voice, "did you—did you do Ma in?"

There was a pause while George, who was putting a new number on the back of his car, came back to the seat beside her, his job done with expert finish.

"She took too much gin fer her age," George said, turning the car back towards the London road, "bottle an' a 'alf a day I've known her swaller. I wasn't there when it happened—so how was I to know? She 'ad her enemies, Ma! Yer might say—she hadn't much else *but* enemies—an' there was Wilfred—when she died—'e 'ad the lot. Never no love lorst between Ma and Wilfred, was there? Lef' everythink she 'ad to Wilfred tho'. She knew wot I thought of her, Ma did. Paid us to live side by side like—but she knew. I never expected more from Ma than wot I took."

Jane gave a little sigh. She must not think of Rundle, as well as not thinking of Elsie; but there was nothing to go back to now.

She glanced again at George. He was sitting hunched up over his steering wheel, his cap pulled well forward over what had once been his ginger-coloured hair. Someone had done a good job of work on George's hair: even the roots were black. His eyes, empty, unconcerned, aloof, were gazing straight ahead. She had not once met George's eyes since he had stopped being Gentleman George.

184

"George," Jane whispered uncertainly, "listen—I gotta know—do you *want* me back?"

George made a sound that was completely humourless, yet it might have been intended for a laugh.

"Well—I *got* you back, haven't I?" he asserted with a satisfaction untinctured by affection.

XXV

Jane longed to know where they were going, what George was doing, and what he meant to do with her. Her mind seethed with questions, but none of them passed her lips. An atmosphere of fierce attention had settled about them—a familiar atmosphere, secretive and tense, which forbade all questioning. Fear lurked in George's cold, shut face, and in the tension of his long, unusually cared-for fingers, gripping the steering wheel as if he were pushing into it the silent forces of his will.

The very car itself seemed spun by fear along a mine-strewn road.

Other cars passed by them, intent on easy errands, business or pleasure—carefree cars, whose drivers had only to think of traffic and the rules of the road. George had other deeper pre-occupations; road traffic meant nothing to him compared to that furtive inner traffic in his own mind. No road signs, or guiding policeman's hands—no traffic lights even—would be any help to George if his own ice-cold wits broke down.

"Turn on the radio", he said to Jane; and she knew what that meant.

"Calling all cars," would be the beginning of pursuit. She mustn't take George's mind off his plans of escape, even for a moment.

It was Fear that regulated their speed or changed their direction; and for three months Jane had been without Fear.

It was cruel to part with Elsie, uninteresting to learn dull lessons, aggravating to feel shut up, maddening to be pushed round by Miss Potter; but all these long three months Jane had been, without realising it—safe. Now she wasn't going to feel safe any more.

The rain-blurred vehicles and figures that they passed; the places they were leaving behind them, or arriving at, must all be adjusted to this new rule of Fear. Nor was it a generalised fear, for other people escaped it; nor was it in the distant hands of governments to increase or assuage; it was in George's hands; and it depended entirely upon George's erratic will how—or if—they escaped what pursued them.

The radio did not say "Calling all cars"; it said very kindly that children were forbidden to take the eggs of song birds from their nests, but that they must not be wholly deprived of less significant birds' eggs. It did not explain how the children were to choose between the eggs of significant or insignificant birds.

When George reached Vauxhall Bridge, he turned sharply along the south side of the river, stopped before a garage and wordlessly dropped the big car into the hands of a mechanic, who appeared to be on the look out for them.

George looked slightly less tense now that he had got rid of the car, and he was sufficiently aware of Jane to say "C'mon!" over his shoulder.

This was not a part of London that Jane knew. You could smell the river all the time, and sometimes see it. Mysterious wharfs shadowed the ends of short dirty streets. Blocks of untidy tenements, or old-fashioned grimy-windowed factories, shot up tier above tier, their advertised wares sailing over the heads of passers by and shining like jewels. Every now and then, between low roofs, Jane caught a glimpse of a tapering mast or the rigging of a nameless ship, like a spun cobweb, between the unseen river and the low, rainy sky.

Before a greengrocer's shop, George paused. Jane thought it a very poor greengrocer's shop to arrest his attention— dusty cabbages, flabby lettuces and disconsolate pinched carrots were flung haphazardly in a heap, behind a window that had not been cleaned for years.

"See? We live over that shop," George told Jane. "If anyone wants ter buy, you can sell things. I git fresh vegs. in once a week. Cover—that's all it is reely. Name of Wilson, if anyone asks you."

"What kind of a relation am I to you now—George?" Jane asked warily.

George took out a key, and with a wave of the hand introduced Jane to the dusty vegetables. Inside the shop, he gave her a doubtful appraising look, as if the question of what relation she was to him had entered his mind for the first time. He seemed to feel a moment's embarrassment before he answered.

"Moll—wife—girl—I dunno! But not farver an' daughter. Might think ter turn yer over ter the police if you said 'daughter'—arsk questions abaht age or education—anyfink!"

George took the card out of the window and slipped it into his pocket, but not before Jane saw that it had "Bed and Breakfast" on it. This too was cover, George explained: they never took anyone in for bed or breakfast.

The shop had nothing in it but a few shelves, on which stood some age-old tins of arsenical looking peas the size of grapes, promising a succulence Jane was sure that they could never perform. A door opened out upon a dishevelled strip of garden with a shed at the bottom of it, backed by a warehouse, beyond which was a slice of darkness that Jane guessed must be the river itself. A second door led up a flight of stairs, into a large sized living room, with a skylight as well as two windows, one of which—as large as a door—opened onto a balcony. The room was clean and tidy, but it didn't have their old furniture in it. It only possessed a kitchen table, two wicker armchairs, three cane ones; and a double bed.

Jane knew now what George's sudden embarrassment meant. This was to be their new relationship. "Moll—wife—girl——" was George's proposition to her.

There was nothing Jane didn't know by now of the vagaries of sex, balanced firmly on the young doctor's scientific explanation. If it hadn't been for that, Jane thought, all that she learned from the other girls might have been puzzling; but she had started off right and couldn't be taken in by any of their romancing. Sex was to all of them alike—whether they knew the facts of life by hearsay or had experienced them by personal contacts—one of three things: a joke—a game—or a complaint. It was never "serious" unless you got caught. Nothing beyond these three categories had reached Jane's mind.

There wasn't much choice open to Jane now—it was only George—or the streets.

Jane realised that she couldn't be George's wife, even if she had wanted marriage; and the opinions of the girls at the Home had varied greatly as to the desirability of marriage. Marriage, they explained, meant risks and responsibilities; it also involved registration, and George never signed anything if he could help it. Yet she hesitated. "If I want to run," she said to herself, "I still can!"

"I got a barf-room", George said loftily, as Jane considered her new prospects. "Modern fittings—I did it meself, and I brought our Fridge erlong, an' I made a kitchenette be'ind that curtain. We got this place to ourselves—see—an' there's three ways aht of it—skylight, an' me new steel-flex ladder 'angs 'ere—stairs—an' barf-room winder drops easy onto a roof—an' there's anuver thing—I got a boat in that there shed in the yard—motor boat, small and easy run—water only a yard or two off it—jest a push and it's in. I got a new line nah—tell you abaht it later——" George broke off.

Jane was no longer listening to him, nor looking at what he showed her. What she saw instead, slowly advancing upon wobbly feet, was a black kitten, insufficiently fed, with bleary eyes and a white star on its breast. With a shriek of delight, Jane sank on the floor beside it.

"Oh George!" she cried, "you thought of it! Yer brought it fer me—it's my kitten!"

It was love at first sight. Nothing else now mattered—and the love included George.

XXVI

J ane did not cry until George had gone to sleep. The big September moon lurching over the dark cavern of a warehouse sent a beam of silvery light through the dirty window pane and lit up George's face. He looked relaxed and happy, and very much younger.

It was not the pain that Jane had minded. George had explained about the pain, and said that it wouldn't happen again. You were only a virgin once; then it was all over and everything would be easy. Nevertheless Jane felt as if she had lost something, and that to lose one of her few possessions was a poor way of beginning this new life with George.

Jane was tough, and without illusions. She knew that films weren't true unless you were rich and could cook things up; but she could not forget the curious sensation that had passed from Mabel's heart to hers when they were lying in the boot cupboard together, and Mabel had told her about Harry. Mabel, in spite of being caught out, and in spite of losing Harry himself, had never given up the feeling that there was something more to Harry than just losing him. There was "the singing, the laughter and the gold".

Even if Jane believed that Mabel was merely a softie, there was the evidence of the far more experienced and frankly materialistic Elsie. Elsie had once said, "Of course if you get a nice boy, that's sweet to you, it's better than nylons or chocolates!" Considering what Elsie thought of nylons and chocolates, this was no mean praise.

Tonight Jane had experienced no magic—just George—and not, Jane thought a little wistfully, George at his best. But she had the kitten, she reminded herself; and it took the place of both nylons and chocolates. She put out her hand cautiously and picked the kitten out of a cardboard box she had placed by the bedside. She had made it as comfortable as she could with a cushion and her skirt, though it had preferred the back of her neck. George had objected to having the kitten in bed, but now he was asleep and wouldn't mind.

The kitten cautiously felt about with its paws till it regained the exact space that suited it, curled up in a warm ball against Jane's neck, and fell asleep; but Jane remained for a long time awake thinking of funny things—that queer, steady look in Miss Bartlett's eyes when she had said goodbye to Jane and told her never to come back; and Snoutie staring after her, for that brief flurried instant on the road, with such a haunting sincerity. Poor little Snoutie! She had counted on Jane, and now what might she not have to face alone in that Approved School, in which there were so many things that could never be approved of!

Jane reminded herself that Snoutie had her red bag, a New Testament in a grey cotton cover, and God. Snoutie had told Jane quite a lot about God—more than Miss Bartlett had ever told her; and Jane hoped that this shadowy, and to her unsubstantial, Figure might be relied upon to stand by Snoutie, now that there was no one else to fight for her.

Although Elsie, too, came into Jane's mind, it was without the urgency of Snoutie, or the steadiness of Miss Bartlett. Jane's heart, having been broken by Elsie, refused to retain Elsie's image. She could remember the pain, but she couldn't remember the joy of Elsie. It was almost as if—apart from having had her heart broken by her—Elsie had no separate existence.

Jane could run away of course, although there was nowhere to run to but the police; without money you had to come up against them sooner or later, and Jane would have to get her hand in again before she made enough to live on out of "lifting". There was a certain sense of freedom in the thought that before long George would go out as usual and leave her to her own devices; meanwhile, there he lay, passive and satisfied. A new idea occurred to her as she looked at him, and a more pleasant one. It was that she, Jane, had made him happy. There she lay, between two creatures whom she had satisfied. They were content—they slept—and perhaps, she thought to herself before she fell asleep, that was not so bad a way of beginning her new life after all.

In a month's time Jane had adjusted herself to George, and transformed the kitten. Its round topaz eyes, exaggeratedly innocent, were no longer bleary. Its coat was satin smooth and bland to the touch; its muscles, sustained by selected and sufficient food, gave the kitten an exquisite and firm control of every movement. Its sex was still indeterminate, but Jane called it Elsie, for it had Elsie's grace and her resilience.

Elsie the cat's character, however, differed in every respect from that of Elsie the girl. She was an adventurous, hard-headed kitten. She knew her place in the world was doubtful, and depended mainly on wariness and claws. Her emotions were secret, suspicious, deep and wild. If offended, she scratched instantly and savagely. She bit, sometimes in an access of affection—for, in her fashion, she returned Jane's love—and sometimes from sheer, desperate, unadulterated spite.

Jane always knew which passion inspired Elsie's bites, but other people took a less discriminating view of her tactics. "A wicked cat", George called her; and indeed, in moments of displeasure Elsie looked wicked. Her ears flattened themselves against her head as if pinned; her black tail fluffed out like a bottle brush; hunching her small round body higher than her head, she leaped forward and backward, every claw spread out with a ferocity that neatly balanced malevolence with ecstasy. Deeply within her minute person, Elsie chewed and spat out what she must have wished to be venom, and yet Jane loved even these witch-antics.

Jane lived with George, but she lived for the kitten. The kitten knew it; in fact her whole person responded to the knowledge of Jane's love. When Jane was alone, Elsie spent all her time with her and revealed the best of her character, but the moment a step sounded on the stair, Elsie would be off, out of the nearest window, not to be seen or answerable to any call of her now familiar name, until by some strange instinct she gathered that the coast was clear.

There was no change in George to meet his new relationship to Jane. By day he was cold, self-absorbed and generally absent; still, there were some slight changes in their way of living in which Jane found advantages. George gave her more money and asked for no account of how she spent it. She could go to the cinema oftener; but, curiously enough, she was not to "lift" any more: instead, she was to learn how to drive a car.

She mustn't revisit Gladys nor try to contact any of Ma's old lodgers who had been Jane's friends; nor was she to make new friends. "You been put away," George explained, "an' all the ole crowd know it. They could put the cops on you, as soon as look at you—nor I wouldn't put it past them."

"How come they fahnd out?" Jane demanded. "I bet you never let on!"

"'Corse I never", George agreed. "Mighta been in the papers, I never read nothing abaht it—I got me own way of picking up things, but Ma fahnd aht. You couldn't never 'ide nothink from Ma. She knew what 'ouse we broke into—an' what we took. I 'ad ter give 'er 'alf them jools ter shut 'er mouf. Got some of them back though—once she'd croaked—'fore Wilfred was on to 'em. Funny thing, Jane, but onct you was took, the whole caboodle like went wrong.

"I 'anded the swag over to Alfie. 'E was my runner that crossed fer me ter Amsterdam. Bloke over there broke 'em up for us—and we got a square deal out of 'im, I will say—but maybe 'e squealed. I dunno—cops got on to it some'ow. Alfie, 'e got cort, wiv the swag on 'im, got a five year stretch—Alfie did—I reckon 'e 'as it in fer me when 'e gets aht. But it wouldn't 'ave been no 'elp ter 'im, my being took too, would it? Ser all that Ma hadn't taken orf me, the cops got. I got kinda fed up with jools. Nah I'm after watches. I get a lot in off the continent—and wiv no duty ter pay—an' three skippers workin' wiv me—I'm in easy street. But I'd be better orf when you learn to drive a car—much bigger pickings ter be 'ad on the road when you know who's going where, wiv what. But you need a partner for the car pick ups. I've given up the Riviera stunt, you and me are not eddicated enough and you gotta speak French like a native. Nah you got ter learn ter drive a car—you gotta drive it good—any car—any speed. You gotta drive like a racing wop—an' keep yer 'ead screwed on the right way fer police traps, while you're doin' it. You'll 'ave ter learn every rule of the road and 'ow and where to break 'em. Mostly I'll drive—but while I'm doing my piece of work you'll take over. Rusty—e's that fella I turned the Jaguar back to—Rusty's good with cars—'e'll teach you. 'E's got more patience than wot I 'ave. Besides, I 'ave ter be busy with them watches. Rusty's no girl runner, 'e won't do you any 'arm ser long as you keep a civil tongue in yer 'ead and don't try nothink on."

"Looked ter me as if he come out of a booby hatch and had orter go back there!" Jane responded tartly, for she had not, at first sight, taken to Rusty. "I wouldn't say he was an oil painting!"

George's new chum had a cast in his eye, hair that looked as if it had been picked out of a dustbin and plastered over his forehead, a long upper lip and no expression whatever. What lay behind Rusty's uncertain eyes was nobody's business; and if nothing lay behind them, no one would be able to guess that there was nothing. Still, he was an expert mechanic, and his garage proprietor thought so highly of him that he could do practically what he liked with any cars that came in. Some of these cars were left for repairs and overhauls, and Rusty let them out to George, for agreed sums and for limited periods. The understanding on Rusty's side was that nothing was to happen to the cars and that they were always to be returned on time; and on George's side that no questions were ever to be asked—or answered, if they were asked, by anyone but George himself.

"I trust 'im O.K.," George explained a little uneasily to Jane, "an' it pays me taking diff'rent cars whenever I need 'em instead of me having me own car all the time, and having to pay for garage. Less easy for cops ter spot too—but yer

194

never want ter trust no one too far, believe you me! Rusty, 'e knows you're my girl—an' wot would 'appen ter 'im if he forgot it. Still, you gotta learn ter keep yer own end up— see?"

Jane saw. "You don't need ter be scared of Rusty", she told George scornfully. "If Rusty an' me was alone on a desert island wiv a boa constrictor I'd take the boa constrictor every time!"

"An' as soon as I can drive by myself", Jane thought, "I'll be free—free as air—that's wot I'll be——" Out loud she said, "O.K. George, I'll learn—I'll learn quickly."

XXVII

J ane did not know that she was happy, but perhaps no one
had ever liked a dull, fog-threatened London afternoon as
much as Jane liked this one. She had got her own way from
a reluctant Rusty, and was driving a midget Morris alone, for
the first time, across Vauxhall Bridge.

The egg-shell car bounced along between giant drays and
uncheckable lumbering lorries, accustoming itself to the light
hand that thrust it so unhesitatingly into the rhythm of the
great stream of traffic.

"In London," Rusty had told Jane, "go with the traffic—but
when the road's free, keep out of it."

Jane paid a great deal of attention to what Rusty told her.
She had never been able to make up her mind whether Rusty
liked her or not; he put up with her for the month of their long,
intensive driving lessons, but when they were over he showed no
regret for their parting. Jane knew that she rather surprisingly
had learned to like Rusty although what she liked in him didn't
belong to her, while what she liked less in George *did* belong
to her. Everything Rusty had belonged to cars: they were his
religion, his love affairs, his undiluted aim in life. If Rusty had
known that he possessed a soul, he would have sold it for a
Bugatti. The steps to buying one were immaterial to him:
he took George's money for lending him cars that were his
clients', or taught a girl under age to drive a car for criminal
purposes, with equal indifference. Still, as far as he could
respect a girl, Rusty respected Jane. She passed her driving
test with credit after a few weeks' lessons; attended minutely to
his instructions; and had an iron nerve. In the parlance of
mountain guides, Jane was "Schwindel-frei"—a knife's edge

over a precipice or a secure and open highway required, and got from Jane, exactly the same unflurried calculation. She was over the bridge now; before her stretched the wide Embankment dimmed by river mist, and heterogeneously crammed, pouring itself steadily forward towards distant towers. Blue as forget-me-nots, the tunnels of great streets flowed and ebbed away from her. Now she had passed Westminster and shot up into Piccadilly, where suddenly there were long flashes of green, striped with black trees, and above them—pieces of sheer open sky. Street lamps began to flare just as she came into the whirlpool of Hammersmith Broadway—a tricky business to choose between the fading light of nature and electricity's harsh glare; but once she had passed the vortex, the traffic ebbed. Here was Chiswick, a village buried in the backwash of a city; and now she touched the tortured edge of Barnes Common and began to look out for Wilfred's big new furniture shop.

Jane had found out where Wilfred lived, and determined to call on him. He was no longer in the district George had forbidden her to visit; and Wilfred would not, she knew, give her away to the police, though Jane would not go so far as to tell him where she lived or with whom. Wilfred had never liked George, even before George took the five hundred off him; but Wilfred and Jane had been on the best of terms ever since Jane had resolutely refused to carry out Ma's schemes by becoming Wilfred's girl. Perhaps she had made a mistake, Jane thought, when she saw his name flashing out above the grandeur of a large furniture shop next to Woolworth's— "Wilfred Best". No more cracked Toby jugs, faked furniture, odds and ends of musty fragments from the dim past, never valuable except for the length of time that they had escaped the dustbin. This shop had smart new carpets, a table lavishly spread with a painted dinner set surrounding spectacularly imitation fruit, flanked by wine bottles that might even contain grapes mixed with vinegar. Alluring bedsteads, covered by shining sham satin, gleamed invitation; armchairs that looked as if they were never meant to be sat in, but could contain elephants, shocked Jane by their stupendous prices. Could women really sit before such dressing tables, spread for their glory, gazing into such unstinted mirrors? George let Jane use his shaving glass, which was a good one, and she could see her head in it, but nothing beneath her small decided chin. These women could see everything, and just sit there looking at themselves all day long—they might even varnish reflected toe nails, Jane thought, and get away with it.

Jane had parked her car at a reasonable distance from Wilfred's emporium, inexpensively in a nearby cul-de-sac; and now she gave herself plenty of time to take in all its splendours.

When at last Jane entered the shop, she was told contemptuously, by a towering, raspberry-lipped blonde, that Wilfred received no one without an appointment.

Jane measured the blonde with a careful eye. Then, giving her a sharp jab with her elbow where she would most feel, and least expect it, she shot swiftly past her. Behind the shop, Jane found Wilfred, drinking tea, in a large ornately furnished office, seated before a walnut wood desk with mock gothic carvings. But was it really Wilfred?—this magnificent young man, whose head stood up on its broad neck like Mussolini's, with chin arranged to cleave the air? Was it Wilfred's crouched stooping figure, now clothed like a would-be fashion leader from an encouraging advertisement, and actually holding itself up? The eyes were certainly Wilfred's—shallow-set, pale blue just not watery, undominating eyes—wavering just as they used to waver whenever they met Jane's, before he had time to exclaim in condescending welcome, "Why—if it isn't young Jane!"

Jane closed the door sharply upon the outraged blonde, sat down opposite Wilfred, crossed her legs and smoothed the new skirt of a suit George had paid rather more for than he had wanted to pay.

"Not so young neither, Wilfred", Jane replied tartly. "How's tricks?"

Wilfred waved his hand in an explanatory benediction upon his prosperous surroundings. It was the same flabby hand, Jane noticed, not really capable of mending the broken cracks in the china Ma had told him to say was the original Worcester.

"Well enough, Jane—well enough!" Wilfred told her in his aggravatingly refined voice.

Ma had sent him to a grammar school, and in consequence Wilfred had always looked down upon Ma and all her friends, even—perhaps mistakenly—upon her enemies.

"But I thought—if you will excuse my mentioning it—that you had been put away, after that jewel robbery George led you into! Where, by-the-by, *is* George?"

"I can't think", Jane replied crisply. "Where should he be? Jes' as you say, I was put away for three months, and then passed out to a good family the Beeks looked up for me; and this being my first free afternoon out, I thought I'd look you up and hear how all Ma's friends was! See?"

Wilfred saw, without appearing to like what he saw. At this moment, a fresh tea appeared for Jane, carried in by a boy with freckles, pushed, Jane suspected, from behind by the blonde, for some of the tea slopped inelegantly, if not purposefully, upon a plate of crumpets.

When the door closed after him, Wilfred told Jane all he knew, and more than he wanted to know, about Ma's former lodgers. Gladys, Jane was glad to hear—for she had a warm place in her heart for Gladys—had married the landlord of the Pig and Lilies, and was expecting.

"I have never had anything more to do with any of them," Wilfred told Jane, "and I should strongly advise you to take the same course. You have now got a chance. You left George young, and you might say, from what I have always understood, more or less innocent. Your having been caught on that first breaking in, you should look on as a blessing in disguise. Now you can start afresh. There's a lot of useful, and even paying things a young girl like you can learn to do."

"I'm learning", Jane told him. "I work in a factory— Glaxo's Milk for kids. You're well paid and I like the work. I don't think I need to learn much else. Are those cigarettes or is it just an ornament—that silver box on your desk?"

It was cigarettes, and Wilfred reluctantly gave Jane one, and lit another for himself. He thought smoking morally bad for Jane, but he was relieved to notice that her shoes must have cost money; so she hadn't come to borrow from him, as he had first expected.

Jane ate her tea politely but with appetite, and listened attentively while Wilfred got some of his new glories off his chest. When he came to a complacent pause, she daintily licked the butter off her finger-tips and asked: "An' what *did* happen to Ma, Wilfred?"

It was like a sudden puncturing of a balloon in full rounded flight. Wilfred gasped, his cheeks sank in, and he turned a pale mauve colour.

"You didn't know?" he whispered fearfully, "God—Jane—I thought someone must have told you! I forgot you were locked up and didn't see the papers. Well Ma—she was done in—George did her in. No doubt of it!" Wilfred added, licking his thin, colourless lips. "But nothing was proved against him. She was found strangled. The verdict was murder by a person or persons unknown. But we knew—we all knew George did it!"

Jane poured herself a final cup of tea with a steady hand, and drank the greater part of it without speaking.

Then she said nonchalantly, "George didn't git anythink aht of it, did he?—Or maybe Ma'd done something he didn't like? Could be! I knew George pretty well, Wilfred, an' I don't never remember his doing nothing to nobody unless he *got* somethink for it. He orften used to say, 'Waste o' time an' risky—doin' people in!' We all know Ma had her enemies! What makes you think George did it? Lots of people had it in for Ma. Way I see it—it needn't have been George—might have been anybody."

"There were things made us know it was George", Wilfred said uneasily. "It was part the way he acted as much as anything. The police didn't know George as well as we all did. Besides, George, he thought out a good alibi. He was seen talking to one of Ma's girls, before anything happened; then he went on and chatted at the Prince of Wales Feather; and Ma was seen alive after he'd drove off in his car. No one saw him come back—till it was all over, and the police was on the spot, and then he drove up—and we *all* saw George coming back as

200

it were! Now Jane, you know George. Ask yourself, even if you saw him go—and that wasn't likely—would you ever see him come back as well? George was just a person you didn't see—not when he was off on his errands."

Jane did not deny that there was something in what Wilfred said, but there wasn't everything. She saw a way out and took it.

"I never knew George", Jane said coldly, "to do what didn't bring him in anythink. What did George git from Ma's having passed on? Why, he even lost his lodgings seemingly."

"He got the jewels", Wilfred explained. "I didn't mention them before perhaps, but Ma had them in her safe—rightly, no doubt, from her point of view—and when things were looked into, the safe—a Chubb safe, you remember, in the wall behind her bed she had it—was empty."

"George isn't the only person that likes a di-mond when he sees it", Jane said, sweeping the crumbs off her skirt. "Well —thank you for a good tea—jes' the same, Wilfred, and I'm glad ter see you doing ser well—jools or no jools, you was the one that got the pickin's, wasn't you? Ta-ta, an' if I wos you I'd keep that blonde's claws orf of you jes' as long as you can manage it!"

Jane felt that she had left Wilfred with the full honours of war; but she was not so happy when she drove back in Rusty's little car as when she had set out in it.

XXVIII

J ane was halfway up the stairs when she saw a light under
the door. The light meant that George was there, and that,
returning unexpectedly early, he would be annoyed to find
Jane out and no meal ready for him.

He would want to know where Jane had been and what she
had been doing, and he would probably have already found out
from Rusty that Jane had taken a car. So she would have to be
careful what she told him. It was never very safe to lie to
George; and it might be downright dangerous if he should discover that Jane *had* lied to him.

She stood quite still feeling her heart swinging against her
side. He hadn't heard anything, for he didn't call out. If
she crept downstairs, and never went back to George, what
would become of her? She had ten shillings in her bag, and
the winter coat she had on had cost seven pounds and might
be sold for three.

If Jane went to Rusty, he wouldn't take her because he was
afraid of George, and lived with his old mother who didn't like
girls, and particularly disliked Jane. If Gladys hadn't been
pregnant, Jane would have gone to Gladys; but it didn't do to
bring trouble on babies, either here—or on their way here; and
George would think of Gladys if he didn't find Jane with
Rusty, and make trouble for everybody all round.

Jane could go on the streets; lots of the V.D.s had told her
how to work it, and though they hadn't managed very well for
themselves, their advice about the preliminary steps was likely
to have been sound. But Jane had not wanted to go on the
streets, even before the V.D.s' advice had been available to her.
Now she wanted to go on the streets less than ever. If only

she knew whether George *had* killed Ma or not! Yet if she knew, would it make all that difference, Jane asked herself? Ma had needed killing.

She stood for quite a long time silent and breathless on the stairs, with her eyes on the strip of light under the door. The faces of Miss Bartlett and Snoutie flickered up into her mind, but she knew that the only real alternative to George was the police. Jane was in the London District, and wherever the police managed to get her put away, it wouldn't be where she wanted to be put. The streets were still her enemies; and George was her friend, whether he had killed Ma or not.

She gave a little sigh, as she found herself mounting the stairs, without guessing that her decision had been taken from the moment she hadn't run down them again. To her surprise George was quite nice to her, when she opened the door, and had actually provided fish and chips for both of them.

George was never very interested in what was going on in other people's minds, so he asked Jane no questions at all. He merely stated that tomorrow she could start working. Her first job would be to take a packet containing gold watches and hand them over to the jeweller's tout, who was to receive them. She would find him outside a bakery in Hillgate Street, a small side street between Church Street and Campden Hill. The young man would be on the look out for her. He would come up to the car and say: "Are you Miss Pringle? And have you got my fountain pens?" Then she was to say: "Yes, Mr. West", and hand him over the parcel. There her responsibility ended.

"One thing you have to remember, Jane", George said earnestly. "You don't want to slop over with these fellers we work with. They pick things up, and might use them against us later on. Say jes' what I tell you to say, and then drive off—an' drive off where you don't mean to stay. You don't want ter come back *here* till you know no one's on your trail.

"I don't mean only police—see—open or shut—in uniform or thinking themselves up as civvies! It's the people who work for us—we want to keep in the clear with, as well. I don't want no one, 'cept Rusty, to know where we live. That was the trouble at Ma's. Everything was too bloody friendly. Think of all them girls—knowing we was burglars jes' as we knew they was tarts—arsking fer trouble, that was! I got things worked nah so that we're pretty snug over those Swiss watches, and no one knows more than they need. Skippers bring the watches to the river. I know where they'll be, and when. The River Police have searched me an' the boat pretty thorough, twice—but it was when I *wanted* them to search me! They're smart boys—those River Police—but I think I'm one up on them—all the samie, Maimie! They're what you'd call 'neutral' abaht me nah—unless they was ter see me—somewhere else wot they was watching! That's where *you* come in. You won't *be* suspect —why should you? They ain't spotted you wiv me yet—nor you won't take the swag ter the same place twice. See?"

Jane nodded. The plan seemed as near fool-proof as George's plans usually were: the maximum of profit with the minimum of risk was George's motto; but she knew now that when you were in it with him, the major profit was on his side, and the major risk on yours.

"There's somepin' else I'm coming to", George said slowly, his evasive eyes suddenly fixing themselves on Jane. "Maybe you think you won't have no fun and games—livin' here, so private-like, over the cabbages, playin' wiv yer pussy cat? But you're dead wrong: I'm goin' ter buy you a cocktail dress, neat and pretty, shoes an' all! Corse I don't want you ter look too gaudy—but I wouldn't say 'no' to a fox fur I picked up the other day—no identity marks, an' looks quite the lady. You'll go wiv me to a dance hall one or two nights a week—good class ones—and whenever I bring you up a young man, and say, 'Meet my friend, Mr. North!' you'll dance wiv 'im, and pass 'im a packet—chemist stuff, size of an aspirin bottle—slip it into 'is pocket, so that no one can see you do it. Think you can do that—the way I taught you ter lift things in shops?"

Jane leaned forward eagerly. "Try me!" she said.

George tried her. They worked hard for an hour, George contriving to act with extravagant clumsiness, representing a nervous young man with clumsy hands, into one of whose pockets Jane had to insert—unseen—the precious packet he was expecting. They went on till George was satisfied; and George was very hard to satisfy. Jane had to think and act for two people, one of whom—George explained to her—would be next door to an idiot, and therefore unpredictable.

"What's in the packet?" Jane asked him, "dope?"

"Never you mind wot's in the packet", George told her rather crossly. "Wot yer don't know can't be held against you —if you're fahnd aht—which yer won't be if you act spry! All you got to remember is—though you can dance wiv any other young man in between times—if I tip you the wink— or wiv me—if no young men don't arsk you—it's only 'Mr. North' that gets the packet. Dames, I'll attend to—they're risky, on account their heads is weaker an' they make more noise."

It probably was dope, Jane decided. There were girls who were dopers at the Home. You took it, Elsie explained, first for fun, and then wanted it more and more, until you had to have it. To supply it should be quite a paying proposition. It sounded cruel too; but Elsie had said you didn't need to take it unless you wanted to!

Neither of these jobs was violent, or need lead, Jane thought, to really wicked things. She began to feel quite comfortable and happy, and George made no objection when she opened the balcony door and Elsie came in and settled down on a newspaper to eat what was left of the fish. Elsie didn't mind being in the same room with George if Jane were there as well. She even pretended to like George and rubbed her back against his leg, provided there was plenty of room all round her to get away if she felt it necessary. When he stroked her, as he sometimes did, Elsie actually purred, but not a deep purr: that she reserved exclusively for Jane.

"I'll want seven pounds for the dress—three for the shoes— and five extra for me bag, and extras," Jane told George, "an' I better have a fur coat too—you got any, George?"

"Could be", George replied almost genially. "But don't run away wiv the idea that you're ter be a rich man's Darling! Nor you ain't no Gorgeous neither, an' I'm not showing you orf as one—See? It don't hurt the eyes any ter look at you—an' that's wot the job arsks—no less an' no more. You play to it, Jane, then we won't neither of us be landed in Queer Street!"

Jane nodded obediently, but the nod was merely a point of conciliation—she still had her hidden dreams. The world was opening up all round her. Jane loved dancing. Beauty shops, Jane thought, could do for her what nature hadn't. She would take the money for this purpose out of the house-keeping. George might not care for her to look like a Gorgeous, but nobody was going to stop Jane from looking as like a Gorgeous as she could.

XXIX

Jane sat behind the counter, her feet on a box of carrots, knitting a twin set. She was uncertain as to whether George might not think bright tan for the cardigan and gold for the pullover too conspicuous; but with luck, Jane thought, she might get away with it.

Elsie sat close to her on the counter, in the centre of a sunbeam. Her eyes were closed and she made a faint humming sound; she was not asleep, but slowly, almost imperceptibly, she was relaxing. She was on a spot she had long frequented without risk, and within reach of the only person she tolerated.

The shop bell rang sharply, and the unwelcome person of George shot into the little room as if expelled by a catapult.

"Here!" George gasped, sweeping Elsie aside with his elbow, "hide this somewheres—look slippy! There's a cop on my tail—I'll be back over the roof ternight ter pick it up! Could search *me*, but can't search here wiv-aht a warrant!"

George was gone before Elsie had recovered herself from the floor, swelled out her tail and spat at him. These movements were simultaneous; but George had slid upstairs, closing the door behind him, before they were over.

Elsie had now to decide, with shaken nerves and no help from Jane, whether she should magisterially sail through the window into the soot-covered garden to sulk, or leap back on to the counter and try to reassemble the scattered atoms of her lost serenity. Instead of saying "Poor Pussy!" and stroking her with a firm and expert touch to help her decision, Jane tore open the parcel and slid each of the twelve well-packed watches under the carrots, carefully covering them over with a thickly spread top layer, until the carrots presented their usual negligent air of being rather small, ignominious vegetables, not likely to sell easily. Even then Jane did not attend to Elsie, who nevertheless decided to jump back on to the counter, while Jane pulled her skirt over the remains of the parcel and took up her knitting.

Jane was a trifle breathless from the speed with which she had acted, but even this slight physical reaction was no longer noticeable by the time the bell rang again and a young man entered.

In spite of his civilian clothes, Jane guessed that he was a plain clothes policeman. Shoulders do not look flabby, even when they are flabby, after they have been firmly drilled; and this man's shoulders had never been flabby; nor did the young man's hatless, casual air deceive Jane into thinking that he did not closely observe everything he looked at. Yet he made one initial blunder: he put out his hand genially to stroke Elsie, who promptly bit him.

"I suppose I asked for it," he said ruefully. "I should have waited till she was used to me."

"She mightn't have got used to you", Jane replied guardedly. "She's a chancy cat."

There was a pause. The room had an untroubled air, as if the cat had sat on the counter, and the girl had knitted behind it, uninterruptedly for hours. Yet if he had been right in his guess—and Henry Dickson was a happy guesser— the man he had been following had disappeared into this very doorway in a state of extreme tension less than five minutes previously.

Henry Dickson would have given much to know how long the other two doors in the room had been shut; one led upstairs, one out into the strip of garden that backed on to the river. Through which of them had George Marsdon gone? Or had Dickson's eyes betrayed him, and was it the next house and not this one in which his quarry had sought refuge? The worst of it was, Dickson had never seen George before, and would not know him if he saw him. He had not even got a photograph of the man he was looking for. He simply had a hunch that this man "George"—but probably not Wilson—in front of him, in a frantic hurry, was the man the Yard most wanted to find. Well—there was no hurry here in this quiet little shop. The only queer thing about it was that the cat, though apparently unruffled, had bitten him. This was curious, because he was a great favourite with cats.

Henry Dickson was also on the look out for George Marsdon's daughter of sixteen. This girl might be nineteen, and she might not be a daughter, but a wife. It is very difficult to tell the difference between a child and a woman. Jane's face was rounded and young, but she had not the eyes of a child. As she left the initiative entirely to him, he had to ask the direct questions he wished to avoid.

"I see the name above your shop is Wilson," Henry Dickson demanded. "Would that be the name of the present owner, and are you his daughter?"

Jane shook her head. She glanced with pride at her third finger. She wore two rings on it, one plain gold, and the other a real solitaire ruby, reset by George. "Anyone can pretend to be married," Jane had convinced George, "but an engagement ring is something else—again—you don't get that for nothing!"

The same idea occurred to Mr. Dickson, except that he thought it too good a ruby for the shop. Still, he almost believed Jane when she said, "I'm Mrs. Wilson, an' me husband's aht. Couldn't say when he'd be in either. Is there anything I could get for you?"

Jane looked politely at two quite eatable lettuces. She had improved the shop greatly—it looked clean, and the vegetables fresh though a cheap type.

George must by now have got on to the roof and be well away.

"I thought I saw a man come into this door as I turned into the street. Who could it have been?" Dickson demanded.

Jane hesitated the fraction of a second. If she said "no one" and he really *had* seen George come in, it would be a mistake.

"Might have been a customer, of course," she replied cautiously, "but should have thought meself that there hadn't been one in for the past few minutes."

"He didn't go out again", Henry Dickson observed gently.

There was a pause. Jane laid down her knitting and looked steadily at him. Her eyes were not large, neither brown nor grey, but curiously bright. Mr. Dickson thought that the brain behind them must work both rapidly and efficiently, but that it would be difficult to guess *how* it was working.

"There's no one in the house but me", Jane said at last. "I only got two shillings an' fivepence in the till—an' I can scream!"

Henry Dickson smiled. "You won't need to scream", he said reassuringly.

Jane took up her knitting again, and Elsie, having decided to take no further notice of the young man after having bitten him, settled down.

"To tell you the truth," Henry Dickson said at last, "I'm a detective officer, and I've been told that your husband might give me some information that would help me, in a smuggling case I'm working on at present."

His eyes rested on Jane's hands; she knitted without pause.

"Smuggling", she said reflectively. "George wouldn't know anything about that. We get all our vegs. straight from Covent Garden—home made, as you might say. We're nuts on the river tho'. We have a motor boat: that's why we took this shop—to be near it. There isn't a free hour we're not on the river. I've seen lots of police boats too—grand the pace they go at! Are you on one of them?"

"I get reports from police boats", he acknowledged guardedly. "Do you mind telling me why you speak with an American accent?"

"'Tisn't so funny when you come to think of it", Jane explained. "My Ma was American born and bred—there was brides before the war as well as after—brides that stuck too, both ways. My Ma liked the British, but she thought they talked all wrong. Dropping their aitches—that was a thing she couldn't understan'—bashed me over the head any time I did it—but of course I don't now. It's low—I've learned better. You might say I gone up in the world since I married George."

The name was George; but George was a very common name, Mr. Dickson told himself, almost as common as Henry. What wasn't so common was the ruby, and the motor boat subsisting on rather poor vegetables. Dickson had known about the motor boat already. He told himself that milkmen are often rich and retire early: perhaps the sellers of vegetables are equally fortunate. There could be very little overhead expenses to a shop like George's. Still, there was the ruby as well as the motor boat.

The young man continued to study Jane. She had a short nose slightly blunted at the top, a wide, generous mouth painted the usual bright raspberry, and she held her head like an American girl, as if, whether she were pretty or not, you would naturally pay some attention to her.

"You're not at all unlike a photograph I've got in my wallet of a girl missing for six months—from a Remand Home", he said in a friendly way. "Girl's name was 'Jane'. 'Yankee Jane' was the nickname she went by."

Henry Dickson laid the snapshot on the counter between them. Elsie opened her eyes and looked up, but as it was neither eatable nor dangerous, she closed them again immediately. It was fortunately only a snapshot taken by one of the V.D.s before they left, so that it was not a convincing likeness. There were three other girls in it besides Jane, one of them—the one who came out best—was Elsie.

"Gee!" Jane exclaimed, "has quite a look of me, hasn't it? But I never wore me hair like that—jes' like one of those towsely dawgs, half rat, half poodle, called griffins, ain't they? Nor I don't think much of the way them girls is dressed —rag-pickers' daughters, by the look of them. What's a Remand Home anyway?"

Was this last question too innocent? The young man replaced the snapshot in his wallet.

"Mildred Jones was me maiden name," Jane told him kindly.

Both George and Jane had thought this a good name, neither high-flown nor uncommon. It had, too, a substantial ring, as if it had really been bestowed on her at a font, making her a Christian.

Jane was pleased to see the young man take it down in his notebook. He swallowed her age too—nineteen—and the date of her marriage. It was a pity to have to give him this date, but a lot can happen to church registers in a year that included the last of the doodle-bugs; and she must *know* when she was married.

"Would you mind my taking a look over the house while I'm in it?" he suggested. "Condemned, isn't it?—all this river side of the street is—but I suppose you took the risk?"

"Well—it lowers the rent, and wouldn't take us long ter turn out if we had to", Jane explained. "I wouldn't mind you lookin' over the house—isn't much to it reely—only one big room upstairs an' a barf room we put in ourselves; but you know how 'tis—George wouldn't half like me lettin' you up there—not wiv him away, he wouldn't. Bit on the jealous side, George is!" Jane gave a light, easy giggle.

She had been badly shaken by Elsie's picture, but she was getting over it. It was better not to let him go upstairs without thinking that she knew he had no right to, unless he had a warrant. George might have left traces behind him in his hurry, though it wouldn't have been like him. He had a safe under the floor of the bath—an ingenious contrivance, since it was indistinguishable from the bath itself; and this was where he kept whatever needed hiding. The skylight had a convenient latch, so that George with a touch could open it, from above or below; but nobody else could open it without considerable trouble and a ladder.

Yet Jane knew that she could not be too careful. This was no ordinary policeman, this polite young man, but one who saw what wasn't there; and made good guesses.

"I'm expecting me husband back tonight," Jane said as he prepared to leave, "but I haven't a notion when. Why not look in ter-morrow morning some time—when you're sure to find him?"

"Thank you," Henry Dickson replied, "I'll do just that. If he knows the river so well and from this point of vantage, he might be able to give me some useful tips on what craft he has noticed. There's been quite a lot of gold watches coming into market lately—we don't quite know how!"

"Just fancy that!" Jane said readily, "and with all those Police boats looking for them too! Well—George would be pleased to see you, whenever you could look in", she added, "I'm sure!"

The watch on Jane's wrist was not gold: it was serviceable steel, not worth smuggling. They both looked at it. Henry Dickson then cast a dubious glance at the cat, but decided to give it no more of his attention.

Elsie sat as if clenched on her favourite spot; her eyes were not closed, they were fixed musingly on a torpid fly. Sooner or later she meant to do for it, but she thought she would wait for the young man to go first; you cannot defend yourself while pouncing upon something else.

Both Jane and Elsie felt a little on the defensive with this quiet young man. It was not his questions Jane had minded, but his listening to her answers.

Jane dropped her knitting and held out her hand to him cordially. "Pleased to meet you, I'm sure", she said, and managed to look as if she was pleased.

XXX

Within half an hour of George's departure across the roofs, Jane was out in the street, a covered basket on her arm, and Elsie resentfully quivering inside it.

A brown blanket of fog hung three feet above Jane's head; a few vague flakes of snow balanced as if unwilling to fall upon the unseen currents of the air. It was so still and cold an evening that even the elements seemed afraid to do anything decisive.

The rush of workers returning home was already over, yet the stream of heavy traffic in the Commercial Road rose higher and higher; drays, lorries, thundering buses, hooting cars, shot by in one unending, moving carpet.

The police might be trailing her, Jane thought, to see if she could lead them to George; but it would be a foolhardy man who tried to follow as she weaved her way to and fro at intervals across the crowded thoroughfare, the wind of the vehicles she evaded by a hair's-breadth, cold against her cheeks. She was not leading the police to George, so it wouldn't do much harm if they did follow her; but she preferred to shake them off altogether. "I don't want 'em in me hair," Jane told herself, "George or no George!"

The lights on the Embankment dimmed to an orange mist. The buses, like shapes of prehistoric monsters, lurched insecurely above a stream of darkness, guided by their shining eyes. In spite of the sparkling lights upon its banks Jane could not see the river; she could only feel its presence moving beside her, as a deeper darkness, and hear the faint lapping of water against stone above the hissing snow. She gave a brief

214

glance behind her; the pavements were empty: no one had followed her across the bridge.

She crossed the Embankment rapidly, and, turning down a side street, saw a thin pencil of light shining beneath Rusty's garage door.

Jane pushed it open, closed and bolted it behind her, without his hearing. All the other men had long gone home, but Rusty lay absorbed and at ease on his back, in a brightly lit circle of tools and oil droppings, tinkering at the complicated entrails of a car he was exposing for treatment. It was nice and warm in the garage, and Jane felt that she had reached a zone of safety. An oil stove burned stickily beside Rusty, and there was a kettle, and two cups without saucers within his reach.

"George is on the run, Rusty!" Jane told him a little breathlessly, sitting down on an upturned bucket.

Rusty paused, tool in hand, gazing up at her with interest but without surprise.

"Cops on his tail?" he enquired. "I fort somepin' was up when you phoned you'd look in. Have a cuppa?"

Jane nodded and put on the kettle.

"Wot I've brought wiv me is me cat," she explained; "carn't take a cat on the run wiv yer, can yer? She might let aht a yell at the wrong time—Elsie—and then George 'ud do fer her. He gave her a narsty look ter-night, so I fort I wouldn't risk it. You take her for me, Rusty. I won't never forget it! Promise ter be good ter her! Promise the way we did at school—'Honest and true, black and blue, Cross me heart, and cut me in two'—then I'll know she's okey-doky!"

As far as a swivel eye can be steady, Rusty's wandering orb steadied itself on Jane's anxious, pleading face, while he slowly repeated her impassioned formula in his own slightly hoarse undertone with no expression whatever.

"I never had no truck wiv cats before," he told Jane after a pause for the oath to sink in, "but I reckon she can stay rahnd 'ere. She may 'ave her uses—rats abaht. There always is near the river. She'll 'ave ter tyke 'er chanct an' rough it

215

like the rest of us—but the men won't mind 'er, an' I'll see that she don't come ter no 'arm if I can help it."

"She's a bit young fer rats," Jane explained, "but 'er claws are good. She ain't everybody's cat, but you feed her well—an' she'll git used ter you—liver an' lights is wot she fancies most, an' I buy 'er a fish's head twice a week. She'll tyke anyfink else you eat yerself—in reason."

"You'll want 'er back when you've settled dahn agin, won't yer?" Rusty asked hopefully.

Jane gave a long slow sigh that might have been relief or despair. "Well—I don't rightly reckon on being settled", she said at last. "Not bloody likely you git 'all this an' Heaven too', wiv George, is it? 'E's on the roofs nah—an' wot's got awkward is that the cops is arfter bofe of us this time—though if they don't *see* George, they don't know fer sure that they *are* arfter him; an' if they don't see him *wiv* me, they don't rightly know if it is *me* they're arfter any'ow! Saw a plain-clothes guy this arfternoon—an' shook 'im! I guess I got them fooled till ter-morrow anyways. George'll come back fer me in an hour or two—at least, he says he shall; then we'll bofe take ter the roofs. He's got ter plant somepin firs', see?"

There was a long silence. The cigarette that hung chronically from the corner of Rusty's mouth burnt its way to his lips, so that he had to spit it out, with an oath. When he had replaced it with another and lit that, he said, "You always goin' ter run rahnd wiv George?"

Jane looked searchingly at Rusty. He had two front teeth missing, his dust-coloured hair was interrupted by a deter-mined cow-lick, his complexion was pasty and had the consistency of leather, and at least one of his eyes was never stationary. No Clark Gable, Jane said to herself, yet there was kindness in that unattractive but not ignoble face.

"Well—wot else kin I do?" Jane said at last. "George—he's tort me all I know, hasn't he?"

"*I* tort you 'ow ter drive a car!" Rusty reminded her.

"Yeah—so you did," Jane agreed, "but I wouldn't say there was any future in me driving a car, would you, Rusty? There's as many people kin drive cars as has 'em."

"There ain't so many girls can drive a car the way you drives one", Rusty unexpectedly told her, for he was no flatterer. "Nor men neither, Jane. You drive it as smooth as if you was strokin' a cat. Any engine 'ud run for a girl like you! Nah George—'e's a good driver if pace is what you're arfter, but 'e's death on engines—'e don't never study what an engine tykes—don't give it time ter breeve 'fore 'e's all aht!—an' corners—Chris'—'is tyres don't bear finkin' of! George got any dough?" Rusty added as an afterthought.

"He don't tell me much abaht wot he gits," Jane admitted, "but I'd say he has dough enuff—salted down somewheres—you don't buy motor boats fer nuffin', an' he's not too close-fisted on me clo'es. This fur coat I've got on—'tain't mink, I grant yer—but it's dam' good musquash—no rabbit in it! He says he has a peach of a car for tonight too! Daimler. How come he didn't hire it orf you?"

"Well, if you want ter know," Rusty said, "I'm bloody well thro' wiv George. I won't split on 'im, nor I won't work wiv 'im ner more, neither! 'E sails too near the wind fer me—George does. I didn't min' lendin' 'im aht a car at times—arskin' no questions an' cashin' in on it. I got ter save if I'm to buy me a Bugatti—wot I want fer racin'. But there is fings I don't 'old wiv. See? Dope—and *you* plantin' it—is one of 'em."

Jane nodded. She was sorry that the slender link with respectability, wavering between George and Rusty, had at last snapped; but not surprised.

She had always known that Rusty was too good for George. There was nothing to wait for now, but her own courage.

"You're George's gal, ain't you?" Rusty suddenly demanded.

"Sort of", Jane admitted, without appetite or conviction.

Rusty's hand shot out from under the car and seized the kettle. "Might as well 'ave a cuppa", he said with renewed zest.

He poured her out a cup and returned to his work, but his mind was still divided between the tricky needs of the car and Jane's dilemma.

217

"I'm not soft on gurls", he told her at last. "Never 'ave been—not got the looks fer one fing—an' any'ow I'm mad keen on cars. I've made a car fer meself aht of spares—she runs beautiful. She ain't no Rolls, yer understan', but anyfink there is in an engine I can git aht of it. Made that way, I s'pose! But I sort a took a likin' ter you, Jane, seein' you can drive the way you do—an' all. If it wasn't fer George, I'd say, 'Stick rahnd—earn somepin'—and we'll see!' But ter tell yer the truf—I'm afraid of George! If you're 'is gal, the man that touches you is arskin' for it."

Jane was pleased. This was her first proposal, and even put in the form of a refusal, it was a matter for pride. George had *not* proposed to her—he had taken her. Rusty would not take her, but he had offered her his heart. Jane had always guessed that there was something she could count on in Rusty: that was why she had brought Elsie to him; but she had not known before, quite, on how much she had to count.

"Nor yer muver don't like me", Jane said after a pause. "I wouldn't say I'd ever bin wild abaht you, Rusty. You ain't no maiden's dream ter me an' even if you had been I'm no slouch of a maiden; an' seein' we'd git trouble bofe ways— George makin' it fer sure, an' yer muver throwin' in her widow's mite—we'd better call it a day—hadn't we? I'm obliged ter you like, Rusty, orl the same—an' always will be. An' now I've had me cuppa—I'd better be gittin' erlong."

Rusty emerged slowly from beneath the car.

"You don't want ter cross George", he said to Jane earnestly. "You know that, don't you, Jane?"

"I know it proper", Jane asserted proudly. "He's that bad, when he is crossed—George—that sometimes I jes' don't know how bad he *is*! Might anyfink happen ter yer!"

Rusty looked uncomfortable. He knew that he was a coward. He should have taken George's place with Jane; and he had funked it. Still, he had agreed to look after Jane's cat; and he stretched out a protecting hand towards the basket.

"Thanks a lot fer takin' care of Elsie", Jane said. "Maybe I kin send fer her one day—and maybe I carn't—but I know she'll be O.K. wiv you, Rusty—an' that's wot I wanted."

218

Rusty slid open the door. The fog had lifted, but it was snowing harder than before, and the night was colder than ever.

"One fing, Rusty", Jane said to him before she plunged into the white whirling mist that curtained the traffic. "S'elp me Gawd—I won't do no vi'lence—George or no George. I seen enuff of it."

"Well—you stick to that!" Rusty advised Jane.

He didn't know what else to say to her, yet he knew that there was more that should have been said.

He watched uneasily while the small indomitable figure made its swift way across the Embankment, and on to the bridge, till the snow blotted it from his sight; then he went back to the flustered and outraged Elsie, who was not one to let him forget what she thought of him for letting go the only friend she had.

XXXI

The wind had come up with the tide, and broken the blanket of the fog. Snow was falling fast, and hiding, as it fell, all traces of man's urgencies.

London wore a totally unaccustomed and affronted air, as if this sudden intervention of ice-white purity, with its consequent slowing up of speed, had shaken her out of her own identity, leaving her—with her temporal aims and gadgets lying useless on her lap—mere "toys of desperation".

Jane gave the river a long, curious stare before she crossed the bridge. This was where beaten people threw themselves, when life was exhausted in them. Jane had never thought about the Thames before except as a floor for traffic; but now, as she saw it moving cold and livid by her side, she felt conscious of its speed and determination, even of its coldness, as if it were a kindred spirit, a part of her own blood. Both of them were escaping towards an unknown sea. Man had caught and used each, for his own purposes, yet neither was permanently a captive. Not locks, nor boats, nor bridges could keep back the river from the sea; neither Police, Approved Schools, nor even George himself could prevent Jane from reaching the depths of her own being.

She was no longer a child warm with illusions and inspired by unattainable felicities. A new sense of her own identity possessed her. She meant to get back to George, but she meant to live her own life with George. She knew that it would be dangerous to cross George, but it was going to be dangerous to cross Jane now—even for George to cross her. She felt that strange truth, known only to people with strong hearts, that when they lose what they love most, they lose fear with it. "I won't never get me a little cat again," Jane said to herself as she crossed the bridge, "but I'll stand up to George."

When she reached the short street leading to the dilapidated house, it seemed to be empty. If the police were watching it, the snow acted as a screen both for them and for Jane.

She found George impatiently shovelling everything he thought he needed into a knapsack.

"You bloody little fool—wot did yer go aht fer?" he demanded ferociously. "Didn't I tell you to wait in till I come—pack—an' cook me an eat? There ain't no time to eat nah. Once them cops start sniffin', it's no use waiting abaht fer them to pounce. Wot yer mean by it, yer double timing little bitch?"

"Keep a civil tongue in yer head, George, or you go alone", Jane told him with cold asperity. "No cops bin followin' me. If they'd tried ter cross a road after me, they'd have been left in strips!"

George spun round and stared at this new Jane. The child he had known was dead; what he heard now was the voice of an unknown woman. But there was no time for challenge or reprisals: the adult Jane must be dealt with later on; at present George had to work with Jane on any terms—even her own.

"C'mon", he said a shade less ferociously. "We got ter git over the roofs nah. I'm takin' no chances bein' held up in the streets. Got a car waitin' in the lane three blocks off. Take yer shoes orf—them heels is death-traps—an' step up to it! You keep yer eyes on this torch in me 'and. I'll hold it so yer can see what's jest ahead of yer. It's no arc light, so you got ter watch it! When I say 'crawl', you crawl—an' when I say 'lie flat' you flatten—an' when I say 'jump!' you bloody well jump—see? There ain't but two or three bad places where the roof don't jine. I'll give you a 'and over them. Rest's a piece of cake."

Jane nodded. She had crossed these roofs before but not in the dark when they were slippery with snow.

She pushed her shoes, skirt and pullover into George's sack, and packed with care her cosmetics in her handbag; as an afterthought she added a towel and a piece of soap. The

221

musquash coat she reluctantly left behind, replacing her skirt by a pair of woollen underpants belonging to George.

Jane had never seen George so hurried as he was while she made her short preparations. He breathed heavily, and interspersed her every action with curses. But Jane took her time; she even drew on an extra pullover before she admitted that she was ready.

"Newmonia ain't goin' ter lighten our troubles", she said severely. "The cops don't know who we are for sure yet—or wever yer 'ere—or in Hell—so what?"

George quieted down, and said almost apologetically, "No knowin' wot cops'll think—nor when they'll turn up. We'll leave all the lights on in 'ere so they'll think we're still abaht. An' Jane, don't you look dahn at the street lights when you're on the roof, fer they won't be no good ter you. Nor we won't start movin' till yer eyes gits used ter the dark."

Jane found the new flexible steel ladder firmer than George's old rope one. She went up it first, while George held it from below. Then with the dart of a lizard he was up beside her, the ladder closed up, and was swept into his pocket. She could only guess at his presence, for she heard nothing but wind and saw nothing but darkness; he had not thought of putting out his hand to reassure her by a touch; but after a time Jane became conscious of the tiny pin-point of light from the torch, which he shielded in the hollow of his hand.

George knew the roofs as a cat knows them: his feet moved with the ease and swiftness of his eyes. His whole body, whether sliding or leaping, or stretched like a piece of elastic over precarious space, was imperturbably certain of arrival.

He did not mind, perhaps he did not even notice as Jane noticed, the difference between the solid darkness of the roofs and the hollow darkness of the empty air. There was always just room enough for George to move where he wanted to move—no more and no less; but for Jane there were no such certainties. She had the torch to guide her direction, but she must act instantly under the flail of obedience: she could not judge her risks. Where the light led she must follow,

222

with no margin whatever for hesitation or dismay. George had taught her to steal with the same implicit swiftness; but what she was stealing now was her own life. Nothingness spread round her on every side, and once, when her foot slipped, it slipped into nothingness.

Chimney stacks comforted Jane here and there like living friends, and she clung to them or to any wandering pipe with an ecstasy of relief; but sooner or later she had to forsake their brief support and find herself on icy slopes, sliding towards flimsy gutters. Occasionally George shot out a hand to steady her, and once the three jumps from roof's edge to roof's edge were over, Jane knew that the worst of the climbing was behind them.

They were on the warehouse roofs now, close to the river; but here the wind and the flying snow became active adversaries. George slowed his pace and increased his caution. The wind clawed and whined at them—and their eyes were blinded by the snow.

"You 'old on nah, Jane", George called back urgently. "Ain't no cops can hear nor see us, but jes' you 'old on! Wind's enuff!"

There did not seem anything else Jane *could* do but hold on. The remaining question was, how long could she hold on? Her wet hands grasped the uncertain slippery surfaces of sloping tiles—a gutter gave a doubtful anchorage to one foot, the other was bent under her.

"I'll go dahn firs' ter keep the ladder steady", George shouted up.

There was a desperate five minutes while Jane held on and waited to find out what George meant by steadiness.

She couldn't see the ladder or George. Suddenly, just beneath the gutter in which her foot rested, something gleamed, like a faintly lit cobweb swaying towards her. She was so near safety she did not dare to think of it. At the bottom of darkness she could see the rear lights of a car. She had been holding on like grim death to whatever she found to hold on to, but she found that there is something grimmer than grim death—there is grim life, and it was to the grimness of life that Jane had now to transfer her precarious hold.

"Nah, Jane—swing on to it!" George called up, his voice harsher and more urgent than before.

Jane saw that it was to this dangling cobweb she must cling while she was launching her whole body into lightless space. She unloosed one frozen hand and fastened it on the thin steel rod, then very slowly she freed her foot from under her and let herself slide downward. Now the other hand caught the top of the ladder, and she was swinging out over nothingness. Her feet fumbled for the still thinner rod beneath them; they found it, slipped off it, and found it again. Now both feet were firmly on the rung beneath her; but they couldn't stay there—one foot had to go on alone as if it was certain that the other one would follow.

The ladder steadied a little under Jane's weight, but it did not stop the wind from trying to pick her off it.

George's voice changed from sharp fear to gruff relief.

"Yer bloody well near dahn", he shouted up to her; and at the sound of the relief in George's voice, Jane found panic had left her.

"Hop orf! yer little fool!" George reassuringly ordered.

But for a long moment Jane's hands refused to let go of the icy rung to which they had clung so long. She could feel her stockinged feet sinking into wet snow, but she could not make herself believe that the solid earth was under her. There seemed to be no room in her lungs for the air to reach her. George snapped the ladder off the roof; half dragged, half pushed Jane into the waiting car; and still she could not breathe properly. It was as if safety itself had locked her away from life; then very slowly Jane began to breathe with less and less difficulty. The car purred steadily on. They had reached the High Street, and the traffic swallowed them. Rusty could say what he liked about George's carelessness with engines, Jane thought, but George could certainly drive.

He slipped into traffic as a South Sea Islander dives under the first low ripple breaking on the shore, imperceptibly submerging and disappearing for so long a time that, when the

224

black head bobs up again, far out in the deep sea, it is impossible to believe that the swimmer is the same man who disappeared so long ago.

George's car, in spite of snow, wind, and traffic lights, never seemed to become stationary like any other vehicle: it was the traffic that became stationary round a fast-moving George.

Before Jane had fully recovered her breath, they were across the bridge and half way down the Embankment. The Strand, Haymarket, Piccadilly, passed them like cards flicked by a rapid dealer; Knightsbridge barracks flung its solid shadow across them; and then the long broad stretch from Kensington to Hammersmith shimmered under them, their wheels hissing over the falling snow.

They picked up the river again at Putney, only to throw it behind them a moment later. Abruptly George turned from west to south, and Jane saw that he was capturing the outskirts of another London. Houses became smaller and streets emptier; George drove more slowly. The snow lay thicker on the road in front of them, and no longer melted as it fell.

"Where we goin' to, George?" Jane at last found it safe to demand.

"I got a 'ouse I can go ter—on the river side," George said nonchalantly. "Light me a cig. will you, Jane? I c'ud do wiv it."

Jane leaned forward with shaking hands and put it between his lips.

"It's jes' the cold that makes me shake", she explained to George. She did not want him to think that her teeth chattered and her hands shook because, now the danger was over, she felt still more afraid than while it was present.

George's white, set face relaxed; his eyes, screwed to a slit from watching darkness, opened a little wider. Danger never came back to George once it was over; it was no more to his inert imagination than a puddle crossed.

"We gotta hide up for a day or two", he explained. "Man the 'ouse belongs to—'e's in stir—watches fahnd on 'im, same as might 'ave been fahnd on me yesterday if I 'adn't

225

looked slippy. An' you too, Jane—I will say, 'idin' them watches under carrots was good! Nah—we've 'ad watches! Too chancy gettin' away wiv 'em arter awhile. You an' me—when we do our next deal—we're goin' ter get somepin bigger than watches."

"Not dope?" Jane asked anxiously. "No good pizenin' people yer ain't got ner quarrel wiv—the way I see it."

George brushed aside this empty, moral reasoning.

"Dope pays swell", he told Jane. "No trouble at all—an' yer do it ter music. Them dance halls is a treat. But the top cops is on to dope somepin' crool. Desguised too—every dance 'all thick wiv 'em. Yer can't even trust a Teddy boy not turnin' into a cop on yer 'ands—knife an' all!"

Jane looked and felt shocked. Why, even Henry Dickson at that rate might turn into a Teddy boy; and look very nice in the costume too.

"Wot you an' me will do next," George went on, between the lulling mouthfuls of hot tobacco smoke, "the cops won't catch on to till it's bloody well worked—an' then they won't be so much wiser—either! Somepin' wot tells no tales, an' 'as no repeat, is what I'm after."

Jane suddenly felt colder than she was already feeling. It is only dead men who tell no tales.

Neither of them said any more till George turned off into the darkness of a side road and stopped the car before the blunter darkness of an unlit house.

It wasn't much of a house. There was no heat in it, no running water, and no food. The raw light of one unshaded bulb in the kitchen merely showed up the dirt. It might have been lived in, but it could not have been cleaned for a long time.

The kitchen contained a table, two empty cupboards, an old-fashioned stove, and a few rickety chairs. Upstairs there were two bedrooms. One had an iron bedstead, with a heap of dirty Army blankets piled on its mattress; the other had only a mattress on the floor, and a fixture washstand without a plug. Between the two rooms there was an unappetizing bathroom, containing, besides a rust-stained bath, a closet without a seat. In the more furnished of the two bedrooms there was a framed picture of a girl in a high-necked long-sleeved nightdress. She was leaning over a rock against which waves broke—waves that appeared to be higher than the rock itself. Her hair was less disarranged than might have been expected, and hung far below her waist. The girl clung to a cross that rose mysteriously from the rocks, and looked unsubstantial, but very well lit.

Jane stared long and curiously at this picture. Sooner or later, she thought, the waves were going to get that girl, cross or no cross; and Jane decided to sleep in the second bedroom that held only a mattress.

George put the car away in a barn, and finding the main, produced a supply of pale brown water. It would soon run clear, he explained, and when they got the stove going they would need it. At present there was nothing to boil in the water, and no fuel to light the stove. However, they could get stores in the morning. It was now well after midnight, and they could do with a little sleep.

Then George noticed that Jane was dividing the blankets. "Wot the bloody 'ell are you up ter, Jane?" he demanded. "We don't want no two beds."

"Yeah, we do, I'm sleeping in the extra room", Jane said firmly. "Ter-morrer I'm goin' ter tell you—jes' exactly what I *do* want, George—an' you can take it or leave it. An' if you don't wonna take it—it'll be *me* that leaves *you*!"

George stared at her speechlessly. This new Jane was like something in a nightmare—unpredictable and menacing. He could of course hit Jane. He could—tho' it would take a fight—have anything he wanted from her; but there was one thing that he saw he couldn't do—he couldn't change Jane. Whatever he did to her, he couldn't make another Jane. He saw by something in her eyes that it would be quite useless to try. The dreadful truth that a woman can be made to do whatever a man wants only as long as she wants the man who is making her do it, dawned slowly upon the unwilling George.

Jane gave it time to sink in. She neither moved nor spoke— she just looked at him. She wore his old pants, there was a black smudge across her face, her eyes were hollowed with fatigue, her lips were set in a thin red line. She did not come up to his shoulder in height, but none of these things made Jane look any less formidable.

"Poor sort of Moll I reckon you are!" George said savagely, going into the room with the picture and banging the door after him.

Jane bolted her own door behind her. Her room was icy cold and smelt of dirt; but she was free, and alone in it. She forced open a stiffly latched window and looked out over the lonely marsh. Not that she could see anything. No star was visible. The wind roared and blustered unimpeded across the flat land. If there were other houses there was no light in them. There was a faint and not unpleasant smell of seaweed and salt water, mingled with the cold freshness of falling snow.

Jane turned away from the window, leaving a small slit of it open behind her. She flung herself down on the thin, uneven mattress without undressing, and drew her share of the dirty blankets over her. All you could say was, Jane told herself before sleep swallowed her, that on a night like this, it was a damned sight better to be under a roof than on one.

XXXII

Half asleep, Jane put out her hand to stroke Elsie's small round head and to receive in return a sharp appreciative nip; instead, her hands touched bare boards, and she remembered that she had no Elsie. She sprang from the mattress to the window to investigate her new world. Three inches of new fallen snow stretched—a shadowless white sheet—covering in merciful oblivion chalk pits, rusty corrugated iron roofs and broken-up motor cars.

The distant low banks of the river were imperceptible behind its screen of rushes. Slowly gliding across the diamond-glinting snow field, a red-brown sail hung between earth and sky.

Where were they? It couldn't be London: there were too many empty spaces between the scattered houses. In the distance sparkled a small snow-covered town, but there was no background except the low grey sky. Worst of all, there was no George; and from the barn to the road there were fresh tracks of a departing car.

Jane fought down the first waves of panic that threatened her. After all, there were houses near them, and must be people in them. She had done enough to annoy George the night before, and he had naturally retaliated by leaving her alone. Meanwhile everything in the house itself was just as she remembered it the night before, neither better nor worse; and on the kitchen table she found a scrap of paper written on by George: "Gone out for some eats. Stay in!" It was not an affectionate message, yet it brought Jane instant comfort. George was coming back; and included her in his future prospects. There was even something to be done in the immediate present to improve their relationship.

Jane washed her face and hands in ice-cold water and unpacked the knapsack. Her handbag was her primary support and she proceeded to put on her make-up and comb her hair, with increasing courage.

It was, Jane felt, less likely for disaster to overtake a girl who was made up than one who wasn't.

George had forbidden her to go out, but Jane decided only to obey George in emergencies; this would show him how she intended to go on; and yet if she used her freedom to add to his advantages, it need not lessen his desire for her company. The main thing was that if George accepted her on her own terms, she *would* go on.

In the barn, Jane found a pile of old newspapers, damp logs, a heap of coal and a bucket. She had already discovered, below the kitchen sink, two battered saucepans and an enamel basin. She could make a fire, boil water and clean the kitchen. Jane was by now very hungry and thirsty, but her premonition of disaster had vanished. She drank two glasses of hot water and felt much better afterwards.

It was four o'clock in the afternoon. Snow had begun to fall again and it was growing dark, yet there was no sign of George. Perhaps something had happened to him? Perhaps her rebuff of the night before had been too severe? It was difficult for Jane, after having cleaned the kitchen for George, not to feel more tender towards him. Jane was still feeling more tender towards George an hour later, when she heard the hum of the returning Daimler.

George came in with a car full of well chosen stores, and in a pleasant frame of mind. One glance round the kitchen showed him that Jane was onto her job. She had collected all the furniture from the rest of the house and arranged each article where she thought that it appeared to best advantage. She had even hung the "Maiden on the Rocks" over the kitchen sink. Best of all, the room was warm, and in half an hour they sat down to slice after slice of well cooked bacon, and eggs scrambled to a feathery lightness. It was not George's first meal, since he had broken his fast at Dartford on reaching the nearest Public House, but it was the first Jane had tasted since her cup of tea with Rusty twenty-four hours ago—as well as the best George had had since Jane last cooked for him. With it they drank cup after cup of bright brown coffee that tasted as good as it smelt.

George actually told Jane where they were. This was a handsome concession from George, for he greatly disliked telling anybody anything. They were on a strip of marsh land between Dartford and Greenhithe, and they had got to stay there till the weather changed.

"I bought a second-hand radio", George explained. "That way, we know what's goin' on, an' don't 'ave to go aht fer newspapers. There's a point I can fix the flex in an' put it up me-self. We can 'ave the Light Programme on all the time. Cheer us up, I thought. We'll 'ave ter lump it 'ere till nex' Friday—Friday being the day I must 'ave fer wot I want, an' the roads not being likely to thaw till then, any'ow. Nor we don't want no nosey parkers turning up wiv milk bottles an' such. I don't want ter cruise abaht in that Daimler either—one thing the road is too bad—an' anuver the car looks too posh fer where we've 'it the hay."

George looked round appreciatively at the room, as if he thought they had hit quite presentable hay.

Jane decided to leave the washing-up till later, and to take advantage of George's pleasant mood.

George took the more comfortable of two ruined armchairs, and smoked peacefully. The feeling of comfort and security between them deepened. It was almost a pity to spoil it by an argument; but, Jane asked herself, why need they have an argument, since what she meant to suggest was for George's own good, and involved at least partially getting his own way. Unfortunately, it involved Jane's getting, at least partially, her own way as well.

"George," she asked, leaning forward anxiously from her rickety chair, "d'you believe in fair do's between you and me?"

She could not have put a worse question in a worse manner.

231

"Wotcher mean 'fair do's'?" George demanded. "Yer got your food—you got your clo'es—you got a roof over yer 'ead. Wot more d'jer want?—di-monds?"

"I'm not complaining", Jane answered mildly. "I work fer my eats, don't I?—jes' like other girls—nor I don't want di-monds—but there's risks I take other girls don't have to take. They don't have ter crawl over roofs at night—nor dope Loonies—nor they don't get the Police in their hair—same as I do. See what I mean?"

George did not appreciate what he was looking at. Still, he decided to give the subject another chance. It might be to his advantage to know what Jane was really thinking.

"Go ahead then—there ain't no 'arm gittin' things orf yer chest!" he said more amiably. "*Tell* me wot yer want? The bloody earth—I take it—same as most women! I fort yer 'ad more sense."

"You're thirty-seven", Jane rather unfortunately reminded George. "While I wouldn't say you're an old man—I'd say you was ageing. You won't always be so spry on roofs as you was larst night—nor able ter git aht of fings as easy as you git into 'em. But you're a clever man, I will say, George. You fixed up that radio beautiful—I'll turn on the Light in a minute: there's a good programme at six—an' wot you don't know abaht locks and keys isn't wurf knowing. How come you don't have enough sense to start a home wiv me—and live decent—before yer teef drop aht?"

"I ain't ole", George shouted indignantly. "There's not a cat burglar under twenty can climb a roof the way I can—nor move so fast an' easy over 'em! Yer don't want strength ter be a cat burglar. You want a 'ead and 'eels, same as I 'ave. Thirty-seven's no age any'ow! An' you're too young, Jane, ter know which side yer bread's buttered—that's wot's the matter wiv you! 'Aven't got yer eyes rightly opened yet—like a kitten."

Jane gave a short laugh. For so slight and brief a sound, Jane's laugh contained a considerable amount of experience, bitterness and self-education.

"I'm a fast learner," she reminded George, "an' I know wot I want—an' how ter git it! That's enuff ter start wiv, I'd say!"

232

"An' wot *do* you want?" George repeated less aggressively.

"I want a home—an' I want a baby", Jane told George with patience and clarity. "You carn't have a baby wiv'aht a home—don't suit 'em." The monstrousness of her suggestion had not yet occurred to her.

George dropped his newly lit cigarette on the floor and let it burn itself out.

"'Oly Moses!" he exclaimed in horror, "Wotcha mean, Jane? Might as well arsk for a n'atom bomb as a baby in our business! 'sides, 'oo wants a baby? Narsty, messy, squalling lil' things—'ave ter be fed every so orften—keeps you awake at night 'owlin' fer wot they don't want when they git it! I've 'ad babies!—an' when you 'it 'em, like as not you git an Inspector dahn yer froat! I jes' don' know what ails yer, Jane. If you was a drinkin' gurl I'd say it was D.T. Seen any Pink Elephants abaht 'ere lately?"

"Not unless *you're* one of 'em", Jane replied tartly. "Lots of girls wants babies, same as I do—an' likes 'em when they've got 'em. Anyhow, that's how 'tis, George. Like it or lump it—that's wot I mean ter 'ave. You know what I'm like—an' I know wot you're like—we c'ud make a do of it better than most. If yer want ter pick fings up on the side—that's all right by me, jes' so long as you don't act vi'lent. I don't hold with vi'lence. I seen enuff of it."

George stared at Jane aghast. He was not only furious, he was horrified. This was not his mascot!—and yet how skilfully she had negotiated the roofs last night, how obediently she had followed him! How cleverly she had staved off the Inspector! How well she had cleaned the kitchen and cooked his supper! He decided to master his rage sufficiently for diplomacy. Jane was little more than a child after all; and perhaps tired.

"You don' know wot 'avin' a baby is", George explained darkly. "You don't jes' go into a shop an' pinch it. Why, it's worse nor an illness! I'd a wife—onct back in the States; you wouldn't believe wot that woman went froo'! 'Avin' babies is tough—an' gittin' rid of 'em when yer don' want 'em before they're born is tough too. Somepin crool—the whole business

233

is! The bes' thing a 'uman being ever did was ter find aht—
same as I showed you—'ow *not* ter 'ave babies! I take my hat
off to the man who fort up that one!"

"Lots of girls", Jane said obstinately, "have babies sooner
than sixteen—some at thirteen! You go ter a good hospital—an'
it's a bit rough like fer a couple of days—an' then you git wot
yer want! Well—I've had it rough longer nor that—and *not*
got wot I wanted!

"I've made up me mind, George. Ef you don't want ter make
a home fer me, there's uvers that will. You an' me *can* stick
tergether, but it's got ter be the way *I* want—as well as the way
you want—or it don't make sense ter me to stay wiv you—
see?"

George started on a fresh cigarette. He smoked it half
through without intermission before he spoke again. He was a
good hand at long silences, and always let the weight of them
rest on the listener, not on himself. However, Jane punctured
his silence by turning on the radio. Jokes broke into the atmosphere of concentration and lessened his power to make it
menacing.

"You don' know what's good fer yer," George said impatiently, "same as a chile pickin' up a pizen pill an' thinkin'
it's a sweet! You're cut aht fer somepin better than 'avin'
babies, Jane! Why d'yer suppose I 'eld onto you an' trained yer
proper ter be light-handed, an' stick on yer toes? Yerse, an' I
risked a stretch—switching you back from those bloody police-
women an' jailer types—that 'ad got 'old of yer. Why? 'Cos I'd
never seen a gurl that shaped better fer wot I wanted. An' that's
the way I *still* want it! Mind you—I might change me mind an'
turn nasty—same as any man might arter the way you carried
on lars' night!—an' I wouldn't want ter fink wot 'ud 'appen ter
you if I did! But you play fair by me, Jane—and I'll play fair
by you! I ain't mean—nor you ain't mean—the way Ma was—
we c'ud make it! Nah—you say you want this baby? Well—orl
I say is yer too bloody young to know *wot* yer want! Nor I'm
not ready to quit yet neither. But that don't mean that I won't
never give yer no baby, if you want one—when you're old
enuff to know wot yer want—you'll git it! An' some day I'll

quit and live quiet. You only gotta wait! An' while we wait, we'll carry on the way that suits me best—same as before—see? Wot I'm onto now is big. You goin' ter quit jes' as I'm onto it? This is wot I trained yer for, Jane—an' 'ad yer tort that car drivin' an' orl! Yer might say I saved yer life fer it, when I picked you up on that desert road squashed like a tomater!"

Jane looked at George waveringly. His eloquence moved her —much of what he said was true. She was used to him. George certainly was not so mean as Ma. They'd just had a beautiful meal together. They liked the same things to eat and the same way of cooking them. There was only one warm room in the house. George had once—of his own accord—given her a kitten. Could he not be trusted, under pressure, later on, to fulfil her heart's desire and provide her with a baby?

"George," Jane said, leaning forward with desperate earnestness, to the sound of a ribald tune, which somehow made it easier for her to make the best use of her earnestness, "you promise—you *reel*, honest ter Gawd—promise you'll git me a house an' let me have a baby—when I'm twenty—say? Nor you won't 'urt it—when it comes—you'll act straight?"

George did not hesitate to promise. Why should he, when the promise would get him what he wanted, and need never be carried out? Perhaps George even believed for a moment that when the time came he *would* keep his promise to Jane; yet his small, shifty eyes stirred uneasily under Jane's gimlet scrutiny. Why did she try to look into the bottom of a heart that was only a muscle with nothing attached to it beyond the power of beating?

Whatever Jane was looking for, George had not got. Yet he took the trouble to go upstairs and carry down the mattress she had slept on the night before, when he might have let Jane bring it down herself.

XXXIII

George had always detested other men; as confederates he had sometimes had to accept them, never as friends; but for women, when he wanted them, George had a brief flowering of affection. Women could fit into his scheme of things. They gave him what he wanted, when he needed it; and could easily be dispensed with afterwards. If he had nothing else to do, pleasing women became for George almost a pastime.

He had, however, never before regarded Jane as a woman: he had thought of her simply as a useful appendage, much in the same light that a dog regards his own tail. He had trained Jane to carry out all that he wished from her, and not to get in his way when he did not need her; but now she appeared to have acquired a life of her own, and in doing so she became desirable to George as a woman.

If Jane had not known George so well without glamour, she might have been deceived by his unexpected and lavish attentions. He even went so far as to buy her a new fur coat and a bottle of scent, on the day that he had to spend in London making final arrangements for the future. This was the George that Adelaide had been attracted by, and Gladys had loved; but beneath the alluring surface, Jane knew that the hard core of the real George remained the same. No woman could touch George unless it paid him to be touched by her. Yet the long week that they passed alone together in snowbound isolation passed in unusual harmony; and if Jane had known what George meant to do, she would have enjoyed their careful preparations for the new venture.

The sky was at last clear and blue. A roaring north wind

followed the thaw for which George had waited. The roads were now free, and they could start on the day appointed; but George had not yet told her where they were going. The marsh land looked more unkempt and dishevelled than usual, lying like an upturned basket of dirty linen in a pool of slush. In spite of a slight feeling of uneasiness, it was an appreciative Jane who took her seat beside George, after locking up the comparatively clean house, which she hoped she might never see again.

During his day in town, George had "lost" their Daimler and "found" instead an inconspicuous but powerfully engined Ford. The Ford, George explained to Jane, had an added advantage, since it was not "wanted" by the police, but simply "borrowed" from a garage keeper, less particular than Rusty, on generous terms with no questions asked. They need therefore have nothing on their minds but the road.

This morning George drove with precise obedience to every traffic law, and at a moderate pace. He did not talk, because he was living out his plan for the immediate future, as a surgeon thinks out every detail of an operation he is just about to perform; and Jane knew better than to disturb George during this process. He only broke the silence when they reached London Bridge.

"Wot you gotta do," he told Jane, "when I git where I kinda slow up, is to watch out for a Buick—U.S.A. 57839. It's a new model Buick easy to spot—an' she'll go fast. We gotta tail this Buick, but not too close. She stops at a Bank—side street back entrance, off Chancery Lane—an' picks up somepin. I'll take yer near enuff fer you ter take a good squint at 'er. Arter that you don't think of anythink else but that Buick! You won't see 'er all the time—you got ter plot abaht where she is when you don't see 'er—before—or be'ind. I'll be watchin' for 'er too—but yer eyes is quicker than mine—an' I got ter drive. We'll be aht of London abaht four o'clock, an' we got ter follow 'er—lettin' 'er feel free. Won't be too easy ter keep where she don't feel us on 'er tail—an' yet keep 'er in sight! We don' creep up on her till arfter dark—See?"

"George," Jane cried aghast, "is this a hold up?"

"Shut yer bloody jaw!" George said fiercely in his old manner; so Jane knew that she must shut it; and that it was a hold up.

All the light of the blue March day vanished. Jane had hoped that they were on a black market job: a black market job would be risky and exciting, but it could avoid violence, and if you had a brush with anyone, it would be with the police, who were their natural enemies: a hold up meant violence to someone against whom you had nothing.

When they passed the Bank there was no sign of the Buick. George had to drive slowly round and round the block five times before they caught a glimpse of the car, and even then the driver got in and out of the Bank so quickly that George had to accelerate and slide forward into the main traffic dangerously far ahead of the Buick. A policeman stood at the corner of the side street, near the door of the Bank, and George had no wish to move slowly under the eyes of a policeman. In dropping back sufficiently slowly to pick up the Buick again, they nearly lost her altogether. Individual alterations of space and time were neither pleasant nor easy to make in the full, ordered swing of London traffic. It was Jane's business to plot the unseen movements of the Buick, as well as to relate what pace was needed in order to catch up with her. Jane could not hear George's curses in answer to her directions, but she could very well imagine them; and she caught herself taking a kindred dislike of the Buick. It was as if the elusive car had now become their common enemy.

Jane had not seen the face of the driver. He had moved too quickly, and her attention had been riveted on the car; but she had the impression that he was a young, thick-set man, shorter than George. She did not want to think about the driver, and she was glad that she had not seen his face.

While Jane was keeping the Buick in sight, George had to attend to the traffic rules and slavishly obey every policeman's white, raised hand. Sometimes the lights were against him, and clear for the Buick. At those moments George dared not over-speed to catch up with her; and it was just as dangerous to fall too far behind, for then Jane could neither see the car, nor plot where George was likely to pick her up again. They were hard moments on the nerves of a nervous man; and Jane knew that George was a nervous man.

Once out of London, it looked much easier to Jane, but the emptier road was not what George wanted. The light was still too clear and there was less traffic to hide in. Sometimes George had to let the Buick slip out of sight altogether, and drive blind. He was sure of her eventual destination, but he could not be positive what roads she would take to get there; and he must not miss her turns.

Jane prayed that they *might* lose the Buick. It was funny, since she had never prayed before, but it seemed quite natural to pray. It would be a miracle—but if there were a God—would He not be specially inclined to mislead George on such an errand? Miss Bartlett believed there was a God, as well as Snoutie; and Miss Bartlett was a sensible woman, not easily taken in. She understood almost everything. She had understood Jane; and no one else had ever understood Jane. Perhaps there really was a God, who wanted everyone to have a chance —even the man in the Buick? Had Jane known St. Theresa's prayer: "O God—this affair goes badly. See to it Thyself!" she would have prayed it. Instead, she uneasily remembered that Miss Bartlett had said in one of her chapel talks that every girl had to do her bit—what came of doing it was God's affair—but the girl's bit, God left to the girl.

"Light me a cig.!" George said out of the corner of his mouth. Jane took a long time lighting it on account of the wind, but got it lit at last, and carefully inserted between George's lips.

"I can't see no Buick yet", Jane told him conversationally.

"Yer don't need to!" George replied with dangerous amiability. "I know where she is nah—there ain't no need ter 'urry for a while—she's on a bit of straight she can't turn off. Wot yet got ter do is ter watch them bloody signposts—every sign there is—mileage an' all. Jes' call 'em aht sure and steady as we pass 'em—See?"

Perhaps putting George wrong about a signpost was Jane's bit? The danger was that George might be watching the signposts too. The Ford was a fast mover. Jane's eyes caught, but only just caught, in the light of their headlamps, every sign they passed. Up to now she had called the names out exactly as she saw them. She was proud of George's dependence on her faultless accuracy.

They caught sight of the Buick again breasting a long hill in front of them, and slowed down. Now she was over the top, and her rear lights dimmed and vanished. This might be Jane's last opportunity—and she took it.

Jane read the next signpost wrong. She gave George a right turn, where there was no right turn. They went on for quite a long way increasing speed before they came to the next signpost. Jane dared not invent the names on it since George might be reading it too, so she read what they actually were; and both of them knew that the names she had read out were all wrong.

George gave Jane one straight look; it was the terrible look of a ferret thwarted of its rabbit.

"You do better next time!" he told her.

George found a place to turn, and drove on without speaking. Sixty, seventy, eighty miles—the needle moved inexorably on. There would be no police traps on so rough a night. Jane gave up God. They were back on the right road again, touching ninety. They were almost on the Buick before they saw her lights. George slowed up, and the Buick vanished; but they were on her heels again now, at a safe distance.

Dare Jane deceive George again? The signposts were hardly visible now as they flashed past them. It was a good moment for misleading George, but something held Jane back —perhaps fear of George; or perhaps the sheer excitement of the chase—the instinct that prevents good-hearted people from remembering that the end of the fox they are so happily chasing is to be torn to pieces.

The Buick left the main road, turning left through a wooded lane. High, leafless trees clashed their bare boughs over their heads. There was so much noise from the elements that the Buick could not have heard the Ford creeping up on her.

George forced the Ford engine to its utmost pace; the rear lights of the Buick shone at them like the red startled eyes of a rabbit. There was a sudden crash—not a terrible crash, just a heavy sidelong lurch—and then the crunch of something breaking up under them.

"Car's orl right—drive on—turn rahnd—and come back!" George yelled at Jane—and was gone into the dark.

Jane heard the other man's voice shouting "What the devil—!"—but now she was in the driver's seat and her hands were on the wheel. The powerful car slid forward. She heard the roar of the wind in the trees, and nothing else. It needed all her strength to keep the big car steady against the wind and on the narrow road, out of the ditches that lay on either side. She must not think of what was happening to the man in the Buick. She must find a place to turn; and Jane went on and on without finding one. Just as at last she reached it, she heard a sharp, metallic sound as violent as the voice of the wind, but toneless.

George had shot the man in the Buick. The excitement of the chase was over. Cars do not race without drivers; revolvers do not shoot by themselves. Only men do dreadful things to men.

Jane got the car round and drove back. She could see nothing, but she heard George's voice with a note of triumph in it.

"'Op aht, Jane. You gotta 'elp me a bit!"

A long dark lump lay in the road that had not been there before.

"Take 'is feet", George told her. "We gotta git 'im into the back of our car—wiv you. 'E's unconscious like. You won't 'urt 'im! 'Old on to 'im like as if 'e was a drunk. I gotta drop 'im furver erlong the road in a ditch. Car's O.K. where it is."

Jane leaned down and picked up the man's legs. He had very good suède bootees on, that must have kept his feet warm and cost a lot of money. It took some time pushing and pulling the inert body into the back seat of the car. Jane could just steady him, when she got in beside him, from rolling onto the floor by letting his head rest on her shoulder and putting an arm round him. He was very heavy to hold. She did not look at his face, but she saw that his hair was quite fair and curled a little.

241

It seemed a long time before George was in the driver's seat again, and the car moving.

"You 'old 'im tight, Jane", George said over his shoulder. "We got ter git 'im away—so the police'll think it's jes' a car smash on a rough night—an' the driver walked off fer 'elp—See? Don't matter if they find 'im later somewhere's else—safe in a ditch—might be anuver man—keep 'em guessing!"

"Yeah—but he ain't safe——" Jane expostulated. "We oughta phone call fer a amblance, George—we certainly oughta!"

"Get 'im in 'is ditch firs'—" George called back, "then phone yer bloody 'ead orf."

George drove rapidly on. Nothing passed them, and they met nothing. The gale blew stronger. They had plenty of petrol, so there was no chance of stopping anywhere. The man Jane was holding did not move unless she pushed him, but he seemed to become heavier all the time.

"George," Jane shouted desperately, "seems as if I couldn't hold him up no more! Wot'll I do if he comes rahnd?"

"You go on 'oldin' 'im up!" George shouted back. "'E won't come rahnd!"

Was he breathing at all? Jane asked herself. The hand she touched was cold.

She shrieked "George! George! he's dead."

George stopped the car. They were in a side road under trees. There was a deep ditch close to them filled with melting snow. George said nothing at all. He simply dragged the man out of the car and pushed him into the ditch. The water closed over him with a splash. The man wasn't visible at all when George had finished with him.

"No! No! George. No! No!" Jane shouted.

George pulled her out of the car and shook her till there was no breath left in her body; then he slapped her face and lifted her onto the seat beside him.

He drove off before Jane could speak again or stop the sobs that were tearing at her as if they came from some will outside her own. He drove very fast; and they had gone a long way from the ditch before he said, "Give me a cig., Jane".

XXXIV

George put fifty miles between himself and the object he had dropped into the ditch before he paused; then he pulled his car off the road, onto a piece of common, high up on the Surrey hills. The wind had dropped, and the sharp air was sweet with the scent of frost-dried heather and bracken.

Jane sat huddled into her seat in a shuddering heap; once or twice she had lurched against George as they rounded a corner, but she had not touched him if she could help it. She had said nothing, and she had been of no help to him on the road. Now all noise and movement had ceased. The cold, impartial night wrapt them in its icy stillness.

They were alone, as Beatrice Cenci once felt herself alone in "the wide, dim, lampless, deep, unpeopled world".

Jane moved at last, but not nearer to George.

"Why did you do it?" she cried out. "Oh George—why did you do it?"

It would have been natural for George to have given her no other answer than a blow, but George's natural feelings had deserted him; he did not feel like hitting Jane. Instead, he wanted to be comforted and to make his peace with her. A strange spiritual anxiety had seized George, as if he must explain what he had done, and find some other human being to share the weight of it with him. Danger emptied itself out of his consciousness, and in its place George found nothing but fear. Yet what had he to be afraid of—without danger?

He said brokenly, "Gawd, Jane, I couldn't 'elp meself—could I? If ever there was a killing in self-defence—that there one was! Why, the bloke asked fer it! There I was—ready to do the thing the way I meant—I 'ad me best voice on—I knew my bit. I come a step nearer to 'im, cosh in 'and—'course I 'ad my gun in my 'ip pocket too—same as I learned 'ow in the States—but all I meant to do, s'elp me Gawd, was to tap 'is noddle! Keep 'im asleep till morning, that would! All snug sittin' in 'is own car—an' then, in a flash, I see 'e 'as 'is gun in 'is 'and! 'E didn't wait fer no explanations like—it was 'im or me! So—seein' it was me or 'im—it 'ad to be '*im*—See?"

Jane ought to have seen, instead of which she repeated in a stupid, agonized voice, "But what did you *do* it for, George?"

"Chris'! Wot would I do it for?" George echoed scornfully. "I did it for a thousand quid—an' there it is—in 'is case at me feet!—money that was ter be paid to men in a factory—all correc' one pahnd notes in a packet. You can change 'em as easy as you want 'em. I'll get rid of the case an' the packet, in a pond I know under the 'ill, afore morning. Safe as 'ouses— that's wot *we* are—an' fer why? 'Cos I got the whole bloody thing planned aht—an' it worked to a treat, didn't it, 'igh wind an' all?"

"But, George—he's dead!" Jane cried out, "an' he didn't do us no harm ever! He's dead! He's lyin' there in that ditch, wiv the water over him, an' we put him there!"

"An' wot of it?" George demanded. "'E's dead—an' water won't 'urt 'im none nah—will it? You don't 'ave ter think of things the way you're thinkin' of 'em, Jane. It's jes' plain soft— an' it don't git yer anywheres! You gotta think of what *can't* 'appen, and what *can*, the way I do! Firs' someone will report that there Buick's empty in the ditch. Man might 'ave walked orf lookin' fer 'elp—mightn't 'e? Bad night—road not ser good —wind enuff ter blow yer ter 'ell—nobody passin'! Next thing, the Factory reports—nuffin' turned up—starts the cops 'unting. By then we're sittin' pretty in Soho. Nice Greek fambly I know there wot'll put us up! Days arfter—maybe a week—ditch dries up an' they find the bloke, an' 'is own revolver wot I dropped erlongside of 'im! Might be suicide by the look of it. 'E fired it all right but wide—arter I got 'im. Might be murder too—seein' they know who's missin'. Takes time fer cops ter put two an' two together. An'—'oo's ever seen *us* anywhere near car or corpse? I turn this car in ter-morrer—no blood on it—nor on you—nor me. 'Cos why? Shot 'im clean fro the 'eart—wrapped 'im tight rahnd the middle, in 'is own raincoat! Never touched nuffin' wiv me bare 'ands. Tyres'll show of course, but wot's one Ford orf the Great North Road? Why, 'undreds of 'em pass every 'our. It's a cinch, ef you arsk me!"

George stopped for Jane's approval; but no approval came. Jane gave a queer little sigh, as if she had lost something she had been looking for, and had reluctantly decided to give up the search. The silence took all that George had said and left it hanging there, unsolicited and unshared.

Girls—all alike, George told himself, savagely; all over you for swag, and no thanks to you for the trouble taken in getting it! Still, George had to admit to himself that he had nothing serious against Jane. She had not cut up rough till it had ceased to matter; and she had kept her head when it did matter. She had acted on his orders promptly and with efficiency. Many girls might have made a fuss handling a stiff; and she had come round smartly with the car, just when he was ready for her. After he had slapped the hysterics out of her, there had been no back talk. Jane was only a kid, after all. What he had to do was to break her in gradually; she'd soon get used to hold ups.

"Nah", George said almost kindly. "We'll 'ave a spot of shut-eye! Too late ter try puttin' up anywheres—might cause talk. Yer get into the back—more room—an' if I'm not awake when it gits light, jes' give me a shake!"

Jane obeyed him with alacrity, but she still didn't say anything. She kept quiet in the back of the car for a long time; only when she was sure that George was fast asleep did she move again.

Very softly her hand closed on the door handle, and Jane slid out of the car into the cold, sweet-scented darkness. She leaned over George without a sound. He did not stir as she removed his wallet from his inside pocket; nor when she put it back again on the seat beside him, closed the door, and slipped away. There had been ten pounds in the wallet, and Jane took three of them. She thought that she had been worth three pounds to George for her night's services, and she needed the money.

There was a feeling of space about her; and in the hushed darkness a curious nearness to the sky. She stood, though she could not see anything, on the top of Hindhead, just above the rim of the Devil's Bowl. A star or two shone out of the clear darkness, and once she heard the deep friendly drone of a plane and saw it winging its way among the stars, with lights redder than their own. Although the wind had fallen, it was just as cold, and Jane had to keep moving, down, down, down the steep, interminable hill, with the backs of her legs wobbling like a jelly. It was no use worrying about the pain in her feet. Her shoes were the wrong ones for walking, but she couldn't take them off in that cold, and try walking in bare feet. She must be able to move quickly off the road into the bracken if she heard a car coming behind her. George might wake up any time and start looking for her.

It was dawn before Jane dropped into Haslemere and found what she was looking for—a call box off the main road.

It was an eighteen-penny call that Jane wanted, but she had the money; it was only the wait that mattered—that—and the right person to answer her call, after it was put in.

When she heard the answering voice, the dizzying world steadied itself under Jane's feet. "Miss Bartlett speaking!"

"It's Jane here", Jane said rapidly, for the light was increasing, and she was afraid of the open road behind her. "I'm in a spot of bother! Can I talk to you? Wot I mean is—can I come to the Home nah, an' not get the cops on me? I got the money; I c'ud come by train. I'm in a norful hurry. I'm wiv a killer—see? I jes' got away from him—but he might be erlong any moment!"

"If you came here I should have to hand you over to the police. I must obey the laws I'm working for", Miss Bartlett's quiet, inexorable voice told her, "but I can come to *you*, Jane, as a private person, without informing the police. Could you get to a London station where I might meet you?"

"Waterloo—First class Ladies! When can you make it?" Jane gasped.

"Eleven twenty," Miss Bartlett answered, without hurry or hesitation.

"O.K.", Jane said, clicking off.

There was hardly any darkness left when she got back into the road, but now the light itself had become a danger. Would George be content when he found Jane missing *not* to look for her? Would not the nearest station be the first place he would look? Yet she must find the nearest station in order to get to Waterloo. She couldn't walk any more. One heel was loose, and she had twisted her ankle once already.

The little station was empty when Jane reached it, but there was a bench she could sit on; and if a car came up, she could hide in the "Ladies" before anyone in the car saw her. It was the cold Jane minded; it crept up her legs and into her bones, till even her new fur coat felt like tissue paper.

Once a lighted train roared right through the station—and Jane's heart raced with it—the flying sparks in the grey dawn warmed her like messages of hope. But in a flash it was gone, and only the cold and the dim shapes of things that didn't move surrounded her.

At last the station woke. A man came onto the platform whistling, and asked Jane what she was doing there.

"Had a car break-down", Jane told him nonchalantly. "Me boy friend's gone ter git a tow—but I gotta git up ter Lunnon fer me work. When's the next train to Waterloo?"

The porter was sympathetic. There was a train to Waterloo just signalled. Jane was in luck, but she dared not trust her luck yet. There were cars on the road in full sight of the station, and any one of them might be George's car.

At last a small, slow train clanked its way in. Never had Jane found a home she needed so much as the warm, empty third-class carriage into which she jumped. Time came to a stop while she waited for the train to start, her head out of the window watching the station road. A milk cart drove up, a lorry, and then a car with two men and a woman in it. The Station Master appeared to signal the train on its journey, and

247

in spite of the gold braid on his cap, Jane couldn't believe that he wasn't George.

When the train moved on at last, and Jane knew that she was safe, she curled herself up into a corner of the third-class carriage and fell asleep as if she were in her mother's arms.

XXXV

The first thing that went wrong when Jane met Miss Bartlett was that she couldn't swallow the lump in her throat. There it was, hard like a cricket ball, taking up all the room, so that the saliva could not pass it; and all that she found to say for the first five minutes, and that in a choked whisper, was: "Thanks a lot!" "Okey-dokey" and "Don't mind if I do".

The next thing was that Miss Bartlett looked such a long way off. How could you talk about murder to a person who looked as if no such thing existed?

Miss Bartlett was, as usual, shiningly neat. She was dressed in a black suit with a touch of grey; not a hair out of place. She got out of a third-class carriage, but looked as if she had been born to travel first. Her gloves, shoes and handbag were a perfect match. It was impossible to find a thing that Jane wanted to change in Miss Bartlett's appearance, in spite of the fact that she attracted no notice at all, and never had wished to attract anyone's notice.

Jane, on the other hand, although she had taken over an hour in the Ladies First-Class before the attendant arrived, and had done simply everything that could be done, including methods of cleaning which no attendant would have allowed— such as washing the mud off her shoes in the hand basin— and something else that was not mud in spite of George's re-assurances—still felt inadequate and grubby, and quite unworthy of the attention that her scarlet lips and finger-nails sought to establish.

Jane had to remind herself—that Elsie had told her—Miss Bartlett had Private Means; that was why she could live in a

Remand Home surrounded by romantic beauty; and why too Miss Bartlett managed at pinches common to her profession, to sugar the bitter pills of girls in adversity.

Jane had no idea that when Miss Bartlett saw Jane's pinched face and the deep purple circles round her eyes, she had instantly realised that this was one of the times when money had to fly, and had said to herself regretfully—for the Private Means were small—"There goes my summer holiday!"

Miss Bartlett merely said, "I think we should be quieter if we took a room in the Hotel. Stations are so noisy."

She seemed to feel quite at home in the vast carpeted hall they entered, and said, to a dressed-up Doll behind a polished desk, who looked as if she were one of those automatic "No-ers" so common in places meant for the convenience of the travelling public, something so incisive as to soften her negative attitude into a submissive, "Yes, Madam. I'll see what I can manage."

A few minutes later they were in a big double room, with a table in front of a big gas fire that gave the appearance of flaming coals, combined with a creditable amount of heat. There were two comfortable armchairs on either side of it, and, through an open doorway, Jane saw a white-tiled bathroom. The bedspread was quilted pink satin.

Jane guessed that it was a bridal suite and must have cost the earth. A waiter appeared, as if by magic, with an immense tray of food. Jane looked at it with helpless longing, for she felt that even the smallest mouthful would stick above the ball in her throat, but she was amazed to find that after a minute or two quite large mouthfuls slid easily past it. The ball got smaller and smaller while Miss Bartlett talked of Snoutie's success at the new school, of Elsie's complete physical recovery, and of the daily adventures of her dog Tito.

Beyond a cup of tea when she had arrived at Waterloo too early to get a proper breakfast, even if she had been able to eat it, Jane had not eaten since the morning of the day before. She emptied the tray set before her, to the last crumb upon it; and then burst into tears. They were the right kind of tears now, easy ones that helped her to speak, just rolling quietly down her

cheeks, instead of the tearing sobs that had shaken her body
the night before as if she were part of an earthquake.

"You don't have to say anyfink abaht what I'm goin' ter tell
you—not ter anyone at all?" Jane began urgently.

Miss Bartlett shook her head reassuringly.

"You are free to tell me what you like—that is why I
came. I took the whole day off, so there is no hurry; and
no one will ever know from me whatever you choose to tell
me."

"It's this way then——" Jane said, after a pause to collect the
violently jumbled images which kept running before her eyes
like a Disney film. "I couldn't stick George any more! Don't
get me wrong. The way I see it, it isn't all George's fault—'cos
he's made that way; and having to git things—orf the record
as you might say—is his profession. But it didn't oughta mean
killing people—I know that same as you do! We hadn't no
quarrel with the man in the Buick neither—good-looking man
he was too—up to the mark and quick at the trigger. It was *his*
business ter look arter the money George wanted, and—if he
had a gun—to use it. But he wasn't ser quick as George—an'
couldn't be expected to be—that was his trouble! I was turning
the car when I heard the shots—so close tergether, I thought it
was only one. I was ter turn the car and pick them up quick, but
it took an orful time turning it against that wind! I didn't know
the bloke was dead—I fort he was unconscious like George
said—an' he was warm at firs'! It was when he got kinda stiff
an' cold while I was holding him up in the car that I felt the
diff'rence. Not all to once I didn't guess he was gone—but I
called out ter George I couldn't hold him up ner more. Then,
when George started pulling him aht—I knew! It seemed crool
all the same to roll him into that deep ditch—an' cover him up
ser quick!"

"Was this the first time George had killed anybody?" Miss
Bartlett asked casually.

Jane looked helplessly at her shaking hands. She had done the
best she could with her finger-nails, but they hadn't the right
look somehow, compared to Miss Bartlett's. Miss Bartlett's
shone as if they had never had anything to dirty them, before

251

she put the polish on. It was a natural shell polish too—not a coloured one. Jane's was bright scarlet.

"I wouldn't say George was a natural killer," Jane said at last, "but he's the kind of man you don't want ter cross: then he gits narsty. Rusty—he's a fren' of mine—he said ter me, 'Don't go fer ter cross George—Jane—not ever!' He knew! An' mostly I didn't cross George. 'Course we didn't see eye to eye always. I oughta tell you—right now, Miss Bartlett—that I ain't a virgin any more. You have ter give way abaht somepin wiv a man like George. Anyhow, I don't know fer certain that he *did* kill Ma. George didn't tell me he'd done her in, though I did arsk onct. Anyhow she *was* done in—an' a good riddance, if you arsk me—whoever done it! Wilfred—that's Ma's son— he *tole* me George did it—but Wilfred, he had all the pickings —so p'raps Wilfred did it hisself—an' I tole him I fort he did —ter protec' George!

"There *was* pickings when Ma died—believe you me—not but what she didn't live poor in a bed-sitter with no one in to clean it—ever—on account Ma drank gin orl the time on the quiet—an' knew she had a narsty temper an' might fro knives, if rarsed. She didn't *want* trouble—Ma didn't—she was rich. She kep' everythink in the Bank too—'cos her lodgers was mostly crooks like George an' me. We never got noffink orf Ma!—an' paid rent. There was some street Ladies in the house too—nice ter me, they was—perfec' ladies some of 'em! An' they was nice to George, I reckon, but they didn't git much aht of him. I will say—George isn't generous."

"He doesn't sound generous", Miss Bartlett commented a little drily. "I suppose it was George you were with before you came to us?"

Jane nodded.

"And George," Miss Bartlett continued, "who picked you up in his car when you were on the way to the school—upsetting the car you were in? Did you expect him to meet you?"

Jane shook her head. "He likes keepin' his plans ter hisself, George does," she explained, "an' nuffin' dahn in writing, he always says. He ain't ever tole me eggsactly what we was going ter do—till we were in it. 'Course sometimes he had ter

give me directions firs'—like on that dope racket at the
dance halls—or how I was ter hand over our gold watches,
what George and the skippers smuggled when we had the
motor boat—ter the jewellers' boys. But mostly George kep'
his contac's to hisself. He said it was safer fer me—an' maybe
it was safer—'cept Rusty—when George wanted him to learn
me ter drive. But Rusty you couldn't hardly say was a proper
contac'—he was pretty straight, Rusty was, tho' he needed
the money. And in the end he shed George—when he fahnd
aht abaht the dope, that was. I lef' my little cat—what I called
'Elsie'—ter Rusty ter look arter fer me, when we was on the
run. An' I will say this fer George, Miss Bartlett, he gave me
that lil' cat orf his own bat, an' 'cos he knew I was mad on
cats—tho' he'd have done it in arterwards if it had got in
his way. An' he got me this fur coat too—real Beever it is—
you can see fer yorself. Not ter say he bought it in a shop,
but he got it cheap from a fur raider he knew, an' brought
me a scent bottle at the same time! P'raps I oughtn't ter have
said George isn't generous—but you can't count on it. He
holds on to money tight. Besides, I earned what I got. I ain't
never been a kep' woman, Miss Bartlett."

"I should imagine that you earned it in more ways than one",
Miss Bartlett murmured half to herself. "Well, Jane, you don't
want to stay with George any more, I take it?"

"No—I don't, Miss Bartlett, an' that's a fac'!" Jane said
with emphasis. "George would kill me if he ever set eyes on
me again anyhow. He isn't one ter stand being let dahn—
an' my runnin' orf like that he'd think *was* lettin' him dahn.
He might fink too, that I'd let on ter the perlice—nor he
wouldn't see the diff'rence! But there *is* a diff'rence, isn't
there?"

"There is indeed", agreed Miss Bartlett.

"Funny thing," Jane said, her tears now dried, "I meant
ter tell you abaht—while we was tailin' that Buick—I fort
abaht Gawd. I prayed ter Him like—I did reely—an' then,
arter I prayed, I tole George ter turn, when I knew there
wasn't no turn. I fort we might lose the Buick that way, but
I couldn't keep it up when we got ter the next signpost.

George, he gave me one of his dirty looks, so I daresen't do it again. But I must say, Miss Bartlett, Gawd didn't do a fing ter help that man in the Buick!"

"He doesn't always do what we hope for, when we ask Him", Miss Bartlett admitted. "He has His own ways of answering our prayers, not our ways of wanting them answered. I think— I don't know, but I think—an awful lot is left to us, Jane, when we know what is right. And if it wasn't left to us, we wouldn't be His children—we should just be His slaves."

Jane listened critically but with a certain amount of respect, due to the fact that she believed Miss Bartlett meant what she said.

"You mean I was a slave ter George—ter do what he wanted, when I knew it was wrong?" Jane asked anxiously.

"In a sense—yes!" Miss Bartlett answered, "but you got away from George when you could, and you would have saved the man in the Buick if you could—wouldn't you?"

"Sure I would have saved him!" Jane retorted promptly. "An' come to that, I should have fort Gawd would! Easier fer Him than fer me—if you come ter think of it—seein' George couldn't touch Him—an' he could kill me."

Miss Bartlett did not dispute this awkward point. She moved straight on to another point more awkward still.

"All that we know, Jane, is what we ought to do ourselves —and even that takes a lot of learning! I think you did quite right to telephone to me, although you mayn't like what I am going to tell you."

Jane sat up. She had begun to feel sleepy, and she knew that Miss Bartlett meant her to use one of the lovely clean beds to go to sleep on, after she took a nice hot bath, because Miss Bartlett had promised it before the waiter brought in the breakfast tray; but suddenly Jane no longer felt sleepy, but devastatingly wide awake. What was Miss Bartlett going to say?

"You don't want to give George away," Miss Bartlett began in her cool, level voice, "and I don't mean to give him away unless you agree to it. I am only going to point out to you that—as you said yourself—George is a killer, and if you wanted to save the man in the Buick, and couldn't, you *would* save anyone else whom George might feel that it was necessary to kill. Have you thought of what it means, leaving a man who kills free to kill again?"

Jane drew a long, deep breath and started shivering.

"Miss Bartlett," she said, "I couldn't do it!—If it meant prison—an' he'd do me in when he come aht—I'd say 'yes'—an' risk it;—but it don't mean prison fer George if I tell on him—it means hanging! Well—right nah I have to tell you—I won't git George hanged—no Sirree!"

Miss Bartlett dropped the subject.

"Well—that still leaves what you ought to do yourself", she suggested. "You've learned how to steal, but you haven't yet learned how to earn your own living without stealing, and stealing always means doing somebody else harm. Even smuggling gold watches means that somebody suffers although you don't know who——! As for dope peddling—that means that you are actually helping people to torture themselves to death. Once you begin harming other people—you don't know where it will stop. I know you don't like murder, but you might get to put up with it—like George does—once you felt you had to have something you couldn't get without murdering someone. As I see it, if you have any decency in you—as I believe you have—you'll give yourself up, and go into an Approved School for three years. You'll learn there what you set out to learn when you left me—how to earn enough to live on, without stealing, and never—never under any circumstances, to harm anyone else as a way of getting what you want.

"There are plenty of other ways of getting what you want, Jane, *besides* harming people, although you may even have to learn to do *without* what you want!

"You have a lot to learn. Am I right in believing that you have the guts to do it?"

Jane was silent for a long time. This talk with Miss Bartlett was nothing like what she had hoped from it. It was almost as hard to swallow as if the cricket ball was still in her throat. Three years loomed up again before her, with women who pushed her round, no men at all—no fun and games—no scent bottles, no Dance Halls! Perhaps Jane might not have answered as she did, except for the night of horror behind her—the man in the Buick, turning cold in her arms—George's face when he had told her what he had killed the man for—and before her eyes again—as if she still saw it—the man's face as George pushed him into the ditch. She looked at Miss Bartlett and met the eyes which believed in her, and said, "O.K.—you win—I'll take it".

XXXVI

THE GIRLS looked at each other with astonished, affectionate yet appraising eyes: "Is this really Jane?" "Is this really Snoutie?" they asked themselves in silence. The seven months that separated them from their abrupt farewell, when George had swept Jane into his car, and Snoutie had been left bleeding on the roadside, had held so much, and such different experiences for each, that they no longer felt themselves capable of instant communication. It was as if the very species to which they had once belonged together had been divided, by a conjuring trick, so that now each spoke a different language: one had the voice of a bird, and the other the bark of a leopard. Yet they still remembered they had once belonged to each other, and had spoken the same language.

When Jane had arrived at Danesbury Close, the day before, Snoutie, crossing the hall, had broken all rules to dash into Jane's arms with the velocity of a bullet. She was instantly recalled by a flat, cold voice saying, "Esmeralda, what are you doing here? Go at once into my office, where I will deal with you later!" And Snoutie had gone at once, while Miss Patricia Duncan, who ruled Danesbury Close, welcomed Miss Bartlett and Jane with haughty indifference.

Miss Patricia Duncan looked larger than life and as if she could have ruled anything; but though she looked as if she could rule anything, she did not look as if she could have led a crusade: she had no enthusiasm.

Jane, who was feeling rather low, had not stood up to Miss Duncan, but let herself be led meekly away by a polite, smooth-haired girl who looked so composed and aloof that Jane failed to

257

discover if she were a fellow criminal or one of the sacred hierarchy who improved criminals. Jane felt as if the girl thought of her as something that might not keep very well if not immediately placed in an ice-box.

It was not till the afternoon of the following day that Jane saw Snoutie again, when she was directed to what was called a Common Room, where besides Snoutie there were several other girls, all behaving properly. Snoutie came forward to greet Jane as if she were a society hostess, and led her to a seat by the window that overlooked the Park.

"We can talk now", Snoutie told her. "This is our Conversation Hour"; and all conversation died between them as if it would never return.

Snoutie was still plain, but her every hair was in place, her clothes were well put on, her nose and her finger-nails were not only clean—they had been clean for a long time, and were no longer bitten to the quick. Most strange of all to Jane was the difference in Snoutie's manner. Snoutie had an air of assured self-respect; she looked both unbullied and unbullyable. She held her head erect and behaved properly: not as if she had to, but as if she wanted to behave properly.

During the seven months that they had been parted, Snoutie had lived in a place where moral, mental and spiritual training took place simultaneously; and by experts; while Jane had become an astute and wary criminal; lost her virginity; and been a sharer—if an unwilling sharer—in murder.

Snoutie was the first to break the strained silence that had risen between them.

"It's not so bad here, Jane", Snoutie began in a strange but not unpleasantly low voice, and with hardly a trace of the broad cockney that had been their common tongue. "Some of the teachers are lovely—they treat us just like friends—young too, so you can fancy they are more human like, and know what you feel. You have to do what you are told, but you're not told too often—and polite like when you are—so you don't feel pushed round. What happens if you don't isn't rough either, but you lose your privileges—and I'd say we have privileges! Why, Jane, we have everything! Television—radio—your own tea-

258

pot at breakfast—a Chaplain that belonged to the R.A.F. and jumped parachute jumping just like the men did! Miss Duncan's always there, of course, but we're allowed to talk to him as if she weren't—and does he speak straight? You'd be surprised!—and jokes too, every kind of joke except rude ones. Most of the girls don't feel rude with him either, and if they do, they don't show it. Blow me if I know why—they don't—it's just the way he is! Not any of us like Miss Duncan. She's not a bit like our Miss Bartlett; she's cold as a fish, and no one gets second chances. But she hasn't got pets, and once you try—she kinda notices—without noticing—if you see what I mean. Miss Bartlett took an awful lot of trouble to get us sent here; there isn't another place like it in England. She always promised that if you turned up again, she'd get you here too, where we could be together. But, Jane, you look awful grown-up now, as if you couldn't be much older than what you are—and kinda sad too. Have you been through Hell?"

Jane considered this question carefully before she answered it.

"I bin wiv George—an' I learned fings too——" she finally replied darkly; but she did not say what things she had learned.

There was another long and awkward silence between them. It was again Snoutie who had the savoir faire to break it.

"They call me Esmeralda here," she said conversationally; and it seemed to sum up the whole situation.

There was an undefinable atmosphere about the old house, as if centuries of culture and traditional living had so sunk into it as to make it difficult to use it as a bear garden. This was not the kind of home in which people had been accustomed to shout, beat each other up or injure the furniture.

Miss Patricia Duncan explained this to each girl on her arrival; and after that the Close itself, and the other girls already tuned to its atmosphere, took over.

"I kin see you're educated", Jane said at last. "How come you got it? An' wot is education any'ow?"

Snoutie found it a little difficult to answer the last question.

She smiled at Jane; and Jane found Snoutie's smile in itself revealing.

Snoutie had always had a nice smile, though she had very seldom had occasion to use it. Now it wasn't only straight from the core of her heart as it had always been: it had a sort of shy pride in it as well, as if whether Snoutie could explain education or not, she really knew what it meant, by the process of acquiring some of it.

"Partly learning things," she said, "partly the teachers their-selves. Most of 'em is real ladies—an' you know it—same as Miss Bartlett. And then you feel free here—somehow. I know there's rules—but you can see the sense of them. I know I oughtn't to have broken that one yesterday. I was on the stairs, which we can use the same as anyone else, and the door opened! I hadn't known you were coming and I saw you sudden like—so I ran——!"

"Ya," Jane agreed appreciatively, "that seemed *you* orl right, an' I was glad. I felt kinda strange—an' I knew I wasn't goin' ter have Miss Bartlett rahnd no more. I guess she fixed it orl up by phone in that Hotel, while I was asleep—but she didn' tell me nuffin'. Only I promised her I'd stick it. Maybe I'll take it an' like it—maybe I'll *not* like it—an' jes' take it! All is, this morning I had to see a raft of folks an' listen to their talkin'—donkey's years!—an' be asked questions. Awkward some of them were, but I managed. Miss Bartlett, she was there—though she's gone now—an' she kep' saying George made me steal, so it don't count ser much. But George didn't do ser much makin' as orl that! You know how 'tis—we lived by it."

Esmeralda nodded. The familiar, debatable land on which she herself had spent the greater part of her short life, where she had hardly known whether she did things because she wanted to or because she had to, was not so far behind her.

"Miss Duncan says," Snoutie cautiously asserted, "here we have a clean sheet. Nothing we've done is going to count against us. Everything here is to count *for* us. We can be just as nice as we want to be—an' we can learn how too—'cos they teach us. That R.A.F. Chaplain—he teaches us loverly; but now, Miss Duncan says, we're responsible. We can't say we can't help it any more, 'cos we can! And if we don't, all of us, now—Miss Duncan won't keep us. She'll send us to some School where they have locks on all the doors and Police whistles an' count the pencils—and no one can feel theirselves any more. Well—I won't say we're perfect here—you'll find out for yourself we're not—but a girl like that Maudie couldn't stay here, not for half an hour she couldn't!"

"We never was like that Maudie—you an' me", Jane said with a sniff.

Jane was not prepared to take virtue too easily or to invite its inroads; but she noticed what it had made of Snoutie; and though she was not yet quite sure, she thought that she liked it.

"An' when we're educated, what'll we do?" she demanded. "I know what I kin do *wiv'aht* education—I kin make me livin' easy enuff—an' I would have, if it hadn't bin fer Miss Bartlett—an'—an' wot happened when I was wiv George. I'll tell you orl abaht that sometime, Esmeralda, but maybe not jes' now! I don't like ter fink of it—an' that's the truv! When I try ter go ter sleep at night, it sorta runs under me eyelids—like a film—an' I can't stop it runnin'. Esmeralda is a long name; I fink I'll call yer Esmé for short. One of our tarts was called Esmé, wot lived at Ma's. Esmé—that's French—so you see I've learned somepin too! She was a Belgian—real nice girl, Esmé was—an' sweet on George. But that didn't do her much good—George not bein' one that took ter foreigners!"

"Esmé is a real nice name", Esmeralda agreed appreciatively. "I'd love you to call me Esmé. Well—most of our girls here— they want to be educated so that they can be Sales ladies in good shops, where they like manners; but some are going to be teachers; and me—I'm going to be a nurse, a real hospital nurse just like you see in 'Lady with a Lamp'. You know that picture? Only of course we have electric light now. And Jane, I want you for my best friend, the same as I always did, but I'm not going to do anything wrong that could stop me from being a hospital nurse—See? What would you like to be yourself, Jane?"

Jane, who had not quite got over being assistant to a murderer, stared dubiously into the distant, unenlightened future. If only she didn't have to see George again, she thought, how beautiful that would be!

Jane said at last, slowly, after a long reflective pause, "How good I'm goin' ter be depends on wot I see I kin get aht of it. But you go on, Esmé, learnin' ter be a hospital nerse if you like it, an' I won't do nuffin' ter stop you!"

XXXVII

Every morning when she woke, Jane found herself pulled between two terrors—the danger she was in if George was not caught; and the danger George was in if he were to be caught. These dangers plagued her simultaneously, and neither cancelled the other out. Nor could she tell which was in the ascendant, for newspapers were not accessible at Danesbury Close; and though the girls could listen to the News on the radio at 8 a.m. and 9 p.m. every day, the News of the World had not so far concerned itself with George. After hearing nothing for six weeks except innocuous information about European crises and Test Matches, Jane stopped listening in. Her fears slowly dulled down; only the man in the Buick persistently haunted her. When was he found in the ditch? And what did the police think of how he got there?

George had had luck, for since the night of the crime there had been fresh snowfalls, followed by a week's rain. Still, by now the ditch must have dried up; and even side roads in so small a country as England receive constant attention.

How much easier her own country was to hide in, Jane wistfully thought, with its enormous empty spaces, ubiquitous Ford cars, and thousands of miles with only oceans for frontiers; and what a pity George had not stayed there!

Then one morning, in the middle of Jane's favourite Grammar class, where she was learning to speak more and more like a Lady, a summons came to her from Miss Duncan herself. There were only two things to be expected from such a summons: a lethal rebuke or a court order.

Miss Patricia Duncan sat, as usual, behind her roll-top desk in her office, signing forms. She did not look lethal, and there was no sign of a Probation Officer; but a man rose up as Jane came in, and to her horror she saw that it was Henry Dickson.

"This is a C.I.D. officer, Jane," Miss Duncan observed in her cold-storage voice, "he wishes to ask you some questions. Please answer them as factually as possible. You may sit down."

Jane and Henry Dickson sat down opposite each other on two small uncomfortable chairs. No sign of recognition had passed between them. During their last interview, Jane had been not unaware of a slight feeling of mutual attraction. They were enemies by profession, but they were not personally antagonistic to each other. Had they been alone together, Jane felt something might have come of this basic attraction; but in Miss Duncan's presence nothing could be done with sex except to suppress it.

Neither of them knew quite where to begin; the Jungle in the person of Miss Duncan—was neutral. Miss Duncan did not like C.I.D. officers talking to one of her girls; nor did she like her girls re-entering their far from lady-like pasts, and sometimes behaving, under police scrutiny, as if they hadn't left them. Miss Duncan went on reading and signing forms with her eyebrows slightly lifted; yet nothing that passed between Jane and the Inspector was going to escape her.

"This time", Henry Dickson began, unable to correct a crooked grin, as his eyes met the unanswering pebbles with which Jane regarded him, "you look less like that snapshot than you did last time I saw you. Yet now we both know that it *was* taken of you, and that you are neither the wife nor the daughter of George Wilson. I believe there is no such person as 'George Wilson' now. 'Thomas Miller' has taken his place— alias George Marsdon—who has just been arrested on a murder charge. We don't know who he was before that, but no doubt there is a further list of borrowed names to his credit."

Jane wished that she had the power of a rabbit to freeze into immobility. She remembered that in a book on crime she had once read, the hands and mouth of a criminal were reckoned as give-away signals, so she kept her own hands lying loosely in her lap, and her mouth in the pleasant, unstressed line recommended by photographers; but she could not control her complexion, which she felt was slowly turning green. George was in mortal danger. One of the dangers she had feared had caught up with her; and she knew now that it was the one she had feared most. George might not have done Jane much harm even if he had found her; but by an inadvertent word Jane could hang George. The question now was which murder had the police tracked down?

"We have followed George's career very carefully since you joined him," Henry Dickson began reflectively. "We know all about the burglary in which you both took part, for instance, when you were picked up in a mink coat, and George got away with jewels worth £6,000, which have not yet been recovered. I propose to tell you now just what we do know, and can prove, so as to play fair with you; and also so as to save myself from having to listen to a pack of lies—like the ones you treated me to last time we met. I shall be much obliged if you will co-operate by letting me have a few plain facts in return."

Jane let her eyes slip away from Henry's. He was a nice-looking young man, but she did not want to look at him any more. He was going to try to make her hang George.

"That was my first house-break," Jane said defensively, "and I didn't get away with it."

Henry ignored this empty plea.

"We know, for instance," he went on, "that since George picked you up, you helped him smuggle gold watches, and peddled dope. You also did some kind of hat trick with George on your way between the Remand Home and this School, which involved risking the lives of two other people and wrecking a car. This enabled you to disappear for seven months under the name of Mrs. Wilson, while running a greengrocer's shop in Lambeth. For sixteen—which I am now told is your real age—that's quite a career."

"It is a career of crime, to which I am sorry that you have to allude", Miss Duncan interjected, looking colder than ever. She did not consider that Henry Dickson was handling his case in a conventional way; and it was only a conventional way of which Miss Duncan could possibly approve.

Jane felt that this gave her a slight advantage with Miss Duncan, and she proceeded to increase it.

"If you've managed to arrest George," Jane said with a touch of pathos, "you've seen him—and maybe you know now that I hadn't much choice. I mostly did like he said—pardon my grammar, I mean, what he said. As for the pick-up, when he got a friend to run down our car—I hadn't a clue!—no more than Snoutie had, as she'll tell you if you arsk her."

"Who's Snoutie?" Henry Dickson demanded, taking out his notebook.

Jane risked a glance at Miss Duncan, and seeing that she looked less sympathetic than before, hastily amended her statement.

"We call her Esmeralda here," Jane explained to Henry, "and she's just my girl friend."

"Esmeralda is her name," Miss Duncan announced haughtily, to the air rather than to either of them, "nor should she be dragged into this very disagreeable affair under any names. Esmeralda was not implicated, Officer; and her behaviour here has always been *most* exemplary. Jane, 'one of my girl friends' is the correct designation! We do not *specialise* in friendships under this roof."

Henry Dickson cleared his throat apologetically, and there was a long silence. Jane thought it advisable to hang her head.

"You were with George at Ma's, weren't you?" Henry broke the silence by asking Jane briskly. "In other words, Mrs. Best. I should like you to tell me when you went to Mrs. Best's and how long you were there—and also any details that you happen to know about Mrs. Best's death. She happened to be murdered too," Henry added drily.

Jane did not like the word "too". Otherwise Ma's death was the least of her anxieties. George had told her that his alibi was water-tight; and it had all happened when Jane was safe in a Remand Home. Her hands took a more natural pose, and she crossed her legs, which was a forbidden attitude, under Miss Duncan's eyes; but they were pretty legs, and

Jane thought that it would do no harm letting Henry notice them.

"Anyone", Jane began cheerfully, "could have done Ma in—and mos' people she knew, wanted to! No need to pick on George. He was away at the time, as I happen to know, and he and Ma were never on bad terms—not that there were any heart throbs between them—far from it! But they knew their onions—Ma and George—that I will say for them! If I'd seen what Ma did to her cat Rundle—that reely belonged more to me than to her—I'd have killed her myself—if I'd had to swing for it! But you can't pin anything on me 'cos I was with Miss Bartlett when Ma popped orf, an' didn't know a thing abaht it, for donkey's years afterwards. As for when I first went to Ma's—it was after George fahnd me—kicked out of camp at three o'clock in the morning by a sky pilot with a face like a raw turnip. A cole night it was—and George jes' slipping orf from a house he'd visited. He saw me shivering-like beside his car; I fought he might give me a pick-up—and so he did—an' that pick-up lasted till I got cotched in the mink coat. So now you know—an' if you want ter know who-dun-it—I mean, did Ma in—I'd say it was her son Wilfred. He'd always got his knife into Ma—seein' he fought his father croaked too sudden—an' I shouldn't wonder if that guy wasn't dead right about his Pa. Anyhow, Wilfred got all the pickings—an' there was some pickings arfter Ma died, believe you me!—ernuff ter set Wilfred up in the furniture world. Furniture King—you might call Wilfred now!"

"You are not speaking at all correctly," Miss Duncan said to Jane severely, "and Inspector Dickson only wishes to hear salient facts—not idle speculations, especially not malicious ones."

Jane blinked and uncrossed her legs. She would gladly have given a year of her young life for a cigarette, and something in Henry's eyes assured her of an equal yearning.

"One other point you might clear up for me about yourself", Henry began again. "This business about your remote past—before you met George, I mean. Could you tell me who your

267

parents really were? And are you quite sure that you were not born in America? You see, we have been checking up on that former story of yours, as well as about those American Camps, which a psychologist you saw thinks never existed. It seems strange to us that we can find no trace of any of your former addresses, no registration of your mother's death, nor any sign of your presence at the schools you presumably attended if you were in this country up to the age of twelve—after which you might perhaps have succeeded in fooling the School Inspectors as to your real age."

"I didn't know what the word education meant till I came here", Jane said with a look of heart-felt gratitude towards the roll-top desk.

Miss Duncan's expression softened. She was not easily deceived by flattery from delinquent girls, but flattery that strengthens our chief aim in life is hard to resist completely unmollified. Miss Duncan really wished to educate her girls; and she thought less favourably of the Inspector and more favourably of Jane from that moment. Jane knew that she had won an ally; and Henry Dickson knew that he had lost one. He cursed his luck and tried again.

"George", he said, "claims that he has never left England or had a passport; and under his various names we cannot prove that he is not stating the truth. Yet there was a man uncommonly like George, called Dawson—also George—who came over from U.S.A. with a girl aged twelve, four years ago. It would help us considerably in our researches into George's past if we could prove that he was this man—and that you were the girl; and I don't see that you can suffer by the change. An American citizen is a pretty good sort of thing to be now-a-days—even in this country—and since you were only twelve when you came over, there isn't anything fresh that can be brought against you."

Jane sat very stiffly on her chair, her eyes turned to pebbles again. Her lips almost formed the words "sez you!" but not quite.

"Yankee Jane", Jane said to herself, "only murdered her stepmother—an' p'raps her Pa—still, that's not a racket I want ter be mixed up in! George won't give me away I guess—nor I won't give him away, but, Gawd, this guy arsks some pretty awkward questions!"

There was a long careful pause before Jane's eyes became human again and she was prepared to go on with her self-made history.

"'Course I went to schools—on an' orf, as you might say", Jane explained. "My Ma and me were what you might call 'migrants', if you know what I mean—here today and gone ter-morrer—though my Pa and I were British and praad ter be! Schooling wasn't my long suit and I lef' orf when I was eleven, looking more than my age, and knowing what I needed. When I was twelve my muver died. I hadn't nothink ter do with certificates, but it was then my Pa—who was a merchant navy man—hooked it. I thought a lot of my Pa—but when I talk I guess I talk like my Ma. Orl I said abaht American Camps is gospel true—like home they was ter me—I jes' took to those guys like a duck takes to water!" "And what's more", Jane told herself triumphantly, "after all that sex business wiv George, no one can prove I didn't! That's the time that psychologist missed the 'bus! Not that I blame him for acting decent to me, but he could have caught me aht that time—now no one can! So I know one of the things sex is good for anyhow!"

"It is not very desirable to open up the subject of Jane's early life unless it is strictly necessary for your enquiry, Inspector", Miss Duncan said warningly.

Henry dropped the subject.

"Exactly what were you doing", he asked, with his pencil poised but his eyes on Jane, not on his notebook, "on March 2nd of this year—when you were seen at Haslemere station in Surrey, at seven o'clock in the morning, asking for a train to Waterloo? There was a heel off one of your shoes, and you looked as if you had been out in the storm of the previous night."

Jane riveted her eyes on her house shoes, heel-less ones that she would never have chosen. She knew that she must give herself plenty of time to answer this question. What she said now might implicate George. Nor did she know if George was already implicated or not. One unnecessary lie might dish them both. She couldn't have walked far on an icy road down that tremendous hill. And from whom was she walking away when she did walk? One thing was certain: George would never wish to be traced to any place where he *had* actually been. It had better, then, be somebody else than George with whom she had passed the night.

"As a matter of fac'," Jane began slowly, raising eyes of gimlet steadiness to Henry's, "I'd had words wiv George the day before—so I'd taken an evening orf wiv another guy—Joe his name was. He had a posh car—one of those Lancias—an' we'd been quite aways—to a roadhouse where there was dancing, on the Surrey side." Jane paused, less for breath than for invention. "I guess I was kinda worried", Jane went on with renewed zest, "thinkin' what George might say when I got back—an' then this Joe guy, wanting to get orf too quick-like on the mark—an' I never havin' meant anythink serious myself—while he was paying the bill, I kinda faded out. You're right, it was a Gawd-awful night—an' I got thinkin' while I was aht in it, all on my lonesome's—wever what I had was worth it. An' when I got the train ter Lunnon, I'd sorta decided not to go back to George at all. So I rung up Miss Bartlett—and she says this was the place for a fresh start—and how right she was —and here I am!"

Jane gave a long breath of relief. She hoped that she had managed to tell a story that would hold water. It sounded good, and Miss Duncan looked pained but convinced by it. Yet there was Henry Dickson with his poker face—not making any notes at all in his notebook, and with one eyebrow hooked higher than the other, like a human question mark.

Telling lies to someone who may know the truth, Jane thought, is like listening to one half of a telephone conversation. You get the gist of what is going on, but you may very well miss the most important point.

"Miss Bartlett tells me you no longer wish to remain with George", Henry obligingly admitted.

"O.K.", Jane replied, drawing a deep breath of relief, "an' if you want to know what put me orf George, it was feeding them loonies dope in the dance halls—shocking, I call it."

This was quite safe, Jane told herself. Henry had already mentioned dope, and both Miss Duncan and Henry would feel sympathy with this reason for leaving George. It sounded foolproof. Miss Bartlett would certainly not have disclaimed it. She would say nothing except that Jane had wanted to leave George. She would say this, if necessary, to Judge, Jury and the Recording Angel—and none of those Powerful Forces would get anything more out of Miss Bartlett, since she had promised Jane to hold her tongue. Morally speaking, perhaps Miss Bartlett had no right to act as an accomplice to a criminal child; but Jane knew that she would act like one; and this was the reason that she loved Miss Bartlett. Nor had Jane known what real love was until she loved her.

Henry Dickson had already been up against Miss Bartlett's inviolability, and knew when he was beaten. He would hear no more about George's activities from either Jane or Miss Bartlett; but he had by no means shot his bolt. There were indirect methods of acquiring information of which he was past master. Henry leaned forward and fixed Jane's attention with his ironic and yet curiously friendly eyes.

"I'm just going to tell you a little story," he said, "and I want you to listen carefully while I tell it, and see if there's anything in it that reminds you of something you already know."

Jane nodded. If he did the speaking it would save her from any further trouble. There was something in the way Henry listened that always disconcerted her; it was as if he knew beforehand that what she was saying was not true. Had her chair been any more comfortable Jane would now have leaned back in it.

Then Henry began to reconstruct the day that they had tailed the man in the Buick. He didn't say anything about the storm, nor how they had escaped out of it across the roofs to the house in the chalk pits, after his last interview with Jane. Perhaps they had fooled him by their flight, and he didn't really know how or where George and Jane had gone; but he made terribly good guesses. He knew all about the man in the Buick. Jane's eyes never moved from Henry's face. She found she couldn't move them. She didn't like to hear that the man in

271

the Buick had a wife and two children. Jane had a vague impression that Miss Duncan had stopped signing things and was listening too.

It was always a quiet school in the middle of the morning because the girls were all at their classes; but there were usually household noises, and now there seemed to be none. Henry began to tell them about what would happen to the man in the Buick if the car that was following him caught up with him. The storm prevented the man in the Buick from knowing that he was being followed, but because he was taking care of other people's money he was always anxious. Then the car crashed into him; and he knew.

From that moment Henry seemed to have seen with his own eyes exactly what took place. Even George's thoughts seemed to be going through his mind; and Jane's obedience to them.

When Henry stopped speaking there was a long silence. At last Jane turned supplicating eyes on Miss Duncan's shocked face. "Please," she said, "now that norful story is done—that don't remind me of nothing—seeing it's worse nor anything I ever saw on the flicks—may I go to the toilet and vomit? I feel kinda sick to my stummick."

Miss Duncan gave a hasty consent.

As Henry Dickson was on his way out, he passed the lavatory door and heard that Jane was really being sick; and then he knew for the first time that the story he had been telling her was true.

XXXVIII

There was no one in the hall as Jane shut the lavatory door softly behind her and stood alone with freedom. She was only entitled to this moment's sudden privacy by the inadvertent advantage of having just been sick. What could she do with it?

It was raining, and the long hall was full of shadows. Standing just below the wide, shallow staircase was a marble statue of Hercules larger than life-size. He was swinging a club and accompanied by a wild boar. Gazing up at him now in his white solitary splendour, Jane wished that she could talk to him. The statue was so heavy and of so little saleable value that it had been left behind by its former owners, and the local council when purchasing Danesbury Close decided that they might be excused from the expense of moving it, by its educational value as a classical subject. Hercules was practically naked, and the girls when they first got there made rude jokes about him. Jane had made some of the rudest; but in the mood she was in, she now clung to the sight of him as a support. If only he could communicate to her some of his muscular strength! Her legs still shook under her, and she was without the reassurance of either a weapon or a wild boar.

Jane, with all her passionate sense of activity at bay, gazed wistfully up at him. Hercules strode forward on his wide marble plinth as if nothing in the world could prevent him from carrying out his purposes. If Jane tried to escape now, she knew that she could not, alone and unaided, reach George; nor was she altogether sure that she even wanted to reach George; but her whole being was bent on somehow or other helping him. There was nothing, however, that Hercules could do about it: nor, at the moment, anyone else. Esmeralda would give Jane her whole sympathy, but Esmeralda knew nothing about the Law. Miss Duncan was part of the Law itself, and would certainly never assist anyone to evade it. Most of the teachers in the School were clever, but they did not seem to be clever in the right way. They would think it clever, for instance, *not* to help George.

By now Jane had stopped feeling faint, and her legs—perhaps stiffened by gazing at the magnificent muscles of Hercules—wobbled no more. She reminded herself that it was quite easy to go back into the cloak-room, drop out of the window into the shrubbery, and keeping out of sight of the house, make for the drive gates. They were not locked; the girls, sufficiently supervised and pleasantly tamed, did not go through them unaccompanied.

Once out on the main road Jane took to her heels and ran. Time was the essence of her problem. She had a few shillings in her pocket; just enough for a trunk call. There was still the danger that Miss Bartlett might be out; but Miss Bartlett wasn't out, and she didn't have even to be told who was speaking to her, or from where. She said at once, as if she had been sitting at the telephone with the receiver in her hands, "Yes, Jane, I've read about George. You know he's only on remand: by our law he is considered innocent until he is proved guilty. He's locked up, but it's not like prison. He will have all kinds of privileges and see his Counsel whenever he likes."

"He's gotta have a *good* Counsel, Miss Bartlett," Jane urged, "the best money can buy—he'll need it. Can you see George for me?"

"I can communicate with him," Miss Bartlett said consideringly, "if it is advisable, through his Counsel."

"You gotta choose a Counsel first", Jane told her. "George is stingy, but he's got the dough. I'll see he pays you back later—you git the best Counsel there is for George. Will you do that, Miss Bartlett?"

There was a long silence at the other end of the telephone as if Miss Bartlett was thinking out her answer with extreme

274

caution, then she said, "I think I ought to tell you, Jane, that George has already appeared before the chief magistrate at Bow Street, and reserved his defence. You see, that means that the police have sufficient evidence for George to be tried for murder and that the Prosecutor's case has been heard by the Chief Magistrate and will now go before the Court at the Old Bailey. This does not, of course, mean that the jury will accept the Prosecutor's case when they have heard the defence; but George is in prison now—on remand—and must stay there until the trial. I *do* know of a good K.C., who is considered one of our most successful defence barristers—Mr. Emery Poulton Waters. If he consents to take George's case he might want to call you as a witness. He would wish to see you first, and Miss Emsley could arrange this for you. Is there anything else you want to ask me?"

"Well—it's this way," Jane said consideringly, "I don't mind getting into this thing wiv George if it'ull help him. I *was* in it wiv him, but if I tell one story and he tells anuver it won't be so good—see what I mean?"

"What have you said so far?" Miss Bartlett asked, "and to whom have you said it?"

"Well—it's that guy that calls hisself Henry Dickson—cop o' course, but plain clo'es—an' talks polite. I jes' seen him. What I said was—that I was wiv anuver fella at a dance hall on the Surrey side—the night of the storm. Couldn't very well help saying I was at Haslemere, 'cos a porter at Haslemere Station gave me away; an' I said anuver fella 'cos George being there hisself—wouldn't want it ter be thought he *was* there— not bloody likely—would he? I beg your pardon, Miss Bartlett, I'm sure, but I'm in a bit of a jam an' the word escaped me. George always says, 'Nothing like bein' somewhere else if anything's traced to you'. Then I tole the guy—that Henry Dickson—I'd lef' the fella I was wiv on account of his being fresh—an' was on my way to you—correc'?"

"Quite correct, the last part of your statement," agreed Miss Bartlett, "and I suppose they can't disprove the first part of your story, though it's always wiser to tell the police the truth, since they are almost certain to find it out, sooner or later.

However, George is not likely to have involved you, unless he went to the station to look for you and got involved himself. Have you envisaged that possibility?"

"Yeah, that worried me a lot, an' he might have done jes' that. I kinda expected he might turn up, while I was at the station waiting—cold as sin it was too—wiv no one abaht. But George has sense; if he woke late he wouldn't go to no station. Stations aren't places you want ter arst questions at. He might drive past like—but if he didn't see me, he wouldn't stop. He'd more likely sprint a bit so as ter git to Lunnon early an' git rid of his car. It wasn't a hot car—but he'd want to turn it in—before questions started at the garridge. Garridges is where cops start early on, arsking questions. One fing I'm dead sure on—we wasn't followed in that storm. An' I don't fink they knew we was in those chalk pits neither! What they followed for quite a while when we lef' Lambeth was a Daimler anyhow! They might have seen us pass the Bank, the day we picked up the Buick; but then it was the Ford we was in. George had ter go kinda slow fer me to catch onto what we were following; but we didn't stop—nor they couldn't know we was spotting that there Buick. Have you got any gen as to what's in their minds, Miss Bartlett?"

"If I had it wouldn't be my business to tell you, Jane", Miss Bartlett said drily. "I am supposed to be on the side of the law. I work for it—but I work for something else as well —another law perhaps. If I can help you, Jane, according to the law of my conscience, I shall do so."

"Well," Jane went on, listening to but hardly taking in what Miss Bartlett had said, "the way I played it was they couldn't prove I *was* wiv George—an' it 'ud be better fer George if they couldn't. But now I'm not so dead sure I was right. Maybe I'd better say I was wiv George all the time—an' cu'd see he didn't do no murder. Whatever happened was in self-defence—or defending me—or somepin'! If I only knew how much that guy *knew*, Miss Bartlett! I'd say all I tole him before was lies ter save myself—but that I couldn't lie on oath—I had to say the truth as a witness; an' then I could fink up somepin' that would save George. Can you git me to the trial? I jes' *must* be there!

Can I git called as a witness? Can you git that there Defence Counsel to ask me somehow, Miss Bartlett?"

"I'm not sure, Jane, either what I can do or what I ought to do", Miss Bartlett said after a pause. "One thing I want you to get quite plainly into your head is that you won't help George by being involved in the murder. You are under age, and were acting under duress. Had you been over eighteen, you would have been called as an accomplice and would have had to stand your trial with George. As it is you are not on trial, and I doubt if your acting as a witness would be of any use to him; it might even prejudice the jury against him. What I might do is to see George's Counsel and tell him that you are prepared to act as a witness in George's defence, if he thinks it would benefit George. But you must face facts. If you tell the truth, it isn't much of a defence; and if you tell lies, they are sure to be found out—and therefore of less than no help to George. Your Counsel will select his own line for defence; he might want you as a witness if you could support the line he chooses. But he certainly won't want a truth that damns George, or a lie that will be found out."

Jane drew a deep breath.

"Wot'll *you* say?" she then demanded.

"I shall say exactly what I have already told Inspector Dickson", Miss Bartlett answered steadily, "that I am not a witness. All I know is that you sent for me of your own accord, asking to be taken to the School where you should have been for the last six months. I have already seen your Probation Officer and the Magistrates you saw before, and I have assured them that you were kidnapped by George, against your will and without previous knowledge, and that you do not wish to lead a criminal life. They have accepted my assurances, and between us all we persuaded the authorities to let you go to the School you are now in, and for which you were already registered. There is nothing very much more that I can do for you—and if you break their rules, I am powerless to help you. What you have told me about George is another matter. I will keep your confidence; but knowing him to be a murderer—I can only see that he is treated according to the law. He shall

277

have a good Counsel—and the Counsel will then decide what value you can be to him as a witness. I shall not be George's witness—but in a sense I am yours, Jane, for I know very well that you could hardly help acting as you did, and that you certainly did not want George to do—whatever he *did* do—to the man in the Buick."

"You're dead right—I didn't!" Jane said passionately. "George hadn't orta!—an' he *knew* he hadn't orta. I tole him wot I thought abaht hold-ups, good an' proper! But that don't mean I want ter see him swing for it! If that man in the Buick hadn't raised his gun, George wouldn't have done him in. I guess I'd better say I *was* wiv George an' saw it all—if they've got the pruv George was really there!"

"Yes—but Jane, you didn't see it!" Miss Bartlett objected. "You don't even know that what George told you was true. The man in the Buick may *not* have fired his gun. You only heard one shot. The Police will find out if another shot was fired or not."

"George would have taken the bullet aht if he hadn't fired it!" Jane explained. "He had a torch. I didn't see what George was doing to the man's revolver: I only heard the splash when he threw it in arter him, but George, he thinks of everything. I cu'd safely tell this Defence Counsel that I *see'd* the man in the Buick shoot too!"

"Oh no, Jane!" Miss Bartlett said with conviction as well as pain. "No good Defence Counsel will advise you to make up a story. You had driven off with your back turned when you heard a shot. If he knows that George committed a murder for certain—a good Defence Counsel would throw up the case."

"Wot's he called a Defence Counsel for then?" Jane asked indignantly. "If you haven't done nothing wrong—wot d'yer want ter be defended for? The way I see it is—George didn't do no cole-blooded murder. This man in the Buick acted quick an' George acted quicker—he had to! Same as you or me might a done! You wouldn't want a man ter be hanged, would you?—fer acting quick—even if you hadn't lived wiv him the way I've lived wiv George?"

There was a perceptible pause before Miss Bartlett answered.

"No, Jane, I cannot believe that any human being should take the life of another human being. But I understand that George is himself a killer. Therefore I cannot want him to escape a murder charge. Nobody obliged him to attack this man in the Buick."

Jane thought this over in silence. She knew that she would like George to be put where he couldn't kill again. She also felt certain that George had killed Ma, perhaps with less excuse if with more reason. Jane could not herself consider killing Ma as far short of a virtuous action; but as there seemed to be no proof that George was implicated in an earlier murder, she decided it would be better not to bring up the subject.

"Well—I guess I gotta go now," she told Miss Bartlett, "gotta be present at six o'clock when they has what they says is a 'Roll Call'. You fink you're freer in that School than what we was at Morely—but they jes' have uver ways of catching you out, that's all! Well—Miss Bartlett, thanks a lot—an' you see I git ter George's trial rain or shine! I guess you done a lot fer me one way or anuver—an' I sure am obliged to you fer it. An' if you could let me know somehow wot's up wiv George—I'd be more obliged still."

"If I can, I will let you know", Miss Bartlett promised, "and Jane, don't try to reach me again if it's against your rules! Remember I'll do the best I can for you, but you and George are up against the law now—and we have to accept it. What is done can't be undone. You are not responsible for George—he is responsible for himself. If you try to break the law to help him, you will only make things worse for George as well as for yourself—and perhaps put it beyond my power to do the little I can for both of you."

"That's fair enuff", Jane agreed. "I'll stay put. You jes' remember, Miss Bartlett, that it's George that's got ter be helped nah—not me!"

Miss Bartlett laid down the receiver without making any further promises to help George.

Jane just had ten minutes in which to run a mile before the clock struck six; and she made it.

279

XXXIX

Jane felt like a man who has been running to catch a train in order to keep an appointment upon which his whole future depends. He just catches the train; and for the moment his satisfaction is so intense that he forgets his fate is just as much as ever in the balance.

Jane had got to George's trial; but George was still to be tried. She sat on a bench set apart for the witnesses, Miss Emsley on one side of her, Miss Bartlett, who had unexpectedly turned up, on the other. The Court was packed; there were rows of benches full of excited people, stretching off into a shadowy entrance, and confronted by an empty stage—empty, except for one doddering old man in a wig playing about with ledgers, who turned out to be the Clerk of the Court, and responsible for everything.

A witness-box, looking like a pulpit, stood to one side of the stage. Miss Emsley anxiously told Jane how to go there when her name was called, and what would take place when she got there; but Miss Emsley could do nothing to help Jane clear the jumbled images in her mind. There was the actual night of the storm and what had taken place in it—and this must be kept perfectly separate from what Jane had invented as a substitute for it; nor must she overlook that the police and the Prosecuting Counsel might have their own pictures of this night not in the least like hers. Whatever Jane said must be untraceable, yet distinctly contradictory to the facts, so that it would steer George safely away from them, and yet not pin him down anywhere else, where it could be proved he hadn't been.

Jane had not realised that there would be a big audience in the Court as well as the law officials and the jury; and she could not understand why all these people who didn't know George should be so excited about him. It seemed funny to her that there should be such a lot of strangers who were quite safe themselves coming to stare at other people whose lives depended upon the verdict reached by twelve men sitting in a box, any one of whom could have been a criminal himself like George, if he had thought of it.

"Why do they want to pick on George?" Jane asked herself resentfully. Could the law—that everybody, even Miss Bartlett, believed in—be trusted to keep the Judge straight when he directed the Jury? Jane had never seen a Judge before and wondered what he would look like. Suppose he had a grudge against Jews—or suppose he didn't like a prisoner who was dark instead of white? Perhaps he had—as some men had—a prejudice against women? Could the law save that prisoner whom the Judge—for no real reason—didn't like? What was the law anyhow? Something a lot of men had made up hundreds of years ago, when there weren't any radios—or motor cars— or aeroplanes—and nobody was in a hurry, or could get any- where quickly if they were? Hadn't anybody ever learned anything more about each other since—or about themselves— so that they could really see why people like George did things and stop them doing them, without having to kill them when they hadn't been able to stop them? Not that there was such a lot to be said for George if you came right down to it—but would that little *be* said? Jane looked anxiously at Miss Bartlett as if to find out what she thought; but Miss Bartlett simply sat very straight and looked particularly grave, and not at all communicative.

Mr. Emery Poulton Waters, George's renowned Defence Counsel, had warned Jane that the only person whose opinion about the case really mattered was the Judge; although the Jury were actually responsible for the verdict, they were unskilled in the law and, wanting to make a fair decision, they were bound to depend upon a skilled man who knew how to sift the evidence for them. "Keep your eye on the Judge", Mr. Poulton Waters had ordered Jane. "Never forget that you have to convince *him*! Whatever you do—don't annoy him! Obey

281

what he tells you instantly! He won't mind your hesitating—he doesn't like a glib witness—and be sure to speak up. Most judges are old, and this one is deaf—though he won't admit it! Speak slowly and respectfully, even to the Prosecuting Counsel —remember he is out to get your goat—and for God's sake don't get caught out in a lie. The rest you may leave to me."

Mr. Poulton Waters had then carefully added that Jane must of course speak the exact truth, as perjury was a punishable offence. Their eyes met, and Jane saw that what Mr. Emery Poulton Waters really meant was that she mustn't let herself be found out when she was lying. What she was going to say was already arranged between them. But how was she going to say it before that vast rustling audience who didn't care about George?

No important person had yet emerged from the inner sanctum of the law. Self-conscious, wooden-faced policemen kept oozing in and out of doors, trying to make themselves inconspicuous and yet control anything that might go wrong or that was out of place. Junior Counsels began to drift onto the stage, careless young men with ill-fitting wigs, and gowns hitched to shoulders that would have liked to shake them off.

It was a surprise to Jane that the men who were going to try George actually dressed up for it, and with the memory of Hollywood strongly implanted in her, she thought that they might have dressed up better. A door opened to the right of the stage, and the "twelve good men and true" filed into a long coffin-shaped box cut off from both stage and audience. Ten of them were men, and two were women. Jane's eyes searched them with the expert speculation she would have employed had she been about to pick their pockets.

The Foreman, who led them in, had a conscientious, over-stimulated, anxious face, "the sort", Jane told herself contemptuously, "that wants to sleep safe in his bed at night, an' never will! He won't be too good for George!—likely to feel better hanging anybody that might give trouble than letting them loose". After him, came as if by accident two loose-witted, wool-gathering types, men of uncertain professions, unbalanced by personal success. "I could take anything off

282

them," Jane said confidently to herself, "and they'd think when they got home they'd dropped it." She was afraid, however, that when it came to making up their minds about George, such types would be glad to listen to anyone who spoke with confidence, and who would let them get home sooner for their tea. The two women came next. One woman looked indignant already, and Jane thought that she looked as if she enjoyed the feeling. Unless the Foreman or the Judge rubbed her the wrong way, George would stand no chance at all with her; indignant women, as Jane had often experienced, being almost always on the side of Law and Order. The other woman looked like a crushed worm, but she might be, Jane hoped, one of those worms who unexpectedly turn—and stay turned—if what has crushed them is pity.

The next two men were harder to place because they wore good clothes, and had intelligent and educated faces. Jane couldn't tell what they were thinking, but she came to the conclusion that even if she could, she wouldn't try to take anything off them. For George's purpose they were, she feared, equally unpredictable. The only thing you could say for them was that if they saw reason to take George's side, they looked capable of standing out for it. The trouble was, would any thinking person find any grounds for supporting George? Next came three rather nondescript men who looked as if they didn't want to be there, but meant to do their duty. They were probably tradesmen, and, Jane thought, more likely to be influenced by the Foreman than the Judge, because the Foreman looked like a tradesman too—rather a prosperous one—and was therefore one of their own sort. All four of these men looked respectable—Jane could see that at a glance—and people who cared greatly for respectability were very unlikely to take a fancy to George.

The last two members of the Jury were not easy to place, socially, but they looked as if they thoroughly liked the job, had never been in any position of authority before and felt that being a juror was a matter of life-long importance. Neither of these two men would be in a hurry to reach a decision. They might not care for George as a person, but they could be trusted

283

to keep up an argument about him in order to prolong their own sense of importance. Seven against, Jane summed up the Jury; five possibles *for*—! Well—even one possible out of the five might argue the others down! Suppose that one woman, both intelligent men and these last two uncertain ones all decided to save George? Then George might *be* saved—but would they?

The funny little Clerk, who had a loud beautiful voice, suddenly announced "Silence in the Court!" Everyone stood up, though Jane had no idea why. What *did* come in, she asked herself scornfully, but an old hen looking as if it distrusted the earth it trod on. The Judge was a lean parchment-tinted old gentleman, who couldn't hide his twig-like insecure legs properly under his gown. His eyes, however, were not insecure; they were small, but remarkably clear, like a piece of glass polished regularly every day by a careful hand.

He sat down, taking his time to arrange his gown and make himself comfortable; and when he had quite finished, it seemed as if something important had already taken place.

There was another stir from the body of the hall; up through a sort of trap door into a little empty box opposite the stage appeared two policemen, with George between them. George looked shrunken and white, as if all his old swagger and speed had leaked away from him, and left nothing in their place. Perhaps it was a good thing that he had decided not to plead for himself and had left everything in the hands of his Counsel. He wasn't "Gentleman George" any more: he was just—George—George as Jane had often seen him in a cold winter's dawn, creep in, after a night of failure; for even George had his failures; and it was in these moments, springing off her bed to heat his coffee over a gas ring, that Jane had come nearest to being fond of George.

She gave a little involuntary gasp when she saw him; and Miss Emsley, who had a kind, romantic heart, patted Jane's hand sympathetically; but Miss Bartlett did not so much as glance at Jane; she looked graver still. It was, of course, the first time she had seen George.

George must have known Jane was to be there, but he did

not try to find her. Instead he looked at the box with the Jurors in it, and started, as Jane had done, summing up his chances.

There was a pause while the large audience resettled itself; and then a long tense silence. George was still standing up; and the Judge leaned forward and rather nicely told him that he might sit down.

Jane was relieved to see that George wasn't handcuffed. The policemen on each side of him looked detached; it was as if they knew that George wouldn't make any unnecessary trouble.

The Prosecuting Counsel, who sat a little below and to the right of the Judge, was what is called "a fine figure of a man"; there was a good deal of him, and he knew how to arrange it to the best advantage. He was the sort of man who as a rule gets on well with women, less well with men, and is considered dull, if not dangerous, by children and animals. Jane took an instant and intense dislike to Mr. Vincent Peel. He wasn't like Wilfred and he wasn't like Ma; but if Wilfred had been a little more like Ma, he would have been like them both. Greed and meanness—qualities used by Ma and Wilfred to achieve what they wanted —had been used for the same purpose by Mr. Vincent Peel, and had left the same marks on him, the only difference being that the things Ma and Wilfred had been greedy about were less expensive things.

The case as he outlined it, smoothly and easily, against George, appeared devastating. It could be proved that George was a lifelong criminal, by turns a cat burglar, a smuggler, and a dope peddler. He had also kidnapped, corrupted and seduced an innocent child. Jane was surprised and indignant to find out that she was supposed to be the child. The Judge interrupted Mr. Vincent Peel several times, and allowed Mr. Poulton Waters to interrupt him, in order to tell the Jury that they were to pay no attention to George's past life. A burglar, a smuggler —even a kidnapper—need not be a murderer, the Judge pointed out, and what they were trying George for was murder; but somehow or other these facts about George slid in and out of Mr. Vincent Peel's speech with the dexterity of eels—not even the Judge could prevent their slipping into the meshes of his hard, unflinching arguments. They were gone as soon as they were seen, but the Jury *had* seen them, and every Juror's face looked as if he had. When it was over, Jane saw that the Jury looked immensely impressed by the Prosecuting Counsel's speech; and antagonistic to George. Jane thought the Prosecuting Counsel would get George hanged, though she noticed he didn't seem to know that George had changed the Daimler for the Ford—nor where they had gone to after their flight over the roofs. Mr. Poulton Waters noticed these omissions too, and brought them out later on with singular force, as if they were direct proofs of George's innocence.

The Judge seemed engrossed in the clean pad on the table before him, upon which he jotted down notes so small that a penny stamp could have covered them.

Jane was so absorbed in listening to the evidence that she would hardly have noticed her own name being called as a witness, if Miss Emsley hadn't nudged her. Miss Emsley had already pointed out to Jane how to go into the witness-box, and what she should do when she got there; and Jane tried to walk all that distance as if the audience wasn't there.

Jane put her hand on the Bible and repeated the oath, wondering, as she did so, if there was anything in the Bible that could upset what she meant to say. She reminded herself that even if there were a God, nothing was going to happen to Him because of what she said, whereas something was certain to happen to George unless Jane could make the Judge believe he was innocent. Jane fixed her eyes on the Judge's narrow little face, and to her surprise found that he was looking at her. It was a very curious look—neither kind nor unkind—it simply went right through her.

Mr. Poulton Waters took her over their story with easy skill. It was wonderful being asked questions you liked rather than questions you disliked. When did Jane first meet George—and where? How did George treat her? What did he make her do? Did she live with George willingly or unwillingly? Did she know what George did for a living? Was George kind or unkind to her?

Jane answered him clearly and slowly. She knew that she must take her time as if she were thinking it all out on the spur of the moment; but of course she knew already exactly what she meant to say, and had practised it with her Counsel. She said she had met George the night she was turned out of the American Camp—she did not know exactly where, as it was on a dark night, and she was only twelve. The Camp was somewhere near Liverpool. Her mother had just died, and George picked her up. He had always treated her kindly. He did not make her do anything; he taught her. He taught her to lift things out of shops. She liked lifting things. She didn't live with George till she was sixteen. She had lived with him willingly. Yes, she knew what George did for a living. She wasn't dumb. Mr. Vincent Peel shot up suddenly and asked her what she meant by "dumb"; he said it was not a word he understood used in the sense Jane was using it: he had always supposed it to mean a person incapable of speech. Jane gave him a long, straight look. "Someways it does", she explained. "Someways it means a person who don't see what there is to be seen." Jane just escaped saying "in my country"; but she went on looking at Mr. Vincent Peel as if she suddenly knew what "dumb" really meant for the first time.

There was a faint titter in the Court, and the Judge frowned. Mr. Vincent Peel suddenly dropped the subject, but he didn't stop his questions; he went on hammering at what George made her do, till Jane said impatiently, "He never made me do nothing. You've got George all wrong. I did what he tôld me because it seemed the best thing to do. We lived well. George wasn't never a rough man!"

She spoke directly to the Judge now, ignoring both the Counsels and gazing at the thin mask of the Judge's face as if there were blood behind it.

"George didn't believe in trouble—and I'd have given him trouble if he'd ordered me about, or bin rough. Believe it or not—George didn't make no trouble for me—never! I'd have told him to go take a walk if he had!"

"Well, I would hardly say that", Mr. Vincent Peel gently reminded Jane. "You remember that night of the Wiltshire burglary at Sir William Despard's? George left you to face the music while he escaped—didn't he?"

"He had to get away with the swag", Jane assured the Judge earnestly. Mr. Poulton Waters heatedly lodged an objection to this question as misleading and irrelevant.

The Judge had frequently upheld objections made by Jane's Counsel to the questions asked Jane. He now frowned ominously.

"Is this past history really necessary to your case?" he again asked Mr. Vincent Peel, who assured him earnestly that it was.

"What do you mean by swag?" the Judge then asked Jane with marked distaste.

"The doings—the sparklers!" Jane explained with care. "What George found in the safe while I was after the mink. An' he had a right to get away with them, 'cos I kinda slowed myself up by wearing that mink, nor I couldn't join George on account of the General turning up unexpected like—an' I'd say there was trouble then, but it was that there General that made it. George—he didn't never believe in vi'lence. I used it 'cos I had to, ter make my get-away. I hit that ole General— right an' left. I hit him hard!"

To Jane's surprise, laughter broke out in the Court. They thought she had meant to be funny, while all she meant was to clear George. The Judge was not amused. He spoke very sternly and threatened to clear the Court if laughter occurred again. He said Jane was not to make comments, but only to answer the questions that the learned Counsel put to her. As if she hadn't been answering his questions! Then the Judge scolded Mr. Peel. He said he did not think this past history was at all relevant to the case. They were trying the prisoner at the bar on a charge of murder only. The Jury must forget entirely what they had already heard as to George's former crimes; or— if they could not forget them—they must discount them. The Judge said he had allowed the witness's evidence as to the prisoner's treatment of her, since it might throw light on what took place later on; but they had already had far too much of it. There must be no more. Very gently, almost casually, Mr. Poulton Waters took Jane's story up again; they moved on swiftly and rapidly for a while, with very few interruptions from Mr. Vincent Peel, till they came to the night of the storm.

Like lightning Mr. Vincent Peel's manner changed. His questions pelted at Jane like bullets, his eyes were fierce, his brows beetled. The night of the storm was hurled at her as if she were to blame for it. Once or twice even the Judge thought Mr. Peel's questions too fast and fierce, and interrupted him to say to Jane with protective courtesy, "You may take your time, Witness, in answering this question of the learned Counsel".

The time this gave her gave Jane just the chance she needed to see the traps Mr. Peel had set for her. Still, the Judge was not on her side. He seemed like a floating iceberg, only the sharp peak of which was visible, so that it was impossible to tell how much more ice might stretch under the surface, or where it would strike next.

Where was she on the night of the storm? Why had she left George—and where? Why had she quarrelled with George? Whom had she met at the Funfair? What Funfair was it? Where had the American airman taken her—and in what? Mr. Poulton Waters drew Jane back into her story, but still Mr. Peel's pitiless questions went on breaking up the smoothness of its texture, till only the jagged points remained.

Jane knew that she had to clear George from passing the Bank at four o'clock in the afternoon in order to chase the Buick. All that these questions really meant was—*when* did she leave George? Mr. Poulton Waters kept trying to stop Mr. Peel's hail of questions—and sometimes the Judge let him, but more often he didn't. Jane had to answer all the questions the Judge said she must, without getting all mixed up.

The airman she had met at the Funfair, Jane said, was called Joe. No, she did not know his other name and had never asked. She had left George at six o'clock at the Elephant and Castle. She wasn't really mad with George—they'd just had words; but she didn't approve of selling dope and had decided to leave him. No, she didn't think it funny not to know what the airman's other name was—why should she ask him? He mightn't really have had the leave he said he was on—and so she could have put the Black on him; and it wasn't funny either that she could remember that he drove her in a Lancia when she'd forgotten everything else, because she drove cars herself, and the Lancia was a peach of a car. No, she didn't know where they went, but couldn't have cared less. They drove out of London, and it was up a pretty steep hill that might have been Hindhead. She knew it was on the Surrey side. She had to walk down the hill later when she ran away from Joe. She ran away from Joe because he got too fresh; that was how she ended up at Haslemere Station at seven o'clock the next morning.

"Perhaps", Mr. Peel said with a sneer, "it may surprise you to know that there were only two Road Houses open in that neighbourhood on the night of the storm, and that neither of these garaged a Lancia or entertained a girl of your age accompanied by an American airman."

"How could they tell Joe was a airman?" Jane retorted. "He wore civvies—not caring to show what he was, nor no one with sense would garridge a car, with an empty road handy; 'cos why pay for what you can put under a tree for nothing? Nor my age isn't no handle to hold on by neither. I'm under the age of consent, when I *don't* consent—and so that airman found out— but I don't need to look it—do I?"

"That is a most improper way in which to speak to the learned Counsel," the Judge told Jane sourly, "and I have told you before that you must not make comments on what took place. You must only state the exact facts, answering the questions put to you, and you must not ask questions yourself. You may proceed, Mr. Peel, if you wish to question the witness further!"

Mr. Peel, it seemed, didn't wish to question Jane further. He was hot under the collar already, and was afraid of letting his exasperation get the better of him. He knew that the Judge had already sensed this and might chaff him about it afterwards; and he had not got—and saw no prospects of getting—what he wanted out of Jane.

Unfortunately Jane looked rather less than her age, and had already won the sympathy of the Court by amusing it. Mr. Emery Poulton Waters was plainly delighted with her. Jane was exactly what he had hoped she might be—a tough and wary witness. Before Jane sat down, he finished taking her over her story of the night of the storm, with sympathetic delicacy. The storm itself died down. There was no Buick. George was safely at the Elephant and Castle playing darts. This he often did: and George was no cinch of a dart player. Ma had taught him. Jane was with the airman showing him where he got off. The trouble, however, still was that Jane didn't know where the police had picked George up or what evidence they had against him. So that she still had to be careful. If only she could have safely put George in the imaginary Joe's place, and successfully established a night long alibi! But she daren't —the police might know better. She could only put George where he *wasn't* at 6 p.m. and hope for the best.

At last Miss Emsley shot up from somewhere and led Jane back to her seat. As they passed near the box the Prisoner was in, George lifted his head and looked at Jane. It was perhaps the nicest look he had ever given her.

Hours and hours passed. One policeman after another gave bits of evidence that fitted into each other like a picture puzzle. The Court was cleared for an hour, and everyone went out for a late lunch. The Prosecuting Counsel made his final speech when they got back; and it was so terrible that Jane daren't look at George. She went on looking at the Judge instead. He looked less human than ever, and Jane didn't think it was a good sign that he had stopped writing notes. He just listened.

Then Mr. Emery Poulton Waters made a magnificent defence speech. After Jane had heard it, she felt that every-thing was explained satisfactorily and that George, far from being a murderer, was one of those unfortunate individuals you sometimes saw on the screen, generously described as: "One of Society's victims". Jane was a victim too—but a fellow victim. George was her protector rather than her seducer; and the alibi at six p.m. fitted in beautifully.

When Mr. Poulton Waters came to the end of his speech, it was extremely difficult to remember that anything lethal had happened to the man in the Buick. He seemed just to have fallen into a ditch and died there—rather carelessly mislaying a thousand pounds that he was meant to guard.

Then the Judge began to speak. All the notes he had made earlier seemed to come into it, and Jane wished he hadn't taken them. His voice was like the drip of a cold tap on a winter day. He seemed to take all the handsome emotion and warmth out of Mr. Poulton Waters' eloquent defence. It was incredible to Jane that the Judge hadn't been utterly convinced in George's favour; but there was no favour whatever in the Judge's voice. He kept saying, "You may believe the witness on this point, or you may not", referring to Jane—but it was quite obvious that the Judge himself hadn't believed her. Still, no one had disproved—if no one could prove—the Lancia, Joe, the Elephant and Castle, the Funfair, the six o'clock alibi! There they all were, floating securely in untracked ether.

The damning evidence came later on—weeks later on, when Jane could do nothing to tamper with it; through some Bank trick, assisted by the police, the money had been traced directly to George. There wasn't much to be said for George after that; but the Judge said whatever there was, and then he came back like some awful automatic sledge-hammer to the things that *couldn't* be said for George. Then the Judge stopped, and gave his cold final charge to the Jury, who went out following their Foreman like a string of ducks across a field.

Miss Emsley put her hand on Jane's arm. Jane had promised to leave quietly the moment she was told to go, but she wouldn't have gone without a scene if Miss Bartlett hadn't been there. It was the pain in Miss Bartlett's eyes that steadied Jane. She could go with pain; it seemed the only safe companion.

They were allowed to sit and wait for the verdict in a little office off the Court.

"The longer we wait the better", Miss Emsley said kindly to Jane.

Someone brought them in three cups of tea on a tray; then they just sat and waited. Just as it was growing dark, a man opened the door and looked in at them without saying anything, and Miss Bartlett went out quickly by herself. When she came back, Jane knew without being told exactly what had happened. The thousand pounds had hanged George; and Jane hadn't been able to do anything to help him.

Jane stood up. The door was open behind Miss Bartlett. Two policemen, with George between them, were in the passage, making for a side door so as to avoid taking George out into the crowd. Jane ran past Miss Bartlett. One of the two policemen raised a majestic arm to stop her, but Jane ducked under it and threw her arms round George's neck. For just one moment her heart beat against his heart, as if she had really reached him; then George threw her off roughly.

"You get away from me, Jane," he snarled, "you never been much good ter me—an' yer none nah!"

XL

Jane and Esmé sat wrapped in blankets on the library roof. They had dropped on it at midnight, after Jane had picked the lock of the bedroom door. She had used an instrument from her manicure set, and managed beautifully.

It was the second night after the trial, and the first chance they'd had to talk it out. Above the black masses of leafless trees the frozen hollow of the April moon stared at them. The night was cloudy and still, with a few dim and watery stars. They would have been frightened if they had not felt so excited. Now they could talk about everything; they could stay as long as they liked; and by clinging together they could balance themselves on the sloping roof, without too much danger of falling off.

The Library had been added on to the Close as a separate building. There was no one above or beneath them. From Jane's lips the whole trial scene sprang in a series of graphic pictures as she re-lived it—with Snoutie clutching her, breathless with sympathy and understanding. Jane left out nothing; all that she had felt, imagined and seen spread round them, peopling the dark. Only one thing she left out: Jane never mentioned that one moment of union between herself and George, when she had felt his arms tighten about her. She could not touch this memory with words; perhaps it was the only moment in George's life when he had given what belonged to him without reluctance or subtraction; and it should remain his own. What he had said afterwards, when he pushed her away, she retailed to Esmé, though she excused it.

"George meant no harm. It was like my little cat Elsie; if you picked her up when she was frightened, she just naturally bit you—an' clawed too something terrible! George—he bawled me out and pushed me at the cop 'cos he was scared. Well—I guess I was scared too—till something that cop said made me laugh. 'Nah then, Miss', he said to me, picking me up sort of careless like, 'enuff of that!' Gawd knows what he thought I'd had enuff of! So we drove back in Miss Bartlett's car—only to the station, she got to get back to Morely—must have driven half the night to get back there before morning. She hadn't said nothing to me all the time. Only when she left me she said: 'It will be in three weeks' time, Jane, and there isn't anything more you can do about it.' She knew that was all I was thinking of—and it kinda helped her knowing. That Miss Emsley—a nice Probation Officer an' I liked her better than I had at Morely—she talked all the time; but I didn't listen—she meant to be kind. But talk don't mean nuffin' to you once you been hit—you're just wondering when you'll be hit again. Three weeks—now I know. Funny when you wake in the morning—it seems a long time and lots you can do in it—and now it's night, I feel it's got sort of short—and I can't do nuffin'—nor no one can—to help George."

"Seems funny to me", Esmé said consideringly, "you're not being in love with George—and he acting so nasty right up to the end—that you have to care so much what happens to him—reely funny it seems to me—that does. You haven't lost nothing in having lost George, Jane."

"I guess I haven't lost so much," Jane agreed with a queer little sigh. "I didn't never want George the way I had him, and I meant to leave him. But losing George isn't the only thing I mind, Esmé—it's jes' George being lost. You wouldn't want a dog to get lost, would you? And dogs don't get hanged when they're lost—they can just run round and pick up things; but George has got to be behind bars—an' they look at you all the time, them guards do—night and day for three weeks feeding you up—and then hanging you. Seems a queer way of doing things, if men are more important than dogs, don't it?"

Esmé didn't point out that dogs didn't shoot men in Buicks either. She could follow the paths of desperation in her own mind and see their finish without flinching; but she couldn't quite see why Jane should feel so badly about what George had done—reasonably from his point of view—and yet so much worse still at what was going to be done to him for doing it—reasonably from the law's point of view. After all, you couldn't just let George go round killing people because it hurt being hanged.

"You thought he killed Ma too, didn't you?" she ventured after a long silence.

When they weren't speaking they could hear the trees creaking a little, as if they were moving up nearer to the Close. They hadn't their leaves on yet, though it was late April, so the trees didn't whisper—they just creaked.

"I reckon maybe he did", Jane admitted. "They didn't go into that. I guess they knew all about it though—that Henry Dickson did, anyway—but George's alibi had stuck; they couldn't bring it home to him no-how. Men like that Henry Dickson—they aren't stupid. That was where we got off the rails—me and George: we thought cops stupider than they are. They keep quiet and just add up and add up till all of a sudden one day they get an answer. George thought he was awful clever—and so he was—never got cotched—thirty-seven, quite an ole man, George was! He didn't keep to one line like most professionals do. First cat burglary—all I know about roofs I learnt from him—you better keep your foot turned in the way I do now, in case you slip—then he shifted to smuggling—and that went good till the skippers weakened; after that we did fine with dope at the dance halls—easiest job I ever took on—but Rusty, my fren' who's a speed driver, he thought it downright low drug-peddling—wouldn't play along with us any more arter that, and he was safe with cars just the way George wanted them; and then George he thought of hold-ups. But once the cops start looking for you in one place, you're the same person when you turn up in another—see?—and after awhile they begin to say, 'Gawd—what's this chap doin'? Funny he keeps turning up whenever a deal's crooked. How come? *He* must be the bug under the stone.' Maybe that Prosecuting Counsel had been well fed by the cops beforehand, and that's why he tried to pile in George's back history—till the

Judge stopped him. The way I see that Judge now—he was out to stop everybody's fun. I daresay that Counsel would have brought up Ma—if he'd been let to. The way I see it is, Ma didn't give them the straight lead to George—but George was there after the murder although he wasn't even tried for Ma— and the cops seen him there. His slate wasn't none too clean anyhow—even then—and they knew that too. They may have took his photograph and waited—and then saw one like it on a passport—different name, but they keep duplicates at those bloody offices, don't they? Then that snapshot after George had picked me up wasn't a good photograph, but could be me! Still they didn't do noffin' and maybe they never would have, after we got away into those chalkpits, if Ma hadn't given George the lead to the man in the Buick."

"But Ma was dead!" Esmé objected.

"Sure she was dead," Jane admitted, "but if George hadn't got away with murder once, he'd never have gone in for hold-ups again at all. He'd tried them in the United States—and he knew they meant vi'lence. 'You start with vi'lence', Miss Bartlett, she said to me, 'an' you end up with vi'lence', an' I guess she was right too! There was that guy Hitler—murdered six million Jews before he was caught up wiv; but I wouldn't er been him, in that rat hole with Russians rolling up all round him—him not knowing proper how to shoot hisself. So some-one else had to do it for him. And then his body burnt up in a garden before they broke in—with that there Eva's—marrying her at the last minute, pore girl, jes' so he could kill her wiv him too, I shouldn't wonder. But George wouldn't do a thing like that! George never told on me—nor I never told on George. 'Course I didn't like taking that oath, and then lying like Hell —but I guess that Bible didn't mean a thing! Anyway I ain't none the worse for it as I can see."

"What's in the Bible's different," Esmé said after a still longer pause. "I don't believe the things they do in a Court have anything to do with it. In the Bible—you save lost sheep— Jesus, He does it all the time—an' even Cain murdering his own brother in the Old Testament—God didn't kill him for it —jes' put a mark like on his forehead, and tole him to travel, so wherever he went they could see he wasn't one to make a home."

"Well—George wasn't neither", Jane agreed. "That's why I'd made up my mine to leave him. I lef' him before he killed the man in the Buick—in my mind I had. When he said he wouldn't make no home till I was twenty, nor have no baby an' settle down the way I meant. I didn't tell him I was leaving straight away. I even sort of gave way that night to please him; but I'd turned—I'd turned the way I meant to turn. It wasn't that I thought of coming back here—I never. I wanted my freedom; but I'd have gone off on my own, and just taken things; it was what I knew how to do, that's all!"

"Yes, I know," Esmé said gently, "and you were cleverer at it than me. I gave it up too—I gave it up because of God and Miss Bartlett—and I'm just going to be a nurse and take care of people now. In a way, it was what you did for me at Morely that started me off! Wouldn't you like to be a professional nurse too, Jane? We could go together to the same hospital then, couldn't we?"

Jane looked at the cold, enticing moon without feeling sure of what she wanted—beyond the one thing—George's safety—which she wasn't going to get. It was clearer now, and she could see a row of advancing trees, like fingers stretched out, with no flesh on them.

"No", she said, after a pause. "Acrobatics is more what I fancy—or I might learn to be a vet. and look after animals. Anyways, I won't steal no more. It's not that I feel the way you do about it, Esmé—upsetting God and all that—nor I'm not afraid of that Henry Dickson, though he's got my photo and for all I know my finger-prints when I wasn't looking. It's just that I don't want to be what people who take things are like."

"Seems a pity you can't have that policeman the way you feel about him," Esmé remarked resentfully, "always dragging him in!"

Jane laughed outright this time, and it made a funny sound in the hushed darkness.

"You shut up!" Esmé urged. Then she added reassuringly, "If anyone heard p'raps they'll think it was a fox."

"Don't worry," Jane told her, "that Henry Dickson won't come in no more. He got what he wanted", she added a little grimly. "He got George! But he didn't get him through me. I'm glad of that! Jees', Esmé, it's colder out here than that Judge's eyes—and we ain't got no fur like them foxes has, neither! Let's hop it!——"

XLI

Long before the day of the execution, Jane saw quite clearly what she wanted to do: she wanted to be there as near as she could get. She wasn't going to be able to see George; Miss Bartlett had tried for her, but it couldn't be worked. If Miss Duncan would have let Jane do it, the Prison Governor—a friend of Miss Bartlett's—couldn't; something to do with her age and not being really kin to George stopped him. But even if the Governor had wangled it, no one could see George when George didn't want to see anyone.

George said from the first to last that he didn't want to see anybody. George was through; he was through with Jane; he was very nearly through with life. Still, Jane had been able to send him word that she would be there standing as close as she could get, taking as much as could come to her. He wasn't to think he was just to be in a Prison having terrible things done to him and no one cared enough to stand outside. It mightn't be much, but would be something which Jane felt George would like to have. That Jesus on the Cross, Esmé kept talking about, had His friends standing by it—three hours that took—and He was going to Paradise—if there was Paradise—and who knew where George would go to? Jane wouldn't stay three hours: it only took about thirty seconds now. "Sure", Jane said to herself, "we learned a lot since then!" But she had made up her mind to be there.

She told no one her intention, not even Esmé, as it might get her into trouble if she knew beforehand and didn't tell; nor Miss Bartlett, who had handed on Jane's letter to the Prison Governor as she had promised—to give to George. It was awkward for Jane to get there, because she hadn't any money and had decided not to steal it.

Fortunately Jane knew where lorry drivers stop for midnight meals, and she found a good-natured one who liked company. Driving through the dark night, after a sausage and mash, to which the driver treated her, Jane had given him the outlines of George's story. It turned out that the lorry driver had had a brother who was arrested because a man died one Saturday night after he'd hit him; fortunately the Jury brought it in as manslaughter, and he was let off light; but it made the lorry driver take an interest in Jane. He went out of his way to get Jane to Wandsworth, right to the Prison gates. He explained that there was a new rule now about people being hanged. They weren't going to put the prisoner's name up outside before the execution and take it down afterwards directly it was over, for fear of upsetting people. But they were going to hang the prisoner just the same; apparently they didn't think that would upset people; and Jane could remember it would be over after the clock struck nine. Then the lorry driver said "cheerio"—and not to forget that there were as good fish in the sea as ever came out of it. And he told her his name was Tom; and that she would know where to find him if she wanted to see him again.

Jane was quite alone now, and she would be alone for the next hour. The Prison stood up stark and grim in the morning light, close against the sky. She couldn't get in; and George was behind the walls, and he couldn't get out. It was a funny feeling because they'd both been so good at getting in and out of places.

There was a surly north wind blowing, but the light was lovely; high above the tainted chimney pots floated clouds just touched with the sun's first gold. A year ago they would have been as free as those clouds. Jane, gazing up at the ugly blocks of stone pushing back the narrow sky, envied the light that could penetrate and yet be free.

They were getting George up now, and they would give him a good breakfast—if he could eat it. And then the Governor and the Chaplain would come in and say things to him that

301

George wouldn't listen to, because his mind would be on what was going to happen to him when they stopped talking. Jane didn't think George would make a fuss. He would keep his eyes open, to see if at any moment there was the faintest chance of escape; but there wouldn't be. It had all been arranged too well, and for too long a time. George would keep quiet because he had never been one to bluster—not from that long ago time he had once told Jane about, when Ma took him in out of the snow—and dealt with him—on her own lines—to that far later moment when Ma found that George was dealing with her—on his lines. But there was no room now for George's skill. George had never been one of the Al Capone sort, who run gangs, but he had known how to take what he wanted. Perhaps few criminals had lived longer than George against the law with such unruffled success; but now the law had got him, and George wouldn't need it explained to him that his skill wouldn't work against the law's final processes.

It was very cold, and Jane moved about a little, and hoped that if people noticed her they wouldn't guess what she was there for. There were not many other people about. George's had not been a sympathetic case; and there had been no Appeal. It was ten minutes before the hour would strike. "It doesn't take long", Jane kept saying to herself. "They'll be as quick as they can! They don't *like* doing it! Why—a man doesn't like killing a dog!"

She began to feel a funny feeling in her throat as if she couldn't swallow very easily. "Lots of men are worse than George!" Jane said defensively to herself. "I wouldn't wonder if the Prosecuting Counsel wasn't worse—nor that Judge. Why —I wouldn't be *his* wife—not if you made me a Queen, I wouldn't! George brought me Elsie just to pleasure me—an' that scent bottle too. He wasn't such a bad man as long as you did what he wanted. Now I guess they're getting him all dolled up, like that lorry driver said, and at the end they cover his eyes—maybe they don't like his being able to look at them, let alone his having to see what they're going to do to him! I don't see why they don't dope them good and proper before-hand, like as if it was an operation. There's a doctor there could give the right injections, and you'd pop off comfortable like an' be none the worse for it! Funny why the law should make you have to take that awful pain that don't do you—nor anyone else—any good; nor it don't even make a show for people neither—like getting hurt in a Football Match!"

"Make it quick!" Jane prayed as the clock began to strike.

It wouldn't be any sense asking God for it not to hurt, for Jane knew that it must hurt. It was hurting her now. She stood half frozen, swaying in the wind and clutching at her throat.

It was not a loud clock, yet in spite of the traffic, standing as close as she could get to the Prison walls, Jane could hear each stroke quite plainly. She felt as if she were the clock that was striking.

When the clock had finished striking, someone touched her arm. She turned round, and there was Rusty.

"Somehow I didn't think you could get here," he said awkwardly. "I thought I'd just pass by like and let you know someone had been about to see the last of George. It's all over nah, Jane! It's all over!"

Jane hadn't been going to cry. She knew there was no sense in crying; and she hadn't even felt like it till she saw Rusty. Rusty took her by the arm and led her to the nearest A.B.C.

"What you want is a good cuppa!" he told her soothingly; and it *was* what Jane wanted, for when she had drunk her tea she began to feel quite hungry, and was glad of the bacon and eggs a sympathetic waitress brought them. The waitress was sorry for Jane. She thought that Rusty had made her cry, and glared at him. This made Jane laugh, for it was his kindness that had set her off: she wouldn't have cried without him. So she explained to the waitress, "This guy's all right—it was something else upset me! I've lost my job", and in a sense that *was* what had happened.

Rusty began to talk to her about Elsie. All the men at the garage had taken a shine to her—she had almost too much fish. There wasn't the faintest chance of Elsie being run over either: she knew the way cars moved as if she'd made them.

"Wouldn't you like to come along now and take a squint at her?"

Rusty had his car parked just outside a doctor's door round the corner where the police would let it stand. A nice little Sunbeam Talbot it was that he was running into shape.

Jane shook her head. "I don't want Elsie upset", she explained. "She's got used to being without me and she'd better stay used. Anyhow, I gotta git back. It's fifty miles or more to the Danesbury Close place, where they board us aht. And I haven't any money to get there. What'll I do, Rusty?"

"I'll take you back in me Talbot", Rusty said proudly. "I only got ter phone the garidge an' take half a day orf. It's not often I want ter get orf—so they won't mind. But, Jane—look—'ere—are you dead cert. you want to go back? Bit rough those Schools, ain't they? I might fix up my Ma—and we might make a go of it arter all! Wot you say? They won't never find you—married an' a new name an' all!—once you're right off—respectable like—an' settled down on the other side of the river?"

Jane hesitated. She looked at Rusty, and he wasn't any different from what he usually looked like. His hands were cleaner; but at the beginning of a day his hands were always cleaner.

"I gotta go back", she said at last. "Thanks a lot, tho', all the same! One thing I promised; an' then—it's a funny thing, Rusty, once you begin to get educated—you kinder want ter go on wiv it."